Praise for *Letters to the ..*

"This book. It made me wince, cringe, chu
doors, shake my head, and maybe utter a 1
unique satire of an American nightmare."

—**Paul Tremblay, author of *A Head Full of Ghosts* and *The Cabin at the End of the World***

"Chaplinsky breathes some much-needed life into the serial killer genre, taking the unique and utterly brilliant angle of turning the focus onto us, and our morbid fascination with these depraved individuals. This book ought to come with a bottle of bleach, to dip your soul in after you're done."

—**Rob Hart, author of *Assassins Anonymous* and *The Warehouse***

"Akin to *Henry: Portrait of a Serial Killer* fucking *Les Liasons Dangereuses*, then strangling it, this sadistic epistolary novel reads like a crime scene smattered in the DNA of Richard Chizmar and Thomas Harris. Better wear rubber gloves when you crack open this brutally captivating book."

—**Clay McLeod Chapman, author of *What Kind of Mother* and *Ghost Eaters***

"You can't see a black hole... only what's around it. Like this brilliant, ultra-vivid book with terrible darkness at the center. Multihued, twistedly funny, and so human it hurts. You'll get sucked right into the horrifying core."

—**Dennis Mahoney, author of *Our Winter Monster***

"*Letters to the Purple Satin Killer* is a morbidly intense and psychologically thrilling page-turner. Once I started it, I couldn't put it down."

—**Stephanie M. Wytovich, Bram Stoker award-winning author of *Brothel***

"Joshua Chaplinsky's *Letters to the Purple Satin Killer* is the freshest, most inventive, and easily the funniest serial-killer novel in years. It says something scary and profound about America itself."

—Nick Kolakowski, author of *Absolute Unit* and *Love & Bullets*

"A wicked feast of serial killer psychosis, *Letters to the Purple Satin Killer* steeps us in the lives of those who accidentally—and purposefully—love a bad, bad man. Told in blistering letters that heap hope, blame, lust and insanity on a monster, Joshua Chaplinsky's haunting new novel will dazzle and trouble you in equal measure. An elegant and horrific epistolary of murder."

—Brian Allen Carr, author of *Bad Foundations*

"Remnants of Dennis Cooper and Bret Easton Ellis at their finest, *Letters to the Purple Satin Killer* is Chaplinsky's best book yet. Cleverly inventive and perfectly perverted, it is deceptively difficult to put down once you get started. Clear your schedules and silence your phones. You've just found your next obsession."

—Max Booth III, author of *Abnormal Statistics* and *We Need to Do Something*

"A fascinating flip of the script here, think *In the Belly of the Beast* in reverse, where a reader doesn't satisfy their morbid curiosity from an incarcerated killer's insight, but instead derives a more dubious satisfaction by stealing the monster's mail. All the expected epistolary pleasures are intact, but here it's highlighted by a more perverse voyeurism, as well as some surprising character arcs from the obsessive penpals and rubberneckers, maybe less an arc but more like that inevitable trajectory that curves down down down into the cognitive gutter."

—David James Keaton, author of *Head Cleaner*

"Filthy, shameful, and so much fun, like an ill-advised late-night tryst with your favorite toxic, psychotic lover. *Letters to the Purple Satin Killer* is a monster in the glossy black mirror reflecting our collective disease, and Chaplinsky catalogues humanity's mordant cruelty with acerbic aplomb."

—Chandler Morrison, author of *Dead Inside* and *American Narcissus*

"The range of emotions that seep into these letters—hatred, love, vengeance, desire—makes for a fascinating (and unsettling) epistolary novel. Transgressive and depraved, funny and sweet, it's *Dracula* via Chuck Palahniuk with a Jack Ketchum chaser."

—Richard Thomas, Bram Stoker and Shirley Jackson finalist

"By turns frightening and funny, Chaplinsky twists the true crime format into an immersive exploration of celebrity worship and humankind's addiction to being heard."

—B.R. Yeager, author of *Negative Space* and *Burn You the Fuck Alive*

"Unlike any other serial killer novel you're likely to ever read. Brutal, original and unflinching, it holds the mirror to who we have become, and who we choose to obsess over."

—Todd Robinson, Author of *Rough Trade* and *The Hard Bounce*

LETTERS TO THE PURPLE SATIN KILLER

Revised and Expanded

by Joshua Chaplinsky

Featuring a new foreword by former
FBI Behavioral Analyst Roddy Perkins

CL◢SH

This book is dedicated to Tina Schoenecker
as well as the victims and their families

TABLE OF CONTENTS

FOREWORD

Born January 12th, 1975, Jonas Williker is considered one of the most sadistic serial murderers of the modern era. The Pennsylvania native brutalized his way into the zeitgeist during the early part of the new millennium, leaving a trail of corpses across five states before his eventual arrest in 2004. All told, he was responsible for the rape and murder of 23 women, and is suspected in the deaths of dozens more. His calling card—a torn piece of fabric found on or inside the bodies of his victims—helped popularize his now ubiquitous nickname.

The Purple Satin Killer.

Law enforcement professionals and true crime obsessives spent countless hours investigating the man and his actions. Their collective pool of knowledge represents an unprecedented study of a diseased psyche. But despite all they learned, one important question remains unanswered to this day.

Why?

What caused Jonas Williker to do all those awful things? Did he come into this world evil incarnate? Or did some confluence of childhood trauma transform him? It is likely we will never know. In fact, the possibility exists he didn't understand the motivation behind his own crimes. Either way, his gruesome story continues to fascinate the masses.

Williker's rise to infamy is a well-documented one. His first attributed murder took place on February 14th, 2000, in Scenery Hill, Pennsylvania, 50 miles from the Murrysville home he shared with his parents. The victim, a 20-year-old college student named Leslie Anne Hawkins, was found strangled behind the supermarket where she worked part-time.

The crime shocked town residents, but barely made a ripple outside the small pond of local news. As far as murders go, it wasn't the most sensational. The purple strip of cloth tied in a bow around Leslie's neck presented an oddity, but in light of the holiday seemed nothing more than a morbid flourish in a crime of passion. Only in retrospect did it stand out as an obvious statement of purpose.

Williker's second killing wouldn't occur until 9 months later, 65 miles away in the sleepy Pennsylvania borough of Berlin. There, on the morning of November 12th, 17-year-old Betty Kaiser's exsanguinated upper body was found by her mother, tucked into bed. The discovery so shocked the woman that she didn't realize until days later that the purple satin sheets atop her daughter hadn't come from the family linen closet. As for Betty's lower extremities, they turned up the next morning, sitting on a bench, waiting for the school bus.

Police didn't make an immediate connection between the murders of Leslie Anne Hawkins and Betty Kaiser. The former remained unsolved those many months later, and a pattern of behavior had yet to be established. But investigators wouldn't have to wait long for the killer to strike again.

Williker's audacious third murder fell on the anniversary of the first—February 14th, 2001. A pair of Homer City teens looking for a place to "park" came across the body of 31-year-old Melissa Wainscott, both her mouth and anus stuffed with the soon-to-be eponymous cloth. When the coroner attempted to remove it, he discovered the two pieces were opposite ends of a single length, measuring over 30 yards. At that point little doubt remained—Pennsylvania had a deranged killer on its hands.

As if in response to this realization, Williker's antisocial attacks intensified, stoking the public's fear. He committed a total of 11 murders that year, each one more shocking than the last, casting a fearful pall over the citizens of southwestern Pennsylvania and the state of Ohio. It prompted a mass exodus, devastating the housing market and crippling the local economy. Those who couldn't afford to leave invested in home security and stopped going out after dark. The sale of handguns skyrocketed. Unintentional shootings tripled as a result. The specter of violence became an everyday part of suburban life.

But the worst was yet to come. Williker finished out the year with the abduction and murder of 22-year-old twin sisters, Hazel and Felicity Coonan, of Zanesville, Ohio. Hazel Coonan went missing on October 17th. After a five-day search effort, volunteers recovered the young woman's body. Despite no external signs of trauma, the autopsy revealed her ovaries had been removed. The family had only begun to process the cruelty of their daughter's death when Felicity went missing. She turned up dead on November 2nd, her sister's ovaries nesting in her ocular cavities. Investigators never recovered the missing eyes.

After this depraved achievement, Jonas Williker went silent. 2002 is often referred to as his "gap year," as no new murders bore the Purple Satin calling card. Investigators believe things got too hot after the Coonan slayings, and Williker didn't necessarily stop killing, he just stopped advertising. Numerous bodies were found in and around the Ohio area that year, which experts think him responsible for, but evidence linking him to the crimes proved insufficient. Despite this, Ohio residents attempted to put him out of their minds and resume a normal life.

But the Purple Satin Killer would return in full force starting on January 1st, 2003. The Indiana Murders, as they were called, weren't as numerous, but what they lacked in quantity they made up for in sheer brutality. They represented a reinvention of sorts. The time taken with the victims and the arrangement of the bodies indicated a confidence in these crimes and what they were trying to convey. They were the work of a madman who fancied themselves an artist. And it was this artistic hubris that led to his ultimate downfall.

The final three murders, those committed in 2004, are the crimes of a man on the run, desperate to escape, but unable to control his urges. During the end of January/beginning of February, Williker fled from Indiana to Nevada. Ironically, he might have given police the slip if he'd laid low, as he did during 2002, but he got careless. They arrested him for attempted assault in Henderson, NV, and he spent 4 ½ months in county lockup awaiting trial. A jury found him guilty, and on November 4th, the judge sentenced him to 18 months in prison. A few weeks later, Indiana extradited Williker and charged him with multiple counts of murder.

As one of the FBI analysts assigned to the Purple Satin killings, it was my responsibility to create a profile of Jonas Williker, who at the time we referred to as PSK. The PSK profile proved a difficult one to build, as certain characteristics distinguished Williker from your typical serial killer. For instance, although he did spend much of his time alone, he could be quite charming when necessary, and had no problem navigating social situations. This, combined with his boyish good looks, contributed to the ease with which he gained the confidence of his victims and eluded suspicion.

Another thing that set Williker apart from many other violent criminals: he had no history of mental illness or violent behavior. He had never undergone psychiatric treatment, nor did he have a criminal record. By all accounts he was a "normal" human being. He just so happened to possess the ability to hide his aberrant nature by flipping it on and off like a light switch. Of course, as anyone who witnessed some of his more erratic behavior during trial can attest, something was indeed deeply wrong with him.

I was permitted audience with Jonas Williker on two occasions. The first took place shortly after his sentencing, during which he maintained full and total control of his emotions. He deftly spoke about his crimes as if a third party had committed them, dancing around his own motivations and any sense of responsibility. When I asked if he thought it a coincidence the murders had stopped after his arrest, he simply stated, "It is a common misconception that serial killers have no self-control." This was years before any of the copycat crimes had occurred.

The conversation revealed little else. At best it served to bolster what we already knew—we were dealing with a monster who rarely took off their human disguise. And although I put in multiple requests, he didn't grant me a second audience until almost two years later, around the time of his public embrace of Christianity.

It is widely believed Jonas's religious transformation was nothing more than a ploy to delay his execution and possibly earn himself a commuted sentence. His direct appeal had been brought before the court and his conviction affirmed in record time (less than a year). His post-conviction appeal, in which he argued he should receive a new trial due to ineffective counsel—even though he represented himself—was largely viewed as antagonistic by the court. Then, instead of filing a writ of habeas corpus, because "it was evident the system was prejudiced against him," he decided to dedicate his remaining time to working on "personal spiritual growth." Those behind the scenes confirmed Williker's legal reach had exceeded his grasp. His meager savings had run out, and no other lawyer wanted to deal with his antics on a charitable basis.

Encouraged by his religious advisors, he admitted to the Pennsylvania and Ohio murders that took place during 2000 and 2001, as well as the 2004 murders in New Mexico and Arizona. But this seemingly altruistic act proved a self-serving one. Although not tried in court, his guilt in these crimes was already a foregone conclusion. What the authorities really wanted were confessions to crimes that occurred in and around Pennsylvania and Ohio during 2002, his "gap year." It is rumored that clemency was offered in exchange for this information, but for whatever reason, Williker refused to cooperate. Indiana's Governor Mitch Daniels allegedly became so enraged at what he perceived as Williker jerking him around, he fast-tracked the execution out of spite.

The reason given publicly, for this and several other last-minute executions at the time, was the impending expiration of the state's supply of Midazolam, a sedative used in the lethal injection process. Indiana and other states were having trouble procuring additional quantities of this and similar drugs, as pharmaceutical manufacturers no longer wanted their products associated with capital punishment. So when faced with the possibility of Williker living to a ripe old age at the taxpayer's expense, Governor Daniels chose to move forward with a warrant of execution.

Jonas Williker spent a mere three years on death row, at a time when the average stay was 10 to 15 years. In an era of ever-lengthening appeals and increased demand for reform, his execution felt almost criminal in its expedience. But despite protests from human rights groups, authorities also faced mounting pressure from the victims' families, as well as senior members of the state legislature. Even President Bush weighed in on the issue, urging the state of Indiana not to let justice go unfulfilled.

Jonas Williker gave few formal interviews. When he did, he revealed little in the way of insightful information. Most books on the Purple Satin killings are a salacious rehash of what is already public knowledge—the court transcripts, the autopsy reports, and certain redacted police and FBI documents (my profile included). His psychological evaluations post-conviction have remained sealed. It would surprise me if they contained anything substantial. No, Jonas Williker was too guarded for that.

During his trial and subsequent incarceration, however, Williker took up correspondence with numerous people on the outside. Even in his letters, he presented a carefully curated version of himself. But what he couldn't control was how those people would respond. There was something illuminating about the distillation of Jonas Williker as presented in the letters written not by him, but to him. A happy accident, an alchemy he could have never predicted. It was the closest thing we ever got to emotional honesty from the man.

Collected here, these letters offer a unique glimpse into a depraved mind through a human lens, including contributions from family, the bereaved, and die-hard fans. They represent a chilling portrait of the American psyche, skewering a media obsessed culture where murderers are revered as celebrities. What it does not include is writing from Jonas Williker himself. Because as we have learned, no truth was to be found in his words. The truth about him was reflected in others. What you learn about the man from these letters will surprise you, as it did me.

Roddy Perkins
Former Behavioral Analyst, FBI
2024

—

AUTHOR'S PREFACE

In the years between his arrest and execution, Jonas Williker received hundreds of letters in prison. Some were from friends and family, others were legal in nature, but the majority of them came from complete strangers—what you might call "fan" letters. Most people find it hard to believe the average citizen would want anything to do with someone who had committed such heinous acts, let alone correspond with them on a regular basis. They become even more incredulous when they find out a large number of these letters are more than congenial—are in fact romantic in nature. People assume the author of such a letter must be as sick as the person they are writing to, if not more so.

Well, having read the entirety of Jonas Williker's written correspondence multiple times over, I can safely say—nothing surprises me anymore. The human desire for social interaction, acceptance, and even love knows no bounds, nor does our capacity for compassion. It is sad, profound, and strangely touching.

Which is not the takeaway I expected going into this project. Putting this book together was not an endeavor I undertook lightly. I knew I would be faced with some of the darkest humanity had to offer, and I'd have to live in that headspace for a protracted period of time. As hard as I might try to compartmentalize, I knew it would impact the lives of those around me as well. It's one thing to subject yourself to the abyss, but it's another to expose the innocent bystander. I did not want my family to become collateral damage in the process.

This concern also extended to the commercial potential of the project, as well as my editorial approach. A complete collection of letters between Jonas Williker and his many pen pals would comprise volumes. Literally thousands of pages. Who would want to read such a thing, other than the truest of true crime fanatics?

So right off the bat I had to make some drastic choices. The project needed a hook. Plenty of historical volumes feature letters *written* by famous public figures, why not publish a book consisting of letters written *to* that person? Letters from those on the periphery would invariably be more palatable, as a whole, than the endless musings of a violent criminal. At least I hoped they would. The lens of the outsider is a unique perspective from which to view a subject—a more truthful one, I would argue. Because the external gaze is not something a person can exert direct control over.

Still, I couldn't just publish every single letter sent to Jonas Williker, either. He received far more than he wrote. Many of them are mad. The bulk of them are maddeningly mundane. So I began looking for a narrative—any narrative—to help guide my editorial shears. Some sort of thematic cohesion. I knew better than to expect a fulfilling character arc from a serial killer in the twilight of their life, but maybe one existed in the people who reached out to him?

I started with the major players. His mother, obviously, as well as Candace Bennington, the woman who would go on to become his wife. Then there was his childhood friend, William Peters. He was a shoo-in once I saw how heart-wrenching his letters were. And who could forget Ginny Goodwinch, the single mother from Chappaqua, New York, who mauled a news reporter on live TV outside of the courthouse? She was a mainstay on the interview circuit for a while, a frequent punchline on late night talk shows, but if you haven't read her letters, you don't know Ginny.

These were easy inclusions. They formed the spine in what could have been an obese body of work. The letters as a whole featured a lot of redundancy, repetition of what I refer to as the Williker Archetypes: the Angry American, the Grieving Family Member, the Religious Grifter, the Prison Groupie, the Fellow Outcast, the Opportunist, the Morbidly Curious, the Torture Merchant, etc., etc. I chose the most well defined of each group, the ones who possessed

a unique voice and provided the most conflict. People with their own minia-
ture narrative arcs, that granted insight into who Jonas Williker really was, as
opposed to the person he was *telling* us he was via his crimes. I also included
a selection of the most entertaining, ridiculous, and mind-blowing one-offs,
to inject a little randomness, because life is random, and I didn't want the
collection to feel too curated. The overall dramatic results are surprisingly
satisfying.

That isn't to say there is a larger purpose behind Jonas Williker's unthinkable
crimes. That would be insulting and disrespectful to the victims and their
families. I'll leave that to the Abigail Tinders and Joseph Oystertons of the
world. No, what I'm saying is human beings are resilient. They have a knack
for overcoming the insurmountable. There might not be any happy endings
in this story, but the people involved do what they can to pick up their lives
and move on. I hesitate to brand them as heroes, because so often we bestow
that moniker upon people who've been through the proverbial wringer, and
it's become shorthand for someone who's damaged beyond repair. I wouldn't
wish the experiences of these so-called "heroes" on anybody. No, what they
are is human. Not the best of us, not the worst, but a good representation
of our species as a whole, and for that they deserve our respect. Their stories
deserve to be told.

So to the friends and families of the victims, thank you.

Thank you to the "fans" as well. You kept things interesting.

To everyone else, thank you for reading. May the book in your hands prove
compelling and insightful.

Joshua Chaplinsky
2024

—

CORRESPONDENTS

Anonymous Shit Poster: A "regular" correspondent whose frequent, excrement-smeared missives somehow always manage to make it through the prison's mail screening process

Judith Williker: Long-suffering mother of Jonas Williker, wife of emotionally-inaccessible factory worker, Frank Williker

Susie Phillips: 10-year-old daughter of victim #5

Ginny Goodwinch: Single mother of two from Chappaqua, NY who doesn't believe all the bad things they say about Jonas in the press

Aaron Tyson: Self-righteous protector of young girls who knows people on the inside

Grant Singer: Former Detective with Columbus P.D., witness for the prosecution, Special Agent on the Federal Task Force for Serial Homicide

Dimitri Novack: Landlord of Jonas Williker at the time of his incarceration

Stacey Santiago (AKA Staci Satin): Intrepid internet pornographer and self-proclaimed #1 fan of the Purple Satin Killer

Captain Andrew Jack Bradford: Former astronaut and one-time political also-ran for whom Jonas volunteered after college

Beverly Flynn: Former high school classmate of Jonas Williker

Candace Bennington: PhD candidate researching hybristophilia at John J. College of Criminal Justice

Mudpie Jr.: Highest ranking player on his Call of Duty fireteam

Lily Anderson: Ex-girlfriend of Jonas Williker, mother of Anna Anderson

Anna Anderson: Daughter of Lily Anderson, born May 19th, 1992

Martin Beaufoy: Autograph hound and collector of true crime ephemera

Wayne McKenna: Avid reader of true crime with some unique theories on serial murder

Aurelius Percy, Esq.: Founding partner in the law firm Percy, Paramount & Bint

Jane Doe (AKA The One That Got Away): The one that literally got away

William Peters: Former childhood friend struggling with numerous personal issues

Ziv Sloan: No-nonsense partner of William Peters

Albert Jefferies: Self-appointed gatekeeper for the pantheon of serial killer greats

Ryland Cochero: 6th grader from London, WI raising money for a school trip to Washington DC

David Manning: Obsessive Truth Sleuth community member who travels for work

Kurt Beckett: Convicted murderer and nemesis of the community organization, Parents Against True Crime

Todd DeFrancisco: Paranormal investigator and host of popular reality show, *Adventures in Ghost Hunting*

Abigail Tinder: Precocious twelve-year-old preacher's daughter from Argos, Indiana

Reverend Wallace Samuel Tinder: Preacher from Argos, Indiana. Father of Abigail Tinder

Joseph Oysterton: Pastor of the Universal Water of Life megachurch

Jason Corbish: Managing Editor of *In Verse* poetry magazine

Miguel Serrano: A man who credits Jonas Williker with saving his life

Antonio Birch: College student, recovering victim of a traumatic brain injury, burgeoning sociopath

Darlene Edmonton: Owner/proprietor of Outside Access, LLC

Elrond James: Bestselling crime fiction author with mommy issues

Vivian Ross: A woman who takes exception to the lack of diversity among Jonas Williker's victims

Larry Hostetler: Owner/proprietor of Murdertown, USA, repurposer of crime-related collectibles

Logan Nester: Owner/proprietor of Macabre Artifacts, chief competitor of Murdertown, USA

SKASM: Serial Killers Against Serial Murder

The Poet: Anonymous writer of troubling/incoherent verse

Wex Durham: Webmaster, The Serial Killer Collective

Morty Friedman (AKA Mortimus): Lead singer of metal band, Black Satan

Buddy Reaves: Corrections Officer, formerly of Indiana State Prison

Jareth Blackbird: Former goth with a history of killer correspondence

Meredith Wu: Juror #6

Citizenry Services: Provider of legally dubious services to the incarcerated and uninformed

Amy Sorenson: Young urban explorer with an interesting story to tell

District Judge Wallace Breheny: The man tasked with signing Jonas Williker's order of execution

Walton Dash: General Manager, Killer Kitchen catering service

Matt Cominsky: Collector of boundary-pushing apparel

Helena Rubinski: Psychiatric researcher and neurocriminologist

Rubix Integer: Senior Advisor, Consciousness Preservation Solutions

Trevor Pence: Brother of Holly Pence (victim #17), member of National Organ Transplant Waiting List

Morley Woodlock: Amateur expert on the history of lethal injection

Martha Randolph: Mother of Sally Randolph (victim #14)

—

AFTER THE INDICTMENT

To: Jonas Williker, inmate #957464
From: anonymous
July 16, 2005

[*Jonas Williker received weekly anonymous letters during his prison sentence, each one similarly soiled. Somehow, they always managed to make it through the mail screening process.* — Editor]

To: Jonas Williker, inmate #957464
From: Judith Williker
July 18, 2005

Dear Jonas,

It's your mother. How are you holding up? Are they feeding you enough in there? I can only imagine what you're going through. One state shouldn't be allowed to just hand you over to another like that. It seems like some sort of civil rights violation if you ask me. Whatever happened to due process? Indiana should have to wait their turn while you serve your time in Nevada. Then they should have to track you down themselves after you've been released. Give you a proper bail hearing and whatnot. I don't care how serious these new charges are, you still deserve to be treated like a human being. At least now you're closer to home. I know you said not to worry about visiting while you were in Nevada, since you only expected to serve a few months, but this here is a whole new ball of wax.

Not much to report on our end. We're in the middle of another heatwave, so your father and I spend most of our time in front of the television with the AC on. When we're not watching the news, we're watching that prison show, *Oz*? Are you familiar? It's very realistic. I don't like all the cussing and the violence, but I wanted to educate myself about your situation. I've already learned so much! I don't know if you're aware of this, but there are men that dress like ladies in there. Can you believe such a thing?

Oh. Your father just reminded me that one of your alleged victims was a he-she. I don't know how anyone can tell the difference. Some of them are quite pretty! Anyway, that's probably the least of your worries right now.

Speaking of Dad, he's still pretty upset about the whole situation. He even had to take a leave of absence from work. It wasn't exactly what you would call voluntary, but in the end everyone agreed it was for the best. Factories are like prisons in a lot of ways. Lots of little cliques. The other employees were constantly picking fights with your father, and distractions can be deadly on the assembly line. One court case at a time is plenty, thank you very much! There are only so many hours in a day.

I'll try to get Dad on the phone next time you call, but no promises. You know how stubborn he can be. I'm sure he didn't mean all those things he said, about you being the spawn of Satan. Not *literally*. In this house we believe innocent until proven guilty. And no matter what you've done, you're still our son. Dad's just never been very good at handling his emotions. You know that.

Sometimes I wonder what young Judy Schoenecker saw in that stoic gas station attendant and his military haircut. I guess I was just happy to have someone show interest in me, even if they did use my father as a go-between. Looking back on it now, my father traded me off like a prize pig. You never knew your granddad. He was… let's just say it was a different time. He passed a few days after the wedding, God rest his soul. I guess he felt he'd fulfilled his obligation by securing me a husband, so he decided to knock off early. Ma didn't seem too upset, but I still miss him from time to time. I didn't even have the chance to tell him he was going to be a grandfather.

The wedding itself wasn't anything special. More of a family gathering, really. You've seen the pictures. A bunch of relatives we rarely saw. A handful of new relatives we'd never see again. And there was never any question of us going on a honeymoon. No, sir. Your father went right back to work the very next day. Honestly, If I'd known he was gonna get laid off so soon after the wedding I would have insisted on that trip to Niagara Falls. Do you know we've still never been? I've heard it's gorgeous this time of year.

In other news, I won third place in the local rose competition. So life isn't all bad. Mary Rogan said it was because the judges felt sorry for me, on account of recent events, but she's just being a sourpuss because she didn't place. She's always been a sore loser, and it's only gotten worse since her husband died.

One time she stopped talking to me for a whole month because your father refused to mow her lawn. It wasn't my fault he said no! Well, technically what he said was she should hire a Mexican like everyone else on the block, but still… She should have known better than to ask. It's not like your father has a history of being neighborly.

Anyway, it's Monday, which means I've got a roast to prepare. As your father likes to say, dinner ain't gonna cook itself! I'll write you again next week. Talk soon.

Love,
Mom

—

To: Jonas Williker, inmate #957464
From: Susan Phillips
July 21, 2005

To: Jonas Williker,

Why did you take my mother from me? I miss her so much it feels like I have a stomach ache. My dad talks about all the bad things he wants to do to you but I just want my mom back. How would you like it if someone took *your* mother from you? Wouldn't you want them to say they were sorry? Dr. Perez says people like you don't feel sorry and that isn't why she's making me write this letter. She says we're not even going to mail it. That's good because I don't want you writing back to me. I would be afraid to read your letter. Dr. Perez says it's good to face our fears but it would be bad for you to know where I live so this letter will go into a special drawer. Maybe I'll read it again when I'm older and it will make me feel better. That's what Dr. Perez says. Right now I don't think it's helping much.

From,
Susie Phillips

[*It is unknown how Jonas Williker came into possession of this letter.* —Editor]

—

To: Jonas Williker, inmate #957464
From: Judith Williker
July 25, 2005

Dear Jonas,

It's your mother. You know what that means, don't you? Another week down! I'm marking the days on my calendar, like tally marks scratched into the wall of a cell. Does anyone actually do that in there? Or is that only in cartoons? I'd imagine the guards frown upon defacement of state property, and are itching for any excuse to dole out a complimentary "wood shampoo," so please be careful.

Your father sure frowned upon me writing on the kitchen calendar. *His* calendar, he called it, so I had to buy a second one specifically to keep track of your time in jail. I got it for 99 cents on account of the year being half over. Not a bad deal! It's a cat calendar, and each month features a cute little kitten getting itself into some harmless, fluffy mischief. Just like you used to. You know, minus the fluffy part. I've hung it on the inside of the hall closet, where I keep my cleaning supplies. Your father hardly ever goes in there. Maybe I'll send you one. That way we can keep track of the days together.

Do they let you go outside at all? Legally I think they have to. The heatwave here finally broke, so I was able to spend some much-needed time in the garden. My award-winning roses missed their momma. They need *lots* of TLC. You'll also be pleased to know the morning glories have started coming in. Grandpa Otts. Your favorite!

What else is new? To be honest, your father and I don't lead the most exciting lives. I didn't really take that into account when I promised to write you a whole letter each and every week. All the exciting things in our lives are happening to you, and I'm pretty sure you don't want me chewing your ear off about *that* stuff!

Is that the appropriate expression? Chewing your ear off? You know, since I'm not actually doing any talking? It's a pretty gross turn-of-phrase when you think about it. What would the equivalent for writing be? Bleeding your eyes dry? I know that's how my eyes feel after I've written an extra-long letter.

Oh. Your father just reminded me that one of your alleged victims literally had their ears chewed off. He said police found the cartilage spat on the ground next to the body. How awful. Personally I prefer not to fixate on such morbid details. It's not healthy.

Oh well. I guess that's it for now. Talk to you soon!

Love,
Mom

—

To Jonas Williker, inmate #957464
From: Ginny Goodwinch
July 28, 2005

Dear Jonas Williker,

My name is Ginny Goodwinch, and I'm a single mother of two from Chappaqua New York. (Bobby is five and little Derrick is three. Mommy loves you!) I've been following your case and I must confess, I find it hard to believe a man with such a kind face could do the horrible things they've accused you of. Abduction, dismemberment, rape—those are crimes an ugly man commits. It's like my mother always says: ugly insides make for ugly outsides. Of course, Mother thinks you're guilty as heck, but you can't be right all the time.

In fact, I read an article that said approximately 40% of all murders go unsolved, so right off the bat the odds are in your favor. That means there's only a 60% chance of your conviction. And that number drops even further when you take the appeals process into account, so chin up! It's like I told Mother, you can't argue with numbers. Of course, she didn't take too kindly to that. Told me there was a reason I flunked math so many times, and if I wasn't careful I'd pull a muscle in my brain. I guess when it comes down to it Mother can argue with just about anything.

The reporter on the news said you didn't have much family other than your parents, so I figured you might need someone closer to your own age to talk to. It must get lonely in solitary confinement, even if it is for your own protection. I know what it's like to be lonely. Sometimes you can be surrounded by people and still feel like the only human being on the planet. Especially when the kids are having an epic meltdown in the middle of the supermarket because you won't let them stick raw spaghetti down their pants. I tried telling them sharp sticks can poke holes in baby birds, but they refuse to listen. Anyway, when stuff like that happens, some meaningful engagement is in order.

So if you find yourself in need of some ME, feel free to write back. You can't believe everything you see on TV, and I'd love to get to know the real you! I mean, what even is coprophagia? Sounds made up to me. Tell me something I won't hear on the news. What are your likes and dislikes? Your hopes and dreams? What does Jonas Williker do for fun?

I mean, under normal circumstances. I don't suppose there's much fun to be had in your current situation. Still, you find joy where you can. Mother says there's no greater joy than friendship. If I'm not being too forward here, maybe I could be that joy for you?

Anyways, it was just a thought. Let me know what you think.

Your potential friend,
Ginny Goodwinch

—

To: Jonas Williker, inmate #957464
From: Aaron Tyson
August 1, 2005

Hey asshole,

I see you looking all confident in the press, but I've got news for you, you fucking piece of shit. You know your upcoming trial's just a formality, right? Your guilt's a foregone conclusion. No jury in the world is gonna put you back on the street, no matter how many liberals they pack it with. If I were you, I'd be more worried about the sentencing. Personally, I feel life in prison is too good for a shit stain like you, but you know what? So is the death penalty. What does Indiana use, lethal injection? Not cruel and unusual enough. Not by a long shot. You deserve so much worse. I'm talking Wu-Tang level shit. Sew your asshole shut and keep feeding you.

Not that it matters. In reality, any sentence you get is gonna be a death sentence. Think you'll be safe in gen pop? You'd be lucky to make it a year. At least two of your victims were underage, and guess what cons hate? That's right. Kiddie fuckers. Don't think they won't find out, either. I know people on the inside. I'll make sure everyone hears what you did to those poor girls. You robbed them of their most precious gift, one that rightfully belonged to their future husbands, snuffing out the lives of potential children and grandchildren in the process. Makes me sick just thinking about it.

It doesn't matter if you're not technically a pedo. Cons don't split short hairs. They get one whiff of chomo, you're a fucking chomo. They're not gonna take the time to pull papers. They'll be too busy turning your face into pulp. You'll have to carry it around in a soup bowl.

If you don't get the death penalty you might as well check in on day one. Don't let pride be your downfall. Otherwise, no space will be safe. Go to the yard? Get stomped out. Sit in the cafeteria? Get stomped out. Try and take a shower? Get stomped out. Then raped. Think you'll be safe in your cell? Only when you're locked in. Every time you come back from rec, someone will have used it as a bathroom. Hosed it down with piss. Wiped their ass with your sheets. Short eyes get pink eye, you know what I'm saying?

Yeah, I can't wait. No matter what happens, it's not going to be easy for you. You're gonna regret ever laying a finger on those girls. Mark my fucking words.

A.T.

—

To: Jonas Williker, inmate #957464
From: Judith Williker
August 4, 2005

Dear Jonas,

It's your mother. Sorry this letter is a few days later than usual, but it's been a trying week. Reporters have been hounding your father non-stop and the stress is really getting to him. He can't even go out to get the paper without someone shoving a camera "in his face." (I've toned down his colorful language, in case anyone else is reading these letters, but you get the idea.) He's also taken to drinking more than usual, and you know how bad alcohol is for his IBS. Plus, with my arthritis, I can't scrub a toilet the way I used to.

At least it gives me something to write about. We hired a Spanish woman named Aretha to help out with chores around the house, but we can only afford to have her come once a week.

Personally, I don't mind the press. You just need to talk to them like regular people. One time they even put me on the evening news! I told them all about what a smart, well-behaved child you were. How much you enjoyed helping me in the garden. I felt like a movie star! Unfortunately your father wasn't too happy about it, so now I'm not allowed to talk to them. It's a shame, because your father isn't much of a conversationalist these days. Not that he ever was, mind you. I tried chatting with Aretha, but she barely understands English. Maybe I'll go dig up some of your old Spanish textbooks.

Worse than the press are all the mean letters we've been getting. I don't understand how people can write such terrible things to someone they don't even know. I responded to the first few, tried explaining how you hadn't technically been convicted of anything, how their anger was misplaced, but it only resulted in nastier letters. After a while I stopped reading them. Some bullies can't be won over, no matter how nice you are. I hope you aren't having the same problem. I would think the prison does their best to weed out most of the hate mail.

Have you made any friends yet? It's always good to have someone to watch your back (I'm learning so much watching *Oz*!). Maybe you could get yourself a little bird friend, like in *The Shawshank Redemption*. Then you'd have someone to watch your *beak*! Your father used to love that movie. Remember watching it together? One of the few things we enjoyed as a family. I really cherish those memories. "Get busy living…" That line chokes me up every time. Never mind the bird, you need to make friends with a wise old black man. Morgan Freeman is just the sweetest!

What else can I tell you? Mrs. Beasley next door got yet another cat. Can you believe it? I think that brings the total up to fourteen. She used to have such bad luck with pets, remember? They were always disappearing or turning up dead. For a while there we thought the neighborhood had a coyote on the loose! It wasn't until sometime after you went away to school that things started turning around for her. Whenever I see her, I make sure to ask how her little fur babies are doing. You think she'd return the pleasantry, but she just growls at me like one of her animals. She always was a little odd.

Well, I guess that's all the neighborhood news that's fit to print. But don't you worry, I'll write again soon. Muchos besos! (That's Spanish for hugs and kisses, by the way.)

Love always,
Mom

—

To: Jonas Williker, inmate #957464
From: Ginny Goodwinch
August 5, 2005

Dear Jonas Williker,

It's me again. Ginny Goodwinch. The single mother from Chappaqua, New York. If the name rings a bell, I apologize, but also, phew! My faith in the United States postal system has been restored. If, on the other hand, the name doesn't ring a bell—holy heck! I must be psychic. Quick! Think of a number from one to ten!

Just kidding. Not trying to be a total weirdo, here. If you're still wondering, "Who the heck is this Ginny broad?" allow me to explain.

Last week I wrote you a letter (which you may or may not have in your possession). A few days after that, the dreaded worrywarts descended. What if I'd forgotten the stamp? Or maybe postage had gone up again, rendering my current stamps insufficient. If so, would my letter be returned, or just thrown on a pile somewhere and forgotten about? Maybe postal employees read those letters to each other for fun? That wouldn't be very nice of them. What if they displayed those letters as a warning to other customers? "Don't be like these dum-dums!" These are just a few of the far-fetched scenarios I imagined might prevent my letter from reaching its destination.

So I decided to send a backup, just in case.

If you've already received the original, I apologize. I'm not a space cadet, I swear. The new version should be more or less the same, so there's no need to read it a second time, unless of course you want to. For me, rereading a good letter is one of life's greatest pleasures, and I write a darn good letter if I do say so myself.

So there you have it. Mailed letter, freaked out, sent duplicate. Typical Ginny! Still hoping to be your friend, though, if I haven't already ruined my chances.

Sincerely,
Ginny Goodwinch

[*Copy of original letter omitted. It was literally word for word.* —Editor]

—

To: Jonas Williker, inmate #957464
From: Grant Singer
August 13, 2005

Mr. Williker,

This has been a long time coming. And although I wasn't directly responsible for your recent apprehension by law enforcement, I'd like to think I played a small part in your indictment for murder.

Maybe you don't remember me. I'm a detective with the Columbus P.D. Back then, they called me Vanilla Pudding, on account of my average looks. This despite 99% of the department being white. Chief loved to crack jokes, used to tell me I should have chosen a life of crime, because no one would ever pick me out of a lineup. Even after I grew the facial hair, he'd say things like, "Who put a mustache on that mayonnaise sandwich?"

I've aged a lot since then. If you ask my ex, she'd say it's because of my unhealthy obsession with your case. So even if you remember what I looked like, you might not recognize me now. What little hair I have left has gone gray. My father didn't go bald until his 50s, so there's that record beat. I've gained a fair amount of weight as well. Ever since I broke the ankle chasing a perp it's been hard to keep off.

But if you don't remember my face, you must remember that night. Out on a secluded stretch of Miller's Highway. I sensed something off the moment I spotted your tan '91 Golf on the side of the road. So I switched on my lights and pulled in behind it. That's when you popped out of the woods, mud up to your knees, a smile on your face. When I asked what you were doing you told me you were taking a leak. "Draining the weasel," to be specific.

I didn't buy it. I followed you to your car and asked for your license and regis-tration. While you rummaged around in the glovebox I shined my flashlight into the back seat. I noticed a length of rope and a black balaclava on the floor. "What're those for?" I asked. You twisted around in your seat to take a look. When you saw what I was referring to you remained calm, casually referring to them as "tools of the trade." When I asked what you did for a living you said, "unemployed hangman," and asked if the department was hiring. Then you tilted your head, stuck your tongue to the side, and mimed yanking an invisible noose.

I left you chuckling at your own joke to run your plates. Everything came back clean. Not even an unpaid parking ticket. No legitimate reason for me to search your vehicle, let alone haul your ass in. But I couldn't shake the feeling you were up to no good. What the hell had you been doing out in the woods? You didn't brave the mud to take no damn piss, that was for sure.

When I walked over to return your ID, you were wiping at your knees with a bit of purple cloth. As I got closer I realized it was a pair of women's undergar-ments, the shiny fabric caked with mud. When you saw the look on my face, you didn't try to hide them. Instead you stretched the soiled panties between two sets of pinched fingers and grinned. "Like what you see?" you said. Then you wriggled your eyebrows like Groucho Marx.

A pretty slick move on your part. You went from unknown threat to run-of-the-mill pervert. I figured you'd been out in the woods jackin' it. It sounds far-fetched, but you'd be surprised how many fellas have an icebox for a wife who won't let them keep girlie mags at home. Rope, mask, panties—those were the personal effects of a horny and repressed individual. And you know what? In that moment I actually felt sorry for you. So I did my best not to touch your hand as I gave back your license, then got myself the hell out of there.

Only after I'd returned to the station and regaled the boys with our creepy encounter did it hit me.

Purple panties.

The next day we returned with the dogs and a twenty-man team to comb the woods. Just like when I ran your plates, we turned up zilch. Not even a stray pube. The guys razzed me for weeks about my deep-woods boyfriend, but I remained convinced—I'd had a run in with the Purple Satin Killer.

I became obsessed. This happened in 2001, right before you took that year-long vacation. I investigated every homicide as if you were the prime suspect. I commissioned a police sketch and reached out to every detective in the state. I had no real proof, but was convinced of your guilt.

For the most part my colleagues were polite, promising to add you to their ever-growing list of suspects. But without hard evidence, there was no reason for them to prioritize you. I spent a long, lonely year waiting for the Purple Satin Killer to strike again. Still, it wouldn't be until 2004, after your assault conviction in Nevada, that people started listening to me. At that point I reached out to the Indiana DA and they began putting a case together.

Like I said, I'm happy to have contributed, despite what it's cost me. My marriage, career advancement, my mental and physical well-being. I'd do it all again if I had to. In fact, I'll continue playing my part as a witness for the prosecution. It'll be interesting to see if you recognize me. If my boring face made an impression. Because I've been obsessed with yours. Hardly a night goes by I don't see it in my dreams. Maybe now I'll finally get some rest. Lord knows I could use it.

Sincerely,
Detective Grant Singer
Columbus Police Department

—

To: Jonas Williker, inmate #957464
From: Judith Williker
August 22, 2005

Dear Jonas,

Es tu madre. Como estas? Te extraño mucho.

I was going to attempt writing this entire letter in Spanish for practice, but that wouldn't be fair to you. It also wouldn't be a very long letter! It's hard enough coming up with things to write about in English. What do I look like, some kind of man of La Mancha?

Maybe you should consider studying Spanish. It's a very useful language. Did you know over 30% of prison inmates speak Spanish? Your father used to complain how none of his coworkers spoke English, but he never bothered trying to understand *them*, so... Maybe things would have turned out different if he'd made the effort.

Spanish can be fun! Whenever your father is being difficult, I look at Aretha and call him a gruñón, and we both have a good laugh. Your father scowls because he knows Aretha and I are sharing a private joke at his expense, but he's too proud to admit he doesn't know what we're saying. I asked Aretha what you could say to a guard to make the Spanish inmates laugh, and she said to call them a "pinchy marycone." She couldn't really explain what it meant in English, but she found it quite amusing. Just make sure you don't say it to a guard who speaks Spanish, otherwise ay yai yai!

Now that we're able to communicate a little better, I've discovered Aretha and I have a lot in common. Did you know she also has a son who's had trouble with the law? It just goes to show, the trials of motherhood are universal. I couldn't figure out exactly what he did, but she kept using the word "ilegal," which is Spanish for illegal. She made me promise not to tell your father. I don't want to give him any more reason to complain, so my lips are sealed. If on the off chance you talk to him, I'd appreciate if you didn't bring it up. Not that I'm worried. You were always so good at keeping secrets.

Talk to you soon!

Love,
Mom

—

To: Jonas Williker, inmate #957464
From: Dimitri Novack
August 23, 2005

Dear Mister Jonas,

Is many month now since I am last receiving payment for rent. Yes circumstances make timing difficult but I remain full of hope for resolution. To make formal vacancy our state insists on signing of letter. This you can provide? Or maybe someone else who is handling?

My preference is always for issues to remain small. Please believe I am never violating privacy even after much complaining of smell. Police make warrant leaving Novack very little choice. They take belonging to Mr. Jonas and treat property worse than wear. Even before police it is sad to say you make apartment hard for living. Quite possible to never rent again. There is requirement of special cleaning at over $8,000 cost! And still there is smell! Pissing from cat is proof of very difficult odor, even after I am insisting on no pet. Stain beneath carpeting ruin floor in very bad surprise. Science police assure me blood is not the type belonging to humans. If sample comes from animal no charges are to be filed. But still so much garbage. Crawling insect and hard cement dropping on floor. Maybe attraction is to spoiling food, but it is right I must pay? Novack is always believing in honor of people. He cannot know about these things they say you do, but he should bear responsibility for mess?

Am I understanding the intention is to discontinue your name as tenant? Please make acknowledgement with writing. Then matters of money can at last be made calm. I would like for things to proceed easy in fashion. You can assist me with this? I am a man who likes no problems.

Thank you sincerely,
Dimitri Novack

P.S. — You have items in storage I am almost forgetting. Big trunk but not so heavy. This I should save? Maybe hand over for police? They are no friend to Dimitri lacking respect of his home. Please you will let me know. Again I thank you.

—

To: Jonas Williker, inmate #957464
From: Ginny Goodwinch
August 24, 2005

Dear Jonas,

I was so happy to get your letter! I've never had a pen pal before. And such a high profile one at that!

Of course I'll tell you a little more about myself. I'm twenty-nine years old (I've been twenty-nine for the last thirteen years now!), and I've lived in Chappaqua all my life. Growing up, I was the only kid in my class who didn't get the chickenpox, which either means I'm immune or destined to die from it. I married straight out of high school, which I do NOT recommend, and got a part-time job as a bookkeeper for the local lumber yard. They haven't fired me yet, so I must be doing something right!

My husband Ronnie was a drinker, and what Mother called a "cooze hound." That scoundrel took off right before I turned twenty-nine for the second time. We never had any kids, and the single life hasn't been easy, what with my thyroid issues. So a few years ago I adopted Bobby and Derrick, two special needs children. The approval process is a lot quicker for specials, because most people just want regular kids, but I'm not picky. They bring so much sunshine into my otherwise dreary life!

But listen to me, complaining! How are things with you? Is your arm feeling any better? I can't believe they let that guard get away with such cruelty. Even if you did threaten to violate the stump of his mother's headless corpse. I mean, those are just words. That man's supposed to be a professional. What's this world coming to?

How's your defense shaping up? That's a rhetorical question, I know you can't talk about it. Justice sure does take its sweet time! What with your arraignments, your bail hearings, your indictments... not to mention the actual trial! As a member of the viewing public, the pace has been excruciating. I imagine it must be even harder on you. One day at a time, I suppose.

Have you read any good books lately? I don't know how well-stocked they keep the prison library, but I'm reading the latest about a lady nurse who goes adventuring through time in the Scottish Highlands. It's sexy and romantic and thrilling and just the thing to pick me up when I'm feeling especially lonely. I'm already on my third read-through. I highly recommend it! Especially if you like a man in a skirt.

I'm enclosing a picture of myself, as requested. It's a few years old, but I don't really have a lot of photos without the kids. This is from the before times, or B.C. as I like to say (that's Before Children), from a solo girl's trip I took to the Jersey Shore. The plan at the time was to celebrate my recent singlehood, but I neglected to put sunblock on my feet (who knew?) and they swelled up like a couple of pink balloons. I spent the rest of the weekend in the hospital with sun poisoning, which was a bummer, because they don't serve margaritas at the hospital!

I hope you don't mind that I'm only wearing a two-piece in the picture. I think I look pretty in it. (Aw shoot, now I'm blushing!) Anyway, I never had anyone to share it with, so I hope you like it.

Do you like it, Jonas?

Your friend,
Ginny

—

To: Jonas Williker, inmate #957464
From: Staci Satin
August 27, 2005

Dear Purple,

You make my cunt ache. I want you to turn me inside out so you can carve your name into it. That way every time I spread my legs the world will know who I belong to. I am a freshly painted bathroom stall waiting to be defaced by your graffiti.

—*Purple Satin was here*

I want to slather your face with my pussy juice. Force the judge to watch as the jury licks it clean on national television. Fuck Bundy, Dahmer, and O.J. Compared to you, those guys are hacks. Rank-and-file amateurs. Yours will be the highest-rated criminal trial of all time. Like a Baroque opera by the Marquis de Sade, starring the inmates of an insane asylum, performed on a stage of rotting flesh.

Oh, how I long to tread the sinewy boards of that stage.

Make me your ultimate victim. I'm begging you.

xoxo,
Staci

—

To: Jonas Williker, inmate #957464
From: Judith Williker
September 12, 2005

Dear Jonas,

Guess what? I learned a new word today! Well, two words, actually. Voir dire. That's French for "to speak the truth." It's what fancy lawyers call jury selection. Look at me, being all knowledgeable! Between this and the Spanish, I'm becoming quite the cunning linguist, as they say.

It's your mother, by the way.

Such a beautiful phrase, don't you think? To speak the truth. That's a jury's job. Makes me feel all patriotic inside!

You know, I was on a jury once. A long time ago, right after you were born. Your father didn't want me to do it, because he didn't want to get stuck changing diapers all day. He told me I should say I hated everyone to get out of it. If the case involved cops, he wanted me to say, "I hate cops!" If it involved Mexicans, then "I hate Mexicans!" You get the idea. It wasn't very nice. Personally, I don't mind the Mexicans. Aretha's Mexican, and she's practically my best friend!

But the truth is, I didn't want to get out of jury duty. I found the whole process meaningful and romantic. So I did my best to be honest, and wouldn't you know it, they picked me! This upset your father, but in the end it didn't matter. He didn't have to take care of anyone but himself. I got your Aunt Lottie to babysit. Don't worry, this was before she had her "issues."

The case seemed pretty straightforward. It concerned an 18-year-old black kid charged with possession of an illegal firearm. It was a first-time offense, and the thing wasn't even loaded, but the serial number had been filed off, which made it a more serious crime. It was obvious the gun belonged to him, even though he claimed it didn't. An eye witness had seen him showing it off to friends, waving it around like Yosemite Sam. The thing is, the police didn't find the weapon on him. Someone had stashed it in a backpack on the ground. The backpack belonged to the defendant, but he said he didn't know how the gun got there.

He seemed like a good kid who made a stupid mistake, but in the end he was technically guilty. I personally didn't think it was in his best interest to send him to jail, but it wasn't my job to determine what was best. It was my job to determine his guilt. I had to do my civic duty and could only hope for the best.

I know in my heart I made the right decision, even if it didn't feel like it at the time. Luckily, we had one of those liberal judges. She went easy on the kid. Hopefully he turned his life around after that. Maybe I should look him up on Myspace?

Sorry. Didn't mean to get all serious on you there. These letters are supposed to lift your spirits, not bring you down.

On a lighter note, I saw that news piece about all your lady-admirers. Your father nearly fell out of his chair, but I'm not surprised. You can be quite the charmer when you put your mind to it. Remember the time Mrs. Edmunds gave you a B+ on that report, and you convinced her to change it to an A? She told me you made a very compelling case and she just couldn't say no. She repeated that phrase a number of times. "I couldn't say no." It made me so proud!

I wonder why Mrs. Edmunds decided to retire so young. Probably found herself a rich husband. It's too bad. She was such a lovely teacher. I know you were fond of her. You had all those pictures. It was like a little shrine!

Oh. Your father just reminded me that Mrs. Edmunds changed her name and moved away, so I guess she did get married after all. Good for her. I should really write her a letter.

Double oh. Your father also says the school refused to give out her forwarding information, which I guess is understandable. Your father doesn't like to talk to anyone from his old job either. Still, you *were* one of her favorite students.

That's it for now, I guess. I'll write again soon!

Love you,
Mom

—

To: Jonas Williker, inmate #957464
From: Andrew Jack Bradford
September 16, 2005

Dear Mr. Williker,

In regards to your request that I appear as a character witness at your upcoming trial, I must respectfully decline. While it may be true that you worked as a volunteer for my West Virginia gubernatorial campaign in 1996, the fact of the matter is I have no recollection of you. Even seeing your face on television failed to jog my memory, and I pride myself on having excellent recall. It was an incredibly busy time in my life, and I considered it a privilege if I got to shake a volunteer's hand, let alone establish a rapport with one. For them, not me. There were so many of you, coming and going, all with the same haircut, I could barely tell you apart. It's just a sad reality of politics. Thankfully that was my first and only foray into said cesspool.

Between you and me, my campaign manager told me I was a shoo-in as a former astronaut, because America loved the space program at the time. It was like patriotic crack. A bald eagle with a booster rocket strapped to its ass. Of course, nothing was the same after the Challenger blew up. You know, I piloted the Challenger on one of its earlier missions. So that could have been me up there. But instead of killing me, the Challenger killed my career. Blew it to smithereens! I was scheduled to command the Columbia in 1986, which would have been a big deal for me, but NASA canceled all space flights after the Big C went kaboom. Damn school teachers. They have no business being in space.

Since then, I have been pursuing opportunities in the financial sector, so I would appreciate you not discussing our shared history with the media. It's hard enough being a political also-ran. I don't need to be an employer of serial killers as well. Nothing against you, it's just an unneeded distraction. I hope you understand.

I see you are a fellow WVU Alum. Might I suggest contacting one of your former professors? Those guys can always be counted on to provide a good word. They love to see their own name in print. Imagine what they'd say to be on TV?

I'm sorry I can't be of more help, but thank you for writing. Don't forget to keep an eye out for Space Jockey brand energy drink, coming soon to select convenience stores in the lesser-greater Denver area.

Sincerely,
Captain Andrew Jack Bradford

—

To: Jonas Williker, inmate #957464
From: Beverly Flynn
September 21, 2005

Hello Jonas,

Yes, of course I remember who you are. We went to the same school for 13 years. You were my lab partner in biology when we dissected those baby pigs. And no, I don't want to be your pen pal. Not after what you've been accused of.

Also, don't think I forgot about the time you followed me into the bathroom at Mary Lou Talbert's makeout party and pretended it was an accident. Instead of turning your back and apologizing you just stood there gawking while I peed. Fifteen minutes later you were on the couch fingering Samantha Preston while she made out with Paul Bixby. She claimed she thought it was Paul doing the diddling, and he was more than willing to take credit (how chivalrous), but like a dozen kids saw what happened. She was forever branded a slut after that. All you ever got were high fives and requests to smell your finger. I feel awful about the way we treated her.

In light of this, your recent arrest makes so much sense. Please do not contact me again. Any mail from you will be marked Return to Sender.

Sincerely,
Beverly Flynn

—

To: Jonas Williker, inmate #957464
From: Ginny Goodwinch
September 26, 2005

Dear Jonas,

How was your weekend? Or is that a silly question? Do you even have week-ends in prison? I mean, I know Friday and Saturday exist on the inside (it would be strange if they didn't), but are they celebrated like they are out here? Is everybody workin' for 'em, like the song says, or does one day just bleed into the next? I feel like if you're not getting dolled up and going out on the town, then the weekend probably isn't that important to you.

Don't worry, it's not important to me, either. I'm usually stuck at home with the kids. My weekdays are more like my weekend, because that's when Moth-er watches Bobby and Derrick while I go to work. That may not sound very exciting, but it's really the only time I get to do any socializing. It's just me and Mimi at the office, the boss's secretary, but we both love to chat, so we make do.

At first Mimi didn't believe me when I told her you and I were pen pals, so I had to show her your letter as proof. That was a big mistake on my part. Mimi's one of those "keeping up with the Joneses" types. When her neighbor got a pool, she had to have a pool. When her sister got a new car, she had to have a new car. When the boss's wife got a boob job, she had to have a boob job, and hers had to be bigger. In fact, when I adopted Bobby and Derrick, she decided *she* needed to adopt some specials, too. Luckily, she was flagged for requesting too many at once (five!), and eventually lost interest.

Anyway, once I showed her your letter, she started going on about how *she* wanted a pen pal, and maybe *she* should start writing to you. Well, I did not like the sound of that. I tried laughing it off, but she just wouldn't let it drop. I finally had to get firm with her. I told her you were *my* pen pal, and if she wanted one so bad, she'd have to find her own. That's when she turned on the waterworks. She said it wasn't fair, me hoarding the best one all for myself, and that anyone should be allowed to write to you if they wanted. She then proceeded to tell me that was exactly what she planned on doing, and there was nothing I could do to stop her.

Well. That's when things got unpleasant. I don't know what came over me. I'm not usually an aggressive person, but she crossed the line. Luckily the repair guy was there servicing our water cooler, otherwise I don't know what I might have done. After breaking up the fight, he and Mimi wound up going out to lunch together, which made her forget all about the pen pal thing. The next day she acted like nothing happened.

Do you think that was selfish of me? I know letters are worth their weight in gold on the inside, but I don't trust that Mimi. She's got a bit of a reputation and, although I could never prove it, I've always suspected her of hooking up with my ex while we were still married. That probably explains why I got so possessive. So consider yourself warned. If you get any letters from her, that's the type of person you're dealing with. She's officially gone from "keeping up with the Joneses" to "keeping up with the Jonases!"

Gotta go. Write back soon!

Your favorite pen pal,
Ginny

—

To: Jonas Williker, inmate #957464
From: Staci Satin
October 8, 2005

Dear Purple,

It's me again. Your #1 fangirl and ultimate fuck slave, ready to degrade myself upon command. Did Daddy miss me?

You are never far from my twisted little thoughts. Every night I recite the names of your victims before drifting off to sleep. They are a holy mantra, sacred, like the 99 Names of Allah: *Leslie Ann Hawkins, Betty Kaiser, Melissa Wainscott...*

Their deaths were a necessity, their suffering ripe with meaning. Like the passion of Christ in all its violent, titillating glory. I look forward to the day they turn *your* story into a film. It will require an artist worthy of your vision, a Mel Gibson to your Jesus of Nazareth.

Unfortunately the media has shown a disturbing lack of insight in their reporting, neglecting to focus on the reverence with which you treated your victims, the weight of their sacrifice. The critical understanding of these so-called "journalists" is predictably narrow in scope. Unworthy of the gifts you offer. Nevertheless, they serve their purpose. As do I.

Tell me, Master, what is my purpose? What can your servant do to please you? You have only to ask.

xoxo,
Staci

—

To: Jonas Williker, inmate #957464
From: Candace Bennington
October 15, 2005

Dear Mr. Williker,

My name is Candace Bennington. I am a PhD student in the Criminal Justice program at John J. College, and I have a proposition for you. Undoubtedly your team has counseled you against giving any interviews until after the trial, but I am not interested in the specifics of your legal woes. I am interested in your perspective on a sociological matter.

I am writing my thesis on the phenomenon of hybristophilia, commonly referred to as "Bonnie and Clyde Syndrome." It is a term used to describe a person possessed of a sexual attraction towards criminals (or those perceived as such). Based on what I'm seeing in the news, this is an area in which you have some experience. It has been reported you receive quite a bit of fan mail, and attendance at your pre-trial hearings has been overwhelmingly female. I'm sure this has not escaped your attention.

Statistically, most hybristophiles are women, due in part to the width of the gender gap amongst prison inmates. Over 93% of federal prisoners are male. But female criminals do have their share of fans, and I feel this is important to acknowledge. Former police officer and Playboy Club waitress Bambi Bembenek became romantically involved with a man on the outside during her incarceration. The couple went on the run together after he aided in her escape. It has also been reported Lorena Bobbitt received numerous marriage proposals despite having severed her husband's penis. If anything were to turn off potential suitors, you'd think it would be a history of penile dismemberment, but no.

So what causes this type of attraction? What leads a person to make romantic choices that fly in the face of traditional logic? Is it a lack of confidence?

Some form of Messiah complex? Unresolved parental issues? The lure of the "perfect" relationship, one that doesn't require actual commitment? These are the questions I seek to answer.

I would love to set up a time to speak with you, if you would be amenable. I suspect this subject arouses your curiosity as much as it does mine. Please write back at your earliest convenience.

Sincerely,
Candace Bennington

—

To: Jonas Williker, inmate #957464
From: Judith Williker
November 21, 2005

Dear Jonas,

Gobble gobble! It's your mother. As I write this letter Turkey Day is just around the corner. Do you have any special plans? Thanksgiving mass in the prison chapel, perhaps? Followed by turkey loaf with all the trimmings? Your father and I would love nothing more than to be with you this holiday, but since that isn't possible, we'll have to settle for being with you in spirit. Or maybe your spirit can visit here with us. That way it gets a nice home-cooked meal. Besides, your dad's spirit doesn't really like to travel.

I know it might not seem like it at the moment, but you still have a lot to be thankful for. So I made you a helpful little list as a reminder. First and foremost, you have a mother and father who love you very much. I know, your father doesn't always show it, but trust me, those feelings are there. They may be buried beneath layers of gruff exterior, but they exist. Like most fathers, he is a man of action, not words. The type that shows love through silent strength. By shouldering the burden of providing food and shelter for his family. It's not easy, you know!

Remember how fascinated you used to be by Thanksgiving? All because of that time President what's-his-face pardoned a turkey instead of the guy who sold all those weapons in the Middle East. You were so cute! You demanded to know what the turkey had done wrong, and why the penalty for its crimes was to be eaten by our top elected official. We all had a good laugh over it.

The turkey's name was Charlie, if you remember. That year you asked to know the name of our turkey because you wanted to know "who you were eating." Your father, who grew up on a farm, found this highly amusing, although if you ask me, it was more than a little morbid. But he insisted it was healthy and gave you the honor of naming the bird. He seemed almost proud. Of course, that didn't last long. He was as shocked as I was when you pulled the name Annette out of the air like that.

What you couldn't have possibly known at the time was your father used to have a sister named Annette who was killed in a freak hunting accident as an infant. The neighbor's kid had been out in the road shooting squirrels. He wasn't a very good shot, and a stray bullet went through the wall and hit Annette in her crib. Punctured a lung, which prevented her from crying out. By the time the family discovered what had happened to her, her tiny body had already gone cold.

Obviously, this was a sensitive subject for your father, and the naming of the turkey after his dead baby sister really set him off. He insisted you knew, that you'd said it on purpose. "Look at his face," he kept saying, but all I saw was a scared little boy. If I'm being honest, Thanksgiving was never quite the same after that. The kid who shot Annette was too young to prosecute, and it *was* an accident, but to your father, the boy got away with murder.

I wonder how one goes about getting a pardon. An actual person, that is, not a turkey. I suppose the president needs to be aware of your predicament, for starters. Then there's the matter of convincing him you deserve to be pardoned. It reminds me of that story in the Bible where the Jews chose to pardon a criminal instead of Jesus, which should never have happened. Still, if it wasn't for them, little boys and girls around the world wouldn't get colored eggs from the Easter Bunny every year. Food for thought.

Well, looks like it's just about time for me to get dinner started. I know I promised you a whole list of things to be thankful for, but we'll have to save the rest for another letter. Really spread those blessings out and make them last. You still have your health, I assume. That's not something to be taken for granted.

Talk to you soon!

Love,
Mom

—

To: Jonas Williker, inmate #957464
From: Mudpie Jr.
November 25, 2005

Dear Murderous Scumbag,

Die.

DIE DIE DIE DIE DIE.

I hope they fry your ass, you worthless piece of shit.

Do not pass go. Take the express elevator to hell, where you can choke on Satan's cock for all eternity.

I'd like to have seen you try that shit in MY neighborhood. Come to my house, I would have put two between your eyes, saved a whole lot of families a whole lot of grief.

But that's how it is with cowards. You never fuck with someone who knows how to defend themselves. You just prey upon the weak and unarmed. Not on my watch. I'm the highest scoring player on my Call of Duty fireteam. Look me up.

Or just fuck off and die. Doesn't make a shit of difference to me.

Smell you later, you fucking bitch.

The one and only,
X_Mudpie_X

—

To: Jonas Williker, inmate #957464
From: Ginny Goodwinch
November 30, 2005

Dear Jonas,

I saw you on TV today. When you looked into the camera and winked, I let loose a scream that would have done young Ginny proud! (I used to be a massive New Kids fan. Mother used to threaten to send me to a shrink, I was so obsessed.)

You looked so handsome in your suit! Was it my imagination or were there an awful lot of women in the courtroom? You better not be cheating on me! (Just kidding.)

Speaking of kids, Bobby and Derek have been driving me up the wall. (You hear me, guys? Mommy's still very upset about her Kristi Yamaguchi commemorative plates!) Sometimes I feel like they're the only thing holding me back from driving across the country to see you. Would you like that? I'd leave the kids with Mother, but she's been confined to a dang wheelchair ever since she broke her hip. (She doesn't think I know, but EMS told me she was fornicating with the gardener in the shower when it happened!)

Sometimes I get so angry over the things they say about you on the news. What happened to innocent until proven guilty? They don't know you raped and murdered all those women. That's for a jury to decide. I wish I knew where that mean old news lady lived, I would drive to her house and give her a piece of my mind!

Listen to me, getting all protective like a momma bear. It's hard for me not to take these attacks on you personally. I feel like we've bonded so much in such a short period of time. Your letters have given me a reason to get up in the morning, not *become* a reason I get up in the morning, like two naughty little children who I won't name. I wish circumstances were different, that we could have met as two regular people on the outside and given our friendship a chance to truly blossom. Still, I wouldn't trade what we have for anything in the world. It is that special to me.

Seriously, though. Why are there so many women hanging around? They can't *all* be reporters. Don't they have anything better to do?

In loving friendship,
Ginny

PS: I've included some new snapshots to keep you company. Can't have you getting bored of me now that you're so popular!

—

To: Jonas Williker, inmate #957464
From: Candace Bennington
December 13, 2005

Dear Mr. Williker

Thank you for your timely response. I will get right to the point by saying I appreciate your concerns. So, as requested, here is a little more about me and my project.

You are correct in assuming my interest in this subject matter stems from personal experience. You see, I never knew my father. He was a career criminal who spent the entirety of my childhood behind bars. My mother, in her infinite wisdom, never allowed me to visit him. By the time I was old enough to do so on my own, he was dead. Stabbed in the throat by a jagged piece of lunch tray. An altercation over a fruit cup.

Despite depriving me of a personal relationship with my own father, my mother corresponded with him often. It drove a wedge between us. I would sneak into her room when she wasn't home and read the letters he wrote her, hidden amongst her silken underthings. It hurt when he didn't ask after my well-being, but somehow it hurt more when he did. It felt like love left on the table.

This project is partly an attempt to understand my mother's motivation. How could she be so obsessed with a man she professed to hate? Was she trying to protect me from him? Or trying to keep him all to herself?

I posit that a father is one of the most important people in a young girl's life. I don't think this is a controversial opinion. Taking that away from her in such a manner leaves an insatiable void, one she attempts to fill over and over again with little success. It is practically a cliche. In lieu of more typical, destructive behaviors, I have chosen to ease my pain with knowledge. Perhaps that way I can help prevent this tragedy from happening to other girls.

I hope this has satisfied your curiosity, or at least piqued your interest. Please let me know if we can meet. I am prepared to clear my schedule to facilitate this. A drawer full of my own silken underthings awaits your written response.

Sincerely,
Candace Bennington

—

To: Jonas Williker, inmate #957464
From: Lily Anderson
December 16, 2005

Dear Jonas,

Is it true, what they're saying about you on the news? I try not to let the speculation get to me, but I've been sick to my stomach for over a week now. It's the same nervous feeling I used to get every time we argued.

I can't look at the TV without hearing the newscaster's monotone voice in my head, reading off a checklist of gory atrocities you supposedly committed. It got so bad I pulled the plug and draped a sheet over the set to shut it up. Now it sits in the corner like a Halloween ghost. It wants to make sure I'm aware of the accusations, that I don't forget, that I never stop thinking about them. The fact that the man I shared my home with, the man who lifted me up at my lowest, who I trusted with my 7-year-old daughter's life, is a violent psychopath who rapes and murders women. And he most likely engaged in these activities during our relationship. While we shared a bed.

It's such an intimate betrayal. How did I not realize something was wrong with you? Sure, I caught glimpses of the darkness within. Vicious mood swings coming out of nowhere. But it would have been a paranoid stretch of the imagination to think this made you capable of murder. To cross-reference the nights you never came home with the crimes happening in and around Pennsylvania. Because yes, you could get angry. You could be cruel and shut me out without explanation. But you could also be exceedingly kind, thoughtful to a fault. Surprising me with flowers or breakfast in bed. Taking Anna to school and letting me sleep in.

I try and reconcile that man with the one who did those ungodly things to all those women, and I can't. Back in high school you got along with everyone. You didn't shun kids who weren't accepted by the in crowd. It's why they voted you most outgoing, most likely to succeed. I had a crush on you, but my shyness rendered you unattainable. After I got pregnant and had to drop out I thought I'd never see you again. When we reconnected 7 years later, I couldn't believe how attentive you were. I thought for sure you'd mistaken me for someone else. But no, you seemed genuinely interested. It was exactly what I needed at the time. I would have never gotten through my divorce without you. Sure, a few friends told me you were too good to be true, but jealousy talks. Finally, I had someone stable in my life. Why couldn't they be happy for me?

And it wasn't just about me. You got on so well with Anna. Picking her up from school, helping her with her homework, just *being* there. She might have needed you more than I did. She still asks about you. "Have you heard from Uncle Jonas lately?" When she finds out, the shock of it will crush her.

Those same friends, the ones who labeled you too good to be true, they never say, "I told you so." Not exactly. They say, "You dodged a bullet. You were one of the lucky ones. God had mercy on you." But what about me was so deserving of mercy? What about all those other women? Did they somehow deserve what happened to them? It doesn't make sense.

What prevented you from hurting us? Were we a cover? A secret you kept from your other self? Is it possible part of you is actually capable of love? Or are you that skilled an actor? I don't know which answer would hurt more. How am I supposed to explain this to a 13-year-old when I can't explain it to myself?

Why am I even asking you? You're probably as clueless as I am. I thought I'd gotten over you, but now the pain is back, and it's so much worse than before. This situation has become so much more than a bad breakup.

I guess there's a chance you're innocent. I have to keep reminding myself. As unlikely as it is, I hope it's true. For Anna's sake. For the sake of my sanity.

I don't know what else to say at the moment. I probably shouldn't have written in the first place.

Sincerely,
Lily

—

To: Jonas Williker, inmate #957464
From: Judith Williker
December 19, 2005

Dear Jonas,

It's your mother. Santa wanted me to tell you to keep your eyes peeled for a special Christmas care package. Nothing too extravagant, mind you. Even Santa has to follow prison guidelines. That means only pre-approved toiletries and snack items. They actually make Santa order them through a specific supplier that's been vetted ahead of time. So while this makes Santa's job easier, I'm afraid the selection is rather limited. Otherwise you'd be getting a batch of your favorite homemade cookies and a nice knitted blanket as well.

Santa was also able to get his hands on those law books you asked for. He had to order them directly from the publisher, which is the only way the prison allows books to be sent. So those should be arriving separately. He also threw in a copy of *How to Win Friends and Influence People*, which he thought might be helpful in your situation. Wasn't that thoughtful of him? Somebody must have been an extra good boy this year!

Even though I'm proud you're taking the initiative to educate yourself, I still think you should accept the help of the public defender. Are you sure you won't reconsider? It's their job to prove your innocence no matter what they think. And they really do seem to care about their clients. At least on TV they do. Otherwise wouldn't they all be high-powered defense attorneys charging tons of money? At the very least you could benefit from their experience.

Oh. Your father just reminded me only crazy people defend themselves. At least in the jury's eyes. So you might want to take that into consideration as well.

Here's hoping these gifts bring you a little holiday cheer! Talk to you soon!

Love,
Mom

—

To: Jonas Williker, inmate #957464
From: Martin Beaufoy
December 20, 2005

Dear Mr. Williker,

Enclosed you will find a collection of newspaper clippings concerning your case. I was wondering if you'd be so kind as to sign them for me? I am an autograph hound and an avid true crime fan. It would be greatly appreciated.

I understand you are yet to be convicted of any wrongdoing, but let's be honest—the evidence against you is quite substantial. Still, if you are uncomfortable embracing the mantle of the Purple Satin Killer at this time, I totally get it. Your legal name will suffice. Remember: just like on a traffic citation, your signature is not an admission of guilt. I used to work in my local County Clerk's office, so I should know.

However, if you choose not to sign, could you still please return the materials? Within six to eight weeks is considered standard etiquette. Either way, I've enclosed a self-addressed, stamped envelope for your convenience. And if it's not too much to ask, please be mindful when you handle the clippings. Oily hands can be quite corrosive. Fun fact: they are the reason the genitalia of metal sculptures are always so shiny, so imagine what they can do to paper! Also, please do not crease or bend the items in any way. And under no circumstances are you to eat while perusing them. I cannot stress this enough. Even without your signature, they are still of value to me. I spent a lot of time scouring local and obscure print publications in an effort to amass this collection. If you choose not to participate at this time, we can always revisit the subject of you signing them at the conclusion of your trial.

Until then, I offer my sincerest thanks for your time.

Sincerely,
Martin Beaufoy
Collector

—

To: Jonas Williker, inmate #957464
From: Ginny Goodwinch
December 22, 2005

Dear Jonas,

I've got a hypothetical question for you. If a person tries to do something nice, but things don't go quite as planned, does the thought still count? You know, like a tree falling in the woods when no one is around to hear it? Would you say that person technically still "did something nice"?

The reason I ask is, I wanted to do something special for you this Christmas, and in typical Ginny fashion, there were... complications. Two of them, in fact. One named Bobby and another named Derrick. So all I'm left with is the embarrassing story of what I attempted to achieve.

I'd gotten the bright idea of dressing up as Santa Claus and dragging my two little elves down to the mall to take some pictures. Sounds simple, right? Well, I forgot how crazy the mall can be during the holidays, and as soon as we arrived it was sensory overload. Bobby got all freaked out after he saw a reindeer accidentally step in its own poop. I mean, what the heck? Reindeer don't belong in the mall! And apparently, neither do Bobby and Derrick.

Bobby started screaming, saying the reindeer was trying to murder its babies. I tried explaining the little brown nuggets weren't babies, that the animal was just making a BM, but he wasn't having it. Then Derrick got it into his head that because it was okay for the reindeer to poop on the floor, it was okay for *him* to poop on the floor, and he proceeded to do just that. He dropped trou right there in the Photomart and let loose, which freaked Bobby out all the more. Even though he'd seen his brother do number two dozens of times, he started yelling at him, saying he wasn't allowed to make babies because he was a boy. Then Derrick started crying, asking me if all number twos were babies, and if every time he flushed the toilet he was drowning his babies.

Needless to say I was mortified. There I was, dressed as Santa, trying to calm two wailing elves while cleaning up a messy BM at the same time. We didn't even get to take any pictures. We were asked to leave, which made the boys cry even more. To top it off, I was told we are no longer welcome at the Photomart. The reindeer, I assume, suffered no such indignity.

Anyway, if it's the thought that counts, then Merry Christmas! I hope my crazy story has brought you at least a little cheer. It's brought Derrick a lump of coal and a second round of potty training.

In loving friendship,
Santa and her naughty little elves

—

To: Jonas Williker, inmate #957464
From: Staci Satin
February 8, 2006

Dear Purple,

How much longer will you make me wait? I've rubbed my pussy raw reading the autopsy reports. Not to get all sentimental on you, but Valentine's Day is just around the corner. You act tough, but I can tell it's a special day for you. I'm sure Leslie Anne Hawkins and Melissa Wainscott would agree.

Sometimes I sit in an ice-cold bath until my lips turn blue, then I lie on top of the covers with my door unlocked, waiting for someone to wander in and find me. Once I ordered food and gave instructions for it to be brought inside the apartment. There was a knock and a faint hello as the delivery person stuck their head in. A shocked gasp escaped them. From the foyer you can see right into my bedroom. I lay there, wet and shivering, for what seemed like an eternity, before the door closed with an audible click. Still, I didn't move, hoping they were in the apartment. I imagined it was you, fantasized about what you would do to me when you found me. Maybe drag a razor blade across my nipples, light as a feather. Or throw a plastic bag over my head and violate me with random household objects. Eventually I couldn't take it any longer. I gave in and made myself cum five times. Then I got up to retrieve my food and locked the door.

Did you make your victims cum for you? Fear can be a potent aphrodisiac. Were they ashamed? Could you see it in their faces in the moments after, right before you ended their lives? Maybe they felt complicit, or that they deserved what was happening to them. Or maybe they welcomed it, because in the end, death is the greatest release of all.

Is that what you're doing? Biding your time until the big goodbye? I know I am. Until then, I'll take as many "little deaths" as I can get.

xoxo,
Staci

—

To: Jonas Williker, inmate #957464
From: anonymous
February 14, 2006

greetings from
   historic scenery hill,
weekend getaway of
   presidents, poets, +
      other persons of note
since the 18th century

jonas williker
inmate 957464
indiana state prison
michigan city IN 46360

To: Jonas Williker, inmate #957464
From: Wayne McKenna
February 21, 2006

Dear Jonas Williker,

How come you don't have a middle name? I thought all serial killers had to have a middle name to avoid cases of mistaken identity. Isn't that like a law or something? What if there's another Jonas Williker out there? Just some regular guy, trying to live a regular life. Things are probably pretty terrible for him right now. Imagine trying to date? How awkward that must be? If you adopted a middle name, it would save the poor guy a lot of undue stress.

Who knows? Maybe it means you're innocent. I don't like dating, personally. Speaking of middle names, you ever hear of The Wayne Theory? Apparently, a high percentage of convicted murderers have the middle name Wayne. Pretty crazy, right? Some journalist made a list and it had over 200 people on it. My name's Wayne. I'm not a serial killer, though. Probably because it's my first name. My middle name's Eustace. I fucking hate it, but at least it's not a serial killer's name. I've found a lot of girls don't like talking about murder on a first date. I try to save it for the second date, but I don't usually make it that far. Making conversation with girls is hard. Mom says I just need more practice.

Now that I think about it, some of the most famous serial killers only had two names. Jeffrey Dahmer, David Berkowitz, Ted Bundy. So I guess there's that theory shot. Still, a lot of serial killers do have three names. Paul John Knowles, Bobby Joe Long. Does Jack the Ripper count as three names? There's also John Wayne Gacy. That's a big one. Plus he's a Wayne, so bonus points for him.

What about Eddie Wayne Edwards? His middle name is Wayne. Not a lot of people have heard of him, and he's one of the most prolific killers of all time.

There's this theory that he was the Black Dahlia Killer, the Atlanta Child Murderer, *and* the Zodiac Killer, all rolled into one. I know a lot of people think the Attorney General from Texas is the Zodiac Killer, but he looks like he couldn't bait his own fish hook, let alone murder someone. Besides, he's too young. I read a whole book about this Eddie Wayne guy. Supposedly his list of victims includes Jimmy Hoffa, Adam Walsh, and JonBenet Ramsey. Pretty crazy, right? Maybe he's responsible for some of the crimes you've been accused of. That'd be convenient, don't you think?

Mom says I read too many murder books. That it's not healthy and I should read normal stuff. I read *The Catcher in the Rye,* but that didn't really do it for me. Mom doesn't know I'm writing you. She says she dated a guy whose middle name was Wayne, and he was mostly harmless. But there was this Walt guy. I was too young to remember, but Mom says he had a real mean way about him. Maybe it's a W thing. Mom doesn't care much for my theories. I don't think I'll tell her about this letter.

I don't think serial killers are good, but they keep things interesting. What if they are the next step in human evolution? What if they kill off all the regular people and become like feudal lords? What if they colonize other planets? Travel through time? Take over the universe? It would at least make a cool book. Quantum serial killing! I've never written to a serial killer before. But maybe in another universe I have?

Thank you for reading!

Sincerely,
Wayne McKenna

—

To: Jonas Williker, inmate #957464
From: Judith Williker
March 20, 2006

Dear Jonas,

It's your mother. Just wanted to drop a quick note to wish you a happy birthday. I know it may not seem very happy, but in my opinion life is never not worth celebrating. You know how they say there's no such thing as bad pizza? That bad pizza is better than no pizza? Well that's how I feel about birthdays. Some people say the same thing about marital relations. For better or worse and all that, but at my age I could take it or leave it. Mostly leave it, if I'm being totally honest. Is that TMI? Life, on the other hand, is a gift to be savored.

Speaking of birthdays, do you remember the weird religious family that used to live in the neighborhood? The Reynolds? I think they were Jehovah's Witnesses or Christian Scientists or something, one of those religions even other religious people think are weird. Anyway, they didn't believe in birthdays. They said birthday cakes were evil because you made a wish when you blew out the candles, and making a wish was like casting a spell, which constituted witchcraft. Seems a bit silly if you ask me. I felt so bad for those kids.

One time I accidentally got them in trouble because I sent them home with some leftover cake. It's not my fault they knocked on the door during your birthday party. Knocking on doors is in those people's blood. What was I supposed to do, not invite them in? Mrs. Reynolds said I was a tool of the devil and had willfully endangered their immortal souls. I never claimed to be the perfect parent, but that kind of talk just doesn't seem healthy to me. There's no way those kids grew up normal.

My point is, try and look on the bright side of things. You're going to need to keep a positive attitude during the trial. With any luck, we'll be celebrating your next birthday as a family, like we used to.

Talk to you soon!

Love,
Mom

—

To: Jonas Williker, inmate #957464
From: Ginny Goodwinch
March 21, 2006

Dear Jonas,

It's your birthday! You know what that means? All aboard the paddy wagon!

You remember the paddy wagon, don't you? Back when I was in school (you hush, it wasn't *that* long ago), whenever it was somebody's birthday, the whole class would line up while chanting "Paddy wagon! Paddy wagon!" and the birthday boy (or girl!) would crawl through everyone's legs on their hands and knees, little bottom raised to receive their celebratory spankings! Everyone loved a good paddy wagon, mostly when it wasn't their birthday. Even the teachers couldn't wait to get their licks in! For me, there was something pleasant about the tingling sensation I felt when I sat down afterwards. Like I had a swarm of bees in my pants. Unfortunately I don't think it's an activity the school board allows anymore.

Now that I think about it, maybe it's patty wagon? Like patty cake? That sounds more like something that means spanking. Paddy just makes me think of leprechauns.

Do you have any plans for your special day? Don't worry, I didn't attempt anything crazy to mark the occasion. I learned my lesson after the Photomart fiasco. Still, I wanted to do *something*. So I asked Bobby to draw you a nice picture. He's quite talented, let me tell you. It seems to be a thing with specials. Something to do with their hyper-focused brains, which I'm also told accounts for how stubborn they can be. Like little mules!

Anyway, even the simplest of plans don't go off without a hitch when kids are involved. I figured Bobby would draw you something appropriately childish, like a T-Rex surfing on a submarine, or a gnome with a big blue butt, but he wound up going in a different direction.

Honestly… I didn't know what to think. As abstract as it was, the resemblance was uncanny. Haunting, even. When I asked Bobby how he knew what Uncle Jonas looked like, he said sometimes you visit him in his dreams. Don't kids say the darndest things? Of course, his brother took one look at the picture and started bawling. Said the man in the picture had visited him in *his* dreams, and made him do bad things. Then he grabbed the drawing out of my hands and tore it to pieces. Personally, I think Derrick's a little young yet to appreciate modern art.

I felt bad for Bobby. He spent a lot of time on that drawing and was really proud of how it came out. So make sure you say something nice about the few scraps I was able to salvage. He insisted I still include them with this letter.

Happy birthday?

Love,
Ginny, Bobby, & Derrick

—

To: Jonas Williker, inmate #957464
From: Candace Bennington
April 17, 2006

Dear Mr. Williker

I appreciate you taking the time to speak with me the other day. Our conversation proved very enlightening. In fact—and please do not take this the wrong way—I must admit you were not at all what I expected. Color me impressed with how intelligently you spoke on the subjects of criminal justice and psychology. Such astute observations. Do you have a background in law enforcement by any chance?

Regardless, I am in your debt. The insights you provided will make a great addition to my project, as will the interviews I conducted with your so-called groupies. They are quite a possessive bunch. It wasn't easy to convince them my interests in you were strictly academic. Good thing I am a skilled liar.

Would it be possible to set up another meeting? I have some follow-up questions. For the sake of convenience, I have relocated to a motel just outside of town. It has hourly and weekly rates, and is appropriately seedy. I've brought along a selection of silken underthings to wear—that is, unless you preferred I didn't wear any underthings at all. Let me know what you decide.

Yours,
Candace Bennington

—

To: Jonas Williker, inmate #957464
From: Grant Singer
April 28, 2006

Mr. Williker,

I have something I need to get off my chest. Not that I've done anything wrong. I just don't like secrets and this one has been weighing on my conscience for some time.

Not long after our encounter on Miller's Highway, I placed a call to your mother. I told her I was investigating a series of crimes and needed to eliminate her son as a suspect. Note I didn't specify what type of crimes. Yet your mother responded by saying, "Isn't what happened to those poor women awful? No, my Jonas would never do anything like that."

Interesting, don't you think? That she jumped to that conclusion?

She went on to tell me all about your childhood. What a smart boy you were, the usual gushing mother spiel. I couldn't get a word in edgewise. But I realized I was more likely to get the information I needed by listening as opposed to asking questions. What she told me voluntarily was more valuable. Plus, I enjoyed talking to her. Which is why a few weeks later I came up with an excuse to call her back.

We've kept in touch ever since. Sometimes your name doesn't come up. She tells me about her day, how your father is doing. She asks me how work is going. Work usually has something to do with your case, so I often change the subject. She's a lovely woman, and she's been through so much.

Don't worry, I'm not trying to turn her against you. She has consistently supported your innocence and never once faltered. It's something I admire. When she talks about you, she is speaking of an upright citizen. I find myself doing the same during our conversations. It is an easy lead to follow.

So there you have it. If you are unhappy with this revelation, please, direct your anger at me. Your mother is a saint and has done nothing wrong. Who knows, maybe you won't think it's a big deal. Either way, I'm glad it's out in the open. The trial's coming up and I want to be able to look you in the eye when I'm on the stand. I look forward to our reunion.

Sincerely,
Detective Grant Singer
Columbus Police Department

—

To: Jonas Williker, inmate #957464
From: Lily Anderson
May 3, 2006

Dear Jonas,

Enclosed is a $25 money order for your commissary, as requested. I don't know why I sent it when I can hardly support Anna and myself. I always did have trouble saying no to you.

I never had to though, did I? At least not the "big" no. The "No, I don't want to see you anymore," no. You just disappeared from our lives. Stopped returning my calls. When I asked your mother where you went, she seemed confused. Turns out, you hadn't gone anywhere. Any time she brought me up you wove her tales of our latest adventures, how great things were going, how happy we were. In fact, we'd recently been on a weekend trip to New York City. News to me, I said, before hanging up on her.

That was mean of me. I regret doing it. But the situation overwhelmed me and I panicked. I couldn't breathe. The conversation was crushing my lungs and I had to escape. I wanted to call her back and apologize, but I didn't want to reveal how pathetic I was. Then I started thinking about the ensuing fight when she confronted you and decided to let her live with the lie. I told myself it was a kindness.

Funny, how much the truth can hurt, yet lies are still what we consider cruel.

If you talk to your mother, please tell her I'm sorry. Make up a good excuse. I can't imagine how hard this must be for her. I know *I* haven't been able to watch the news coverage. Not with Anna in the house.

Who am I kidding? Even if Anna wasn't here, I doubt I could physically watch it. It's too much for me to handle. Too intense. In fact, I still haven't plugged the TV back in. I'd hide it in the back of a closet if it weren't for the inevitable "Why?" it would trigger from Anna. Maybe I'll say it broke, and we can't afford a new one. Not having enough money is something she understands. There wouldn't be any follow-up questions to that.

Speaking of Anna, I have to go and pick her up from school. I miss having you around to help with stuff like that. I miss having you around for so many reasons.

Take care of yourself, Jonas. And please remember to tell your mother I'm sorry.

Sincerely,
Lily

—

To: Jonas Williker, inmate #957464
From: Staci Satin
May 11, 2006

Dear Purple,

I wish I could have seen what you did to their bodies. Tell me, did you fuck them before or after you cut their eyes out? Maybe you set the detached orbs aside so they could watch? A private performance for a captive audience.

Which one was your favorite? Betty Kaiser? Or maybe Sandra Hamilton? My money's on Sandra. Her friends called her Sandy. The autopsy report said you dug up her body days later and went back for seconds. Remember how her husband broke down when he found out? It was deliciously pathetic. She must have been one sweet peach. Soft, juicy, and ripe.

Would you like to do those things to my body? Run around with my tongue in your pocket, use my severed breast as a pillow? Probe my ocular cavities at your leisure? They never found Sandy's left eye. It's obvious to me what happened. You were consumed by her, therefore you consumed her. That way she could be a part of you. At least until you shit her out.

Because that's all any of them are.

Picture her eye as a camera, traversing your body from one end to the other, recording the journey and transmitting it beyond the grave for her soul to witness, the degradation following her through eternity. I'll be thinking about that as I fall asleep tonight, fingers gliding gently between my thighs.

Sweet dreams, my love.

xoxo,
Staci

—

To: Jonas Williker, inmate #957464
From: Martin Beaufoy
May 23, 2006

Dear Mr. Williker,

I am writing in regards to the materials I sent for your signature on Tuesday, December 20th, 2005. I have yet to hear back from you and we are well past the customary eight-week return period. If you do not intend on signing, I would greatly appreciate the return of my property. As I stated in my previous letter, I put a lot of effort into obtaining those clippings. It really is the least you could do. Don't be an asshole.

My sincerest thanks for your time,
Martin Beaufoy
Collector

—

To: Jonas Williker, inmate #957464
From: Judith Williker
June 12, 2006

Dear Jonas,

It's your mother. What on earth has gotten into you? How could you possibly ask your own mother such an inappropriate question? Not that it's any of your business, but no, I have NEVER been unfaithful to your father. Never! Where is this even coming from? Didn't I tell you last time I no longer had any interest in marital relations? That includes the extra-marital variety!

Honestly, I'm too flustered to have anything resembling a normal conversation right now. If I were you I'd tear this letter into pieces and flush it down the toilet. Just the *thought* of someone else reading it mortifies me. Please, Jonas, let us never speak of this again.

With love,
Mom

—

To: Jonas Williker, inmate #957464
From: Aurelius Percy, Esq.
June 15, 2006

Dear Mr. Williker,

What you hold in your hands is not the standard introductory letter we send to prospective clients.

It is a lifeline.

At Percy, Paramount & Bint, we specialize in sentence reduction for high-risk defendants. A recent feature in *Trial Lawyer* magazine labeled us one of the "Top 10 Up-and-Coming Firms Representing Unsympathetic Offenders." Some of our recent success stories include Hit-and-Run Harry, the Foghat Flasher, and orphanage arsonist Giles Groovy. When it comes to violent crimes, we successfully negotiated a charge of involuntary manslaughter for Brad Kellerman, the man accused of smashing his neighbor's head with a sledgehammer, in what is quickly becoming known throughout the legal profession as "The Gallagher Defense."

Now don't get me wrong, I've been watching the pre-trial hearings and you've proven yourself more than capable. I think you made the right decision firing the public defender. Those court-appointed flunkies don't have what it takes to win a big case like yours. Most of them couldn't litigate their way out of a parking ticket. That being said, you're going to have a lot on your plate once the trial starts. And most defendants in a case like this have a whole team of lawyers. Wouldn't it be nice to have a professional in your corner? At least for the sake of appearances?

At Percy, Paramount & Bint, we understand the value of appearances. You are obviously a man who takes pride in his public persona. With our firm behind you, you wouldn't have to worry about your authority being usurped. Our legal team is content playing a supporting role in your fight for justice. And if finances are an issue, we would be more than happy setting up a payment plan. Our foremost concern is victory.

You can still be your own hero—with the strength of Percy, Paramount & Bint behind you. It's a decision you won't regret.

Sincerely,
Aurelius Percy, Esq.
Percy, Paramount & Bint

—

To: Jonas Williker, inmate #957464
From: Jane Doe
June 22, 2006

Hello Jonas,

It feels strange to call you by your name, even in writing. I didn't learn it until they caught you. No one did. Just like no one knew what you looked like until the police released the footage of you trussed up like Hannibal Lecter.

I had to practice saying your name out loud before I could commit it to paper, rolling it around on my tongue before I sealed the envelope with my spit and sent it on its way. I wanted my handwriting to properly convey the tone and cadence of how it felt in my mouth. I wanted it to sound just right in your head when you read it, as if I were saying it to you that night on the side of the road.

"Jonas…"

I remember your rough hands grabbing my arm, threatening to dislocate my shoulder. I gasped, my breath suspended there in front of me, your face obscured by it like a surrealist painting. In my mind you were a cloud until the day they showed you on the news. I still picture you that way from time to time. The human face doesn't fit.

Experts say in order to establish a rapport with an attacker you must identify yourself, personalize yourself, so they view you as more than an object. If they see you as human this creates empathy, and hopefully diminishes their urge to hurt you. I didn't know your name at the time so I attempted to tell you mine. I only managed half a syllable before you shoved a bundle of slick cloth into my mouth. Was it enough? Is that the reason I got away?

These are probably details you enjoy hearing, but it doesn't curb my desire to talk to you about them. It's different than paying a disinterested party to listen while I recite my fears like a dour litany. You're invested in the listening. It's personal to you, same as it is to me. A shared experience. Who can understand what I went through more than you? What harm can it do if you get your jollies from my confession? You wouldn't be the first to do so.

But I suspect hearing from me also upsets you. You were too comfortable. You got careless. Made mistakes. Or maybe I got the better of you. Outplayed you. It was bound to happen sooner or later.

Does it make you angry, Jonas? I hope it does. You thought yourself so superior. I was a plaything, weak and nonthreatening. I should have wound up in the ground with all the rest of them. United with my sisters in death. But it wasn't meant to be.

You'll hear more from me soon. I promise. I've been hearing your voice in my head for so long, and I've grown tired of letting you do all the talking.

Sincerely,
The One That Got Away

—

THE TRIAL

To: Jonas Williker, inmate #957464
From: William Peters
July 14, 2006

Dear Jonas,

This is Billy Peters. I used to live down the block from you? We hung out all the time when we were kids. The summer before sixth grade we were practically inseparable, riding our bikes everywhere, wandering the woods for hours. It's amazing how much freedom our parents gave us. All that mattered was we made it home in time for dinner. These modern, helicopter parents would get ulcers just thinking about it. Different times, I suppose. Lack of supervision was commonplace. Some of my most cherished memories are from that summer.

I hesitate to call myself your best friend, since it was obvious you didn't need the social interaction. It wasn't the air you breathed like it was for me. That doesn't mean you weren't good at it when you had to be, though. My biggest fear was one day the other kids at school would realize how cool you were and you wouldn't be "mine" anymore. You'd be too popular.

I know it sounds pathetic. I spent a lot of time and money hashing it out with my therapist over the years. Looking back on it now, with 20/20 hindsight, I was a beard of sorts. A token friend to please your parents, so they wouldn't think their son was a weirdo. I was an easy enough kid to get along with and our friendship served a purpose.

It devastated me when my family moved away. I wanted to stay in touch but my parents didn't make it easy, and although I wrote a couple times, you never responded. It's so obvious why, now. You had no use for me anymore. Did you replace me? Never mind, don't answer that. I couldn't bear to see it in writing. I hope whoever you chose was as suitably innocuous a friend as I was.

I wasn't sure I should write this letter, but once I had a lock on your location I couldn't resist reaching out. Your case has been a real head-fuck nostalgia trip. Like a Stephen King coming-of-age story. All those summer days poking roadkill with sticks don't seem so innocent anymore.

Remember the sleepovers we used to have? Always at my place, never yours. We'd stay up all night watching cheesy horror flicks. It's funny, I loved those movies, but you always seemed bored out of your mind. Even *Faces of Death*, which left me traumatized (I *still* have nightmares about monkey brains), barely got a reaction out of you. Once you found out the filmmakers faked most of the footage, you lost interest.

Eventually I'd fall asleep and you'd watch surgery videos on cable access. (I can't imagine what you would have gotten up to if the internet existed at the time.) I thought you were just this weird, smart kid who would grow up to be a surgeon. When I first saw your mugshot on the news all these years later, I immediately flashed back to you watching those videos.

It wasn't long after your arrest my dad brought up something he'd never told me before. One of those nights, after I'd fallen asleep, he caught you masturbating to some sort of post mortem exam. Something real gnarly, where a person's entire face had to be reconstructed. I'm talking puzzle pieces for bones, skin pulled back like a cheap mask. When I woke up the next morning you were gone, and when I asked where you went, my dad said he'd had to drive you home because you'd gotten a stomach ache. We moved not long after.

Did you realize you were different from other kids? Or were you blindly following your feelings like the rest of us, and they happened to take you down a different path? You know how some people say they knew they were gay from the time they could walk? (And I am NOT equating being gay with being a serial killer. Please, let's not go there. Yeesh. This question is more about self-awareness as opposed to causation.)

Not that I'm expecting an answer. You never answered my other letters. I should probably tear this up and toss it in the trash. Start a journal instead. Or better yet, go back to therapy, which would make my partner happy. Still, I can't help but wonder what it would be like to hear from you after all these years. Maybe I'll find out? At the very least I hope you look back on the past with the same fondness I do.

Here's to more innocent times (even if they weren't).

Your friend,
Billy Peters

—

To: Jonas Williker, inmate #957464
From: Ginny Goodwinch
July 15, 2006

Dear Jonas,

Well, I certainly had myself a day.

It all started with the best of intentions, as most days do. I recently found out about this organization called the Innocence Project. Have you heard of them? They're a non-profit committed to exonerating the wrongfully accused. Sounds too good to be true, right? That's because it is, as they so rudely demonstrated when I called this afternoon.

A pleasant enough sounding woman answered the phone, but before I could get a word in, she immediately put me on hold. And there I sat for a good half hour, listening to the same God-awful piece of muzak over and over again. It was maddening. On top of that the kids were in rare form, bouncing off the walls like a couple of circus monkeys.

When the woman finally came back on the line she asked what I was calling about, so I started explaining your situation. She cut me off right there. Turns out they only accept case submissions by mail. "I wish you would have mentioned that before you put me on hold for forty minutes," I told her. Make no mistake, I have no problem putting pen to paper, as you are well aware, but they should have been more forthcoming with that information. Still, I didn't want to be nasty about it. They are a charity after all. "It doesn't matter," I told her. "It's a high profile case. I'm sure it's on your radar." "Oh? Which case?" she said. "The Jonas Williker case," I told her.

The phone went silent. I thought she'd hung up on me. "I'm not familiar," she said, finally. Can you imagine working for a legal organization and not being aware of such an important trial? But like I said, I was trying to be nice. So as distasteful as I find it, I had to use the colorful nickname the media gave you. And that's when she laughed.

Can you believe it? She *laughed*. The audacity.

"Did I say something funny?" I asked her, and she got real quiet, because she knew she'd messed up. "Well?" I asked again. "Did I?"

And then she put on this real condescending voice, like she was a teacher and I was some stupid kid. "Ma'am," she said. "We only consider post-conviction cases, ones which have already lost their appeal." "Well that doesn't seem fair," I told her. "Ma'am," she said. (I did NOT like the way she kept calling me ma'am.) "Jonas Williker has yet to be found guilty, so it would be premature to claim a miscarriage of justice."

I hate to admit it, but she had me there. Still, she didn't have to be such a b-word about it.

And that wasn't even the end of her disrespect. "Furthermore," she said. "The Innocence Project only considers cases where there is physical evidence which, if tested, will exonerate the defendant. From what I understand, there is plenty of physical evidence in the Williker case, and I've got news for you— it ain't gonna point to his innocence!"

And with that she hung up. I was so steamed I almost put the phone straight through the wall. I actually swung my arm back and hit poor little Derrick in the head. Boy, did he ever howl! Then his howling set Bobby to howling. Like a chorus of wolves, those two. I really wanted to call back and give that woman a piece of my mind, but the kids refused to settle down. And in light of what she told me, despite how rude she was, it's probably better if we keep the Innocence Project in our back pocket, just in case the trial doesn't go our way.

Sigh.

So that was my day. How was yours? The boys are finally asleep and I'm relaxing in my robe with a nice cup of rooibos tea, thinking of you.

Sweet dreams!
Your ever-faithful Ginny

—

To: Jonas Williker, inmate #957464
From: Judith Williker
July 17, 2006

Dear Jonas,

It's your mother. I hope you're doing well. I'm feeling a little down in the dumps myself. You remember our cleaning lady, Aretha? Turns out she speaks English a lot better than she let on, and she's been speaking it to the press. Can you believe it? Your father saw an interview with her on the news. The caption read: "Williker Housekeeper Airs Dirty Laundry," which was confusing, because she told us she didn't do laundry. It was one of her stipulations: no laundry.

Boy, did your father ever pitch a fit. Started hollering about the cleaning lady being on TV. I thought he was having one of those senior moments until I saw it for myself. Lucky for Aretha, it was her day off. I mean, the odds were good. Most days were her day off, since she only worked one day a week. Lord knows what your father would have done if she'd been here. He had me call her house and fire her on the spot. It was one of the hardest things I've ever had to do. I feel like I've lost my best friend. Muy triste!

Your father threatened to sue, although he's too cheap to actually go through with it. He says the government should provide public defenders to the families of those on trial, because they're the real victims. What can I say? The world isn't fair. I didn't say that to your father, of course. He says it often enough when it comes to other people's problems (usually foreigners like Aretha). You think he'd see the hypocrisy in his own complaining.

It didn't help when a bunch of kids egged our house the following night. I could have really used Aretha's help cleaning up the mess. Although come to think of it, I don't think she did windows either, so maybe it wouldn't have made a difference. Someone also spray-painted "murder parents" on the sidewalk. That hurt. You'd think with all the reporters milling around, *someone* would have seen something, but apparently not. All I know is plenty of them were there to film your father's meltdown after the fact.

Which reminds me… You might want to mute the TV if you come across that footage. Or leave the room if you have to. I know the remote control plays an important role in inmate hierarchy, and you've only been there a short period of time. Anyway, your father had been drinking and said some things he didn't mean, things that could easily be misconstrued. You know, the whole "No son of mine" routine he does when he gets mad at you. He probably doesn't even remember saying that stuff, so best to let sleeping dogs lie.

But enough about us. The trial seems to be going well so far, all things considered, although I don't understand why the prosecution always gets to go first. It's like giving the bad guys a head start. They should at least flip a coin like they do for the Super Bowl. Otherwise the first thing the jury hears is a bunch of personal attacks on your character. In your case the prosecutor even had the nerve to bad-mouth my mothering! Me, an old woman unable to defend herself!

You know I'd be there if I could, but your father isn't well enough to travel. It's that dang IBS of his. Every time it looks like he's in the clear he's hit with another flare up. It really is an awful affliction. And now without Aretha around I couldn't possibly leave him on his own. I promise once he's able to leave the house with confidence we will come and visit you.

Speaking of your father, I should probably start getting dinner ready. The man's got an appetite you could set your watch to. As always you are in my prayers. No need to return the favor, but if you've got a few to spare for your father I'm sure he'd appreciate it. He's been extra cranky because of the low

FODMAP diet the doctor put him on. And you know how much your father loves his FODMAPs.

Talk to you soon!

Love,
Mom

—

To: Jonas Williker, inmate #957464
From: Candace Bennington
July 20, 2006

Dear Jonas,

Considering the intensity of our recent meetings, I wasn't sure I'd be able to control myself going forward. The prison's "no touching" policy is nothing short of puritanical fascism. State sanctioned torture both unusual and cruel. Thankfully you continue to surprise me with your resourcefulness as well as your charm. There aren't many men who could transform a visitor's cell into such a seductive tableau. Where did you find the time? I can only imagine how many favors you had to call in. Candlelight, music, drinks—color me impressed yet again. That was the most balanced toilet wine I've ever tasted. Surprisingly soft and full bodied.

Like me.

Okay, maybe I'm exaggerating the quality of the wine. It went straight to my head and left me with a killer hangover. Did we even discuss my thesis? I honestly can't remember. The whole thing's a blur, imprinted on my psyche as a series of moods and gestures. There's no way we didn't exceed our allotted hour, yet I felt as if I'd only just arrived when the guard came knocking, telling me our time was up. Like being awakened from a dream you never want to end.

The more I think about it, the more the whole thing feels like a carefully constructed fantasy. Almost too good to be true. They say the first step in avoiding a trap is knowing one exists, which begs the questions—is this a trap, Jonas?

Not that it would make any difference.

Maybe it's one of my own design. Have I sabotaged my thesis by inserting myself into it? How can one effectively and objectively make a case study of their own actions? You either wind up skewing the data or being led by it. Like a bull by the ring in its nose, or a man by his cock.

Do I still even care about my thesis at this point? It seems to grow less important with each passing day. Maybe it never existed in the first place? I'm sure that wouldn't matter to you on a technical level, but the implication—that I made it up—there's an interesting idea.

One of us is setting a trap here. I can see how you'd think it was you. It gives us something to discuss next time I visit. Because make no mistake—I will be seeing you again. I'm curious to see what you come up with for our next date.

Yours,
Candace Bennington

—

To: Jonas Williker, inmate #957464
From: Lily Anderson
July 24, 2006

Dear Jonas,

Well, I broke down and called your mother. And guess what? It's something I should have done a long time ago. She sounded genuinely happy to hear from me. Told me she didn't remember me hanging up on her, but understands why I did (if I did). She apologized profusely despite having done nothing wrong. Told me how much she misses Anna, how she still thinks of her as a granddaughter, and that we need to visit her. Then we both had a good cry.

I'm telling you, it was such a relief. I don't know what I was so afraid of. Judith is such a warm, caring person. Makes me wonder how you turned out the way you did. Guess we'll have to blame Frank's side of the family. Not saying Frank ever acted unkind towards me or Anna. He treated us with more of a detached indifference.

As much as I'd love to bring Anna to visit your mom, it would require me telling her the truth about you, and I'm just not ready. Besides, something tells me Judith hasn't come to terms with the enormity of your situation yet. Maybe when all this blows over and Anna's a little older the three of us can confront this thing together, *Steel Magnolias* style. I don't think any of us can handle it on our own right now.

Your mother says "hello," by the way.

Sincerely,
Lily

—

To: Jonas Williker, inmate #957464
From: Staci Satin
July 25, 2006

Dear Purple,

I took these pictures of my pussy for you. The tattoos are temporary, but that doesn't mean they didn't hurt, because they hurt like fucking hell. We used my own blood as ink, pulled from my veins and scratched into my skin. It will eventually be reabsorbed by my body, hence the temporary nature of the art, but the sentiment will live forever. I am the property of Jonas Williker.

These images are part of a larger series based on your life's work. DVentlust. com heralded them as "a bold, transgressive statement on the status quo of kink," while Jezebel dismissed them as "the very definition of internalized misogyny externalized." I consider them my crowning achievement as an artist and a monument to your greatness.

Do you have access to a computer? If so, you can see more at my personal website, www.stacisatinxxx.com. Maybe you could mention it the next time the cameras are rolling. It would help further spread the gospel, and I can't be expected to do *all* the spreading, can I? As gauche as it is to say, art is not self-sustaining. The ugly truth is it requires patrons. To put it bluntly, money's tighter than my pretty pink asshole, and my manager is expecting a return on his investment, if you know what I mean. I would love to be able to continue creating art in your honor.

xoxo,
Staci

[*Although not included here for legal reasons, these images are readily available online.* —Editor]

—

To: Jonas Williker, inmate #957464
From: Jane Doe
July 27, 2006

Hello Jonas,

It's me again. The nameless one.

I never went to the cops. After you flashed that badge to lure me in, how could I? The fear held me back. Besides, what would I say? I spent most of the ordeal blindfolded by a purple cloth. What little I saw wouldn't help. Your face was a cloud, remember? A mist of condensed breath. It would have sounded ridiculous. It still does. I used to feel guilty about not coming forward, as if it somehow made me complicit in your subsequent crimes. But I doubt my fantastical account would have contributed to your arrest, so I try not to dwell on it.

It took seven more murders for them to catch you. Practically by accident. More carelessness on your part? Or were you getting bored? Tired? They say deep down most criminals want to be caught, but I'm not so sure. Most victims want to escape, at least in the moment, but many find themselves wishing they hadn't as the years go by. Life doesn't go back to normal after an experience like the one we shared. For the hunter or the prey.

Psychologists recommend keeping busy to distract the mind so I've taken up gardening. You're a bit of a green thumb yourself, if I'm not mistaken. Mother's little garden gnome. It's part of your mythology. I used to hate getting my hands dirty, but now the sensation of earth under my fingernails soothes me. I like to bury my hands in the soil and hold them there. I can feel the vibration of the insects, the roots reaching out to caress me. I put my ear to the ground and listen. They want me to join them.

Confined spaces comfort me. I sleep with a weighted blanket on my bed, blackout curtains over the windows. When things are really bad I'll curl up in the back of my closet. Sometimes I leave the doors and windows wide open, a giant invitation to the world.

But not to you. Because you're locked away in a cage. You don't know who I am or where I live. Of all the things I fear, you are no longer one of them.

You are the one who should be afraid of me.

Writing to you puts you in your place. I used to see you in shadows, around every corner, in other people's faces, but now I know where you are at all times.

And I'll be watching. Just like everybody else.

Sincerely,
The One That Got Away

—

To: Jonas Williker, inmate #957464
From: Albert Jefferies
July 31, 2006

Dear Jonas Williker,

You must think awful highly of yourself. I can see it in your eyes. That smug sense of satisfaction. You're the type of guy who thinks their shit don't stink, even though they've smeared it all over the walls and everyone in the room is choking on the smell. Well I've got news for you, buddy, you need to pay your dues if you ever want to enter the pantheon of the greats. A list of names that has stood the test of time, crimes that are studied by experts. Classic killers like Dahmer, Ramirez, and the notorious BTK.

Of course, the real greats are the ones who were never caught. The ones who killed for love of the game, not the notoriety. People like Jack the Ripper, the Zodiac Killer, and the Moonlight Murderer. Those guys didn't necessarily have the highest body counts, but tales of their exploits continue to inspire terror in God-fearing Americans to this day. Sure, they also inspired movies and pop culture and folklore, but that wasn't their intended goal. They were men of principle.

Don't get me wrong, you've got a great hook. The whole purple satin thing. But if I'm being honest, it kinda feels like a gimmick. A gift from you to the press. Which means the name didn't come about organically. You pushed it on us. It smacks of desperation. Like you were crying out for attention.

Most of the greats, even the lesser-known ones, received their nicknames from the public. It's an honor you can't bestow upon yourself. Like an English knighthood. It signifies acceptance, recognition of a job well done. These nicknames are a perfect encapsulation of a killer and their MO.

Take Charlie Chopoff, for example. There's a name that still strikes fear in the loins of young boys everywhere. Or the Doodler, who would sketch his victims like a fancy French girl before having his way with them. And who could forget the hyperbolic-but-still-amazingly-named Servant Girl Annihilator, or gay serial killer the Rainbow Maniac, or the Bible Salesman, who committed unholy acts with the holiest of texts? Those guys earned their nicknames. They didn't seek fame, fame sought them.

I'm not saying you can't one day become one of the greats. Despite this faux pas you've had an impressive career. The public loves you. My advice? Slow your roll. Don't speak about your crimes, let your crimes speak for themselves. You've built a substantial following in a short period of time, but now it's time to hand over the reins and let nature take its course. When it comes to the long game, you don't want to force things.

Look what happened to Alfonso Ferreira. He was a young up-and-comer who got a big head and lost it all. He had a unique fetish—tearing out his victims' pubic hair by hand while they were still alive. The press went nuts for it. But he was impatient. He dubbed himself "The Brazilian." It was the perfect moniker, but the press didn't take kindly to him jumping the gun, and he paid the price. Although unique, you rarely see his crimes referenced these days.

Ultimately, you are the captain of your own ship. But remember, to know your future is to know your past. Learn from those who came before you. You may think you can control public opinion, but eventually public opinion winds up controlling you.

Respectfully,
Albert Jefferies

—

To: Jonas Williker, inmate #957464
From: Candace Bennington
August 3, 2006

Dear Jonas,

I had the strangest dream last night. I opened my eyes and there you were in my motel room, looming over me like a shadow. I went to embrace you only to find myself unable to move, as if I'd been tied to the bed. When I attempted to speak my voice came out soft and muffled. You stood there, watching me as I struggled, a hint of a smile glinting in the dark. It was erotic, but also terrifying.

When I woke up this morning I turned on the news to find out you'd escaped. I have to admit, after the initial shock wore off I couldn't help but smile. Did all my talk of traps inspire you? Could it be you were afraid?

I should probably pack my things and head home, but I can't help but feel we have unfinished business between us. You've most likely disappeared back into our nation's collective fear, never to return, but as you know, I don't like leaving love on the table. So on the off chance you return don't hesitate to reach out. I can't promise I'll still be here, but I can't promise I won't be, either. Love is strange, don't you think?

Yours,
Candace Bennington

—

To: Jonas Williker, inmate #957464
From: Judith Williker
August 7, 2006

Dear Jonas,

It's your mother. I'm writing this under the watchful eye of 24-hour police surveillance. I think you know why. If you happen to show up here like they expect I'll save a stamp and hand this letter directly to you. It would be lovely to see you again, even if only for a few minutes. Maybe the police would let you sit and have dinner before they took you back. They would be more than welcome to join us for their trouble.

Speaking of trouble, you sure are in it. Although I couldn't help but chuckle when the details of your escape were revealed. Somebody's face must sure be red, leaving you alone in a first-floor bathroom with no bars on the window. I could have told them that was a bad idea! You always were a wiry little scamp. You started climbing out of your crib at 9 months old!

I hope this isn't because we haven't been able to visit you. Normally shenanigans like this would have your father apoplectic, but he's really taken to the police presence. For one thing, the house hasn't been vandalized since they've been here. They've also got a nightly poker game going, if you can believe it. I even caught Dad regaling them with stories from your childhood!

Remember that time he took you fishing and you capsized the canoe? Well usually that story makes him madder than a bag of bees. You know how he likes to insist you intentionally tried to drown him. The way he told it this time you'd think it was one of his most cherished memories. I've never seen him laugh so hard!

So don't get caught on your father's account. Wherever you are I hope you're staying warm and getting enough to eat. And please, be careful. Law enforcement probably won't be too gentle should they come across you. You made them look like Keystone Cops, and they're not likely to forget it. But don't tell them I said so!

One way or another I hope you get this letter. Talk soon!

Love,
Mom

—

To: Jonas Williker, inmate #957464
From: Ginny Goodwinch
August 9, 2006

Dear Jonas,

That was the most nerve-wracking week of my life! I'm glad you're okay, but don't ever scare me like that again, mister! You could have been killed! Fortunately you didn't look too worse for wear when the state police brought you in. For a guy who spent 7 days living in the woods, that is. I hope they treated you with the dignity and respect due a man yet to be convicted of a crime. I'm a firm supporter of the police, but some of those law enforcement boys have a real chip on their shoulder. I'm sure they all want to be the one who bagged the big bad Jonas Williker.

Anyway, sorry I didn't write while you were "on the lam." I know it would have been nice to come home to a long letter from your Ginny Bird (and I use the word "home" loosely), but I couldn't bear to think of our personal correspondence in the hands of those mean-ole screws. Those letters are private! Especially the pictures! Besides, I was glued to the TV the entire time. Barely got any sleep. The damn kids went coo-coo bananas! Turned the place into a pigsty. (I don't care how special you are! You two are gonna get it, you hear me?) I whipped out my pen and shot off this letter as soon as I saw you were captured.

You know, a part of me hoped you would show up here. That you'd traverse the country to be with me. I don't know how long it would take to get here on foot, but by the third night I imagined every creak of the house was you coming through the front door. Every sputtering engine was you in a hot-wired car. I'm not going to lie, it was a little intimidating, the thought of our first meeting. I made sure to wear my best nightgown to bed. The one you like, from the photos? I'm a little embarrassed to say I sweated clean through it in one night, and had to resort to sleeping completely nude! Imagine what the kids would have thought if they walked in! They've seen me going toilet, but I don't think they're ready for the full reality of my womanhood.

Oh my, now I'm blushing. Where was I?

I was sad that you were caught, but also a little relieved. I believe in your innocence, and as much as I want you here with me, I want you exonerated. I don't want to live in fear. I want to enjoy our life together. Maybe I'm being naive, but I believe in the system. There's no way a jury with half a brain would find you guilty. I'll just have to be patient and let justice run its course.

I guess I better let you get some rest. You're gonna need all your strength for the battle ahead. Stay strong, my sweet.

Love,
Ginny

—

To: Jonas Williker, inmate #957464
From: Candace Bennington
August 12, 2006

Dear Jonas,

I know I come across as a strong, independent woman who's got her shit together, but when I first heard you'd escaped it felt like I'd had the vomit-stained motel rug pulled out from under me. As I lay there on the floor, staring at the cracks in the ceiling, my emotions ping-ponged back and forth between "this is for the best," and "why is he doing this to me?" And while I'm not normally the type of person who makes everything about themselves, I must admit I wallowed in self-pity for a couple days.

But after that brief period of uncharacteristic self-indulgence I was back to my old self. And the old me set a deadline. I pre-paid for one last week at the motel with the stipulation that if you didn't turn up by then, it was a sign I needed to move on with my life. I was literally packing my bags when I saw the news of your apprehension.

I understand you're disappointed to be back under lock and key, but our reunion yesterday was exquisite. Even with the guard watching us through the door. I could tell by his smile he enjoyed himself just as much as we did.

Relax, I'm joking. But don't get the wrong idea—I don't belong to you. Just because I sign my letters "yours," it doesn't mean I'm your property. In fact, I never even bothered unpacking my bags after you were caught, because somewhere in the back of my mind I know this relationship of ours could end at a moment's notice. Your escape proved as much. And if anyone's going to break things off it's going to be me. If you haven't realized by now I like to be in control.

Don't get me wrong, what we have is good—really good— but all good things must come to an end. Eventually I will have to return to the real world.

My doctorate awaits. You've contributed to my education in more ways than you can imagine. I'd love to stay on indefinitely, but let's be practical. We both know this isn't going anywhere. I mean, I hate to say it, but *you're* not going anywhere. Another thing your escape proved. And a girl can't wait around forever.

Unless you can think of some other reason I should stay? Something I may have overlooked?

But no, I've made up my mind. I'm not sure when I'll be leaving, exactly. Could be tomorrow, could be a week from now. Perhaps I'll wait for the trial to resume. Make one final showing of support before I depart. We'll see.

I did leave you a little something to remember me by, though. Perhaps you found it? One of those silken underthings you're so fond of. I hid it inside myself when I visited yesterday. The guard had no idea. Until I pulled them out, that is. You had your back turned, but he saw.

Yours,
Candace

—

To: Jonas Williker, inmate #957464
From: Jane Doe
August 14, 2006

Hello Jonas,

My last letter must have struck a nerve. Unless there was some other reason for your little disappearing act? You don't have to explain yourself to me, I understand. You were scared. You panicked. You're used to being the one in control. Take that away and you're not the Purple Satin Killer. You're just a man named Jonas. And Jonas is a coward.

What exactly were you trying to prove with that stunt anyway? No cage can hold you? I'll never be safe while you're still alive? Did you expect me to break down when I heard the news? Retreat to the back of my closet and curl up into a ball? I told you, you are no longer something I fear. Besides, you're already back where you belong. Even if you had somehow managed to avoid capture you would have never found me. As far as the rest of the world is concerned I don't exist. I'm a voice inside your head. One you better start paying attention to.

And right now that voice is saying you're going to be in jail for the rest of your life. The sooner you come to terms with that, the better. Otherwise it will destroy you. Only after I embraced my trauma was I able to move forward. You can't leave it behind. You have to pack it up and take it with you.

Are you ready to move forward, Jonas? Or are you stuck in the past? Never mind being ready, are you even capable? That's the real question. Are you capable of moving forward?

Think about it.

Sincerely,
The One That Got Away

—

To: Jonas Williker, inmate #957464
From: Lily Anderson
August 15, 2006

Dear Jonas,

Jesus jumping Christ! If you're trying to convince people of your innocence you're going about it the wrong way. And if you're trying to give me a panic attack, mission accomplished!

Your escape freaked me out so much I left town and checked into a motel, and you know I don't have the money for that kind of thing. Anna thinks it's because the landlord had to fumigate, but the truth is I couldn't stay there while you were on the loose. What with our recent correspondence, how was I supposed to feel safe? What if you showed up and demanded shelter from the police? Or needed a quick murder fix and were like, "I know just where to find some easy prey"? No way was I waiting around for either of those things to happen.

I don't think I want to hear from you anymore, Jonas. Especially if you're going to keep pulling stunts like this. Life is hard enough as it is. I'm a single mom whose ex is an alleged serial killer. Do you even understand what that's like? First dates are a minefield. Long-term relationships are a nonstarter. If job applications required romantic histories I'd never work again. All I want to do is regulate my anxiety and take care of my daughter, and you are making both of those things more difficult than they need to be.

Please, Jonas, leave us alone. I can't take much more of this.

Sincerely,
Lily

—

To: Jonas Williker, inmate #957464
From: Staci Satin
August 17, 2006

Dear Purple,

Welcome back! Did you enjoy your little vacation?

While you were out gallivanting I came up with an idea for a new tattoo. I was at the gynecologist of all places, gritting my teeth through a rather unpleasant exam when it came to me like a bat out of hell. I couldn't wait to share it with you.

The design is based on one of your "unsolved" murders, which, let's be honest, has your name written all over it. As someone who literally has your name written on them I should know. The only reason they haven't charged you is because you can't technically have a murder without a body, and all they've got is a body part. One that can't provide any concrete identifying characteristics like fingerprints, or teeth (although the idea of one of these with teeth is a common enough trope in cautionary folk stories). Yes, I'm talking about vagina dentata, and yes, I'm also talking about the infamous Moore Creek crucifixion.

So here's my idea: a woman's flayed genitalia, nailed to a cross like a butterfly pinned for exhibition. The labia spread wide like the arms of Christ, pierced by metal spikes on either side, with a third spike at the base, going through the perineum. The clitoris, drooping forward in exhaustion, will be ringed by a razor-sharp crown of thorns. Instead of rays of light, maybe we add a few stink lines.

I'm gonna get my tattoo guy working on a sketch right away. I'm thinking a full thigh piece. Maybe set the cross in a graveyard amongst the tombstones, just like Moore Creek Cemetery. What do you think? Pretty sexy, right?

xoxo,
Staci

—

To: Jonas Williker, inmate #957464
From: Ryland Cochero
August 18, 2006

Dear Mr. Williker,

My name is Ryland Cochero. I am a sixth-grade student at Middleton Elementary School in London, Wisconsin. My class is having an auction to raise money for our graduation trip to Washington D.C. and I am writing to ask if you have anything you would like to donate.

I wanted to write to someone really popular because the student who raises the most money will win a picture with the Vice President. A lot of my classmates are writing to boy bands and reality TV stars but I think it is better to write to someone adults like because if an adult wants something they buy it. Like when my dad bought a riding mower even though my mom said he couldn't.

A lot of good ideas have already been taken. Sawyer Stevens called dibs on Kanye West and my friend Harper is writing to Kobe Bryant and The Rock. I don't really know what adults are into so I looked on the computer and your name came up. It is one of the most popular search terms on Google.

I have already received some cool responses from other people. Jim Davis sent a signed picture of Garfield. A lot of my friends are into web comics but I prefer the old kind. Especially Garfield. He hates Mondays and loves lasagna. Lasagna is my favorite too. What is your favorite food?

I also wrote to the Department of Defense to see if they had any old Space Command stuff. Space Command was the coolest. It was created in the 80s to protect America in outer space. That means it was their job to fight aliens. Their motto was "Guardians of the High Frontier," which is awesome even though my dad says the only thing they were guardians of was satellite TV.

They were shut down in 2002. I hope the new president brings Space Command back. When I grow up I want to draw comics like Jim Davis or be a general in Space Command.

I read that you collect things called "mementos." I would love a memento for our auction. It doesn't even have to be one of your favorites.

Thank you for your time.

Sincerely,
Ryland Cochero

—

To: Jonas Williker, inmate #957464
From: Ginny Goodwinch
August 19, 2006

Dear Jonas,

I haven't heard back from you since before your escape. You never even responded to my letter about those jerks at the Innocence Project, and that was
over a month ago! Is everything okay? The worrywarts are running amok (as
are the children) and I'm starting to have my doubts about the U.S. Postal
Service again. If you think you're missing any letters please let me know and
I'll fire off some duplicates, ASAP.

If this is about the woman who flashed her breasts outside the courtroom,
don't worry—I'm not mad at you. It's not your fault women are attracted to
you. They see you as a hunter, an alpha male. It's only natural. If anything that
woman's ample bosom helped raise awareness about your situation, especially
among men ages 18 to 24, which is a key demographic.

So please write back soon. I know I get to see your face on television, but your
words bring me so much comfort. Whenever I get a letter from you I turn on
Court TV and turn the volume down so I can read it out loud and pretend
you're talking to me. Of course, it breaks my concentration when they cut to
that ugly old judge, and the children don't understand sometimes Mommy
needs "private time," but it's all I have. Please. Just thinking about it makes
me burn inside!

And no, that burning has nothing whatsoever to do with anything unsavory. If you must know, the only man I have ever been with is my
ex-husband, and even though it has been quite a few years, I recently
paid a visit to the doctor to make sure the bum didn't leave behind any
unwanted guests.

So please, write back soon. I've enclosed another snapshot as incentive. It's a bit naughty, so don't let the guards see. I had my Bobby take it. For a little guy he's pretty good with the camera! Anyway, there's plenty more where that came from.

Love always,
Your Ginny Bird

—

To: Jonas Williker, inmate #957464
From: David Manning
August 19, 2006

Dear Jonas Williker,

My name is David Manning. It's a pleasure to make your acquaintance. Like everyone else in America I've been obsessively following your story. In my opinion it's shaping up to be one of the Great Narratives of the 21ˢᵗ Century. Something about it has cut through the fog of everyday life, jarring this sleep-walker out of his stupor.

What can I say? When I'm into something I go all in. Which is how I came upon the website TruthSleuths.com. It's a forum for amateur true crime in-vestigators. I've been a member of their community for a while now. They have an entire section devoted to PSK's so-called "Lost Year," wherein they try to pin various unsolved murders on you.

I'm surprised law enforcement doesn't rely on them more as a resource. They are extremely thorough in their methods. Luckily for whoever committed those crimes, cops are an insular bunch that don't communicate with one another, let alone outside agencies. It's like they're not interested in the actual truth. Instead they pick the most convenient truth and stick with it.

I'm not a cop, but I live in the greater Ohio area and travel a lot for work. It has allowed me the opportunity to visit many of the towns where the murders took place. I even made a pilgrimage to your childhood home in Murrysville. Don't worry, I didn't knock on the door or anything.

I've managed to speak to quite a few people involved with the case under the banner of a Truth Sleuther. It's a name that loosens tongues. I have a map with the locations of all the murders marked down, and I check off each one as I go. Sometimes I imagine I'm the Purple Satin Killer. They say getting into the mindset of the killer is essential for any good investigator. Probably why so many of them are as fucked up as the people they pursue.

Not that I'm trying to solve any crimes. I don't have some sort of moral agenda. Sleuthing is more of a hobby. Something to keep my mind occupied while I'm on the road. It gets lonely out there. Sometimes I meet up with a fellow sleuth, but mostly I keep to myself. Those people are an odd bunch of ducks. I met up with one self-proclaimed expert who wanted to re-enact one of the crimes, which led to a pretty memorable one-night stand. I gave her a call the next time I rolled through town, but she stood me up. Perhaps she felt our little tryst crossed a line.

I'm gonna be in your neck of the woods in a few weeks, and it's a long shot, but I was wondering if you could put me on your visitors list? I already went ahead and filled out all the necessary paperwork. I've learned a lot of interesting things on the road, stuff I wouldn't feel too comfortable putting into a letter. I think it might be worth your while if we spoke. And since you are more or less representing yourself, our conversations would be considered private under the umbrella of attorney/client privilege. So we could, you know, *talk*.

Who knows, if we hit it off, maybe I could help out in other ways. Like keeping an eye on your interests in the free world. I can follow up on leads, do research, surveillance. I doubt the court has been ponying up for PI expenses. It would be like having the whole of TruthSleuth.com at your disposal. Someone who isn't afraid to get dirt under their fingernails, so to speak.

Either way, I'm going to try and make it out there before the trial's over. I hope to talk to you soon.

Sincerely,
David Manning

—

To: Jonas Williker, inmate #957464
From: Judith Williker
August 22, 2006

Dear Jonas,

It's your mother. Congratulations on getting married! I must admit, I wasn't sure what to think at first. I was as shocked as anyone when you proposed on live TV. There I was, thinking Candace was just another in a long line of character witnesses, and you go and pop the question. I spent the short recess that followed fantasizing about what the wedding would be like. Would it take place in the prison chapel? Would I be able to attend? What would I wear? So you can imagine my disappointment when the trial resumed and it was announced the judge had performed the ceremony in his chambers during the break. I understand the impatience of young love, but I wish I could have been there. With all those cameras you could have at least had someone document the moment.

But that's just me being selfish. Candace seems like she's a good fit. You're going to need a smart woman to take care of you after your mother's gone. It just goes to show, it's never too late to turn things around. You might make a grandmother out of me yet!

Unfortunately I also have some bad news. Your father is in the hospital. He didn't take too well to the news of your happy day. In fact, he got so worked up he burst a blood vessel in his head. Right in the middle of the news coverage! Luckily the hospital had a TV in the waiting room. Did you know channel 12 is doing an exclusive wedding special? They've already contacted me for an interview!

Anyway, I know you and your father don't always get along, but please keep him in your prayers. A boy needs his father. Every decision I've made as a mother has been to provide you with the best life possible, including who I married. Maybe you think I chose poorly, but I did the best I could with the options I had. As a newly married man this is something you will come to understand.

So hopefully your father has a speedy recovery and we can visit soon. You make sure to tell Candace she can always reach out to me if she needs anything. I can't wait to meet her!

Love always,
Mom

—

To: Jonas Williker, inmate #957464
From: Ginny Goodwinch
August 22, 2006

Alright Buster,

I don't know who this Candace slut is or what kind of spell she's got you under, but I will tear her fucking eyes out. Imagine my surprise when I turned on the TV, all set to get a little well-deserved alone time with my man, only to hear you propose to some random bitch in open court. Go ahead, imagine it! I hollered so loud the kids woke up thinking the evil leprechaun was back. (Long story. I should have never let them watch that stupid movie.)

Are you doing this to spite me? Is it because I couldn't be there with you? Well guess what? I left the kids at Mother's while she was asleep, and by the time you read this I'll be halfway to the courthouse. No stops. I've got plenty of snacks and a Tupperware to pee in.

You know the part in the wedding ceremony where they say, "If anyone knows of any reason this couple should not be joined, speak now or forever hold your peace?" Well you're lucky I wasn't there for that part, because I would have had a whole lot to say on the matter!

Do you think this whore knows you like I know you? Do you think she sees through all the fame and the bullshit to the vulnerable person you really are? I was there for you when no one else was. I don't care if you *did* kill all those women, you have brought so much joy into my life, and I am not about to let that go. So you tell this piece of trash I'm coming for her, and if she's still around when I get there I'm going to destroy her world. Consider this marriage annulled.

Other than that, can't wait to see you!

Your rightful wife,
Mrs. Ginny Williker

—

To: Jonas Williker, inmate #957464
From: Candace Bennington Williker
August 25, 2006

Dear Jonas,

Did you have to go and attack that poor guard? You're supposed to be on your best behavior. Now I feel guilty for teasing you about him.

That being said, part of me is flattered you'd be so possessive. Although maybe protective is a more appropriate word? Something instinctual inside me recognizes this as a desirable quality in a mate. That's right, I referred to you as my mate. Because I just got home from the doctor's office and it's official—we're pregnant!

I guess it's a good thing you went and made an honest woman out of me, huh? If you hadn't I'd be on the other side of the country with my legs in a pair of stirrups by now.

Don't get me wrong, I'm over the moon we're starting a family, but being a single mom finishing a PhD was not on my list of life goals. I am a responsible woman who makes responsible choices and I take family planning very seriously. But having a husband in my corner makes all the difference. We are a team. And unlike my own mother I will make sure my child knows their father. They'll be there with me every visiting day from the moment they're born.

So make sure you work that out with the warden. Studies show a mother's temperament affects the health of her unborn child. Did you forget you were married to an academic? That means the more anxious I am, the more anxious the baby gets. And the idea of my baby not being able to visit their father stresses me the fuck out.

Can't wait to see you!

Love,
Candace

—

To: Jonas Williker, inmate #957464
From: Jane Doe
August 26, 2006

Hello Jonas,

I saw on TV you got married. Have you told your new wife about me? The unrequited kill that keeps you up at night? Frankly I'm amazed the judge allowed it, let alone performed the ceremony himself. Don't you think we're taking this whole "rights of the accused" thing a little too far? I'd say it's not fair you get to enjoy these milestones of normalcy while I can't even look another person in the eye without having a panic attack, but what you're doing isn't exactly normal, is it? I don't think you've ever led a normal life. You've only pretended to.

Still, sometimes I miss intimacy. The last true intimate moments I experienced were with you, for better or worse. That's not to sexualize them. I don't think they were sexual, even for you. Not in the typical way. The armchair academics talk about power dynamics, and sure, that's part of it, but does anyone really understand why people do the things they do? Do you? Maybe that's what you were doing. Searching for an answer to that question. Some self-actualization. And the fact you thought you might find it in me? I find it flattering.

Of course, you wouldn't have found what you were looking for. Not in me or my death. You certainly didn't find it in your next six victims. Did you find it in lucky number seven? Is that why you let them catch you afterwards? You finally found the answer to your question? It doesn't explain the new wife though, does it? Maybe you've found the answer in her. Maybe *she's* the answer.

Or maybe you'd gut her like a fish given half the chance.

Either way, I'm happy for the both of you. I'm not gonna lie, it did make me a bit jealous when I first heard the news. An unconscious surge of anger I almost didn't recognize welled up inside me. Like you were my lover, not my attacker. It took a minute for my brain to regain its emotional equilibrium and correct the mistake. It's funny how easy it is to trick oneself. I'm sure your new bride understands.

Sorry I couldn't attend the ceremony. Do share where you've registered, though. I already know where to send the gift.

Sincerely,
The One That Got Away

—

To: Jonas Williker, inmate #957464
From: Lily Anderson
August 26, 2006

Dear Jonas,

I sent you another money order. Unfortunately for you it will be the last. Now that you're a married man you can mooch off of your wife.

Do I sound bitter? Because I feel like a fool. Not that I entertained the possibility of us getting back together. I wouldn't want that in a million years. Still, I found myself falling into the same old emotional patterns. As I'm sure you're aware, the line between caring and codependency has always been a blurry one for me.

But that's not the impression I get from your new wife. From what I've seen on TV (yes, I plugged it back in), she carries herself with confidence. I didn't think confident women were your type. She must have something you think you can exploit. Why else would you bother?

We all have a type whether we want to admit it or not. Did you ever notice when people refer to someone's "type" it's generally framed as a negative? Why is that? I suppose if your type is "conscientious and committed" you get it right the first time, thus avoiding the negative pattern associated with people who date the same person over and over.

Ugh. This letter is a disaster. I don't know why I'm writing it. I guess that's just the type of person I am. It's a hard box to break out of. You were always so good at putting people in boxes. I hate being so predictable.

Sincerely,
Lily

—

To: Jonas Williker, inmate #957464
From: Staci Satin
August 28, 2006

Dear Purple,

Funny, I hadn't pegged you for the marrying type.

Don't worry, I'm not jealous. That Candace is a certified piece of ass. Does she like girls? I'm already blocking out scenes in my head. Your first time together must have been INTENSE. How do you manage to control yourself, I wonder? Are you capable of keeping things within the acceptable boundaries? I picture your strong hands grasping her windpipe, your mouth leaving bites and bruises in hidden places. Marks other people won't see.

I want to press my lips against those scabbing wounds, reopen them with my teeth and feed from them. Feel their wetness on my face, nourishing me. You'd like that, wouldn't you? Presenting your wife to me as a gift, messages written on her body in a code only the two of us can decipher. We can trade her back and forth until there is nothing left to say, no space left in which to say it, and her vitality is all used up. Sounds decadent, doesn't it? Tell Candy I said congrats.

xoxo,
Staci

—

To: Jonas Williker, inmate #957464
From: Ginny Goodwinch
August 30, 2006

My Dearest Jonas,

I don't know if you've heard the news, but I went and got myself arrested. Now don't you worry, they're treating me just fine. I'm actually enjoying the downtime. No screaming kids, no overbearing mother telling me how I'm ruining my life. It's given me time to reflect. I realize it probably wasn't the best idea for me to show up at the courthouse like that. And I do feel bad about biting that reporter's cheek. I saw a pretty face and I snapped. They told me I threatened to "suck her soul out through her eye sockets," but honestly I don't remember much. After the taste of blood hit my tongue it was all a blur.

You've allegedly tasted human flesh. I can see how people could get used to it, if there was nothing else. Not that I'm insinuating anything. Just thinking out loud, is all.

Anyway, I hope the trial is going well. I'm on what they call "psychiatric hold," and they don't let me watch the news or read the paper. I'm not even supposed to be writing you, so I don't know if you'll get this letter. It's more an exercise for my own mental health. But if by some chance it makes its way to you, I want you to know I'm sorry for embarrassing you. The last thing I want is to hurt your chances of being exonerated.

In other news, Mother called and told me the state put Bobby and Derrick back into foster care. (Sorry, guys! Mommy still loves you!) I know we never really talked about kids, so it's probably for the best. Right now I need to concentrate on getting better. Then I can concentrate on relationships. The kids were just a distraction. Despite the locks on the doors here, I feel free for the first time in my life. And I owe it all to you. I hope one day we can still meet. Maybe even have ourselves a torrid little fling. I've never done anything like that, and it sounds like fun.

Love you!

Always and forever,
Ginny

—

To: Jonas Williker, inmate #957464
From: Kurt Beckett
September 1, 2006

Dear Mr. Williker,

Hello, fellow felon here. Although I'd never presume to put myself in your league, we do have one thing in common: the ire of the dreaded PATC.

Now I'm not sure how closely you follow what goes on outside prison walls, but that stands for Parents Against True Crime, and man do they have it in for you. They've been picketing your trial like nobody's business.

Of course, a pessimist like myself doesn't view this as activism in effect. To me it smacks of opportunism. Because you can't blame the popularity of true crime as entertainment on actual criminals. That's just silly. It's a totally separate issue. At that point you might as well change your name to Parents Against Crime, and what parent isn't? What rational person, for that matter? Unless they're, you know, a professional criminal. If the group is truly against crime as entertainment as they claim, why are they protesting you, a man who has nothing to do with the entertainment industry?

To answer this question I'll have to tell you a little bit about myself, and how PATC came to be.

I'm currently serving 25 to life for the murder of my wife, Ellie. I guess that makes her my ex-wife. She was my wife at the time of her death, so it's not like we got divorced, although I admit that would have been a more prudent course of action on my part. I wonder: Are you still considered a widower if you kill your wife? Never mind.

It was your typical crime of passion—she cheated and I lost my cool. I'd never been a violent or angry person, but three times in three years? Come on. As the husband, they cast me as the main suspect from the start, but I covered my tracks well. It took investigators almost five years to scrounge up the evidence to charge me. But credit where credit is due—once they had me, they *had* me. Dead to rights. When asked how I'd avoided arrest all those years I jokingly told police I read a lot of true crime.

Well my mother-in-law latched onto that like a bull terrier. When you spend so much time being angry about something it's hard to let go, even after justice has been served. Hate is an addiction. The fact that I was being punished for my crimes didn't satisfy her. She needed a bigger baddie to rail against. A reason for my actions, something more than jealous rage. She wanted to wage a war against the world, and needed a scapegoat.

Thus, Parents Against True Crime was born, or PATC, for short. Their stated goal was the curtailing of America's obsession with true life violence as entertainment. Of course this degenerated into a finger-pointing platform, advocating for the censorship of any materials they deemed deviant, including TV shows, horror films, and the ever-popular boogey man of heavy metal music.

The media smelled blood in the water and increased their coverage, giving PATC a huge boost. Some claimed to do so in the interest of parity, but it was plain to see they did it in the interest of ratings. The cause became more about the cause than the actual cause, if you get my meaning. Now they've latched onto the biggest murder trial of the century—yours. They aren't so much protesting you as they're protesting your media coverage. If you ask me they're jealous, and want their fair share.

When confronted with the fact that protesting so vociferously only brings more attention to the things they are trying to denounce, the argument always comes back to me. I started this whole mess. A man killing a woman. And who was going to tell a mother she wasn't allowed to protest the killing of her own daughter? Not me, and I'm the guy who killed her! A pretty clever tactic, in my opinion. Because no matter how big the cause gets they can ratchet focus back down to a point no one wants to argue against.

Maybe it is my fault. I should have kept my glib mouth shut. Because if I've learned anything from this whole situation it's that anything you say can and will be used against you. Something I would have realized if I'd been the true crime fan I'd professed to be.

It doesn't stop there, though. Most recently PATC spawned the offshoot group SKASM, or Serial Killers Against Serial Murder. Their aim is to enlist the aid of actual killers, such as yourself, who claim to have reformed, to speak out against the crime of multiple murder. As if it's just a matter of persuasion. "Oh, this guy said slaughtering innocent people ruined his life? I guess I won't go down that path." Ludicrous.

I figured they'd be reaching out to you, if they haven't already. You'd think no self-respecting person would fall for such a feeble gimmick, but look at the Berkowitz conversion. Evangelicals actually claim him as a member of their tribe. I'm not sure what he gets out of the deal. It's not like he's ever getting out of jail. Maybe he enjoys the attention.

So I'd avoid them if I were you. That's really all I've got to say on the matter. I'm trying not to engage with PATC in the public arena. I don't want to aid my mother-in-law's cause by playing the role she's cast me in. That's exactly what Marsha would want, and I don't want to give her the satisfaction.

Feel free to write me back with any interesting developments.

Sincerely,
Kurt Beckett

—

To: Jonas Williker, inmate #957464
From: anonymous
September 5, 2006

INDIANA STATE PRISON

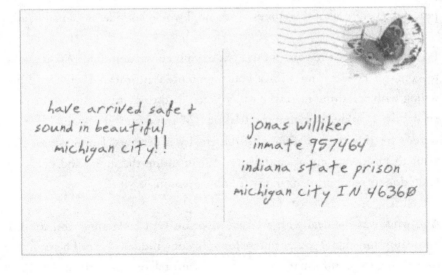

have arrived safe +
sound in beautiful
michigan city!!

jonas williker
inmate 957464
indiana state prison
michigan city IN 46360

To: Jonas Williker, inmate #957464
From: Judith Williker
September 11, 2006

Dear Jonas,

It's your mother. I'm not going to dwell on today's disappointing verdict and neither should you. The most important thing for you to do right now is to stay positive. The road to acquittal is a long one and this trial was just the first step in that journey.

I haven't told your father yet. He's been so peaceful since he got home from the hospital, and I didn't want to aggravate his condition. He spends most of his time out back in his wheelchair, watching the squirrels. I just "set him and forget him," like on those infomercials. He'd probably spend all night out there if I let him. He doesn't watch much TV these days. Not even the news. Too much violence, he says. And he totally gave up on *Oz*. Not that I'm blaming you, but I think your situation kind of ruined it for him. If he happens to pass peacefully before all of this comes to an end, I would consider it a small mercy.

I don't want to lecture you, but in light of your conviction, maybe you ought to consider cooperating with a court-appointed attorney? There's nothing wrong with accepting help when it's offered, and this isn't a game to be taken lightly. Frankly, watching the trial on TV, sometimes it seemed like you weren't treating the situation with the gravity it deserves. I understand you want to project an air of confidence, but insulting the judge and cracking jokes doesn't seem prudent in my humble opinion.

And what was the deal with the detective you kept badgering? You think I know him somehow? I've got news for you, cops and lawyers call here all the time trying to get information out of me. I can't tell one from the other. They all sound exactly the same. And judging from that guy's face, they don't have very distinguishing physical characteristics, either.

You're a married man now, responsible for others. You know that silent strength we talked about? Shouldering the burden of family? It's time you started taking that seriously. Like your father. Once he's doing better you should reach out to him, take advantage of his years of experience as a patriarch.

Please think about what I said. I'll talk to you soon.

Love always,
Mom

—

To: Jonas Williker, inmate #957464
From: Lily Anderson
September 14, 2006

Dear Jonas,

Well, Anna finally found out. It was only a matter of time. I went to pick her up from school and she burst into tears the second she got in the car. Apparently she'd seen your picture on the cover of the newspaper, veins in your neck bulging as you screamed at the jury, the word "GUILTY" looming over you in gigantic letters.

You'd think teachers would know better than to leave those things laying around where kids can see them. It totally freaked poor Anna out. She demanded to know why they'd put Uncle Jonas in jail, and if that was the reason you'd stopped spending time with us. I caught a glimmer of hope behind her pain. Maybe you still wanted to be with us, but you weren't able. If you got out of jail things would go back to normal.

So I told her why they arrested you. I gave her the sanitized version, of course, as sanitized as the defiling and dismemberment of women can be. I told her you wouldn't be getting out ever again. You were a bad man who did bad things, and as much as it hurt, we were better off without you in our lives.

And guess what? That was the easy part. Because then she asked if I knew you were a bad person when I welcomed you into our family. Such a loaded question for a kid. The truth is I had no idea. But still, I had to think about it before I answered her.

You should have seen the look in her eyes. It wasn't that she didn't believe me, she just couldn't understand how a person could be so naive. She experienced a realization. Her mother wasn't perfect. She was a flawed person capable of horrible mistakes.

When I walk down the street I feel like people know I was so emotionally dependent I thought nothing of putting my daughter in harm's way. Because a real mother would have seen the signs. Would have recognized you for what you were, and not let her child within a thousand miles of you.

Please tell me you never did anything to hurt her. I torture myself with nightmare scenarios, trying to account for every second the two of you spent alone. Sometimes she catches me staring, and when she does, she smiles, and I have to fight not to burst into tears. I don't want to alarm her, make her think her mother's cracking up. And I wouldn't dare ask her, because I don't want to plant the idea in her head. The awful idea that someone she loves could hurt her in such a way. She isn't aware that kind of betrayal exists, yet. Or maybe she is. The thought of resurrecting some suppressed trauma within her terrifies me. I wouldn't be able to handle it. And what good would I be to her then?

What if I'm reading the entire situation wrong? And every time she asks about you it's not because she misses you, it's to reassure herself you're gone, and you can't hurt her? The tears in her eyes at seeing your face on the newspaper were born of fear. The glimmer of hope I thought I saw was a moment of vulnerability, quickly buried.

But no, there's no way. If something had happened I would know. I have to believe I would. The alternative is too awful to bear.

Please tell me I'm right.

Lily

—

To: Jonas Williker, inmate #957464
From: Jane Doe
September 15, 2006

Hello Jonas,

The was fast. What did it take them, three hours? Including lunch? Must be some kind of record. Even the judge seemed surprised, though not as surprised as when you demanded he "send them back to think about it some more." Did you catch the expression on his face? Priceless.

All that leaves is the sentencing. I was thinking, maybe a little reunion is in order? Do you think you'd recognize me if you saw me sitting there in the courtroom? Would you feel my eyes burning holes into your skull? My gaze wending its way into your brain like hungry worms? Would it soothe you? Excite you? Make you nervous?

Sometimes I think about what it would be like to confront you. Even for a moment. To look you in the eye, peer through that puff of smoke. Would it live up to the nightmare? Or would it be like seeing an old friend?

Who am I kidding? Maybe you don't remember me. Maybe I'm not the only one who escaped and kept silent. Maybe this character I've fashioned doesn't exist. Maybe the real me died that night, out on the side of the road, and I'm just a ghost, risen from a satin-lined casket, unable to move on to the afterlife. If I was a ghost, I could walk right into the courtroom, wave my hands in front of your face, and you wouldn't see me. No one would. Not the judge or the jury or the journalists. Maybe that's the price of keeping my story to myself. Insignificance.

But you, you've made a mark. Left a legacy. You'll be remembered. More so than any of your victims. People want the gory details of what you did to those women, they don't care who they were. Fucking misery tourists. They want a day trip to wallow in the muck. Then they'll go back home to their comfortable lives like it never happened.

And despite all the horrible things you've done, your gregarious smile and courtroom shenanigans will be remembered most. Your attractiveness will be your epitaph—*How could such a handsome man commit such awful crimes? He looked so normal.*

As for me, no one will ever know my name. Not even you.

Sincerely,
The One That Got Away

—

To: Jonas Williker, inmate #957464
From: Ryland Cochero
September 15, 2006

Dear Mr. Williker,

Thank you so much for your donation to our class auction. The drawing you sent that you named "Exquisite" was a big hit. When I first saw the folded-up piece of paper I was disappointed. Even after I opened it and saw the portrait I didn't know what to think. I have never seen something like that before. The parts on each square look like they belong to a different person but together they make up a whole face like a Frankenstein.

When Mr. Feldspar saw the drawing he got very excited. He took it from me and called the other teachers. He said he recognized the woman in one of the squares from just the eye. He said the rest of the squares belonged to "possibles." I don't know what that means but it made him very happy. He told me we couldn't use the drawing in our auction because we had to donate it to the FBI but I would still get to have my picture taken with the vice president.

I'll be honest Mr. Williker. You're no Jim Davis but your drawing was pretty cool. I told you adults liked you. Thank you for helping with our auction.

Sincerely,
Ryland Cochero

—

To: Jonas Williker, inmate #957464
From: Judith Williker
September 18, 2006

Dear Jonas,

Wow. The death penalty. I know I told you to stay positive, but as your mother this hit me hard. It almost doesn't seem real. Your father has always been such a vocal proponent of capital punishment, but I never really gave it much thought. No one sheds a tear when a random convict is executed, but everything changes when that convict is your son. I may have to rethink my whole stance on the issue.

Of course, if the time comes and your father is physically able, we'll have to make the trip to say our goodbyes. He hasn't said as much (he can't say much of anything at the moment, half his face is paralyzed), but I know he regrets missing all those school recitals when you were a kid, and he'd want to be there front and center for your final performance.

Such a strange thing to write about. Out of all the thoughts that ran through my mind the first time I held you in my arms, out of all the grand futures I envisioned, this certainly wasn't one of them. I don't think there's a mother alive who could say that. You were such a happy baby. So well behaved. And talk about smart! You were what they call a precocious child. It made me sad I could never give you a little brother or sister to play with. Not that we didn't try. Unfortunately your father suffered from what the doctors call low motility.

Maybe it was for the best. I always tried to be a good mom. I hope you know that. Sometimes it's hard not to blame myself for what's happened. Constantly thinking of what I could have done better. If I had only realized…

But it's too late for that. Too late for a lot of things. If it's any comfort, I pray for you every night. You are still my son, and I will always love you.

Sorry to be such a downer. I promise next letter I will be back to my old, bubbly self.

Love,
Mom

—

To: Jonas Williker, inmate #957464
From: Jane Doe
September 21, 2006

Hello again Jonas,

Well I guess that answers my question, whether you remember me or not. I have to say, although I found your antics highly amusing, I don't think you did yourself any favors. Spending half your allocution making veiled threats against a woman who doesn't exist wasn't the best use of your time. And if you think for one second you've scared me off, I've got news for you. YOU. CAN'T. FUCKING. TOUCH. ME. You're a cloud and I'm a ghost, remember? Neither of us are substantial enough to make an impact on the physical plane. That's how I was able to waltz into the courtroom and sit front and center.

Sure it was unnerving when the judge asked whether the gravity of your situation had escaped you, and you looked directly at me as you said, "Nothing escapes me." Like you were trying to expose me for the world to see. Even the women sitting on either side of me felt it. They squirmed in their seats as if you were speaking to them. But you weren't. You weren't even speaking to me. You may have thought you were, but in reality you were speaking to hear the sound of your own voice. You were trying to convince yourself you could still have me.

"Nothing escapes me."

Those are just words, an empty threat. Because I did escape. And no amount of theatrics is going to change that. The smoke has cleared, and I see through the facade to the scared little man you are.

You hear that? The clock is ticking. This is what it's like to be human. Enjoy knowing you're going to die.

Maybe I'll reveal myself after all. Go on a press tour. Do the talk show circuit. Humiliate you on national television. Then I can attend your big going-away party. I want to be the last thing you see as your life fades away. Because I'll still be here when you're gone.

Sincerely,
The One That Got Away

—

To: Jonas Williker, inmate #957464
From: Anna Anderson
September 25, 2006

Dear Uncle Jonas,

Mom doesn't know I'm writing you this letter. Please don't tell her. It can be our secret, okay? Now that I'm 14-years-old, I shouldn't have to ask her permission for every little thing.

I'm sorry I didn't write sooner. I just found out you were in jail. I guess Mom didn't want to tell me. She doesn't like the bad things people say about you. They make her cry. Don't worry, I don't believe any of them.

The police came to our house to ask us questions about you. I told Mom not to let them in but she said she had to. They wanted to talk to me alone but she wouldn't let them. That was good because I was afraid. So Mom held my hand and helped me with my answers. The cops wanted to know if you'd hurt me. I told them you would never do that but they kept asking. They said they wanted to make sure. They said sometimes people forget the bad things that happen to them. Sometimes they forget on purpose. Like how sometimes I forget to clean my room. Mom told them I never forget to clean my room. It made the police mad.

Finally Mom said no more questions and sent me to bed. I pretended to go to sleep and listened from the top of the stairs. She kept telling the police to keep their voices down but they talked real loud. They asked the same questions over and over. It made Mom tired. She said stuff I didn't understand. Like sometimes you did things to her. Things that hurt. Like playing tie-up.

I remember playing that game. You would pretend to be a bad man and tie me to a chair. "Oh no, here comes the train!" you'd say. Then I'd try and escape while you laughed and twirled your imaginary mustache.

Sometimes playing tie-up made my skin scratchy but I still thought it was lots of fun. I don't know why Mom didn't like it. Some games are for kids and some are for grownups, I guess.

Mom said sometimes she woke up at night and you were under the covers with a flashlight like an explorer. Is that a grownup game? After the police left Mom asked if you ever played explorer with me and I told her no. Then she asked if I was forgetting on purpose. I told her I didn't think so and it upset her even more. I wanted to know what you were looking for under the blankets but she wouldn't tell me.

I don't understand. Are you a bad person like they say? Have you done bad things to me? Even though Mom says I shouldn't miss you I still do. I can't help it.

Do you miss me? I hope you do.

Love,
Anna

—

To: Jonas Williker, inmate #957464
From: Staci Satin
September 29, 2006

Dear Purple,

Come on, dude! And I'm not talking about my tits here. What I mean is come-fucking-on already! In case you haven't noticed, I'm really putting myself out there with this shit. Throw me a bone, will ya? And no, that's not a euphemism either. This isn't a fucking AC/DC song. I'm talking quid pro quo. Isn't that a thing with you serial killer types? The give and take? I write you some dirty letters, fellate that ego of yours, and you help me promote my business? You could at least write back so I have something to show for my efforts.

You think I like this gore-girl schtick? It's demeaning and depressing. I only do it because you encroached on my brand. That's right, I was Staci Satin long before you came along. But it was either adapt or get left in the dust by some fresh-faced starlet with an ass like an altar boy.

Plus my manager-slash-boyfriend keeps threatening me, not that that's gonna motivate you. You probably get off on the idea of him beating the shit out of me. This whole stupid thing was his idea. He's obsessed with you. All he does is hang out in serial killer chatrooms and on message boards, trading morbid theories with a bunch of basement dwelling weirdos.

He claims it's research for the business, but I know he gets off on it. He's always asking me to role play as some dead girl or run grotesque torture scenarios. It's too much. What the fuck was I thinking? God only knows what he's doing when he's out of town for work, if he even has a job anymore. I have a sneaking suspicion he got fired months ago, which is why he's pushing this web shit so hard. I wouldn't be surprised to turn on the TV one day and find out he's been arrested for murder. Anyway, I've said too much. What the fuck do you even care?

You know what? *I* don't care. Fuck it. I'm done. With both of you.

Good luck finding someone half as entertaining to fantasize about while you punish your pud, because I'm over this.

Enjoy what's left of your rotten existence, loser.

Staci Satin

—

To: Jonas Williker, inmate #957464
From: Aurelius Percy, Esq.
October 2, 2006

Dear Mr. Williker,

Our condolences on the outcome of your trial. We understand how devastating a guilty verdict can be, especially one that carries such harsh consequences. That being said…

It didn't have to be this way.

No disrespect to you or your litigation skills, of course, but you didn't have what it takes. Thankfully this is America, and we have this long, complex institution called "the appeals process."

Percy, Paramount & Bint would love to throw our hat into the ring once again. We've already started brainstorming, and are prepared to mount a robust defense. We believe the route with the best chance of success would be to appeal your sentence. Because let's face it, everyone thinks you're guilty. Your only hope now is to marshal the liberals in a fight against the death penalty. Compared to death, life in prison doesn't seem so bad now, does it?

We are standing by, should you decide to retain our services.

Sincerely,

Aurelius Percy, Esq.
Percy, Paramount & Bint

—

To: Jonas Williker, inmate #957464
From: William Peters
October 3, 2006

Dear Jonas,

You wrote back! I was starting to think you'd forgotten about me. Don't worry, I understand you have a lot on your plate. My condolences on the outcome of the trial, by the way. I tell myself I'm not supposed to feel sorry for you, but I can't help it. Sure what happened to those women was awful, but I wasn't friends with any of them. To me they're unlucky strangers, names on the news. But you... you were my friend. I'd like to think you still are.

But back to your letter. I got so excited when I saw it, I swear I had some sort of out of body experience. There I was, 12 years old again. I'd just moved to a new neighborhood and every day I'd wait for the mailman to arrive, hoping for a letter from my best friend. Your recent letter *was* that letter. The first of many. I lived an entire lifetime in a single moment. We continued to write and talk on the phone, my parents begrudgingly driving me to see you every so often. It wasn't much, but we made it work.

Things became easier once I got my license, and we were free to hang out whenever we pleased. We picked up right where we left off all those years earlier, exchanging bikes for cars, juice boxes for beers. We helped each other navigate the college years, and remained friends into adulthood and beyond. None of that awful, other stuff ever happened. It was like the final episode of a TV show, where they jump ahead into the future. An alternate life lived in fast forward. I read your letter three times in a row.

Then I had to come back to reality.

Still, what you wrote resonated with me. That you never considered yourself different, just normal in a unique way. "Alternative normalcy," you called it.

Taken out of the context of your current situation, it's something to aspire to. I envy your self-awareness.

Personally I've always struggled with who I am. My partner blames it on my conservative upbringing, which is such a cliche. Or as they like to call it, a clich-*gay*. Although I abandoned religion as an adult, I found myself sucked back in, joining one of those "pray the gay away" men's groups for a short time. It's embarrassing. The average person recognizes an organization like that for what it is. (My partner calls it "prey the gay away.") But a desperate man is willing to try anything. And at that time in my life I was desperate to be anything other than what I was. Who I am.

Your recent media ubiquity has brought some of those old feelings back to the surface. I realized I never felt more myself than when we were together. Does that make you my first crush? Nothing remotely romantic ever happened between us, as far as I can remember. Believe me, I've wracked my brain. I don't think I was even aware of my own sexuality at the time. I felt so at ease in your company, so un-judged.

Which sounds nice, but has given rise to all sorts of unhealthy conflations between who I am and who you are. The rational part of me understands it's a false equivalency, but I can't shake the idea that we are somehow the same.

I haven't told my partner I'm writing you. They'd freak if they found out. They know we were childhood friends, and have even teased me about my first "boyfriend" being a serial killer, but they aren't aware of my current struggle with what our friendship meant. Like I said, I had no idea what you were at the time. If you suspected I was gay, it didn't seem to concern you one way or the other. I'm thankful for that much, at least.

Sorry if this is all over the place. My thoughts are a fucking mess. Your letter triggered a manic whirlwind of emotions inside me. I probably should have taken some time to compose myself before responding, but I wanted to get these feelings down on paper. I wanted to be honest, with you and myself. Plus I wanted to take advantage of my partner being out of the apartment. I suppose at some point I'm going to have to be honest with them about this as well, which is not a conversation I'm looking forward to. I don't suppose you have any advice?

As crazy as they are, my thoughts are with you. What are yours?

Your friend,
Billy Peters

—

LIFE ON DEATH ROW

To: Jonas Williker, inmate #957464
From: The Welcoming Committee
October 5, 2006

In God We Trust - Invest in Luck

1. *Rat Fuck Randy*
2. *Harry Arsole*
3. *Alfred Southwick, DDS*
4. *CO Piedmont*
5. *Dick Trickle*

Dear Inmate,

Welcome to Death Row! Are you in need of a little luck? This chain letter was created in the tradition of the Lucky Letters of the Dust Bowl era and the Send-a-Dime letters that preceded them, in the hopes of spreading good fortune amongst the people that need it most—convicts!

It was started by an inmate named Templeton Bailey, who had his death sentence commuted less than 3 months later. Another inmate, Buck Fisker, was promoted to Head Cook with full privileges after participating.

The way it works is simple: Omit the top name on this list and put your own at the bottom. Then make five copies of this letter and pass it on to five inmates who could use some luck.

Then instead of *sending* a dime like they did in the old days, you're going to *drop* a dime. Write down a crime you have committed and deliver it to the person whose name you omitted. This puts everyone on equal footing and ensures the integrity of the chain. To this day, not a single secret has been revealed outside the community.

If you do not do this within 48 hours your luck will take a turn for the worse. DO NOT BREAK THE CHAIN! The last man who did was found in the showers with his throat slit and a bar of soap shoved so far up his ass his neck was blowing bubbles.

Thank you for participating. Good luck!

[An example of one of the less-intimidating initiation rituals awaiting the newly-incarcerated at Indiana State Prison. —Editor]

—

To: Jonas Williker, inmate #957464
From: Ginny Goodwinch
October 6, 2006

Dear Jonas,

Guess what? I figured out a way to get my letters to you. Obviously, duh. Wanna know how? I went and got myself a man on the inside, that's how! He's an orderly here at the hospital and he's literally "my man," so hands off, ladies! I know, I can't believe it either. I don't mind telling you, I am tuchus over tea kettle! As you are well aware, it's been a long time since I've had a man. Or *had* a man, for that matter. Far too long. But now I have! In both senses! I hope you're not upset. I'm not trying to make you jealous or anything. You *are* married, after all. It's only fair I move on.

But let me back things up a bit. Last letter I told you how I'd been put on psychiatric hold for attacking that reporter. (Mercifully, she isn't pressing charges. It seems she's experienced quite the boost in popularity since the incident.) Anyway, at the end of that 72-hour period, which I barely remember, they decided to extend the hold for a full 14 days of "intensive psychiatric treatment." It sounds scary, but it wasn't so bad. I was able to get plenty of rest, and they gave me some nice medicine that made me feel all floaty. There were also lots of people to talk to, when I found myself in the mood for company. A bunch of kindred souls who know what it's like to be lonely. And of course I met my Guy.

That's his name: Guy. And he's a dream! He saw how worked up I was getting over my letters and offered to mail them for me. When I told him I didn't have any stamps he said all I had to do was "stamp those pretty little lips of yours right here," and tapped himself on the cheek. Talk about a smoothie. I would have swooned right out of my bed if I wasn't strapped into it. Let me tell you, kindness is such a turn on!

Anyway, he leaned in so I could pay for services rendered, but instead of kissing him on the cheek I somehow found myself locking lips with his hungry mouth. It all happened so fast. I don't know who started kissing who first, but one thing was for certain, neither of us could help ourselves! Also, I think I might be into bondage now?

Obviously I've been in here more than two weeks. At the end of 14 days it was recommended I remain for further treatment, and I whole-heartedly agreed. It's like being on an extended honeymoon! And I can tell the therapy's really working. Normally I'd be blushing beet red telling you steamy details about me and Guy, but I am cool as a cucumber in the hands of a skilled lover.

Oh shoot. *Now* I'm blushing. But at least I'm making progress!

I hope things are going well with you. I asked Guy for an update on the trial, but he said he didn't want to compromise my treatment, and it was something I should discuss with my doctor. I'd love to remain platonic pen pals if you're interested, as long as that's okay with your wife. A gal can't have too much meaningful engagement. And Guy has agreed to continue mailing my letters. Isn't he the thoughtfulest?

Hope you're doing well. I gotta go line up for morning meds, but I promise I'll write again soon.

In loving friendship,
Ginny Goodwinch

—

To: Jonas Williker, inmate #957464
From: Candace Bennington Williker
October 7, 2006

Dear Jonas,

Sorry I didn't get to see you this week. I wasn't feeling well for a couple days, there. Morning sickness is a bitch. I tried to visit you on Friday, but they told me I wasn't on the list. I didn't recognize the CO on duty, so I told him there must be some mistake. I stopped short of going full, "Don't you know who I am?" but he just gave me a sheepish look, as if to say, "It's out of my hands, lady."

What the hell's going on over there? You need to straighten this out with the warden. You are his most high-profile inmate, after all. Until then, make sure you call me. I have lots of baby stuff to tell you.

I'll try again next week, after I've had my sonogram. That way I'll have a solid idea of the baby's due date (although I'm pretty sure I can do the math). The chances of the state granting you furlough are slim-to-none, so I've been looking into the possibility of giving birth at the prison hospital. Glamorous, I know. Has anyone ever done that? You know, outside of the 2000 incarcerated women annually who don't have a choice?

Maybe you could make a few inquiries. I'd love to get a tour of the facilities. I'll be bringing the midwife along to make sure they're up to snuff. You missing the birth of our child is not an option.

Can you believe the little cocktail shrimp is already 2cm long? That's crown to rump, as they say. Life sure is a miracle. I can't wait to meet ours!

Your pregnant wife,
Candace

—

To: Jonas Williker, inmate #957464
From: Judith Williker
October 9, 2006

Dear Jonas,

It's your mother. I hope I'm not spoiling the surprise, but I just can't contain myself. I'm going to be a grandmother! Which means you're going to be a father! Surely Candace has told you by now. It's already all over the news. I'd be a little insulted the press found out before me if I wasn't so elated. You know in my day we didn't tell anyone outside the family until at least the 12th week, just in case (knock on wood!). I suppose infant mortality rates aren't the concern they used to be thanks to modern medicine. Either way, I'm thrilled to hear the news and will be telling anyone who'll listen. Even strangers!

I have so many questions. When? Where? How? On second thought, don't answer that. It's like our own little immaculate conception. A genuine miracle. Do tell Candace to reach out if she needs anything. I'm sure her mother is all over it, but when it comes to children you can never have too much help.

Have I mentioned how excited I am? Because I am very excited. I can't think about anything else, so you'll have to wait until next time for your normal dose of news. Talk soon!

Love,
Mom

—

To: Jonas Williker, inmate #957464
From: Todd DeFrancisco
October 11, 2006

Dear Jonas Williker,

My name is Todd DeFrancisco. I am a paranormal investigator and host of
the popular reality show, *Adventures in Ghost Hunting*. Ring any bells? Dollars
to donuts you've seen our Alcatraz special on the ghosts of 14D. The show's
pretty popular in the pen. I should know, I get a ton of mail from the inside.
Requests for signed photos, questions about my workout, stuff like that. You
guys are true fans. As my father used to say, there's no folk like prison folk.
Probably because he was one.

Anyway, what with your current popularity, we're considering a special themed
episode focusing on the victims of the Purple Satin Killer. The idea is to hit a few
of the major crime scenes and try to contact the souls of the dearly dispatched.
Definitely the location of the first murder, the abandoned supermarket in Scenery
Hill. Some of the spots of the more notorious killings, too. Like the farmhouse
where they discovered Kirsten Swallows. In my experience, the more violent the
death, the angrier the spirits tend to be, and the better chance of them reaching
(or lashing) out. I like when they come at me. It gets me pumped! That's what
inspired me to get "I ain't afraid of no ghosts" tattooed on both my biceps.

This is where you come in. I was hoping you could provide some insight
into the psyche of the victims at the time of their death. Maybe share a
few key phrases that would help trigger a response. A lot of these spirits
tend to exist in a sort of fugue state, and need to be shocked into action.

Are there any odors you would associate with specific events? Ghosts are attracted to familiarity coupled with strong emotions. It's kind of the reverse of
burning sage to scare them away. Shit and piss are old standbys. The smell of
gasoline, flowers, perfume.

Semen is another big one, although I try to avoid it. Neither me nor the other guys like to contribute our own fluids, to avoid the possibility of a rogue spirit forming an attachment. Accidental bonding is a real hazard of the job. Our cameraman, Danny, was once followed home by a succubus that took months to exorcize. He and his wife still can't conceive. That spectral bitch drained him dry.

But enough about Danny's desiccated balls. Any information you provide would be greatly appreciated. And if there's anything you'd like us to pass on in the event of contact, any sort of personal message, please don't hesitate to ask. Closure is hard to achieve in these situations, and if we can help facilitate that for either party, we consider it a privilege.

Sincerely yours,

Todd DeFrancisco

Actor-Writer-Director-Producer-Paranormal Investigator-Amateur Body Builder-Ordained Minister

—

To: Jonas Williker, inmate #957464
From: Lily Anderson
October 12, 2006

Dear Jonas,

There's the cruel streak I remember so well. I bet you couldn't wait to unload that hurtful little secret, could you? Although like everything else, it seems so obvious in hindsight.

I'm such a fucking idiot.

My hands are shaking so bad I can barely write. Do you know I still double and triple check the stove before bed every night? A Pavlovian side effect of your help-ful "reminders." Sometimes I even wake up in a cold sweat, convinced I smell gas. I flash back to the paramedics wheeling Anna away, clear plastic mask strapped to her face. How easily you convinced me to blame myself, despite the fact I'd never made a mistake like that before. Despite the fact we hadn't used the stove all week.

You never missed an opportunity to pile on the guilt. At the time I thought I deserved it. The abuse prevented me from making the same mistake twice. But my only mistake was trusting you.

It's a relief knowing I didn't almost asphyxiate my daughter. But that's can-celed out by the fact I exposed her to something far more deadly than natural gas. I can understand you wanting me dead. But I'll never forgive you for almost killing Anna.

It's a small comfort, but I'm glad they gave you the death penalty. It's the least they could do. You deserve so much worse. They should be able to kill you once for every life you've taken. I don't know the current method of execution in Indiana, but my vote is for the gas chamber. Whatever they decide, the end result will be the same—you rotting in hell for eternity.

I want to make this perfectly clear: do not contact me or my daughter ever again. Any goodwill I felt towards you is gone. I'm looking forward to the end of this whole fucking ordeal.

Lily

—

To: Jonas Williker, inmate #957464
From: William Peters
October 13, 2006

Dear Jonas,

I'm not sure how to take your advice on what to do about Ziv. I think you were joking, but sometimes it's hard to tell in a letter. Anyway, it gave me a good laugh, but if anything I think *they're* going to be the one that murders *me*. This is the exact type of scenario Ziv's paranoid brain would concoct—me dumping them for a straight guy on death row. I can picture them jumping up and down on their therapist's couch shouting, "See? I told you so!"

Poor Ziv. I may drive them crazy, but they were halfway there when they got in the car with me. I mean, what's the harm in writing a few letters? This is me dealing with my issues head on, which is what my therapist and Ziv are always telling me I should do. There's no rule that says I have to share every little detail with them, right? Other than the arbitrary one they made? Isn't the point learning how to take care of myself?

Sometimes I wonder exactly how helpful this whole therapy racket is. In a way it's not much different than religion. It's so easy to get caught up in the technicalities and forget the intent, which is supposed to be helping people.

How about you? Do you have access to any mental health services? Might be worth your while, especially if the State's footing the bill. The amount of money I've spent on therapy over the years is obscene! Not that it's made much of a difference.

For real, though. If you have any serious suggestions on what to tell Ziv, I'm all ears.

Your friend,
Billy Peters

—

To: Jonas Williker, inmate #957464
From: Candace Bennington Williker
October 13, 2006

Dear Jonas,

You haven't called in a while. Have you taken care of the visitor issue like I asked? They turned me away again this week. Do I need to get the lawyers involved? The officer on duty acted pretty smug. I'm starting to think something's wrong.

You are missing out on important milestones in our child's development. Next week the fetus will be the size of a kumquat, and the week after that, a lemon. You don't want to miss lemon! I know you've got a lot going on with your appeal, but establishing a pattern of neglect before a child's birth sets a bad parenting precedent. And remember what I told you about stress. I'm doing my best to stay calm, but there's only so much chamomile tea I can drink. The baby may be getting bigger, buy my bladder sure as hell isn't. I've got a stream like a racehorse on steroids!

Please fix this. And call me.

Your agitated (and pregnant) wife,
Candace

—

To: Jonas Williker, inmate #957464

From: Abigail Tinder

October 14, 2005

Dear Jonas Williker,

Allow me to introduce myself. My name is Abigail Tinder, and I am a twelve-year-old preacher's daughter from Argos, Indiana. I am writing to inform you that although you are a despicable sinner who has committed heinous crimes, it is not too late to save your soul from eternal damnation.

Of course, fear of hell is not, in and of itself, a valid justification for redemption. As it says in the book of Romans, you must renounce your sin, and believe with all your heart that Jesus Christ is Lord. Only then can you truly be saved.

It is that easy.

If you are interested, I have enclosed some literature containing a simple sinner's prayer for you to recite. I think you'll get a kick out of it. It's one of those popular cartoon gospel tracts. This one's about an elementary school student who murders his classmate in a rage after finding out Santa Claus isn't real. He grows up to become a terrorist on the FBI's most wanted list, second only to Osama Bin Laden, and is eventually executed for his crimes. It's a poignant story about the dangers of false idols presented in an accessible form. If you have any questions after reading it please don't hesitate to reach out. I am always available to further instruct you in the ways of righteousness.

I believe your conversion would be a valuable testimony to the saving grace of our Lord and Savior Jesus Christ. You have the potential to become the next David Berkowitz. David gave his life over to Christ and is now a shining beacon for the Lord. A perfect reminder of God's master plan, even where senseless slaughter is concerned. It would not be a sin for you to follow in David's footsteps in that regard.

Yours in Christ,
Abigail Tinder

—

To: Jonas Williker, inmate #957464
From: Jane Doe
October 16, 2006

Dear Jonas,

I've been thinking a lot about what you said to me at your sentencing. "Nothing escapes me." Three little words that convey so much. At the time I dismissed it as bravado on your part. A reaction to the shock of seeing my face. I felt so powerful in that moment, confident you could never touch me. But now I'm beginning to wonder if I didn't take your words a little too literally. If I didn't willfully misinterpret them.

Because I came to a realization the other day. Try as I might, I can't picture my life without you. You've shaped who I am so thoroughly I fear excising you would leave me gutted. An empty shell. I thought I had the upper hand that day in the courtroom, but the truth is I made myself vulnerable. I exposed myself. I willingly squandered my greatest asset—my anonymity.

It hit me on the courthouse steps as I was leaving. Standing shoulder to shoulder with the press and the gawkers and the rabble I should have felt hidden, but I felt exposed. Recognition flashed in every passing set of eyes, greedy to exploit my secret. One reporter singled me out, shoved a tape recorder in my face, and asked my thoughts on the judge's decision. Demanded to know my name. At least that's what it seemed like. All I remember is I panicked, fumbling over my words before fleeing into the crowd like a frightened animal.

But the damage was done. Something followed me home that day. Lodged itself in my brain. I'm starting to think you were right, maybe I didn't escape. Maybe you allowed me to live. And by allowing me to live you sentenced me to a different kind of death.

So I guess this isn't goodbye after all. Despite what I tell myself I'm going to keep writing to you. Because our futures are intertwined. As long as you're alive there is purpose in my life. I'd be a fool to throw it away. At this point it's all I have.

Sincerely,
The One

—

To: Jonas Williker, inmate #957464
From: Jason Corbish
October 17, 2006

Dear Jonas Williker,

Due to public outcry, I regret to inform you that *In Verse* magazine will no longer be publishing your poem, "The One That Got Away," in our upcoming Incarcerated Artists issue. While the initial concept of the theme was inclusive of any and all individuals living behind bars—for whatever reason—to provide as wide-ranging a field of viewpoints as possible, it seems the writing community has taken exception to this and decided on a narrower interpretation they feel is more appropriate. Under the threat of boycott the publishers of *In Verse* thought it prudent to acquiesce to their demands.

This was a unanimous decision agreed upon by the entire editorial staff, and not one we take lightly. There was much deliberation, but ultimately we chose to honor our obligation to our readers. They are the ones who support us, and they deserve to have their feelings honored in such matters.

On a more personal note, I was never quite comfortable with the content of your piece, and will not miss its inclusion. Your take on the subject of victimhood left much to be desired. If I am being honest, your poem has already served its purpose—drummed up invaluable free publicity for our tiny publication, which was most likely the intent from the start. Of course I cannot speak for everyone on staff here at *In Verse*, but many of my co-workers are quite media savvy.

Thank you for submitting to *In Verse* and trusting us with your work. We hope it finds a home elsewhere, and we look forward to hearing from you in future open calls.

Sincerely,

Jason Corbish
Managing Editor, In Verse Magazine

—

To: Jonas Williker, inmate #957464
From: Ginny Goodwinch
October 18, 2006

My Dear Sweet Jonas,

I just heard about your conviction and sentencing. I am so, so sorry. And here I was, selfishly oblivious, rubbing my happiness in your face like the stereotypical evil ex. I feel awful about it. Truly. I used to be one of your biggest supporters, but now I barely know what's going on in your life. Just the thought of it is enough to send me deep into a shame spiral. When you needed her most your Ginny Bird was nowhere to be found. She'd flown the coop.

I heard the awful news during one of my weekly therapy sessions. The doctor said I'd been making such good progress that I was ready to confront the specter of the trial's outcome. Shows what she knows. I only had a complete and utter meltdown. Fearing for her tender cheek flesh, the doctor quickly locked herself in the bathroom and called security. They had to restrain me and dope me up but good. So when I say I just heard about your conviction, that was probably like three semiconscious days ago. My head's still a bit foggy. In light of my reaction the doctor thinks it's a good idea if my stay here remains indefinite. There is work yet to be done on ole Gin Gin.

What about you? What's the next step? Will you be handling your own appeal? Is it time to get the Innocence Project involved? Not that they've proven very helpful. I wish I could do more, but like my doctor says, I can't fix other people's problems until I fix my own. Still, my heart is with you. Stay strong, Jonas! Everything will work out in the end. I can feel it.

Your stalwart friend,
Ginny

—

To: Jonas Williker, inmate #957464
From: Candace Bennington Williker
October 20, 2006

Dear Jonas,

Okay, now I *know* something's wrong. I went to see you today and the warden told me I have been permanently removed from the visitors list, per inmate request. Me. Your wife. The mother of your unborn child. I've never been so humiliated in my life. The walk back to my car was worse than any so-called walk of shame. I barely managed to keep my composure until I was behind the wheel.

What the hell is going on? Is it because I'm pregnant? Are you afraid I've somehow developed a fragile constitution and can no longer withstand exposure to the harsh realities of prison life? Let me tell you something, buddy, I'm no delicate flower. Pregnancy makes incarceration look like a walk in the park. My body is an actual jail of flesh, and in a little over 6 months its occupant is going to stage a prison break via my most intimate of areas.

Or maybe you're suddenly concerned about your son growing up with a con for a father. As if that's the worst thing in the world. Remember who you're talking to. As someone who grew up unable to visit the father she so desperately loved, I can affirm that refusing to see your child will have serious negative effects on their emotional well-being. You'll be knowingly and willfully fucking them up. Are you going to make me tell our child that their father was a selfish piece of shit who wanted nothing to do with them? Don't think I won't!

You better call me and straighten this out. If you don't want to be a part of this family anymore you're going to have to try a lot harder than that. You're going to have to act like a man and tell me to my face. Tell *us*. And you better have a damn good reason. None of this "the first step in avoiding a trap is knowing one exists" crap. You better not try and throw *that* back in my face. That was roleplay and you know it. Sexy talk to spice up our letters. And it fucking worked, because newsflash—I'm fucking pregnant! Now it's time for you to do *your* part. I'm not going to continue playing these childish games with you.

I'm serious, Jonas. Call me.

Candace

—

To: Jonas Williker, inmate #957464
From: Judith Williker
October 23, 2006

Dear Jonas,

It's your mother. I hope you're keeping your spirits up during the appeals process. It seems like the media coverage has died down a bit, which is a blessing. Used to be I'd catch someone peering over the back fence at least once a week. Now I'm lucky if the paperboy waves hello as he rides by on his bike. I have to say, I kind of miss the interaction. Nothing gets the heart pumping like chasing trespassers with a broom! He'd never admit it, but I bet your father misses it too. It gave him something new and exciting to complain about.

Speaking of complaints, Candace tells me you've taken her off your visitor's list? That can't be right. She said she's yet to hear it from you directly, so I'm assuming this is all just a misunderstanding. Some sort of clerical error on the prison's part. Is there anything I can do to help? Poor Candace sounded so distraught I told her I'd look into it. Stress isn't good for a woman in her condition, so try and keep her happy. That's my grandchild in there!

Talk to you soon.

Love,
Mom

—

To: Jonas Williker, inmate #957464

From: Miguel Serrano

November 1, 2006

Dear Jonas Williker,

My name is Miguel Serrano. You probably won't remember me, but about a decade ago you saved my life.

You were working as a phone operator at Charleston's Suicide Crisis Center at the time. But back then you weren't Jonas Williker. Per company policy you didn't use your real name. You went by "Teddy." Watching your trial all these years later, I experienced a feeling of déjà vu. I closed my eyes and it was like being on the phone with Teddy all over again.

I was at my lowest point. Lower than low. They say when you hit rock bottom there's nowhere to go but up, but I proved them wrong. I'd been drinking heavily and decided to take a whole bottle of aspirin, but I was scared, and wanted to make sure it wouldn't be a painful death. At the time I assumed it was equivalent to overdosing on sleeping pills. So I called what I thought was a medical hotline (at least that's what I told myself), and asked the nice-sounding young man on the phone about the side effects of salicylate poisoning. That's the clinical term for an aspirin overdose. You taught me that.

Well, the man on the phone said he wasn't an expert, but we could find out together. A clever tactic. Something they taught you at the center? You realized I was beyond wasted, so you kept me on the phone while you did "research," talking to me for hours, until I'd sobered up enough to realize I didn't actually want to kill myself. Because the details of taking too much aspirin were not pleasant. Burning in the throat, high fever, chills, hallucinations, seizures, intense stomach cramping, loss of bowel control, projectile vomiting. A little hyperbolic, perhaps, but regardless, it didn't sound fun.

We spoke multiple times over the following months. Every time I called I asked for Teddy. My guardian angel. You helped me shovel through a lot of shit that year. I found myself in a much healthier place when you finally told me you were thinking of moving on. That you had a new career opportunity but wanted to make sure I'd be okay before you took it. That you didn't want to abandon me. It meant so much. And I'm forever grateful.

When I realized your true identity all these years later, it was hard to reconcile the man who did all those terrible things with empathetic young Teddy at the call center. Had it all been an act? Some sort of human roleplay, to prove to yourself you could move among us undetected? This happened a year or so before your first murder. Had you not crossed that line yet? I find it hard to believe the Purple Satin Killer didn't already exist inside you. Why did you help me? And how were you so well-versed in the ways of kindness?

I have to admit, I thought about hurting myself after I found out. But instead I wrote this letter. It's taken a while (I've been working on it for a couple months now) because I wasn't sure what type of letter it should be. Am I angry? Of course I'm fucking angry. I feel betrayed. I feel like a fool. I'm sad, hurt—all of it. But I'm also thankful. Thankful I'm alive. And I'm alive be- cause of you. What that means to you, I'll never know—if it means anything at all—but that's a pretty big deal, being responsible for saving someone's life. Out of all the awful things you've done, you've also done a tiny bit of good. That's got to account for something.

Who knows? I wanted to talk to you one more time. To remind myself of what you're capable of. Maybe to remind you, too. Do you consider it a blem- ish on your spotless record of evil? Does it drive you crazy? That wouldn't be such a bad thing. In fact, it would be a damn good reason for me to continue living, don't you think?

Do you need someone to return the favor? I'm including my telephone num- ber at the end of this letter. I don't want to speak to Jonas. The thought of doing so terrifies me. But if Teddy ever needs someone to talk to, please let him know I'm available.

Sincerely,
Miguel Serrano
[phone number redacted]

—

To: Jonas Williker, inmate #957464
From: William Peters
November 15, 2006

Dear Jonas,

You ever wonder what things would have been like if I'd never moved away? If we'd remained friends all these years? I'm not talking about the stuff of idyllic daydreams, like the scenario I wrote about in one of my earlier letters. More on an existential level. I guess what I'm asking is, do you think my influence could have changed your trajectory at all? Could our continued friendship have made enough of a difference in your life? I'd like to think so, but I was never the most assertive person.

If anything I would have been the one sucked into your world, out of my devotion to our friendship. And that frightens me. My only consolation is, despite my love of horror movies, I'm pretty squeamish when it comes to real blood. One time I passed out having a zit lanced at the dermatologist. So I don't think I'd make the best thrall.

Would you have been able to hide who you were from me? Would I have been oblivious? Willfully ignorant? Would I have had the guts to confront you? Turn you in? These are questions I can't answer.

You know what? Something awful just occurred to me. Mrs. Beasley's cats… It was you, wasn't it? It's so fucking obvious now. How you always seemed to know where to find the remains. Oh God that poor woman. I think I'm going to be sick…

Wouldn't it be great if puking your guts out purged your mind as well as your body? Like how sometimes when you eat something gross or you've had too much to drink you make yourself throw up so your stomach feels better? Shouldn't stress-puking do the same for your mind? Wipe your memory and reset the anxiety meter to zero? That way you can recuperate and get some sleep, instead of feeling physically wrung out while your thoughts bounce around your skull like a lunatic in a padded cell.

Ugh.

I think I need a nap. I'm going to lie down and try not to dream. Wish me luck.

Your friend,
Billy Peters

—

To: Jonas Williker, inmate #957464
From: Antonio Birch
November 23, 2006

Dear Mr. Williker,

My name's Antonio Birch, but you can call me Ant. Most people do. I'm not much of a Tony guy. Growing up I had to make a choice: either be a Tony guy or an Ant guy. Since Tony's what my mom calls her husband when she's angry, I went with Ant. Having the same name as your stepdad is awkward enough as it is. My Meemaw calls me TJ, but I don't let anyone else use that name. Only her.

Anyway, I'll get to the reason I'm writing.

I'm currently in the hospital recovering from a traumatic brain injury that left me partially paralyzed. How'd that happen, you ask? Good question. My stupid stepdad had recently installed a hot tub in the backyard and I was lured home from school with the promise of extreme relaxation. Long story short, I should have spent the weekend on campus. As I was stepping into the tub for my inaugural soak, I slipped on the deck and cracked my head wide open. It took over 2 dozen staples to close me up and I spent the next three weeks in a medically induced coma.

One of the nurses told me I would scream in my sleep every night at 11 P.M. on the dot. A throaty, honking noise, like someone squeezing a goose with all their might. That's how I woke up. Honked myself right out of that coma. I have no recollection of any dreams or what might have caused me to make such a sound. Pretty weird, right?

I'm getting to the point, I promise. Which is this:

Ever since I woke up I haven't felt the same. It's like something's missing. The doctors keep telling me that's normal, and I have to give it time—which is super condescending and frustrating. Doctors never actually listen, you know? They think they know everything about everything, but they don't. Just like my stepdad.

Have you heard of acquired savant syndrome? There was a story making the rounds not too long ago, about a guy who became a musical genius after falling down a flight of stairs. He'd never touched a piano in his life, and then BONK! He's flipping sheet music upside down and playing these complex compositions in reverse. There was another guy who got struck by lightning and woke up speaking fluent Spanish. Not the Mexican kind, either. I'm talking full-on European Español. He didn't realize no one could understand him and eventually reverted back to English in the middle of a conversation.

There was also a guy who had a stroke and claimed it turned him gay, although the jury's still out on him. Dude might've just been a closet case looking for an excuse. My point is weird shit happens all the time and doctors just shrug. We understand very little about the human mind when it comes down to it.

I'm not saying I'm a savant now, but brain trauma has a slew of other side effects. Things like behavioral shifts, mood disorders, and even violence. Look at poor O.J. Simpson. The man took one too many hits and turned into a world-class stabbing machine.

Again, I'm not saying this is what's happening to me, but maybe it is? I've always been a happy, outgoing person, but ever since my accident I've been feeling pretty aggressive. I'm not just talking ticked off here, I'm talking really fucking angry. I mean, sometimes I get so angry I start thinking awful things. Horrible thoughts about hurting people I love. Stuff that would make the old me sick to my stomach. But now I find myself dwelling on those things, focusing on the details, and it's scaring me.

I keep asking myself, is this how it starts? Am I going to lose control and start killing people? I don't want to become a murderer, but then again, maybe

I do? My brain is all, "That's an interesting proposition, Tony," and like I said, nobody calls me Tony. If they do, my stepdad quotes that stupid movie. "There can be only one!" It's super fucking annoying.

I haven't brought this up with my doctor yet. He'd laugh it off because it doesn't fit the typical narrative of my injury. It feels a lot more natural discussing it with someone in your situation. Did you ever experience a traumatic head injury as a child?

Maybe I'm going stir crazy. Being confined to bed sucks. I guess writing letters is as good a hobby as any. Is it weird you're the person I chose to write to?

I'm sure you receive tons of letters, so thanks for taking the time to read mine. Assuming you do. I guess I won't find out unless you respond. In any case, take care.

Sincerely,
Ant

—

To: Jonas Williker, inmate #957464
From: Grant Singer
November 30, 2006

Mr. Williker,

That was some trial. A real three-ringer as the circus folk say. I hope there's no hard feelings. I made sure to wait a while before writing again, just in case. Despite agreeing with the jury's decision I want you to know I take no pleasure in it. You treated me with nothing but courtesy, professionalism, and respect on the witness stand. As a member of law enforcement I appreciate that. Seeing how you butt heads with the judge, I know things could have gone a lot different. Luckily for you Judge Mathers is both level-headed and even-handed. I also think you reminded him of his son, who's had his own issues with the law, which could account for the man's abundance of patience.

Still, I don't think you went easy on me. A less experienced investigator might have cracked under the rigor of your cross examination. Looking back, I can't help but chuckle when I think about how hard you grilled me over my friendship with your mother. Demanding to know my intentions like I was some kind of suitor! I probably should've never written you that damn letter, but like I said, I didn't want to seem like I had something to hide. In the end I think that line of questioning did you more harm than good. Instead of establishing a conflict of interest it made me look honest to a fault. So even though that wasn't your intention, I wanted to thank you.

We did have our lighter moments, though. Am I mistaken or did I catch a gleam in your eye when we discussed the purple panties? Same as when you showed them to me out on Miller's Highway. You then repeatedly referred to them as a "sham wow" in an attempt to trip me up, but I've told that story so many times I could recite it in my sleep.

It reminded me how once my ex handcuffed herself to the bed, wearing nothing but matching purple undergarments, and demanded I have my way with her. I suppose she saw it as a way to connect with me, incorporating my obsession into our failing sex life, but things didn't go so well. It was the one and only time I ever got rough with a woman. Not something I'm proud of. It signaled the beginning of the end for us.

How are you settling in? I imagine prison takes getting used to. It seems neither of us are cut out for retirement. Since the trial I've accepted an offer to head a special federal task force on multiple murder. I guess I'm considered a bit of an expert in the field now. I don't suppose they reached out to you for a reference?

Your mother tells me you're keeping busy with the appeal. That woman is a pillar of strength, and you're lucky to have her in your corner. The fortitude it takes to cope with your incarceration and care for an ailing husband must be extraordinary. I am not ashamed to say I admire her.

Take care of yourself, Jonas. For your mother's sake.

Sincerely,
Special Agent Grant Singer
Federal Task Force: Serial Homicide Unit

—

To: Jonas Williker, inmate #957464
From: Darlene Edmonton
December 1, 2006

Dear Jonas Williker,

Thank you for your interest in Outside Access, a personal social media manager and online secretarial service for the incarcerated. We have gone ahead and submitted your information to JPay for State-approved email/payment transfer access. Once we receive confirmation we will forward it to you. Then it is just a matter of scheduling.

While you are waiting to be connected, please consider some of our other services. We specialize in:
- Setting up/maintaining personal blogs, Myspace, and Facebook pages
- Connecting inmates with pen pals via both snail and electronic mail
- Providing stock quotes/sports scores/"Lost" spoilers
- Creating and managing dating profiles
- Research assistance for writers

What we do NOT do:
- Post anything that can be construed as threatening or harassing
- Post anything that would aid in any enterprise of an illegal nature
- Post pictures of genitalia, commonly referred to as "dick pics"

May I inquire how you found out about us? I'm assuming someone passed you one of our business cards, or posted a flier in a common area. Or maybe someone on the outside made a recommendation? Either way, we appreciate you reaching out. Outside Access is a small business run by a single mother who herself is the partner of someone on the inside. We believe maintaining relationships and forging personal connections is essential to the rehabilitation process. As statistics regarding repeat offenders have shown, imprisonment on its own has not proven to be an effective deterrent of crime.

Thank you very much for your time. We know it is your most valuable asset.

Sincerely,

Darlene Edmonton
Outside Access, LLC

—

To: Jonas Williker, inmate #957464
From: David Manning
December 3, 2006

Dear Jonas Williker,

I appreciate you taking the time to meet with me while I was in town. I'm told you're very selective about who you see, so I consider it an honor. Especially since it was during the climax of your trial. My fellow Truth Sleuthers would lose their minds if they knew (not that I plan on violating your trust).

Which reminds me, you definitely should consider posting some of your poetry on the boards there. I think it would be really well received.

It's a shame the verdict didn't go your way, but I'm interested to see what the future holds. If I can be of any further use, please let me know. I'm back on the road but I promise to keep in touch.

Sincerely,
David Manning

—

To: Jonas Williker, inmate #957464
From: Abigail Tinder
December 4, 2006

Dear Mr. Williker,

I have yet to receive a response from you, which leads me to assume one of two things:

You believe you deserve hell. If that is the case, let me remind you we ALL deserve hell. It is only by the blood of Christ, his sacrifice in our stead, that we are washed clean of sin and permitted entry into the gates of heaven. The egregious nature of your crimes notwithstanding, very little difference exists between you and I. There is no reason we cannot one day break bread in the hereafter.

Either that or you are a prideful man who takes pleasure from spitting in the face of God. Such defiance can only result in destruction. Proverbs Chapter 16 Verse 5 says: "Everyone who is arrogant in heart is an abomination to the Lord; be assured, he will not go unpunished."

Do you think you are too good for the grace of God? You will burn in hell for your arrogance, along with all the unrepentant homosexuals and baby-killers. Consider yourself warned.

However, if you've already responded as of the time of this letter's arrival, you may disregard the above recrimination. I'm hoping this is still the case, and I receive word from you soon.

Yours in Christ,
Abigail Tinder

—

To: Jonas Williker, inmate #957464
From: Elrond James
December 7, 2006

Dig this scene,

The body of Helen James was found naked on the side of the interstate one hot June morning in 1975. Elrond James was ten years old. You'd just been born, so you're off the hook.

What, did you think I wasn't going to make this about my mother? I put a photo of her corpse on the cover of my first book, for Christ's sake. This is what the people expect from me. I'm not stupid. I'm aware of my place in the food chain.

Back to our pathetic story. Her body lay cooking in the sun until some hippie deadbeat tripped over it while trying to hitch a ride. He freaked out, but people kept on driving. Nobody wanted to stop for a raving lunatic screaming at a dead body. Eventually a passing trucker radioed the police. He pulled to the side of the road and made sure the hippie didn't go nowhere. Cops determined the hippie wasn't the culprit. My life would have turned out a lot different if he had been.

By the time the police showed up at my house I'd been alone for over 24 hours. It's the kind of time that makes a kid realize something's wrong, and I spent the whole time fantasizing just how wrong. The longer it took, the worse the fantasies became. And even when it wound up being the worst thing I could imagine, the actual telling was so much worse.

This moment defined my life. Put me forever on the side of the victim, but always in the mind of the killer. Cops told me my mother had been choked to death. Years later I discovered there was a lot more to the story, and that she'd suffered immensely.

Having no father I bounced in and out of foster homes for the next eight years. Those were formative times. I learned never to trust anyone. I learned how to fight. Rage dominated me. Violence became my everything. At the age of 18 I joined the police force, because hey, why not? Made it three years. My first wife kicked me out on my ear (that's right, cameo appearance! Blink and you'll miss her!) I prowled the streets, waving my dick at the moon. I spent the entirety of 1986 drunk off my ass. When by some miracle I emerged at the other end I had a book, or at least the semblance of one. A messy pile of scrawl covered pages. My agent took it and turned it into something coherent. Still not sure how she pulled that off.

But let's be real. Credit where credit is due—there was something there. The pain, a realism I could never duplicate. It's the reason none of my other books have sold as well. Don't get me wrong, they SELL—I'm fucking rich—but my debut was a publishing anomaly. As for dear old Mom, the police never caught her killer. Hell, they barely bothered looking. Just another bottom feeder nobody would miss. More important people needed their help. People with privilege. Fucking cops. Makes you wonder why I joined the force. Maybe I thought I could do a better job. Boy was I wrong.

Let me tell you something—closure is a hell of a drug. It's the only drug you can become addicted to without having a taste. It's like a thought crime. The idea of it is dangerous. Causes a perpetual state of junk sickness while you chase that invisible tail. The shakes and sweats never go away. Sure, sometimes you get a reprieve, a moment of placid relief, but before you know it the pain is ratcheting up again and the agony becomes your world.

Which makes me the perfect person to write about sick fucks like you. We're a lot alike, you and I. Our relationship is symbiotic in nature, our egos feeding off one another, regurgitating the same morsel of food, passing it back and forth between our mouths with diminishing nutritional returns.

So open up and say ah! I'm writing a series of stories based on —surprise!— my mother's murder. Each one will be told from the POV of the perp, a revolving door of real-life sickos, and you, my friend, are high on my list of potential leads. Guess you ain't off the hook after all. Yeah, yeah, you were a twinkle in your daddy's nutsack when Mommy Dearest kicked it, but this is a conceptual exercise, you dig? By revisiting the details of my mother's case through the tried-and-true M.O.s of our most zeitgeisty killers, I'm hoping to gain a morsel of fresh insight. Perhaps breathe some new life into her cold, dead cold case. If I'm lucky, the sonofabitch is still alive. Maybe he's got a library card, and he'll avail himself of said public resource and read my book. Maybe he'll think, "That's not the way it happened! You've got it all wrong, Mr. James. Let's touch base and clear the air."

Hey, you never know.

Listen, I'm not asking for permission, here. I'm not even expecting you to write back. It's all part of my process as a writer, and, let's be honest, part of the reason I'm not in the clink alongside you.

Huh. That gives me a great idea. A version of my mother's murder where I'm the killer. I can call it, *If I Did It*. Yeah, that could fucking work.

Thanks, shitbird. You've been most helpful.

Peace out.

Elrond James

—

To: Jonas Williker, inmate #957464
From: Jane Doe
December 13, 2006

Dear Jonas,

I want to tell you the story of how I escaped. I want to fill in the gaps between the moment you discovered my absence and the moment I re-entered your life in the form of a letter.

But I can't. Because I don't remember most of it. One minute I was stumbling blind through the woods and the next I was waking up in my bed, purple cloth covering my eyes. At first I thought I was still inside the box. Once I realized I was home, I thought maybe I'd dreamt the previous night's ordeal. But then I felt the pulse of the cuts and the bruises, a network of injuries throbbing in unison. And of course there was the blindfold. I ripped it off, then threw back the covers to reveal torn clothes, caked in dirt and blood, the sheet bunched around shoes I hadn't taken off.

It all came flooding back, everything from before the escape. How you came upon me out of nowhere, flashing a badge. How you stuffed me in the trunk of your car and drove around for what seemed like hours. How I wasn't the only one in the trunk, just the only one alive. How I whispered to that person in the dark, making assurances, stroking their hair. I reached for them when you pulled me from the trunk, not wanting to be separated, having bonded over our ordeal. I'd learn her name weeks later, after the discovery of her body, and finally get to see what she looked like.

Kira Wagner.

For all I know we were out in the middle of nowhere, miles from where I lived. On top of that I couldn't see shit. So how did I make it home? It doesn't seem possible. Maybe there's more to this story. Maybe *you* should be the one filling *me* in.

Days passed before I got out of bed. I took a scalding shower, clothes and all. Then I got back under the covers soaking wet and slept some more. I existed in a trance-like state for weeks, doing the bare minimum to maintain my existence. Eventually the fog thinned enough for me to pick up a pen.

I think you know the rest of the story.

But where does it go next? That's the real question, isn't it? I've got to admit, I don't have the answer.

Do you, Jonas?

Sincerely,
The One

—

To: Jonas Williker, inmate #957464
From: Vivian Ross
December 18, 2006

Dear Jonas Williker,

I was watching the news the other day when it hit me. None of your victims were Black. In fact, unless you count that one Greek woman, none of them even came close to being a person of color.

Why is that? Are the sisters not good enough for you? I mean, look. I'm not saying I would have preferred it if you'd been more inclusive and targeted Black women. We've got plenty of other problems, believe you me. But it's hard to look at the demographics and not be reminded of a larger, systemic issue—our collective invisibility.

We're ignored on the street, ignored in the boardroom, and ignored in our own homes. We're ignored in the mass market, ignored in politics, ignored by justice—and now we have to put up with the indignity of being ignored by a murderous shit-stain like you? I'm not having it.

I'm not going to let YOU make ME feel like less of a person for being alive. Just because you're a twisted deviant with some VERY specific kinks doesn't mean Black women aren't beautiful. That's bullshit. We're out here fighting for bandwidth like everyone else, except we're fighting twice as hard.

Open your eyes and take a good look. Because I want you to see what you've been missing, what you'll never have. And that's not a slight against us. That's on you. Never forget that. I hope it haunts you every day until they fry your ass, or whatever it is they've got planned for you. We are here, and we will not be ignored. Not in any arena.

Signed,
Vivian Ross

—

To: Jonas Williker, inmate #957464
From: Candace Bennington Williker
January 2, 2007

Dear Jonas,

It's a new year, and my New Year's resolution is to not give up on my husband, even though I haven't heard from him in months. I'm not going to lie, this pregnancy has been extremely challenging, both mentally and physically, and I've almost thrown in the towel multiple times. The only thing preventing me from leaving this cesspool of a motel and heading home is the thought of you holding our newborn child in your arms. No matter how slim the chance, I don't want to risk it. I don't want to be the one to deprive them of that.

That alone would make all of this worthwhile. Some women claim they enjoy being pregnant. Not me. In my opinion those women are either crazy, liars, or a dangerous mix of both. There was a brief period where I stopped getting morning sickness and was able to live my life like a normal person, but as the second trimester came to a close I could barely summon the energy to drag myself out of bed. My feet and ankles ballooned up the second they touched the floor, never mind cramming them into a pair of sensible shoes.

Then there are the random sporadic uterine contractions that almost always decide to happen while I'm asleep. The first time I experienced one I thought a meth head had broken into my room and kicked me in the stomach. I'm constantly hungry, but also constantly tired, so no matter how bad I want to eat or sleep, it's a non-stop tug of war. Just going to the refrigerator takes a Herculean amount of effort and leaves me out of breath. I've taken to ordering in most meals, because the thought of going food shopping makes me want to curl up under the covers and cry.

What else? Oh yeah, the fucking hemorrhoids. You have no idea the wear and tear pregnancy wreaks on the body, and that's before you squeeze a human watermelon out of it. Oh, it's real cute when they tell you the baby's the size of a sweet pea or a raspberry—how adorable—but they never think to warn you about the produce farther down the chart. The coconut, or the eggplant, or the pineapple. Why would they include a spiny fruit on the list? For Christ's sake, couldn't they choose a less abrasive alternative?

But yeah, the hemorrhoids. Why do women have to bleed from every available orifice? It doesn't seem fair. Men should have to do some of the bleeding.

But enough complaining. Soon this whole ordeal will be over, and when it is, I would like for you to share in the joyous results. Even if you don't deserve to. So please write or call me. Give me some indication your family means something to you. That you still want to be a part of our lives.

Here's to a fresh start in the New Year.

Your wife,
Candace

—

To: Jonas Williker, inmate #957464
From: Judith Williker
January 15, 2007

Dear Jonas,

It's your mother. Did you clear up the issue with Candace's visitor status? I haven't heard from her recently, so I assume all is back to normal. No news is good news, as the ostrich says!

In other news, I was recently invited to join a support group for family members of violent offenders. Now before you get all upset, don't worry, I turned them down. We are in the middle of an appeal, after all. I didn't want to give the impression I'd lost hope, but it was nice to be asked. Margery, one of the founders, said the sooner I come to terms with your guilt, the better, which I thought was a little presumptuous on her part. Still, I didn't want to make a big deal out of it, because she really was rather pleasant, and I don't have many friends these days.

We got to talking and it turns out we have a lot in common (besides the obvious). We both enjoy nature, working in the garden, and chatting on the phone. She also makes something called a podcast, have you heard of this? It's like a radio show but on the computer. Any subject you can think of, there's people talking about it on these podcasts. Gardening, movies, snack foods. There are even podcasts completely devoted to you! Isn't that crazy? It's like you're famous or something.

There's also this group that's against the podcasts, or at least the ones like Margery makes. They say listening to them promotes violence, but I think most people just like a good mystery to take their mind off things. To me it isn't any different than watching *The Shawshank Redemption*, or even *Oz*, as gruesome as it can be. A good story is a good story whether it's real or made-up. Of course, I personally don't want to listen to stories about alleged crimes committed by my son, but I'm sure somebody out there does. Who am I to judge?

Margery's going to teach me how to make phone calls over the computer. With video, like I'm from the future! I just have to make an appointment at the library. It really is amazing what you can do with machines these days. I wish you had one so I could make video telephone calls with you. Then I wouldn't feel so bad about not being able to visit. It would be like I was right there with you inside your cell. I'd love to see what you've done with the place!

I'll let you know how the lesson goes. Talk soon.

Love,
Mom

—

To: Jonas Williker, inmate #957464
From: Larry Hostetler
January 25, 2007

Dear Jonas Williker,

Allow me to introduce myself. My name is Larry Hostetler, and I am the owner/proprietor of Murdertown, USA™, the biggest re-purposer of crime-related collectibles north of the Mason-Dixon line. We host one of the largest public inventories of murderabilia, and believe no one has the right to dictate a consumer's personal ethics. Our mission is to provide a safe space for the discerning true crime aficionado to indulge in their fascination with the darker side of life.

In addition to the buying and selling of collectable assets, we also act as intermediary for incarcerated artists looking to broker sales of their work to the general public. For example, we hear you are something of an amateur poet. Poetic verse by "People of Interest," as we like to call our true crime creatives, is a big seller on the open market. We could move such work with ease, regardless of quality (although I'm sure you're quite an accomplished writer).

Now I know what you're thinking: Son of Sam laws prevent the convicted from profiting off of their crimes. This is a common misconception based on outdated information. The original New York law was successfully challenged by Simon and Schuster in 1991, in a battle over the book *Wiseguy* by Nicholas Pileggi, basis for the classic mob movie *Goodfellas*. Approximately 15 other states have either repealed, replaced, or struck down their own version of this draconian law as a First Amendment violation. We do not conduct business in any of the five states with active bans on the sale of such items.

As a show of good faith, I would love to begin our relationship by purchasing some autographs for my own personal collection. We have heard through the murderabilia grapevine that Logan Nester of Macabre Artifacts claims to have numerous newspaper clippings with your signature on them. Of this I am dubious. I personally know Logan to be a snake and a crook, and wouldn't put forgery past him on a good day. Can you verify these items are authentic? Have you knowingly signed anything for Logan or any of his associates? If you haven't, I would caution against getting involved with that fink. There was a time when we were friends, but then he left me high and dry with a knife in my back, and I have very short arms. That man is not to be trusted. Ask around.

Murdertown, USA™, on the other hand, is a name that inspires confidence. We would be proud to represent you in all of your artistic endeavors. All you have to do is ask.

Sincerely,
Larry Hostetler

—

To: Jonas Williker, inmate #957464
From: William Peters
February 8, 2007

Dear Jonas,

Did you ever kill anyone who wanted to die? Maybe someone who didn't realize it at first, but sort of accepted it as the reality set in and embraced it? Would that enhance the experience or ruin it for you? I suppose the whole point of taking someone's life is the actual taking. If it's given freely, as a gift, it's not quite the same, is it?

The reason I ask is, one time, at my absolute lowest, right before I met Ziv, I went out cruising a known hookup spot at a local park. This wasn't something I normally did, but as I was at odds with my identity at the time, the anonymity of the situation suited me. Unfortunately I had been drinking, and wasn't as discerning as I should have been. I came upon this nervous looking kid with a shaved head and should have realized something wasn't kosher, but I threw caution to the wind.

He kept leading me farther and farther into the woods, insisting there were too many people around, even though I didn't see anyone else. Finally I got him to calm down a little and backed him up against a tree. I started kissing him to shut him up. Then I dropped to my knees and started unbuckling his pants. Just as I was about to pull his cock out he grabbed my wrist. Annoyed he might be getting cold feet I looked up, and that's when the night exploded into stars.

I remember counting the punches, like counting reps at the gym, trying to break a personal record. Each hit caused the world to drift a little bit farther away. "I'm not a fag!" a distant voice kept repeating, and I couldn't tell who it belonged to, me or him. By the 7th or 8th punch, my face felt pleasantly numb, and I'd started considering maybe this is what I'd wanted all along. By lucky number 13 I'd passed out.

I woke up in the park the next morning, face swollen so bad I couldn't see, flies making a meal of my blood. I stumbled my way to civilization where a group of bystanders took pity on me and drove me to the hospital. That's where I met Ziv, who worked there as a registered nurse.

Somehow they knew the right questions to ask, and got out of me what no one else could—the truth of what happened. I remember telling them I thought the kid was gonna save me. "Save you from what?" Ziv asked. I gestured to the walls, the staff, myself. Ziv put a hand on my shoulder. As I met their gaze I thought to myself, *Maybe this person can save me instead.*

Did you ever feel like you were helping people? That you were their savior?

Your friend,
Billy Peters

—

To: Jonas Williker, inmate #957464
From: Antonio Birch
February 20, 2007

Dear Mr. Williker,

Thanks for writing me back. I wasn't sure you would. You must have a lot of time on your hands. Trust me, I know the feeling. I'm still stuck in this damn hospital bed. Even when I go to physical therapy, they wheel me there in the fucking bed! I appreciate the change of scenery, but it's like I'm flying there on the world's smelliest, most uncomfortable magic carpet.

Did you study neurology? Because you sure know a lot about the human mind. I had no idea that a specific part of the brain controls empathic response. It makes sense that if it were damaged a human's capacity for empathy could be damaged as well.

It also makes sense that a person could be born without that part of the brain, like they could be born with one lung or no eyes or extra fingers. I read somewhere that when people who are considered "psychopaths" are confronted with the threat of pain, a certain area of their brain lights up, showing fear. But when they witness pain inflicted on others, the area doesn't light up, as it would in a "normal" person. In fact, certain areas in the pleasure center of their brain light up instead.

I found this fascinating. It made me think: if lack of empathy is a condition someone is born with, wouldn't calling them psychotic be discriminatory? Shouldn't we come up with a more acceptable term, like we've done for the mentally retarded? Prostitutes prefer to be called "sex workers," drug addicts suffer from "substance-use disorder." All the former dregs of society have been rebranded and are now considered valid. Isn't it time we humanized violent criminals as well, and separated the stigma of the behavior from the person? Isn't the psychopath just empathically atypical? A person with non-traditional moral boundaries? And should they be held criminally accountable for actions related to their condition? Isn't it time they received treatment as opposed to punishment?

And what about people in my situation? People whose personality has been altered by an accident or injury? Especially when doctors continually ignore their concerns. Who is responsible if I hurt someone? Me, the person who is unwell, or the doctors whose negligence puts other people at risk? What about the people who installed the hot tub where my injury occurred? Or my stepdad, for hiring them?

Just thinking about this stuff makes me so angry, I want to punch Tony in the goddamn mouth. Same goes for that doctor. Maybe then they'd take my disability seriously.

At least I have someone I can talk to about this. I appreciate you taking the time to listen to me, and I hope to hear from you again soon. Any tips on navigating society for the newly neurologically challenged?

Your friend,
Ant

—

To: Jonas Williker, inmate #957464
From: Stacey Santiago
April 3, 2007

Dear Jonas,

It's Stacey Santiago, AKA Staci Satin. I wanted to let you know I'm still alive and kicking despite your best efforts, or lack thereof. Not that I think you care, but because I didn't want you getting off on the idea of my broken body lying in a ditch somewhere.

Turns out David doesn't have the killer instinct after all. He didn't even seem upset when I told him we were through. Fucking loser barely gave me a black eye for my trouble. Afterward, he packed his shit and took off. Where to, I don't care. All that matters is he's out of my life. Most likely he's living out of his truck, looking for some other poor, damaged woman to take advantage of. Someone he can really glom onto and feed off of, like the parasite he is.

Since David was in charge of all the tech shit, I assume stacisatinxxx.com will drift away into the archives of obscurity. We have a decent number of subscribers, but without a constant influx of new content people will lose interest pretty quick.

As for me, I'm leaving porn behind. At my age I really have no choice. I was never a huge player, and since it's still a male-dominated industry, the chances of me making the leap to directing or producing are pretty slim. There's always the convention circuit, but the idea of being pawed at by awkward civilians all day isn't very enticing. I can't decide what's worse: the obligatory groping or the bored look in their eyes as they do it. It reminds me of an old industry adage: What are the three most devastating words you can say to an adult actress? Answer: *I remember you.*

That's what people are going to say about you. "Oh yeah, I remember that guy." Or, "Hey, wasn't he the guy who…" Then they'll dredge up some half-remembered, inaccurate factoid, or worse—give you credit for someone else's shitty work. Maybe they won't even remember your name, and attribute your so-called artistic triumphs to some amateur hack. That would be worst of all, wouldn't it? All that work for nothing. Welcome to my world.

But time moves on. Wounds heal. My body is no longer "your property." Your claim on me is slowly fading, like the temporary ink etched into my vulva. Of course, I'll have the permanent reminder of keloid scarring due to David's inexperienced tattoo hand. I don't relish having to explain those marks to future partners, but at least I'll no longer be branded with your name.

I'd say it's a shame it had to end this way, but who am I kidding? We both know I'm better off. So enjoy what we had while you still can. Me, I'm going to enjoy moving on with my life.

Sincerely,
Stacey Santiago

—

To: Jonas Williker, inmate #957464
From: Grant Singer
April 9, 2007

Mr. Williker,

I just got off the phone with your mother. It seems you've been telling tales out of school. I hate to be the one to break it to you, but no one likes a rat. Considering your current location, it's a lesson I would've expected you to learn by now.

I could have saved you the stamp and the trouble, because Judith knows all about my relationship with my ex. We're friends, Jonas. That's what friends do. They share things with each other. So yes, I have discussed my past with your mother, even the unsavory bits. The parts I'm ashamed of. Just like she's shared things with me. The trials of her day-to-day life. Caring for your father, the indignity of wiping his ass.

Of course, she doesn't describe it that way. She's much too polite to use such harsh language. But she does enjoy a good jaw session. We've spent countless hours talking about her hopes and dreams, her fears and doubts. The prospect of a future without a man in the house. Yes, Jonas, we've gotten to know each other quite well.

I must admit, I found some of your biographical embellishments highly amusing. That I had trouble performing sexually in the absence of purple undergarments. Or that random purple objects would give me a spontaneous erection, even in public. Judith and I shared a hearty laugh over that one. She has a wonderful sense of humor, your mother.

The whole conversation brought to mind that Alice Walker novel. I don't remember the exact title. The idea that God gets upset when humans don't take the time to appreciate what he considers his most beautiful creation—the color purple. Of course, purple also happens to be the color of bruised skin, which has its own troubling narrative implications. It's a thought-provoking book. You should check it out.

Don't worry, I won't hold these acts of slander against you. I understand why you would resent my friendship with your mother. I understand your need to discredit me in her eyes. It's another topic we've talked about at length. Obviously she knows you better than I do, although I do think I bring a unique perspective to the table, which she appreciates. A kind of devil's advocacy. Although technically, in my opinion, she's the one advocating for the devil. The God of the Bruise, as it were. Between the two of us we've got a pretty good idea of what makes Jonas Williker tick. If I were you I'd take comfort in that.

Take care of yourself.

Sincerely,
Special Agent Grant Singer
Federal Task Force: Serial Homicide Unit

—

To: Jonas Williker, inmate #957464
From: Darlene Edmonton
April 17, 2007

Dear Jonas Williker,

Thank you once again for choosing Outside Access for all your online secretarial needs. It looks like your JPay setup is complete. Please let us know if you experience any difficulties.

In addition, we have posted your poem, "The One That Got Away," on the Truth Sleuths message board as requested, and it has garnered quite a bit of feedback. See comments below.

COMMENTS

"I can see why In Verse passed on this. I'm not even sure it belongs on this board. Mods?" **citizensleuth**
— "not a fan of free speach, comrade?" **underworldUSA**
— "if it isn't spelled correctly, is it even protected?" **grandsonofsam**
— "IV is a private company. They can publish whatever they want. As for the boards, how is the writing of an actual serial killer not relevant?" **cerealkiller**
— "this is why we can't have nice things." **hallseatoates**

"This can't be legit. How does this guy have access to the internet?" **marlowe76**
— "how do YOU have access to the internet and not know the answer to this question?" **hallseatoates**
— "u kno u can get anything on the inside, rite?" **TS138**
— "I can get you a toe by 3 o'clock." **walterppk**
— "with nail polish" **banshee**
— "he probly has some lonely bitch on the outside, stuffing her face with Cheetos and her twat with the wrong end of a hairbrush while she posts." **cerealkiller**

— "Not cool, dude." **citizensleuth**

— "If he has someone posting that means he has someone reading." **underworldUSA**

— "oh shit, it could be any one of us, just like in The Thing. I'll go get my flamethrower... **cerealkiller**

"I've definitely been put on an FBI watchlist after reading that." **jayjaygee**

— "You think that shit's dark? Check out www.myspace.com/black satan" **metalmorty**

—"NO SPAM. Mods?" **citizensleuth**

"What's the deal with the box imagery? Some sort of metaphor? I don't remember anything like that from any of the other murders." **barryboy3**

— "Police don't always release all the information they have. It's a common investigative technique used to weed out attention-seekers and crackpots." **grandsonofsam**

— "No shit. I was just thinking out loud." **barryboy3**

— "well then fuck me for trying to help." **grandsonofsam**

"I dunno, it's kind of evocative? At the very least it's a window into a depraved mind, for those brave enough." **manx**

— "uh... yeah." **hallseatoates**

— "It's halfway decent, which is why I think I find it so disturbing." **barryboy3**

— "Agreed. Very conversational. Like the author is speaking directly to me." **dman**

— "Really? Given the opportunity, what would you say in return?" **hallseatoates**

— "IDK. something about Schrödinger's victim and never knowing whether she's truly gotten away until the box is opened?" **dman**

— "..." **hallseatoates**

— "jeez" **marlowe76**

— "Oh Mr. FBI man, can you come over here for a second? I have someone I want you to meet." **cerealkiller**

END COMMENTS

FYI: As of this writing, "The One That Got Away" still appears on the Truth Sleuths website. Still, I'd be careful about drawing negative attention with this kind of provocative content. We do not offer refunds.

Sincerely,
Darlene Edmonton
Outside Access, LLC

—

To: Jonas Williker, inmate #957464
From: SKASM
April 26, 2007

Dear Mr. Williker,

Are you a convicted serial killer plagued by regret? Have the poor choices you've made wreaked havoc on your life? Well, it might not be too late to turn things around. Become a member of SKASM: Serial Killers Against Serial Murder, and show the world you've learned the error of your ways.

SKASM was formed to shift the media's focus from sensational crimes and provide incarcerated killers with an outlet to give back to the communities from which they have taken so much.

Unlike similar programs, which aim to scare potential offenders into the waiting arms of the police force or the military, SKASM has no ulterior motive. We are not a tool for religious recruitment. We simply wish to demystify the glamorous lifestyle of the serial killer and prevent impressionable young people from starting down what we refer to as "the psycho path."

How can you aid in our endeavors? Simply by being yourself. We are standing by, waiting to connect you with a concerned parent, so you can pump a healthy dose of fear into their potential little deviant. If they think you are a good fit, they will provide you with a name and address where you can write their child. The rest is up to you.

Not sure what to write about? Show them the unvarnished truth the media glosses over in their coverage. The burden of leading a double life, the constant fear of capture, the insatiable hunger of your unnatural desires. Take them straight into the heart of darkness.

And let's not forget the consequences of your actions. A life of incarceration, stripped of freedom. The daily degradation of being told what you can do and when. The mental, physical, and sexual abuse at the hands of your fellow inmates and the authorities charged with your well-being. Feel free to describe what would happen to the child if they were locked in a cell with you. We find this to be highly effective, so don't hold back on the gory details.

In certain, extreme cases we have found it necessary to fly a family out for an in-person visit. Regulations vary state to state, but we find a tour of prison facilities really adds to the realism of the situation and drives our message home: the life of a serial killer is not all it's cracked up to be and should be avoided at all costs.

Interested in participating? We would love to have you, and hope to hear from you soon.

Sincerely,
SKASM
Serial Killers Against Serial Murder

—

To: Jonas Williker, inmate #957464
From: Candace Bennington Williker
May 15, 2007

Dear Jonas,

I am writing to inform you of a momentous occasion. A milestone in both your life and mine.

A week ago today your son was born. Jonas Sean Williker came screaming into this world at 2:32AM on Tuesday, May 8, 2007. His birth was a miracle, and you fucking missed it.

Even though it feels like you've abandoned us, I still did you the honor of naming baby Jonas after you. He is your son, after all. I understand fatherhood can be a real head trip, so I'm hoping you just need some time to adjust to your new role. I'm optimistic you will come to your senses and do the right thing. That I didn't name him Sean, after my own father, should give you an idea of how seriously I take your paternity.

Both Jonas and I are doing well, although the road to recovery hasn't been an easy one. My labor lasted over 34 hours. At hour 10 I begged for an epidural, but it stopped working after 45 minutes. Poor needle placement, the doctor told me. Apparently the anesthetist was a trainee. By the final 4 hours I was delirious from exertion. The last thing I remember before passing out was the doctor saying something about an emergency c-section.

I awoke hours later in excruciating pain. They pumped me full of enough morphine to sedate an elephant, which only made me nauseous and incoherent. I demanded to see Jonas Jr., worried I was missing out on essential bonding time, but they refused. I remember weeping uncontrollably, convinced my newborn son would reject me, like his father had. I couldn't understand why the doctors wouldn't let me see him. Maybe he'd died and they weren't telling me. Maybe they killed him and were covering it up.

It turns out I'd suffered a complete uterine inversion, and my abdominal muscles clenched up so tight the doctor couldn't get the damn thing back inside me. It lay completely outside of my body like a discarded sock. It took a dangerous cocktail of drugs and three nurses to remedy the situation. There were literally four hands in my abdomen, pulling on the muscle wall with all their might, while another pair forced the organ back into place.

Afterwards, the doctor compared my vagina to an exploded cigar, like in a Bugs Bunny cartoon. Said he had to rebuild it from the ground up. He claimed he made me "better than before," which I found incredibly demeaning. Forget about the husband stitch, he said, he'd given me husband *stitches*. The father of my future children was a lucky man. Later I found out the genius had trouble locating my clitoris in the aftermath, and was about to cut his losses when one of the nurses pointed it out. I felt like Frankenstein's monster, impotent and disfigured.

The delivery wasn't easy on Junior, either. Because of how long and stressful it was, he experienced what is called meconium aspiration, which occurs when the fetus expels fecal matter into the womb, which then mixes with the amniotic fluid and is breathed into the lungs. The contaminated fluid had to be suctioned out, and they put Junior on a breathing machine and heart monitor.

I'm not trying to shock you with the details, or make you feel guilty. I just want you to understand what I went through. Because in a way you're partially responsible. And as hard as the birth was, it pales in comparison to the pain of you not being there. Instead of having my husband by my side to help me through it, I had to do it alone. The midwife was there, but it wasn't the same.

Our son is beautiful. I want him to know his father. Please allow us to visit you.

We are still your family.

Yours forever,
Candace

—

To: Jonas Williker, inmate #957464
From: Abigail Tinder
May 18, 2007

Mr. Jonas Williker,

I received your response to my letter, and I must say, it did not amuse me. I might have preferred if you hadn't answered at all. Your opinions on the sincerity of Brother Berkowitz's conversion were uncouth and uncalled for. Do you think me so naive because I am a child? Incapable of recognizing deception? Or do you just doubt the healing power of God's forgiveness?

Moreover, your graphic description of his crimes and detailed assessment of his efficacy as a killer did not impress me. David is not proud of the sins he committed. He holds repentance in his heart. You obviously do not. You revel in your atrocities. Every drop of blood and bile. I see that now.

This is not a game. If your intent was to frighten me off you did not succeed. There is nothing new under the sun, and believe me, as a soldier in the army of God, I have seen my share of carnage. My loins are girt about with truth and my breastplate is forged of pure righteousness (not that a young girl's loins or breasts should be any of your concern). I am washed in the blood of Christ and fear no evil.

Not even the retribution of the satanic cabal who would silence the message of Brother David. Do you count yourself amongst their ranks? Your weak-minded adherence to their principles suggests you do. You may think your allegiance to the Prince of Darkness protects you, gives you power, but you are merely a pawn. Otherwise wouldn't he have delivered you from incarceration and what will ultimately be death?

Maybe you think you will live on through the memory of your deeds. But the Bible says, *It is appointed unto men once to die, and after that, the judgment.*

You are quite adept at writing visceral descriptions, so let me leave you with a few of hell. The Bible says the smoke of your torment will go on forever and ever, and you will have no rest, day or night. It is a place where the worm dies not, and the fire is unquenched. A place of eternal darkness, filled with weeping and the gnashing of teeth.

Doesn't sound so pleasant, does it?

I pity you. You will burn forever for your sins. Now if you'll excuse me, I have other souls to minister to. I have wasted enough charity on you.

Yours in Christ,
Abigail Tinder

—

To: Jonas Williker, inmate #957464
From: Judith Williker
May 21, 2007

Dear Jonas,

Thank you thank you THANK YOU for finally making me a grandmother! I have to say, it's about dang time! I am literally beside myself with joy. I can't wait to start answering to Gam Gam, Nonna, Meemaw—anything little Jonas Junior is able to pronounce! He can call me Moo Moo for all I care! He is the most darling thing I've ever seen in my entire life. I couldn't ask for a more perfect gift. Okay, maybe having my son back home, but I have to be honest—now that I have J.J., I don't see how I could possibly give him up. And I haven't even seen him in person! He looks so much like you in the pictures it's uncanny. He has those same piercing eyes. I remember them staring up at me the first time I held you, watching me even as I nursed you. So intense! I'm sure you can't wait to meet him.

It's a shame you weren't able to be there for the birth, but from what Candace tells me it may have been for the best. Having babies is a messy business and the delivery room is no place for the squeamish. Some might say it's no place for a man. I used to be one of those people. I made it through the whole ordeal by myself just fine. Granted, things were different back then. But your father was there for everything that came after, and that's all that matters in the end.

You know, I don't think Dad ever expected to become a grandfather. When I first broke the news of Candace's pregnancy, he twisted his face into the most skeptical looking expression, although that could have just been paralysis from the stroke. Then he mumbled something about a DNA test, but I think he just needed time to process the information. Trust me, now that he's gotten used to the idea, he's as excited as I am. I can tell.

Here's to Jonas Junior!

Love,
Meemaw and Pep Pep

—

To: Jonas Williker, inmate #957464
From: Ginny Goodwinch
May 22, 2007

Hello Jonas,

I know it's been a while since I've written. I'm especially sorry I missed your birthday, but after my previous episode the doctors have really cracked down. Even Guy started playing things by the book. He told me it wasn't healthy to continue writing to you, so he stopped mailing my letters for me.

That was back in October of last year. A lot has happened since then. I received my "certificate of sanity," for one. That's right, I've officially been discharged from the psychiatric hospital. It was a day of mixed emotions. Naturally I didn't want to be away from Guy, but I always knew the day would come, and I assumed we'd make things work. Turns out, Guy had other plans.

As soon as I checked out he ceased all communication with me. He refused to see me in person and wouldn't return my calls. I even tried writing, and you know how persuasive I am with a pen. So one day I stormed the psych ward and confronted him. He told me point blank he didn't want to see me anymore. Just like that. The old me would have eaten the nose right off his face, but I somehow managed to contain myself. I found out through the grapevine he's seeing a new patient, some bitch named Lena, and that he's been seeing her since *before* I left. I can't tell you how much this betrayal hurt. In fact, I'm still considering violence on a daily basis.

Despite all this, or maybe because of it, the doctors agreed it would be a good idea for me to continue out-patient therapy. As long as I maintained my distance from Guy. So I moved into one of those extended stay motels. The hospital helped me get a job at a local supermarket bagging groceries. It's mindless work, but the manager seems to like me and there are plenty of people to talk to. I help them to the car with their bags and send them on their way with a smile!

Every once in a while a reporter knocks on my door, but for the most part they've forgotten about me. I try not to think too much about your appeal. My doctor says if I become too invested it could trigger another episode. I'm not supposed to be writing to you, but I wanted to let you know that I'm okay. I didn't want to leave you hanging, wondering what became of poor old Ginny. And I wanted to let you know I'll always be here if you need me.

Of course, Mother is mad as all get out. She keeps demanding I come home this instant, but I'm through being bullied by her. I need to do what's right for me. And right now that means continuing my therapy and living my life. I hope you're doing well. I heard you recently became a father. Congratulations! There is no greater joy in life than having children. I miss little Bobby and Derrick terribly.

I know this letter has been a lot about me, but that's what I need to concentrate on right now. I'm sure you understand.

Be well, Jonas.

In loving friendship,
Ginny Goodwinch

—

To: Jonas Williker, inmate #957464
From: Logan Nester
May 23, 2007

Dear Jonas Williker,

Logan Nester here. Of Macabre Artifacts. I don't like foreplay, so I'll get right to the point. Word on the street is Larry Hostetler's been sullying my good name in your neck of the woods. Let me tell you something about Larry. He is three things: a nogoodnik, a liar, and a goddamn crook. We used to be partners until that dirty double-crosser ran off and left me holding the hairy bag. Ever since I extricated myself from his shady enterprise, he's been fixin' to ruin me.

He claims I've been selling fake autographs, but that ain't true. Every one of my pieces is verified and authenticated. We don't currently have anything graced with *your* signature, but we'd love to change that. I could pick up the phone and have half a dozen buyers by this afternoon. Easy!

Another popular item, especially among the fairer sex, is hair. You'd be amazed how far a good head of hair can go towards influencing a jury. Yours appears thick and lustrous from what I can tell. Frankly, I'm surprised you were convicted. I know plenty of collectors who'd jump at the chance to own a lock or two. I also sell toenail clippings. All the better if it's a full set. We shellac 'em and package 'em in a fancy little display case for 100 bucks a pop. Toenails!

Already made a deal with Larry? We'll beat it. I'm a capitalist, through and through, and see no reason you can't sell to both of us. That's twice the market saturation. Just be careful in your dealings with that worm. Larry is what we refer to in this business as "small time." He doesn't have the reach we do at Macabre. Our customer list is long and our clientele have deep pockets. Last month I moved a pair of chopsticks used by Issei Sagawa for a tidy sum. He didn't even eat anybody with 'em! I've got original Ramirez doodles no one has seen. Ass and titty stuff. Super fun. I've got a line on an ultra-rare used tampon from Aileen Wuornos if that floats you. Larry, on the other hand, couldn't sell Ed Kemper's pubes if he was offering them two for one!

So if you're in the market for a rep that'll look out for your interests with none of the bullshit, drop me a line. I look forward to hearing from you.

Logan Nester
Macabre Artifacts

—

To: Jonas Williker, inmate #957464
From: Anonymous
May 25, 2007

dear recipient,

following is such sweet swallowing
when mired in a complicity of efforts
like a copy disregarded
unrestrained
a revenant
in namesake only
to which i aspire

sincerely,
the perpetual oligarch hanging from a wire connected to a thin branch about
to break

—

To: Jonas Williker, inmate #957464
From: William Peters
May 29, 2007

Dear Jonas,

Wow. What do I say? I hadn't considered I might be able to visit you, or that you'd even want me to. My heart nearly jumped out of my chest when I read your letter. I spent the next hour checking hotel availability and mapping out directions. It wasn't until Ziv came home and I slammed the laptop shut that I realized what I'd been doing.

Lucky for me, Ziv started unloading some dumb work shit as soon as they walked through the door, and didn't notice how suspicious I was acting. I remained completely distracted during dinner and all through sex night (yes, Ziv likes to schedule our love-making. Another of our therapist's brilliant suggestions). Afterwards I lay awake in bed, mind racing, while Ziv snored beside me in a post-coital coma.

By the time the sun had risen I'd made my decision, despite knowing I couldn't pull it off without Ziv finding out. But I'll worry about the details later. Right now I'm too excited to care. This morning I zipped around the kitchen making breakfast, which seemed even more suspicious, but it thrilled Ziv. I can't believe I'm going to see you face to face. There are so many things I want to talk about, letters worth, but I don't know where to begin.

It's been too long. I can't wait.

Your friend,
Billy Peters

—

To: Jonas Williker, inmate #957464
From: Jane Doe
June 2, 2007

Dear Jonas,

My home has become foreign to me. I long for the familiarity of the box. Technically it was an old steamer trunk made of leather and wood, but that's what you called it. *Get in the box*, you said. So I did. You'd already broken two of my fingers—bent them farther than they were meant to go—and covered my body in shallow little cuts, so I knew better than to argue.

I felt safe in the box. Grounded. Because as long as I stayed inside you wouldn't be able to hurt me. You wouldn't be able to fulfill all the promises you made before you shut the lid. Promises about what you planned to do to me once you dug me back up, whether I drew breath or not. You emphasized that last part, as if it were the real threat, but I remember praying for it. That I would pass out and never wake up. Once my soul left, what you did to my body didn't concern me. I never considered what I'd be leaving behind if I somehow escaped. Escape wasn't a viable option.

No matter how far back into the closet I burrow, no matter how many blankets I pile on top of myself, I never feel as safe as I did in the box. The womb from which I was reborn. Do you have any idea what that's like? Constantly chasing something you can't recapture? The frustration involved, the resulting emptiness? The utter helplessness? When you know there is no point in trying, but you can't stop yourself?

Something tells me you do.

Sincerely,
The One

—

To: Jonas Williker, inmate #957464
From: Wex Durham
June 5, 2007

Dear Jonas Williker,

I am writing on behalf of the Serial Killer Collective, an online fan club of true crime obsessives. We provide fans with a dedicated forum to discuss, dissect, and debate, away from the prying eyes of social media reactionaries. They can't seem to get it through their thick skulls— just because we're obsessed with serial killers, it doesn't mean we condone their actions.

One of our more popular features here at SKC is the Friendship Questionnaire—a list of 13 mundane queries that reads like a dating show survey. It started out as a joke, but then inmates began responding and it became a huge hit with our members. Would you be interested in participating? The questions are listed below. I've also included the answers given to us by the notorious Brian James Fitzpatrick as an example. We like his sense of humor, and it gives you a good idea of the potential of the format. So have fun with it!

Who was your childhood hero?
Real estate tycoon, hotelier, and all-around business genius, H.H. Holmes.

What do you view as your crowning achievement?
Stretching out my mother's cervix with my giant head.

What is your biggest regret?
That she survived.

What is your greatest weakness?
My love of ice cream, which indirectly led to my arrest.

What is your favorite food?
A nice, rare rump roast.

What is your favorite movie/TV show?
Television rots the brain. I prefer the films of Bergman and Tarkovsky.

What is your favorite book?
The Bible, *Atlas Shrugged*, anything by Anais Nin.

What kind of music do you like?
Jazz, classical, and K-Pop.

What do you look for in the opposite sex?
Long legs and low self-esteem.

What is your ideal night out?
Freebasing and fucking under the full moon, baby. Awooo!

What is your most prized possession?
My crooked dick.

What is something not a lot of people know about you?
I'm a cold heartbreaker fit to burn and I'll rip your heart in two.

Where do you see yourself in 10 years?
Living in a place where nobody knows who I am, leading a quiet double life.

—

Great stuff, right? We look forward to reading your responses!

Sincerely,
Wex Durham
The Serial Killer Collective

—

To: Jonas Williker, inmate #957464
From: Antonio Birch
June 13, 2007

Dear Jonas,

Well, I finally I did it. I gave that know-it-all prick of a doctor a piece of my mind. I'm pretty sure I gave him the damaged piece, too. The one that used to regulate my empathy. It's not like I need it anymore.

It was the cherry on top of a shit week here at the hospital. The food sucks, my bed's uncomfortable, and I'm bored out of my fucking mind. They don't take my condition seriously, so why am I even here? It's like I'm being held against my will. My stepdad keeps complaining about how much this is costing him yet he won't let me come home. Not until I can shit without help, he says. I told him I can make it to and from the bathroom on my own now, but he was too busy chuckling at the idea of me shitting myself to listen.

So I decided to revolt. I started by refusing my meals, throwing the slop they call food on the floor where it belongs, demanding better. After a few days of this the doctor came to see what my problem was, and I responded by slamming a lunch tray over his head. It wasn't hard enough to do any actual damage, but it sure got his attention. Now maybe they'll treat me with a little more respect around here.

I gotta tell you, I felt so good afterwards, I thought maybe I don't have a condition after all. Maybe I just need to stop putting up with life's bullshit. Either way, I'm not letting them off the hook. Someone's got to hold these quacks accountable.

I've got a new creed: If it looks like a duck, and talks like a duck, then I don't give a fuck. Put that on a t-shirt, you fucking ghouls!

I'm gonna continue acting out. I don't care what my stepdad says. What is he gonna do, ground me? I'll keep you posted on how things develop.

Your friend,
Tony

—

To: Jonas Williker, inmate #957464
From: Jason Corbish
June 14, 2007

Dear Jonas Williker,

I am writing in regards to the publication of your poem, "The One That Got Away," on the website TruthSleuths.com. Please forgive me if I was unclear in my previous letter, but according to your signed contract, *In Verse* magazine owns the first publishing option on said poem for a period of 18 months. So although we pulled the poem from publication, you are still not allowed to publish it elsewhere for another year or so.

I believe the confusion arose from the line, *We hope [your poem] finds a home elsewhere,* which is part of my standard rejection and shouldn't have been used in said email. See also the line: *and we look forward to hearing from you in future open calls,* because we most certainly do not. In fact, the longer we can prevent this poem from seeing the light of day, the better.

So please do us all a favor and remove "The One That Got Away" from TruthSleuths.com for the duration of our contractually agreed upon time period. I'm sure your lawyers have plenty to keep themselves busy without having to worry about a matter as tedious as this. We thank you in advance.

Sincerely,
Jason Corbish
Managing Editor, In Verse Magazine

—

To: Jonas Williker, inmate #957464
From: Candace Bennington Williker
June 17, 2007

Dear Jonas,

I've been thinking a lot about my father lately. How little I actually know about him. What few memories I have that weren't filtered through the lens of my mother's spite. His trial wasn't a cause célèbre like yours, so there isn't much info out there. A few local news articles and some court documents. That's about it. No interviews or national headlines or televised footage. Not for a petty thug charged with accessory to armed robbery. A glorified lookout man. Still, it was his third or fourth offense so they threw the book at him.

My mom had a few snapshots, which she kept hidden away with the letters he'd written. Only one of them included me, sitting on dad's lap wearing a diaper, my face caught mid shriek. I couldn't have been more than six months old. In it, Dad has one hand around my chubby waist, a half-smoked cigarette in the other. He looks like he's just woken up, stubble unshaved, greasy hair sticking straight up. A steaming cup of coffee sits on the table in front of him, just out of my reach. It is a photo of details, not least of which is the carefree grin on my dad's face. It's like he's saying, despite the hot coffee, lit cigarette, and chaos in his lap, everything is under control.

I loved that picture. One time, before I knew better, I stole it from my mother's dresser and hid it inside my pillowcase. When my mom went to sleep or passed out drunk I would burrow under the covers and study it with a flashlight. I would stare at it for hours, trying to divine the mystery behind the smile. It felt like I finally had a piece of my father all to myself.

One morning I woke up and found the picture missing. Enough time had passed that in my mind the picture belonged to me. Some childlike version of "possession is nine-tenths of the law." I casually asked my mother if she took it, no fear, like I hadn't stolen it from her in the first place. Looking back, I'm lucky she didn't smack the shit out of me. Instead, she simply stated the picture was back where it belonged, and what did I want with an ugly old picture of myself anyway? It would only remind me of why my father left.

After that I never took anything from her again. Still, I would sneak into her room and look at that picture whenever she wasn't around. If you're thinking, how often could a young child get that opportunity, you don't know my mother.

Father's Day has always been a sad day for me. I'm afraid it's going to be a sad day for our son as well. This realization has made me reconsider cutting my mother out of my life. So what if my mother and I have issues. It doesn't mean Junior should suffer. Every parent's dream is to give their child more than they had growing up, and I never met any of my grandparents. They were all dead by the time I was born. So surely it makes sense to allow Junior to have a relationship with his grandmother. It would give him a leg up on his mother.

Happy Father's Day, Jonas. Whether you choose to celebrate it or not.

Candace

—

To: Jonas Williker, inmate #957464
From: Judith Williker
July 16, 2007

Dear Jonas,

It's your mother. Sorry it's been a while, but I've been struggling to come up with things to write about. There's only so much neighborhood gossip to go around. Your father says I'm putting too much pressure on myself, that a letter every couple of months should be more than enough, but I know what a lifeline communication can be.

Still, I might be over-thinking things a bit. I've found myself making decisions based on the story potential of the outcome. Why just the other day I contemplated picking up a scruffy looking hitchhiker because I thought it would make an interesting anecdote. Never mind the fact he looked like he belonged in a police lineup. Good thing I came to my senses before I did anything rash.

But I had an epiphany the other day. I had just gotten back from my weekly trip to the grocery store. You know how much I love food shopping. It always puts me in a good mood. But for some reason that day I was feeling particularly down in the dumps. I started thinking about how awful the food must be where you are, and how little I could do about it. It got me so upset I almost broke down and cried right there in the freezer section. Not even browsing the ethnic food aisle cheered me up, and for me that's like going on vacation!

I spoke to Margery about it, and it turns out prison cooking is a whole art unto itself. Who knew? She invited me to a special "prison potluck," where everyone shared their favorite recipes. Sure, most of the dishes just take a popular food and put the word "prison" in front of it, but familiarity is part of the point. It's meant to bring comfort. So from now on, whenever I'm at a loss for words, I'm going to send you instructions on how to make yourself a tasty little treat. Here's one of the most popular to get you started. All of the ingredients should be available in the prison commissary.

Mackerel Mash
1 bag potato chips
1 can chub mackerel
1 generous helping of apple sauce
2 packets relish
1 bag oatmeal mix
Hot sauce to taste

So the first thing you should do is crush your potato chips inside the bag. That bag is going to serve as your mixing bowl as well. Isn't that clever? Then you add the mackerel, water and all. Don't drain it! Nobody likes a dried-out mash. After that, go ahead and add the other wets, your apple sauce and your relish. Mix it up good. (If you don't have any implements, you can mix your mash by massaging the outside of the chip bag. Just be careful not to pop it. Otherwise you'll be left with a mackerel mess!) Once all those ingredients are good and integrated, start adding your oatmeal, a little at a time. This is what gives your mash its consistency. Continue to "mix" throughout. The key here is to achieve a light gray paste. The more even the mixture, the better tasting the meal. Finally, add some hot sauce if you like things spicy, or if you find the finished product particularly inedible.

I know it doesn't sound great, but it can't be worse than that punishment loaf they serve in solitary. You could grout a bathroom with that stuff!

Bon Appetit!

Love,
Mom

To: Jonas Williker, inmate #957464
From: Reverend Wallace Samuel Tinder
July 20, 2007

Mr. Jonas Williker,

My name is Reverend Wallace Samuel Tinder. I believe you have been exchanging letters with my daughter. As I am sure you are aware, she is a minor, which is why I have put an end to your correspondence. Abigail is a bright girl, and ambitious to a fault, but her limited years on this earth have rendered her ill-equipped to provide the spiritual guidance necessary for a man in your situation. Frankly, I am doing you a favor. Your immortal soul is at stake, which is why I'm offering my own services as your personal spiritual advisor.

Perhaps you feel you are beyond forgiveness. That due to the nature of your sins you cannot be saved. I am here to tell you this is not the case. God's love washes away ALL sin, even those as horrific as yours. It just takes a little extra scrubbing, is all. And while dedicating your life to Christ might not be a "get out of jail free" card, it will certainly get you out of spending eternity in hell.

Think God won't understand? Look at it this way. You've killed a lot of people. You know who's killed more? God. Many of 'em babies. Last I checked, he's got you beat there.

So what have you got to lose? Other than your eternal soul, that is? If you're interested, I have enclosed a tract with a simple sinner's prayer for you to recite. An adult tract, not one of those childish comic books Abigail is so fond of. I am also available to further instruct you in the ways of righteousness should you so desire. I believe your conversion would be a valuable testimony to the saving grace of our Lord Jesus Christ, and a boon of peace for your final years. My daughter was not incorrect in her comparisons to Brother Berkowitz.

Yours in Christ,
Reverend Wallace Samuel Tinder

—

To: Jonas Williker, inmate #957464
From: Ginny Goodwinch
July 23, 2007

Hello Jonas,

There have been some new developments in the continuing adventures of Ginny Goodwinch and I wanted to give you an update. Drumroll, please… I've started a secret love affair with my manager at the supermarket! Isn't that exciting?

For now he must remain nameless, as it is technically against the rules for management to date employees, and I will do anything to protect our love. When we are not stealing glances across the frozen food aisle we share clandestine encounters in the walk-in refrigerator, away from prying eyes. Sometimes he even visits me at the motel after hours. It's been quite the morale booster! Especially since he's so much younger than I am. He's a mere sapling at 23 years old. Scandalous, I know! He calls me his sexy work cougar. *Raaar!*

My therapist has noticed the change, but of course I can't tell her why because she would not approve. It's funny how often you have to lie to people when it comes to the true nature of happiness. Especially those in charge of your supposed well-being. It's like they want you to be happy, but only on their terms. It's so restricting.

The best part is this young buck doesn't care about my past. Not that we have time to talk about it, what with all the love-making. But I can only assume he knows, since my employment is part of a social rehabilitation initiative, and is contingent on my continued good behavior.

How are things with you and the family? Fatherhood agreeing with you? I can see myself settling down again one day, but for now I'm enjoying my freedom. Still, sometimes I envy you. There is comfort in stability, after all. Remember that.

Your friend,
Ginny

—

To: Jonas Williker, inmate #957464
From: Dimitri Novack
July 24, 2007

Dear Mr. Jonas,

What is this you are trying to pull? An old man's leg? I write again because of never receiving letter I request. Are you making notice for vacation? You still owe many months of rent. Also for making clean blood and pissing of cat. Apartment is requiring much work to make good for living at great personal loss.

Why do I hear nothing from you in return? Even after making gift of special trunk to nephew in good faith. At first I decide no, you are owing too much, but nephew write check so I hand it over. I tell him only you have key, I am never trying to open, although maybe when you are not paying I should. I tell him breaking locks is easy for me if that is his wanting, but he remain polite. Trunk is only weighing a little. It is not necessary to break inside.

I make mistake trusting this nephew. His check good only for bouncing and leaves me with nothing. No trunk, no money, no room for rent. I tell name of nephew to police. Maybe Devin, right now I forget. I also tell police information about trunk. Is maybe something bad from crime? I pray for it not to be true, when all the while I keep safe in my home near wife and daughter who are precious to me.

Wife still very upset to learn of your fame for making murder. Try and say I must have known better! If that is possible? Telling me there are always strange feeling in you, not liking when you make smile for our daughter.

Is too much for thinking about it. Please make contact so our business can be final. Even when things are looking bad, I am trying to help you.

Sincerely,
Dimitri Novack

—

To: Jonas Williker, inmate #957464
From: Antonio Birch
July 26, 2007

Dear Jonas,

Things sure have been lively on this end. The doctors ran a whole battery of tests in response to my outburst. MRIs, bloodwork, psych evaluations, you name it. My stepdad is freaking out over the insurance costs. It's gonna take a while to get all the results, and even longer to form a consensus. There's no current method to diagnose chronic traumatic encephalopathy in the living, although they have experimental PET scans capable of detecting abnormal brain tissue. So we'll see how things go.

In the meantime I'm going to maintain a full court press. Acting out has been so liberating, I'm going to keep it up as long as I can play the brain injury card. I took your advice and expanded my target from the doctors to the nurses and other care workers, like technicians and janitors. And as you suggested, I've added a psychological element to it.

There's this nurse that's always parading around in her tight scrubs, cleavage bursting from the neckline. I can tell she gets a kick out of flaunting her stuff in front of weak and restrained men who couldn't act on their impulses if they wanted to. I kept in good shape before my accident, and I can tell she likes what she sees. The flirtation was fun for a while, but I'm sick of her thinking she's wielding this power over me. So I gave her a little surprise. The other day, when she leaned in to take my temperature, thrusting her big ole chest-bubble right in my face, I hocked up a slimy wad of phlegm and spit it right between her tits.

She jumped back, shock on her face. "Antonio!" she said. "Why would you do something like that?"

"Because I want to stick my cock between those fat tits of yours," I told her.

She gasped and just stood there. She wasn't expecting that one. I bet no one's ever spoken to her like that before. Not even in bed. I grinned as my saliva dribbled down her chest and disappear into her cleavage. When she still didn't move I reached out and grabbed one of her huge fake tits and squeezed.

That got her attention. She smacked my hand away and fled the room in tears. I leaned back, hardon throbbing between my legs at the thought of her flesh balloon bursting in a shower of blood and saline. Writing this letter has brought it all rushing back. I think it might be time for a little "physical therapy," if you know what I mean.

Your friend,
Tony

—

To: Jonas Williker, inmate #957464
From: Judith Williker
August 6, 2007

Dear Jonas,

It's your mother. How are things? I've been keeping busy, myself. Since I can't leave your father alone, I started hosting the ladies from the prison group once a month. Don't worry, I haven't joined. Technically it isn't considered an official meeting. Just an informal get-together where we chit-chat and exchange recipes. I hope you don't mind. Your father doesn't like having company, but I just wheel him out back, so there's really nothing he can do about it. We spend so much time cooped up, just me and him, it really puts my sanity to the test. I'm sure you can relate.

Hosting is the only contact I have with the outside world, other than my video chats with Margery at the library. Those are a godsend! I'm telling you, Margery should have been a therapist. She is so easy to talk to. Sometimes I feel bad because she just sits there and listens while I go on and on and on. As you know, I can talk a blue streak, especially when it comes to family. It's so rare these days to meet someone who actually pays attention to a conversation. Sometimes she even asks follow-up questions, to make sure she's got all her facts straight.

She especially likes my young Jonas stories, so I've been dusting off some of the old favorites. Like that time when you were three years old and I caught you walking around the backyard clutching a dead squirrel like it was your baby. You were holding on so tight its insides had squirted out all over you. I had to call your father to pry it out of your tiny hands. You got so upset you pouted the rest of the night. It was adorable!

I don't suppose they'd let you have any pets in there, would they? I've heard rats can be quite affectionate, although they're probably full of parasites.

Whatever you do, don't become one of those people who puts a cockroach on a leash and starts calling it Fido. Roaches give me the willies!

Talk to you soon.

Love,
Mom

—

To: Jonas Williker, inmate #957464
From: Darlene Edmonton
August 8, 2007

Dear Jonas Williker,

As always, thank you for choosing Outside Access for all your online secretarial needs. Below please find the most recent comments on your poem,
"The One That Got Away."

COMMENTS

"What the fuck did I just read?" **brackishwater**

— "Do we think he's for real here? I mean as far as we know there are
no survivors associated with PSK. Wouldn't they have come forward?"
marlowe76

— "cue all the men who never had to deal w/ anything like this saying
they'd come forward." **citizensleuth**

— "depends. could be too traumatic/humiliating." **barryboy3**

— "especially if Jonas was already in the bag. why put yourself
through something like that?" **damageink**

— "what if he hadn't been caught yet?" **goldenfisherman**

— "then hell no. he'd come after me for snitching."
XTC1969

— "good point" **goldenfisherman**

— "I totally think there could be a survivor out there. This poem is about
cleaning up loose ends." **dman**

— "gonna be hard to do that from a jail cell." **XTC1969**

— "maybe he's got followers?" **brackishwater**

— "am I gonna have to break out my Thing reference
again?" **cerealkiller**

— "couldn't hurt." **damageink**

— "Quote: 'You are every woman staring back
at me from the gallery.' Seems like a shitty metaphor

to me. Also, he rhymed 'back at me' with 'gallery.'
That might be his worst crime yet." **marlowe76**

— "*I'm every woman…*" **cerealkiller**

    — "That's what he's gonna sing as he gets reamed in the showers." **banshee**

    — "Not cool. Rape is never funny." **citizensleuth**

    — "even if the person deserves it?" **hallseatoates**

— "You have to read between the lines. Poetry is a higher form of communication. A cipher waiting to be solved." **Dman**

    — "college boy over here…" **cerealkiller**

    — "Poetry is all about interpretation. You get out what you put in. You see what you want to see." **barryboy3**

    — "I see dead people." **banshee**

    — "I C U P" **cerealkiller**

    — "we really need stricter moderators." **citizensleuth**

END COMMENTS

Sincerely,
Darlene Edmonton
Outside Access, LLC

—

To: Jonas Williker, inmate #957464
From: Jane Doe
September 11, 2007

Dear Jonas,

Do you believe it's possible to will something into existence? Not in a new age, *if you conceive it you can achieve it,* kind of way. I'm not talking about sending out positive vibes in an attempt to influence the universe. That's too rooted in the Christian notion of prayer for my tastes. No, I'm talking about using the power of thought to physically manifest something that has mass and occupies space.

No? Me neither.

Which leaves one of two potential explanations for what showed up on my doorstep the other day.

The first and most plausible explanation is that it was a hallucination. Obviously I must be experiencing one of my more lucid moments to even suggest this. Not counting the specter of your presence, I spend most of my time alone with my thoughts, most of which are extremely dark. I don't eat or sleep well and exist in an almost constant state of dissociation. In addition, I have a large stockpile of psychiatric medication left over from my years of on and off again therapy, which I self-administer with no consistent schedule.

The second possibility is that it was a gift from you. Of course, I don't know how you could have pulled off such a thing. You're locked away in a maximum security prison and, even though you've seen my face, you still have no idea who I am or where I live. Figuring that out would take no small amount of detective work on your part.

Whatever the reason, I am grateful. My only fear is waking up from an extended delusion and finding the box gone. Its loss would be too much for me to bear. But so far that hasn't happened, lending more credence to option number two. I suppose time will tell.

Here's to getting a good night's sleep.

Sincerely,
The One

—

To: Jonas Williker, inmate #957464
From: Morty Friedman
September 15, 2007

Hey dude,

The name's Mortimus. Lead singer of the bleakest, blackest, black metal band to ever come out of Kokomo, Indiana— Black Satan. In case you couldn't tell, we kind of named ourselves after you, except, we changed "purple" to black, because nothing's darker than black, and we changed "satin" to Satan, because Satan rules, and satin is kind of soft and girly.

Don't get me wrong, you're still a gnarly dude. Totally evil. But today even true artists like myself have to take branding into account. It's just a fact of death. (Take that phrase, for example. Something I coined. Like calling something a "fact of life," but I changed the word "life" to death, because death is brutal. Clever, right? Hopefully it catches on. Feel free to take that bad boy out for a spin.)

It's amazing you've gained such notoriety without the aid of a PR team. It's like the bodies you left behind were your press releases, and law enforcement helped promote them by talking to the public and investigating. They're practically doing the work for you! It goes to show, grassroots tactics still work. So fucking savvy, dude. Straight up.

It would be awesome to collaborate with you on some promotional ideas for the band. Adapt the serial killer model as a form of distribution or something. The way you started local, then expanded your reach, and by the time people caught on to what you were doing you were on to the next thing. The way purple satin was your calling card, instantly recognizable, even as your methods evolved, never using it the same way twice. Reliable yet unpredictable. That's the key to longevity. You know, your arrest notwithstanding.

If anything, I'd say your incarceration represents an important turning point in your career. Like when Dylan went electric, or the Beatles discovered LSD. There's no shortage of potential victims in prison, just new and inventive ways to kill them. Murder is your art, and the best artists adapt.

Anyway, check out our latest EP on Myspace if you can. It's called *Sacristy of Butchery*. We tracked live to cassette tape in one night at the abandoned farmhouse where they found Kirsten Swallows' remains. It was supposed to be 4 songs, but somebody called the cops and they shut us down, so it's one short. I think Kirsten's pain really comes through in the recording. You probably don't have access to the internet, so I've taken the liberty of including an excerpt of the lyrics below.

Yours in eternal darkness,
Mortimus of Black Satan

Sacristy of Butchery

The stench of death fills this abattoir,
God's whore, redesigned
Entombed and enshrined
The tightening of the holy stole restricts her cries
Nowhere to run
My will be done
Soiled virtue, spilt seed, maggots' thrall, lust & greed
Benediction held at bay
Forever within these hallowed halls

—

To: Jonas Williker, inmate #957464
From: William Peters
September 24, 2007

Dear Jonas,

Well, that was inevitable. My nosey partner found out about my plan to visit you. They were not happy about it either, let me tell you. I had to promise to go back to therapy to keep them from packing their bags. If it sounds like emotional terrorism to you, that's because it is.

It wasn't so much that I wrote to you, but more that I'd kept our correspondence a secret.

My partner is one of those "my life is an open book" types, and when you're with an open-booker, your life automatically becomes part of their story. No more distinction between books. It's like having a significant other who wants to combine movie collections, but more personal.

Also, some of the subjects I wrote about are touchy ones for them. My partner can be a little "queerer than thou" sometimes, and has some pretty firm opinions. Me, I'm just a guy who grew up watching horror movies. I'm not looking to fixate on the negative subtext in *Sleepaway Camp*, I'm out to have a gory good time. If pressed on *Silence of the Lambs'* cultural impact on gender, I'll err on the side of empowered monstrosity, and say it's a shame we as queer people can't have nice things. But not everyone agrees.

Especially when it comes to true crime. While I might be inclined to crown Jeffrey Dahmer the Queen of Serial Killers, my partner would argue that the fact that he preyed on gay men is what prevented his apprehension for so long, because society doesn't care about dead fags (hello, AIDS crisis), thereby indirectly contributing to the body count. Then, once they did catch him, there was this toxic idea that his crimes were so much more aberrant because of his sexuality, which... I can't say my partner's wrong there. And so many of his victims were Black as well as gay, which is a whole other can of worms.

Meanwhile, an assumed straight white male such as yourself might be elevated to a pop-culture pedestal, any traces of queerness in their crimes—if they exist—stricken from the record. (And don't think my partner hasn't analyzed the fact that one of your victims was transgender, and although the media has branded it a case of mistaken identity, you had more than enough time to realize, yet you still engaged in your usual, protracted torture session.)

The conversation is enough to make my head spin. Sometimes I have a hard time keeping track of what's supposed to offend and what's supposed to empower. To top it off, my partner is concerned I have a lot of internalized hate, which is why I'm always looking for a "reason" I am who I am, and I can never "just be."

The only time I can remember "just being" is when we hung out as kids. Funny how I keep coming back to that.

It doesn't matter. You might not even get this letter. One of the concessions I had to make with my partner was giving them full editorial control over our correspondence. They are standing by with their red pen as we speak. I told them if they are so concerned with their own views being represented, they should write their own damn letter.

Big mistake.

Apologies in advance,
Billy

—

To: Jonas Williker, inmate #957464
From: Grant Singer
September 26, 2007

Mr. Williker,

Thank you for your recent letter. I wasn't sure I'd be hearing from you again. It makes me happy to know we are still on speaking terms. I suppose your mother deserves most of the credit for smoothing things over? Or maybe you just enjoy talking to me.

Your newfound admiration for my skills as a detective is quite flattering. Although flattery normally has an ulterior motive, wouldn't you agree? Still, in the interest of politeness I will take your compliments at face value. Yes, detectives and killers are both "master hunters" as you put it, although I would make the distinction that the two hunt for very different reasons. I hunt out of a sense of justice, to protect the innocent. Killers... well, I don't want to speculate on the specific impulses *you* were trying to sate. Maybe you can enlighten me?

I'm sorry. Old habits. I'm not trying to interrogate you, I swear. How about we split the difference and say there's a good amount of obsessive behavior on both sides?

In answer to your question, I hadn't planned on writing a book. At least not any time soon. Sure, the exercise might prove therapeutic, but it could always have the opposite effect. It could reignite my obsession. Your offer to write the introduction is... well, I'm not entirely sure. It raises certain moral and ethical questions. While it is true there are convicted killers who have co-authored confessionals or proclamations of innocence, those are generally viewed as sensational and self-serving. I don't think I would be taken seriously as a true crime writer if I allowed the subject of my book to pen the introduction as if we were colleagues or old friends.

Although, it does appear that we're developing what could be considered a type of friendship, wouldn't you agree? Life sure is strange.

Have you considered writing your own book? Maybe an analysis of famous serial killers by a self-proclaimed expert on the subject? That is, unless you plan to go the innocence route. I don't know how much of a market there is for a book like that, to tell you the truth. Last I checked not many people were questioning your guilt. At the very least your mother would buy one, God bless her. But what the hell do I know? I'm not in the publishing business. From what I've heard those are shark infested waters. Let me know if you decide to take the plunge. Maybe *I* could write an introduction for *you*.

Sincerely,
Special Agent Grant Singer
Federal Task Force: Serial Homicide Unit

—

To: Jonas Williker, inmate #957464
From: Antonio Birch
September 28, 2007

Dear Jonas,

I'm glad you got such a kick out of my last letter. You were my inspiration, so it's only fitting. My stepdad, on the other hand, was not so thrilled. He's threatening to divorce my mother so he doesn't have to deal with me anymore. If that bastard breaks her heart I will fuck him up. There can be only one.

I would have written sooner, but I got into quite a bit of trouble after that stunt with Nurse Funbags. They put me in restraints and sedated me heavily for a few days. My brain is only starting to come out of the fog now. I have to admit, there was a moment in my drug-fueled stupor, kind of during the in-between phase where I wasn't totally incoherent, that I felt sort of guilty for what I did. But now that I'm back to my old self, I realize it was just the effects of the drugs, not authentic feelings of remorse. In other words the bitch got what she deserved.

In fact, I've got plans for her, should she ever show her big-titted face around here again. She's been replaced by this short, fat bitch with no chest who looks like she can fight. I'm sure they did that on purpose. Well it doesn't matter how ugly this bitch is, she's gonna get some. All I have to do is get her into the bathroom. My physical therapy's been going a lot better than I've been letting on, so I'll have the element of surprise. I took a page from your book and tore a swatch of my sheet to gag her with. It's not purple satin, but it'll have to do.

I'll let you know how it goes. Unless, of course, it goes too well, in which case you might never hear from me again.

If that happens, it was nice knowing you, Jonas. Take care.

Your friend,
Tony

[Antonio Birch disappeared from the hospital the day after he sent this letter. The nurse in question spent 2 weeks in ICU. Antonio's stepfather left his wife and moved out of state. —Editor]

—

To: Jonas Williker, inmate #957464
From: Anonymous
October 1, 2007

tell me, uncle

does my wayward lust slick sick the empire? this is a thing machines choose
to ignore

for sometimes a dog they bite and pain rings hollow
even in the aftermath
when the very idea has been put to ground with the trembling lips of an
apostate's contrition
a celebration of the tooth wet with venom
a putrid cuspid
an ivory pedestal upon which fraternity seats secure
one holy site of many on an infinite pilgrimage

with regards,
your loving nephew wormwood

—

To: Jonas Williker, inmate #957464
From: Buddy Reaves
October 3, 2007

Dear Mr. Williker,

We've never met, but I used to be a corrections officer at Indiana State. I loved that job, but was transferred a few years ago due to "disciplinary issues" after one of my sergeants started dating my sister. Are you familiar with Henry Piedmont? He ruined my life, and I want something bad to happen to him.

Don't worry, no one else is gonna read this letter. The fucks over at IS are too lazy for that. I should know, I was one of them. They just check the mail for titty pics for the wall.

You're familiar with the Wall of Fame, right? Every prison has one. Nude photos are considered contraband, and it's prison policy to confiscate any and all prohibited material. It's supposed to be logged and filed in the "evidence" locker, but most of it gets divvied up between the boys (after the higher-ups take their cut, of course).

Most COs confiscate nudes for the Wall and leave it at that, but old Hank is a grade A scumbag. He peruses the letters, and if he comes across a woman with a decent body who lives in the area, he reaches out—in an official capacity, of course—and informs them their pics have been intercepted, and by sending them they have technically committed a crime. Then he lets them off with a warning, because he doesn't want to see such a sweet, innocent thing get into trouble. He then proceeds to inveigle his way into their vagene.

You're probably thinking, *Why the hell would this guy care*, and you're right—I didn't. Until it happened to my sister.

It's partially my fault. I made the mistake of mentioning the Wall in front of her, and how horned up these lonely women get for convicts. I knew my sister was a serial dater, but I never considered her desperate. Anyway, one day her tits showed up in the mail and found their way to Hank's desk. Hell, I might have been the one who put them there! I try to tell myself I couldn't have known. I didn't read the letter, and what person would recognize their own sister's titties? I mean, another sister might, but a brother?

I'm getting off track here. Unbeknownst to me, Hank and my sister started… dating. I found out when she brought him over for dinner. Any time one of my sister's relationships lasted more than a few weeks, she brought them over for dinner. You should have seen the shit-eating grin on Hank's face. I launched myself across the table and ruined my wife's signature casserole.

The next day at work I got the scoop. The entire department was in on it. Needless to say it became a very hostile work environment. He told me it was on account of her prowess in the sack, but I think Hank kept the relationship going just to spite me. That's the kind of guy he is. He doesn't need a reason to be a dick. It's part of his nature.

But once my sister got pregnant, he became a ghost. I realized something was up because he went from frat boy to Mr. Professional at work. He even took my sister's picture off the Wall.

I'd love to put this whole situation behind me, but my stupid sister insists on keeping the baby. She claims her biological clock is ticking and this might be her last chance to have a child with a guy that has such a strong jawline.

Fine, she wants to have the asshole's kid, so be it. But I can't go another day knowing he's out there, laughing it up, doing this to other women while my sister raises their baby on her own. Which is where you come in. I don't care how you do it. Maybe he can have an accident. Maybe he can slip and fall and a mop handle can accidentally break off in his ass. Something humiliating and painful. I'll leave the details up to you.

I know, what's in it for you? With that jerk out of the way, I'm free to transfer back to Indiana State. In fact, I'm pretty sure I'd be up for his job. And it never hurts to have an ally on the inside. You know what I'm saying?

Do me a favor and think about it.

Buddy

—

To: Jonas Williker, inmate #957464
From: Judith Williker
October 15, 2007

Dear Jonas,

It's your mother. I've got another recipe for you. This one takes a beloved Italian classic and reimagines it for the incarcerated!

Prison Pizza
2 sleeves of Saltine crackers (or Ritz, or one of each if you're feeling adventurous!)
Hot water
Onion powder
Ketchup packets
Cheese wiz
Slim Jim (pepperoni)
2 Empty chip bags
Hot sauce (just in case)

First put your crackers in a chip bag and crush them into as fine a powder as possible. Then add your hot water, being careful not to over fill. Then mash the mixture within the bag for 10 to 15 minutes, until you've got a nice, doughy paste. Let that settle a bit, then carefully slice open the bag and lay it flat. Do the same with the 2nd empty chip bag and lay it on top of the exposed mixture. Then use your hand to flatten the dough between the two bags. Fun tip: not all pizzas have to be circular!

Now comes the tricky part. Depending on your setup, this could mean the difference between a delicious meal and an inedible mess. If you have access to a microwave or hotplate, cook the dough for 4 to 5 minutes. (If you are lucky enough to have a microwave, please remember to remove the dough from between the two chip bags, as those are made from aluminum coated plastic, which can melt or cause sparks.)

If you don't have access to a microwave, lay your pizza across whatever heat source you have, be it hotplate or radiator. Cooking time may vary, depending on how stingy your specific facility is with the heating.

Once it's nice and toasty, spread your ketchup and cheese whiz across the top of the crust. Add a dusting of onion powder and whatever toppings you desire: Slim Jim (pepperoni), veggies (relish packets), anchovies (mackerel). And don't forget, if it tastes terrible, that's what the hot sauce is for!

Bon Appetit!

Love,
Mom

—

To: Jonas Williker, inmate #957464
From: Ginny Goodwinch
October 16, 2007

Dear Jonas,

You are never going to believe this, but it turns out I've been living next door to your wife and son for the past 6 months!

Let me put your mind at ease up front and state I have no animosity towards them. In fact, I think Candace is lovely, and we've become fast friends. And little Jonas Junior is so scrumptious! I could just eat him up, nom nom nom nom! I've been missing Bobby and Derrick something fierce recently, and your little boy really fills that baby hole. It's been an absolute pleasure to look after him while your poor wife gets some well-needed time to herself. It can't be easy raising a child all on her own. Believe me, I understand. He ain't even special! I mean, he's special, but he's not *special*. You know what I'm saying.

Anyway, it's a funny story. She thought I was a prostitute because I had all these strange men coming and going (they were reporters), and I thought she was a drug addict because she was always sneaking around in a hat and glasses like a vampire afraid of the sun. One day we ran into each other by the vending machine, and you know how friendly I can be… When I finally got a good look at her I knew exactly who she was. She is so pretty! Even prettier than on TV. It's kind of intimidating. I can see why you fell for her.

Anyway, she was wary of me at first, which I can understand, her trying to keep a low profile and all. But I was just as scared of telling her who I was. I thought once she knew I was the woman who bit that reporter's face she'd want nothing to do with me, but it seemed to have the opposite effect. We bonded over our mutual experience, and, frankly, our relationships with you.

I know, I know. Apples and oranges. We were pen pals. You guys had a *relationship* relationship. Hence Jonas Junior. Still, Candace and I have a lot in common. Talking to her has helped give me clarity on this whole situation, and on life in general. She says you two aren't really on speaking terms at the moment, but I thought you'd like to know someone is out here keeping an eye on her and Junior. So rest easy! I'll keep you posted!

In loving friendship,
Ginny

—

To: Jonas Williker, inmate #957464
From: anonymous
October 16, 2007

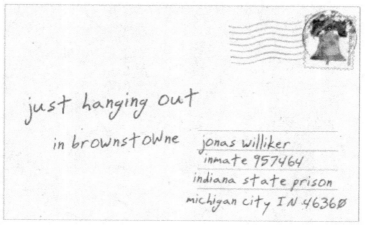

[*A postcard found among Jonas Williker's possessions after his execution. The murder of 27-year-old Mary Landsfield (victim #19) took place on October 16th, 2003 in Brownstown, IN. Her body was found hanging from a bridge by a noose made of purple satin and her own intestines. One of her nipples had been chewed off and her mouth was gagged with a pair of urine-soaked panties. A copycat killing took place there in October of 2007. —Editor*]

To: Jonas Williker, inmate #957464
From: Larry Hostetler
November 6, 2007

Dear Jonas,

Hope you are doing well since we last spoke. Not trying to make a nuisance of myself here, but I've got an update on the Macabre Artifacts situation for you.

I was at a convention this weekend and ran into one of Logan Nester's exes. Not that bitch he seduced out from under me, who stole my collection of rare, William Suff Garfield sketches. And not that piece of Texas jailbait who turned out to be his second cousin. I'm talking about Lexi, who, despite her poor judgment when it comes to men, never did me no wrong. In fact, we even dated for a short while there, bonding over our mutual, Logan-related misfortunes. What can I say? The murderabilia scene is an incestuous one, wedded kinfolk notwithstanding.

Where was I? Lexi told me Logan's current girl, Edna, told her Logan claims he's a cunt hair away from signing an exclusive deal with you. Is there any truth to that? This ain't even about me. The important thing here is you don't make a decision you're going to regret, one that'll dictate your legacy for decades to come. I'm serious, DO NOT get into bed with Logan Nester. He will fuck you in a way you will not like. Just ask his exes. He's only in this game to make money. He don't give two shits about the community.

Maybe this is just a case of Logan's girl running her mouth. Maybe it's a case of Logan running his mouth to impress his girl. Either way, you owe it to yourself to think things through. I'd advise caution, as I do to anyone considering getting involved with Logan. If you've got any specific concerns, you can always come to me for advice, free of charge. Pro bono, as they say in your circles. The way I see it, you don't deserve to be conned just because you're a con.

Sincerely,

Larry Hostetler
Murdertown, USA™

—

To: Jonas Williker, inmate #957464
From: Jane Doe
November 8, 2007

Dear Jonas,

I fear my delusions may be getting worse. The box remains a tangible object, for which I am grateful, but I've gone and taken things a step further. Out of the depths of my loneliness I've conjured myself a friend.

He appears normal enough. Normal, as opposed to some romantic ideal, so there's one thing in favor of his existence. He showed up on my doorstep, much like the box. Maybe they came from the same place? The same wellspring of hope and desire? He claimed to know my identity, but I told him that wasn't possible. Nobody knew who I was, which made him a hallucination. He smiled at that. Hadn't he seen me outside the courthouse? Wasn't I "The One That Got Away?"

"That name has never been uttered aloud," I told him. "Which definitely makes you a hallucination."

He's been here ever since.

Together we reimagine your crimes as a type of passion play, with me cast in the role of the victims. Sharing their pain helps me feel closer to them, like less of a fraud, an imposter because I survived. Like somehow I'm channeling their voices, allowing them to live again, if only for a while. I'd gladly die in their stead, would my visitor let me, but there is always a last minute reprieve, a sacrificial angel appearing from nowhere. Each death is a postcard, lovingly framed, a note-perfect ballad composed in your honor. An exquisitely crafted work of art. A brilliant line of poetry. I'm incapable of maintaining a normal relationship, so why deny myself this? To be touched. To experience something. I deserve at least that much.

Do we have your blessing, Jonas? Please say we do.

Sincerely,
The One

—

To: Jonas Williker, inmate #957464
From: Stacey Santiago
November 21, 2007

Dear Jonas,

I saw that TV movie they made about you. What a flaming pile of trash. Did you watch it? The actor they got to play "Jordan Hilliker" was *too* attractive. I mean, you're a good-looking guy, but he was distractingly hot. Total Playgirl material. Too bad he couldn't act for shit. I wouldn't be surprised if he's done porn. His civilian resume only has a couple of soap appearances and some modeling on it.

Did you really take your shirt off every time you were about to kill someone? Or was that just a plot contrivance? I like how they tried to justify it by saying your character was fastidious about leaving evidence. They used that word almost as often as Jordan flexed his pecs. Fastidious. It began to lose all meaning. Just like Jordan's crimes. He seemed to have no motivation other than: *you pretty, me kill.*

Who was this shit even made for? 1950s housewives? Wannabe pickup artists? The lighting and set design scream *Master the Art of Seduction in 3 Easy Steps.* Almost all the murders take place offscreen. I've seen more violent beer commercials. Your average game of golf has more injuries. Why did they even bother?

Honestly, it's kind of insulting. You better hope none of your prison buddies see it. You don't want them thinking you're a softy. I'd watch my buns if I were you.

Sincerely,
Stacey Santiago

—

To: Jonas Williker, inmate #957464

From: Darlene Edmonton

December 11, 2007

Dear Jonas Williker,

As always, thank you for choosing Outside Access for all your online secretarial needs. Below please find the comments on your most recent poem, "A Purpose Served," which has been posted to the Truth Sleuths website.

On a personal note, I consider myself fairly objective and open minded, but I debated about whether I should post this poem. While presented as fictitious, some of the details ring a little too authentic for comfort. I went ahead and posted it anyway, since you'd already paid, but I've made the decision not to post any of your future poetry. It doesn't feel right to me, and I'd rather not risk my business. There are law enforcement agencies that monitor what I post. They have reached out and told me as much. I expect you'll hear from them on this matter.

COMMENTS

"This is next level fucked." **manx**

— "seriously, what is the point of posting this? The guy's just getting his jollies knowing people are reading it." **citizensleuth**

— "the real question is what does this tell us about the case? Because he's definitely trying to tell us something here." **thequantummechanic**

— "us?" **manx**

— "yeah, he's trying to tell us he REDACTED that woman's REDACTED with a REDACTED and then he REDACTED her REDACTED with a side of REDACTED." **cerealkiller**

— "as disturbing as this is, it's def relevant. It's not like we're some fancy literary journal. This is a true crime board. He could be describing unsolved murders." **grandsonofsam** "is this supposed to be a continuation of the last poem? Because there's no mention of TOTGA, but doesn't it feel like he's jumped inside that character's head? And that character is jealous he's out there killing other women? I dunno. spitballing." **marlowe76**

— "there *have* been some recent Ohio Valley murders reminiscent of PSK." **dman**

— "You know the rules. Start another thread if you're gonna speculate." **hallseatoates**

— "Not speculating. One of them was in Brownstowne." **dman**

— "where are you getting this information? and why hasn't it been in the news?" **hallseatoates**

— "amateur question. and it's BROWNSTOWN." **cerealkiller**

— "You guys are taking this way too seriously. It's just bad poetry." **goldenfisherman**

END COMMENTS

Sincerely,
Darlene Edmonton
Outside Access, LLC

—

To: Jonas Williker, inmate #957464
From: Elrond James
January 7, 2008

What's up, J-Dog?

Elrond here. I wanted to bounce some ideas off you, like Jack Nicholson bouncing that ball in *The Shining*. That's what we writers do when avoiding the chair (not to be confused with the chair you're trying to avoid). We bounce. Whether it's a tennis ball against a hotel wall or ideas against an unresponsive audience. So tell me what you think. Or don't. But for your information, you're the only living subject who hasn't given me feedback on their characterization in my book.

Oh, and if it sounds like I'm amped, it's because I've been popping Bennies like grapes.

—

So check it out, you're a depraved lunatic out on the prowl, dick throbbing so hard it hurts. (Newsflash: if priapism lasts more than four hours you should seek medical attention.) Daddy needs his medicine—a ripe, young Betty out late, unescorted. The pain is overwhelming, the mindset animalistic. Still, the façade is there. The edges are frayed and some holes need patching, but you're charming enough for her to overlook it. She's got *her* needs. A different sort of desperate. She's got a little boy at home, but you don't know that—you wouldn't care if you did—and you sure as shit ain't gonna ask.

An easy mark, you think. It ratchets up your disgust. How could she be so irresponsible? She's got a kid, for crying out loud—maybe she *did* tell you, I don't fucking know. She deserves to be punished for being so careless. You're in awe, you worship her, but she's filth. The things you'll do to her, the rituals

you'll perform, the pain will cleanse her. She'll have plenty of time for self-re-
flection. Plenty of time to think of the scared little boy, home alone in pissed
Jockeys, lacking the sense to take them off. How's he supposed to survive
without her? A kid that dumb doesn't have a chance. But you don't know this.
You see it in her eyes, but for all you know she's wasting her regret on herself,
crying tears of self-pity, soiling herself with fear.

And she has good reason to be afraid. You start slow, giving her an idea of
where things are headed, intent on taking your time. But before long the lust
takes over. Everything else becomes a blur. This will be the part the media
focuses on.

What they won't focus on are the moments after, the reverence with which
you treat the body, the ritual of the purple cloth, the sorrow of having destroyed such a perfect thing. Collateral damage be damned! The victim exists
in a bubble of loss. What a waste, they'll say. She was so pretty. Such a shame,
what happened to her. What kind of perverse creature would do such a thing?
But they won't see the love with which such horrors are committed. Will
never understand the motivation behind them. Will never understand the
repercussions outside of a pretty girl's death.

That's why they'll never catch you.

Each victim is a work of art. An attempt to create life. An attempt to raise
the dead. The dead housed within yourself. Multitudes of unclaimed bodies,
heads down, shuffling towards oblivion.

—

Well? What do you think? Am I hitting near the mark? Do my intuitions
pass muster? I understand it's uncomfortable looking inward, but this is your
chance to course correct, have some control over how you're represented. I
don't offer this opportunity out of courtesy—fuck courtesy!— I offer it in the

pursuit of truth. Truth is the only authority I recognize. I kowtow to no other. Truth in art equals truth in life. You can quote me on that.

Maybe I'll hear from you, maybe I won't. Until then, stay frosty in there.

Elrond James

—

To: Jonas Williker, inmate #957464
From: Judith Williker
January 21, 2008

Dear Jonas,

It's your mother. I've really gone and done it this time. Remember all those video chats with Margery from the support group? Turns out, what I thought were private conversations between consenting adults were actually podcasts in disguise! I feel so betrayed! I opened my heart to that woman and she stomped all over it. She didn't even take her shoes off first! I thought she was my friend, but she was just using me to boost her stupid ratings.

I know you think I talk too much, that I'm too friendly with reporters and police, but I promise, I didn't say anything that might hurt your appeal. I didn't even tell Margery any of the *really* embarrassing stories, like what a nightmare your potty training was. You probably don't remember, but even after I got you to consistently go #2 on the toilet, I didn't dare take my eyes off you. If I stepped away for even a second you'd be elbow deep in your own mess, smearing it all over the walls and on your face. One time you managed to escape the house like that and had to be returned by Mr. Carlson from next door. Needless to say I was mortified. When I opened the door there you were, grinning ear to ear like, as Mr. Carlson so insensitively put it, a little "shit-caked minstrel."

The worst part is I found out Margery doesn't even have any violent offenders in her family. The closest thing she has is an uncle who was convicted of mail fraud, and he got off with time served! Why do I have such bad luck making friends? First Aretha, and now this. Thankfully your father doesn't know. I'd really be in for it if he did. At least I got some recipes out of the deal. Have you tried the prison pizza yet?

Talk soon.

Love,
Mom

—

To: Jonas Williker, inmate #957464
From: Morty Friedman
February 11, 2008

Hey dude,

Greetings from the land of ice and snow, the midnight sun, where the hot springs flow! A Scandinavian paradise of mountains, glaciers, and coastal fjords. That's right, I'm talking about Norway! The band and I went on a little pilgrimage to the motherland, the frosty birthplace of Black Metal itself. We booked ourselves a mini-tour, opening for all-female metalers, Lily's Hammer. Don't let their gender fool you, these babes are totally brutal! They shred like nobody's business, and shredding *is* my business. The vocalist, Wilfa Grindr, pulled out her tampon and threw it into the crowd at every performance! 10 straight shows! No wonder she's so angry. She's always on her period! Even though metal has a rich history of misogyny, especially in the U.S., Norway is a super progressive place. As usual, Europe is way ahead of the curve.

And you *know* we had to check out the notorious *Helvete* record shop. Wilfa and the gals took us to the basement of this metal Mecca where the inner-circle of the scene once congregated. Standing amidst the satanic graffiti and concrete walls it was easy to picture Euronymous and Grishnackh plotting their latest arson while Dead got wasted (RIP). I can only imagine what other gnarly shit went down. Animal sacrifices, demon summoning rituals, blood orgies. The whole thing was pretty inspiring. Afterward we all went out for a nice curry.

I'm telling you, man, Norway's where it's at. Especially for someone with your "interests," if you know what I mean. They had a guy over here, a former nurse, who was convicted of poisoning 22 people (although it's believed he killed over a hundred), and they only sentenced him to 21 years in prison! That's less than a year per person! To top it off, he got out after 12 for good behavior. Can you imagine? He's off somewhere living a peaceful life under an assumed name. Definitely not killing anybody. Talk about progressive. Even Varg Vikernes, the infamous church burner and poster child for Norwegian Black Metal, served 15 years, and he only killed one measly guy! (Sorry, Euronymous. No offense.)

For the record, I'm not really down with the burning of churches. I mean, I am and I ain't. It's complicated. Don't get me wrong, Christianity sucks. It's a colonialist cancer on the colon of the world. But it's also produced some amazing works of art. As a creator of art, this is something I can't deny. So as much as I'd like to see Christianity wiped from the face of the earth, I also can't condone the destruction of historical pieces of architecture like 100-year old churches. I approve the sentiment but not the practice, you dig?

Anyway, this trip has been one of the greatest privileges of my musical career. Every self-respecting metal fan should visit Norway at least once. I've been posting pics online, and my scene cred is through the roof. All hail Black Satan!

Don't worry. Norway also has plenty to keep non-metal fans occupied, like the Viking Ship Museum in Oslo. Very impressive, and still kind of brutal. Vikings raped and murdered the shit out of everyone they met. There's also the famed Holmenkollbakken ski jump, which opened in 1892. Try saying that three times fast! I'll send you a post card!

Yours in eternal darkness,
Mortimus of Black Satan

—

To: Jonas Williker, inmate #957464
From: Anonymous
February 14, 2008

venerable sir,

whosoever fucks their way through time's squalid artifice has proven themselves worthy of esteem

wouldn't you agree?

—

To: Jonas Williker, inmate #957464
From: Ziv Sloan
February 22, 2008

Dear Mr. Williker,

This letter is in regards to my partner, Will Peters. Let's just cut right to the chase, shall we?

What the ever-loving fuck?

If you were anything like the friend he described from his youth, you wouldn't be filling Will's head with such nonsense. You'd recognize he is in a vulnerable state and was reaching out to you for help (as warped as that decision might have been). And let me be clear, the you he reached out to was the you from then, idealized over time, molded into a saint, not the sorry excuse for a human being you currently are. So I'd appreciate if you ceased all communication with Will and allowed him to move on with his life.

Maybe you should turn that discerning eye of yours inward for a little critical self-evaluation? I know your type. Don't think I can't see what the media has glossed over in their attempts to make you as appealing to a mass audience as possible. Beneath the handsome, jocular veneer, where your crimes cease to be vague and sexy, ugly details paint a picture of who you truly are. You're not a dangerous ladies' man run afoul of his appetites, you're a festering pile of misogyny and self-hatred. You take out your insecurities on the innocent in an attempt to convince yourself you're a virile devourer of women, when in reality you're an impotent little child. And the only way you know how to confront this is to lash out.

You need to ask yourself why you hate women so much. Whatever you're blaming them for, you'll most likely find it within yourself. Locked away in a tiny box you've convinced yourself can't be opened.

Leave my partner alone. He needs to heal. And dealing with your bullshit isn't helping the situation.

Fuck you in advance,
Ziv Sloan

—

To: Jonas Williker, inmate #957464
From: anonymous
March 3, 2008

bloomingtonis
wonderfull this
time of year

jonas williker
inmate 957464
indiana state prison
michigan city IN 46360

[*Another postcard found among Jonas Williker's possessions. The murder of 24-year-old Kira Wagner (victim #16) took place on March 3rd, 2003 in Bloomington, IN. Her bloated body was found floating in a motel pool with bruising so severe the coroner referred to the then-Jane Doe as Veruca Salt. A copycat killing took place there in March of 2008.* —Editor]

To: Jonas Williker, inmate #957464
From: Jareth Blackbird
March 3, 2008

Dear Jonas Williker,

I used to go out with this goth chick back in high school. She was a bit older than me and had already graduated. Looking back, I'm not sure what she saw in me, other than a lump of wet clay to mold. I didn't even have a car. She'd pick me up after school and we'd drive around smoking cigarettes, blasting the radio.

Music had been my in. Social interaction didn't come easy for me, but at the time I naively believed I could convey a sense of myself with nothing more than a cassette tape. Who needed words when you had emotion? If you occupied the same space as me, a space dominated by a song, you'd be able to feel exactly what I felt. And if two people shared such a powerful experience, there was bound to be a connection, right?

Of course, it usually resulted in some poor girl with her fingers in her ears, trying to have a normal conversation with me while I was all, THIS SONG IS THE PERFECT REPRESENTATION OF THE COMPLEX EMO-TIONS ROILING INSIDE ME.

But it was a lesson I had yet to learn. So when this girl offered me a ride in her banged-up Ford Escort, I popped in a mixtape and cranked it like I owned the place. The look on her face said, *Not what I expected, but I can work with this.*

You know how you can become so wrapped up in someone else's world it overtakes your own identity? For me it started with the music. She reverse-engineered my tastes to fit her aesthetic, from the pop-tinged punk bands of the 90s to their forerunners—bands like Siouxsie and the Banshees and the Cure, as well as darker acts such as Bauhaus, Sisters of Mercy, and Christian Death. Music that was atmospheric, existential, and morbidly romantic. Music that reflected the emptiness within. She'd put her head to my chest and tell me she heard it reverberating inside me. I started going by the name Jareth Blackbird. Can you imagine?

She claimed to be a witch. She liked to keep vials of blood and semen in her refrigerator for ritualistic purposes. When we weren't driving around we'd hang out at her place and write letters to serial killers, a favorite hobby of hers. She'd invent a persona and attempt to make desperate people fall in love with her. She'd be whatever they wanted her to be—gay, straight, male, female, all of the above—it didn't matter. As long as she got inside someone's head. She enjoyed having control over them. Sort of the early equivalent of the whole fake identity thing happening on the Internet these days.

She made me write this one dude whose claim to fame was eating people's skin and collecting dicks in jars. I wasn't into it, but she'd get all riled up when I read his replies out loud, so I played along. You'd think prisons would monitor communications better, but they don't. So much gets overlooked due to understaffing, underfunding, and good old-fashioned negligence. This guy would write about murder like your uncle telling an anecdote. Murders that hadn't even been solved. He'd tell me about all the fucked-up things he'd like to do to me. How we were soul mates. It started to weird me out. I told the girl I didn't want to do it anymore and she broke up with me. By the third breakup I was done. I made sure to dump my jizz down the sink, just in case. I let her keep the blood, though.

Sometimes I still think about that girl. I recently read an interview with her online. Turns out, she still likes to write letters. She and her husband have been communicating with serial killers for the past decade, pretending to be these made-up characters, and they unloaded the whole of their correspondence at auction for over six figures. No mention of how fucked up it was that they spent years toying with people's emotions, even if those people had committed horrible crimes. Makes you wonder about some of the letters you've been getting, doesn't it?

That article inspired me to write this letter. Kind of a bookend to that period in my life. Maybe a part of me felt bad and wanted to confess? Or maybe I was feeling nostalgic.

What kind of music would I hear if I put my ear against your chest? A melancholic symphony of strings? The operatic works of Wagner? What about something more modern? Like the proto-thrash of Venom, or some Norwegian black metal? For all I know it could be Donna Summers. To each his own, I suppose. Chances are it would be the same hollow silence that plays inside the rest of us, which is the scariest option, when you think about it.

Although now I kind of like the idea of you dismembering corpses to the sounds of "MacArthur Park."

Anyway, thanks for listening,

"Jareth Blackbird"

—

To: Jonas Williker, inmate #957464
From: Grant Singer
March 5, 2008

Mr. Williker,

I appreciate your insight into the recent Ohio Valley murders, unprompted though it may be. It gave valuable perspective on the killer's motivation and helped our team generate numerous alternate avenues of inquiry. Despite this I cannot share the files with you. And under no circumstances am I able to secure approval to escort you to the crime scenes. It doesn't matter how many sets of chains you wear, how many hoops you jump through. Those types of things may happen in TV procedurals, but my superiors would never allow it. Still, if you have any further analysis to share I would be interested in hearing it.

I'm curious. Why the sudden interest in helping the authorities? And why these cases in particular? The information made available to the public has been minimal, yet you managed to extrapolate some pretty specific details. The fact that these crimes are connected, for instance. You referred to them as "practice runs," and "a tentative first step towards something larger." As if you knew the first crime scene was staged and no actual homicide took place. If I didn't know better I'd say someone fed you that information. But that couldn't be possible. I'm your only connection on the task force. I'll just have to work under the assumption that you really are an expert when it comes to the subject of serial killers, like you've claimed so many times on TV and in letters.

I'll keep you apprised of any future breakthroughs. Unless, of course, someone else beats me to it.

Sincerely,
Special Agent Grant Singer
Federal Task Force: Serial Homicide Unit

—

To: Jonas Williker, inmate #957464
From: Joseph Oysterton
March 8, 2008

Dear Mr. Williker,

Allow me to introduce myself. My name is Pastor Joseph Oysterton, shepherd of a little flock out of Indiana called The Universal Water of Life Church. Maybe you've heard of us? Our weekly services average over 50,000 attendees a week, with over 10 million more tuning in via satellite from over 100 countries. I am the bestselling author of over two dozen books, including *Peekaboo, Guess Who? It's Me, Jesus*, which has been translated into 47 languages.

Or perhaps you are familiar with the series of comedic Internet videos featuring my sermons overdubbed with embarrassing bodily noises? They go by many names: The Flatulent Father, The Ripping Reverend, The Effluvial Evangelist. They are crude and silly, but I'll be the first to admit they are indeed humorous. My own family gets quite a kick out of them. I'm not endorsing them as part of my ministry, but I do believe they've had the unintended effect of raising awareness, especially amongst young people. They may come for the farts, but they are being crop-dusted by the Word of God.

I don't normally reach out personally, as my flock is quite large and I have a capable team of Assistant Pastors, but the Lord spoke to me and told me yours is a special case. So if you'd be so inclined, I've made myself available to further instruct you in the ways of righteousness. I believe your conversion would be a valuable testimony to the saving grace of our Lord and Savior Jesus Christ.

It also couldn't hurt your image. I've been following your appeal. Numerous members of the Indiana State Judiciary also belong to our church, and I'm sure they'd agree it would be foolish to destroy a potentially powerful evangelical tool in the name of retribution. For doesn't the Bible say, "Repay no one evil for evil, but give thought to do what is honorable in the sight of all?" Wouldn't restitution for sins yield a more beneficial result?

These are questions you need to ask yourself, questions that must also be asked of the leaders of our community. I am praying both parties arrive at complimentary answers.

Yours in Christ,

Pastor Joseph Oysterton
The Universal Water of Life Church

—

To: Jonas Williker, inmate #957464
From: Judith Williker
March 10, 2008

Dear Jonas,

I've got one final recipe for you. Since it's almost your birthday, I thought it might be fun to try your hand at making a cake!

Correctional Cake
1 bag of Chips Ahoy
1 bag of Oreos
1 carton of milk
1 packet of mayo

First heat up your milk by any means necessary. Again, if you don't have access to a microwave or hotplate, place the carton on a radiator or run it under hot water. While you wait for the milk to steam, crush both bags of cookies into a fine powder and mix them together in one bag. Then pour the steamed milk into the mixture and stir. Add mayonnaise and continue to stir until thick. Slice open the empty cookie bag and lay it flat. Pour the mixture out and shape it into a thin brick. (The thinner it is, the faster it will cook.) Place the brick on your heat source. Cook for three to five minutes. Allow cake to cool before eating.

And if you want to be a fancy pants and make yourself a latte to go with it, use some of that steamed milk with your instant coffee instead of water! Just don't let it heat too long, or it starts to curdle.

This recipe came from Margery herself. Boy, did she have me fooled. Hopefully your cake is not as bittersweet as the memory of my friendship with her. No amount of hot sauce can fix that.

Have a happy birthday!

Love,
Mom

—

To: Jonas Williker, inmate #957464
From: Meredith Wu
April 2, 2008

Dear Jonas Williker,

How have you been? I've been better. Life just hasn't been the same for me since the trial. It's funny, when I first found out I had jury duty, I immediately started thinking up excuses to get out of it. I wrote a list: I'm a full-time homemaker, a mother of three, an active member of my HOA, I have a thriving eBay business. But when I found out it was going to be a murder trial, THE murder trial, I quickly changed my tune. Here was my chance to be a part of something historic, something larger than myself. What me and my fellow jurors did that day was meaningful. I believe in my heart justice was served.

And then it was over. Suddenly normal life didn't seem so exciting. I spent weeks thinking about nothing but the trial, and after it ended I couldn't stop. I missed the feeling of walking into the jury box, every eye in the room on me. The throng of reporters vying for my attention. The buzz it gave me. It's like when you discover a new favorite food and you want it all the time, and with each bite you think, this is *so* good, it will never *not* be this good, and one day out of nowhere it isn't. All of a sudden you can't imagine taking another bite. It's that jarring.

Since then I've read every scrap of writing about the trial, from the books to the magazines to the internet message boards. I'm a lurker, as distasteful as that is. It consumes me. When people pass me on the street, I want them to recognize my face, quiz me about the trial, demand information like they used to. Sometimes they do, and I get a little taste of how things were, but mostly my presence is ignored. Sometimes I catch a glimmer of recognition, followed by a moment of panic at the idea of having to interact with me.

I've spoken to my fellow jurors about this and they feel it too, although most of them are happy the trial's over. They've reintegrated back into their lives, picked up where they left off. Some of them are writing books, and that's how they're getting their fix. Me, it's like I'm a stranger in my own home. Like I'm living a lie. A life that belongs to someone else now. I'm not sure who, but whoever they are, they're not me.

When I first brought up the idea of writing to you, the other jurors were aghast. Why the hell would anyone want to? they said. I've learned to broach the subject casually, laugh it off when they're appalled. I expect it now, but can't understand for the life of me why the idea is so outlandish to them. How is it they weren't affected by the trial like I was? Why didn't it leave a gaping hole inside them? Maybe there's something wrong with me?

Do you think there's something wrong with me? I passed judgment on you, so turnaround's fair play. I'd be curious to hear your opinion. Do you hold any personal animosity towards me? Now that it's all said and done, maybe you're glad we found you guilty? Yes you are appealing the death sentence, but in your heart you know what you did and didn't do. Unless you have completely separated those parts of yourself. You might not *want* to die, but do you feel you deserve death?

I'm not sure why, but I find myself thinking more and more about *your* feelings these days. In a way I have more of a connection to you than the victims at this point. They are gone, but you're still here. You can answer my questions. They can't. I can't help but be curious.

Have any of the other jury members written you? They all claim they wouldn't dare, but you never know. I'd be pretty ticked off, but it'd also be kind of a relief. Just don't tell any of them about this letter. I'd rather they hear it from me.

I hope you write back. Even if it's to tell me to go to hell.

Sincerely,
Meredith Wu
Juror #6

—

To: Jonas Williker, inmate #957464
From: Ginny Goodwinch
April 17, 2008

Dear Jonas,

Well, it looks like I'm no longer lucky in love. Wesley and I broke up.

Yes, that's his name, Wesley, although these days I prefer to call him the Wea-sel. I'm through protecting that little two-timer's identity. Can you believe he left me for a younger woman? A girl, really. One his own age. I'm starting to wonder if I'm not better off alone. How much heartbreak is one person supposed to take?

Fortunately, Candace has been a godsend through all of this. I've started calling her Candy because she's so sweet. She talked this weary cougar off the ledge, reminded her she used to be a bird with wings, one that still has the freedom to fly! She also gave me some great advice on what to do about Weasley Wes. After he dumped me, I was sure I'd lose my job, but Candy made me see that *I* was the one who held the power, not Wesley, and she helped me draw up my demands. In exchange for keeping our relationship a secret Wes promised not to fire me. In addition to that, I got a thirty cent raise out of the deal, and weekends off, so now I can spend more time with baby Jonas. That Candy really knows what makes men tick, but I'm sure I don't have to tell you. It's a shame you two still aren't talking!

In fact, Candy and I have been getting along so well we've decided to move in together! Isn't that amazing? We've hired a realtor and have been looking at apartments in the area. The motel really isn't the best environment to raise a child, and the meth heads are starting to overrun the place. I feel bad that I'm always crying on Candy's shoulder, complaining about my boy troubles, especially since she barely mentions her relationship with you. I guess she's just a lot stronger than I am. Still, my fingers are crossed you two work things out. For Jonas Junior, at the very least. Don't worry, I'll put in a good word! More news soon.

In loving friendship,
Ginny Goodwinch

—

To: Jonas Williker, inmate #957464
From: Jane Doe
May 1, 2008

Dear Jonas,

my companion ~~where's~~ wears your face? bloody teeth behind a slit open mouth, stained sheets suspended from a clothesline, tracking time's passage, months divided into weeks divided into days, each square a piece of rotten pulp encased in enamel. i can't remember the last time i had my period. i don't eat much and rarely produce waste. what little i do is harmless and inoffensive. clothes hang loose on my body, my skin hangs loose on my bones. my skeleton folds up like a marionette inside its box. neural pathways lead me down dark, earthen tunnels full of blind things that crawl. synaptic singularities contract and expand as moments become ~~lifelines~~ lifetimes. i burrow out of time, living other lives, communing with my decaying sisters, the anonymous victims. tapestries of flesh adorn the walls, hollow white faces, weightless breasts, each mouth breathing a cloud of smoke, an evanescent spirit making its escape. a rapping of knuckles summons me

the one

—

To: Jonas Williker, inmate #957464
From: Candace Bennington
May 15, 2008

Dear Jonas,

These are the last words I will ever write you. And once they are committed to paper, I will do my best to erase them from my memory. I don't know why you turned your back on your wife and son. Maybe I put too much pressure on you, expected too much. Or maybe this was another way for you to get your kicks torturing women.

Whatever the reason, I'm not going to spend the rest of my life trying to figure it out, begging the silence for answers. I once claimed I'd chosen to fill the father-sized hole in my life with knowledge instead of the typical surrogates, but that turned out to be a lie. Trying to mold you in my father's image was a fatal mistake, and I accept responsibility for it.

Jonas Jr. is doing well. It won't be easy raising him as a single parent, but I will do my best. My plan is to teach him to treat people with kindness, and above all to respect women. That way, even though he doesn't have a father figure in his own life, he can still grow up to fill the role himself. When the time is right I will tell him all about you. At that point you won't be able to hurt him. You'll be dead. A memory. A life lesson. An example of how not to be.

The day will be here sooner than either of us think. Junior is growing so fast. Yesterday he said his first word. "Dada." He was pointing at his diaper, alerting me to the fact he'd taken a shit. It brought a tear to my eye, but I didn't correct him. He'll figure it out. So close but yet so far.

I don't think there's anything else to say. Any future communication will be sent via my lawyer.

Goodbye, Jonas.

Sincerely,
Candace Bennington

—

To: Jonas Williker, inmate #957464
From: Logan Nester
May 16, 2008

Dear Jonas Williker,

Logan Nester here. Again.

What the hell did that fool Hostetler say to you? I can't believe you let him queer our deal! That sonofabitch can't keep my name out of his goddamn mouth. It's like he's obsessed with me! I swear, one of these days he's gonna choke on my name like he was throating a stallion! My ex Lexi says he's been harassing her at conventions, demanding details about my personal business. It's beyond unprofessional—it ain't right!

Do you know who came up with the idea for Murdertown, USA? ME. Who provided the startup capital? ME. Who took us from the basement to the convention circuit to international mail order? That's right, ME. Logan P. Nester. I taught Larry everything he knows! Treated him like family! And when I turned my back for a second, what did he do? He buried the knife right between my shoulder blades. Took everything I had and left me for dead.

He claims I stole his wife and we conspired to steal his Garfields? Horseshit! She left him because he treated her like property, just another piece of memorabilia to add to his collection. He only married her because she'd gone on a date with Ted Bundy and lived to tell the tale. The truth of the matter is he gave her those drawings as a wedding gift, so they were hers to take.

The murderabilia scene is a small one. A man like Larry Hostetler might call it incestuous, but I don't like to use language that makes my customers look like deviants. It's bad business, and Larry should know better. Still, his ignorance on the matter doesn't surprise me. He doesn't care about the community. He's only in it for the cabbage.

I've said my piece. You're gonna do what you're gonna do. I wish you luck in all your future endeavors, even if you decide to partner with a scumbag like Larry. But if you ever change your mind and find yourself in the market for a more trustworthy partner with business bonafides, my barn door's always open.

Until then,

Logan Nester
Macabre Artifacts

—

To: Jonas Williker, inmate #957464
From: Citizenry Services Inc.
June 1, 2008

Greetings Citizen,

Are you a sovereign individual whose rights have been stripped by an illegitimate governing body? Do you languish in prison while your freedom is traded as collateral between an international cabal of Zionist financiers? Don't worry. It may seem like a hopeless situation, but you are not without recourse. All you have to do is buy back the judgment levied against you using U.S. issued treasury bonds.

These are the same bonds used by the government to open off shore bank accounts in the names of the unlawfully incarcerated, allowing them to accrue interest on your identity while your body rots in jail. They don't want you to know how easy it is to buy back these debts, thus releasing the lien on your person, but the information is hidden in plain sight within the convoluted Code of Federal Regulations. Once you assume ownership of your personhood, they are obligated to set you free.

It may sound far-fetched, but this diabolical scheme dates back to the establishment of the Federal Reserve in 1913. Positioned as a way to monitor risk and alleviate crisis in our financial system, the Fed was in actuality a Trojan Horse packed full of shylocks and other vermin poised to suck America dry. An ever-increasing yoke of involuntary servitude foisted upon the average citizen, striking down all those who rise in opposition. It was followed up by the Emergency Banking Act of 1933, and the creation of the FDIC, which only further strengthened the government's stranglehold on working-class Americans.

Many citizens have bought back their lives. We will help you secure and submit the appropriate bonds, and act as intermediary between you and the corrupt entities that hold sway over your future. All you need to provide is your social security number and a one-time fee of $5000, which includes the cost of buying back your judgment from the so-called Justice Department.

If our services are not within your budget, you can opt to purchase our $500 Sovereignty Reclamation Kit, which includes a detailed guidebook and all the necessary information to write and file your own motions.

Act now, before the government decides to modify the existing laws.

Sincerely,
Citizenry Services Inc.

Disclaimer: This information is for advisory purposes only. We are not licensed attorneys and the letter you are holding should in no way be construed as binding legal advice.

—

To: Jonas Williker, inmate #957464
From: anonymous
July 4, 2008

[Another postcard found among Jonas Williker's possessions. The murder of 29-year-old Francine Kilshaw (victim #9) took place on July 4th, 2001 in Austintown, OH. Her mangled body was found in a local farmer's cornfield. A copycat killing took place there in July of 2008. —Editor]

To: Jonas Williker, inmate #957464
From: Grant Singer
July 10, 2008

Mr. Williker,

I'm going to be honest with you. I do not believe the Ohio Valley murders exonerate you, or even cast doubt on your guilt. The Purple Satin Killer is not "out there running free while an innocent man rots in jail," as you so claim. These are copycat crimes, plain and simple, influenced by your own. A deranged tribute, desperate for your approval.

In fact, I wouldn't be surprised to find out you were pulling the strings, manipulating some impressionable protege from the comfort of your cell. It'd be damn near impossible to prove, but it would explain your fascination with these crimes. You knew they were related to your case from the start, before any of this was made public. That's pretty suspicious if you ask me.

I'm sending a couple of my boys up there to speak with you. If you're smart, you'll give them your full cooperation. They'll have the Ohio Valley files, and I've instructed them to give you full access, like you wanted. If you're serious about helping us catch this guy, this is your big chance.

FYI: I haven't mentioned any of this to your mother. The Ohio Valley murders don't seem to be on her radar, although I'm sure that's about to change now that you're involved. Still, she's been through enough, and the longer I can shield her from this the better. So I'd appreciate if you didn't discuss any of this with her.

Sincerely,
Special Agent Grant Singer
Federal Task Force: Serial Homicide Unit

—

To: Jonas Williker, inmate #957464
From: Meredith Wu
July 12, 2008

Dear Jonas,

Thank you for writing me back. I can't help but notice you avoided answering most of my questions, but that's okay. Maybe you aren't ready to open up about those things. Or maybe your lawyer has advised against it. Although, correct me if I'm wrong, but aren't you your own lawyer? Either way, I won't hold it against you.

Oddly enough, I enjoyed hearing about your day-to-day life. It seems... well, like it could be worse, to tell you the truth. My impression is you've adjusted quite well to your circumstances. They say children are resilient and can adapt to almost anything, so it's good to see that quality still exists in some adults. Just because you're being held accountable for your crimes doesn't mean you have to suffer, although I'm sure plenty of my fellow jurors would disagree.

I find it interesting that you are as obsessed with the cultural ramifications of the trial as I am. We've read many of the same books. Don't tell anyone I told you this, as it hasn't officially been announced, but Vincent Maronek (Juror #2, who is a chef in real life) has just signed a publishing contract for his memoir about the trial. It's called *Serving Justice* (bad pun alert), and will be the first book written by a jury member. I haven't read it yet, but he did interview me for the project. Don't worry, it was before you and I started corresponding. I'll save these letters for my own book, if I ever write one.

I asked Vincent if he'd reached out to you. Turns out he hasn't, and doesn't plan on it. When I asked him why he said there was no need. He already knew what you would say, and didn't want to give you a platform to further profess your innocence after we'd already proven your guilt.

Proven.

The word feels so absolute. Don't get me wrong, I still believe we made the right decision, but I don't know how anyone can be 100% sure about anything these days. A product of sitting on a jury, I suppose. Or maybe it's the internet's fault.

I told Vincent that sometimes I think about writing to you, and he laughed and told me that's because I'm a woman. I didn't appreciate the sexist implications of that, but having thought about it a little more, if it's because he thinks women are more empathetic than men, that's not necessarily a bad thing. I happen to be an exceptionally empathetic person. It's part of what the prosecution liked about me. Whether I'm empathetic because I'm a woman, that's another story, but I'll take it as a compliment.

Do you think it's true what the psychiatrists said in their testimony, that you are incapable of empathy? I refer back to my earlier comment about proof. I can accept 99% incapable, but there's got to be a tiny part of you that feels for your victims. Or is at least aware of the harm you have caused. Maybe the feeling has waned over the years due to your increased transgressions, but you must have started out with some degree of empathy.

Right?

Please tell me I'm right.

Sincerely,
Meredith Wu
Juror #6

—

To: Jonas Williker, inmate #957464
From: Ginny Goodwinch
July 14, 2008

Dear Jonas,

In my last letter I told you how Candy and I were planning on moving into an apartment together. Well, we just signed the lease on the cutest little two bedroom, not far from the grocery store and within walking distance of my therapist's office. Much nicer than the crummy old flop house we were living in. I can't believe I stayed there so long. Like a lobster in a pot of boiling water, I suppose. I didn't realize how bad things were getting. Thankfully I got out before it was too late, and I owe it all to Candy.

Sorry I missed your birthday again this year. This time I can't blame it on crappy men or the U.S. Postal Service, either. Truth is I just plum forgot. I wonder... how come the plum is the forgetful fruit? Why not an apricot? At least that rhymes. Apricot forgot. Maybe it's because people always forget plums exist. I know I do. Come to think of it, I don't think I've ever had a plum. I'll have to remedy that. I do work at a grocery store. Anyways...

If it makes you feel any better, all my celebratory energy was funneled into Jonas Junior's birthday, which is a couple months after yours (like I need to tell you your own son's birthday!). I know he probably won't remember it, but I sure will! He had such a blast playing with the balloons and opening presents. What was inside those presents wasn't even important, but the opening was sublime. And let's not forget cake! You should have seen his face when he tasted the frosting. I swear I could pinpoint the exact moment all that sugar hit his tiny brain. Such a wonder to behold! Pure, unadulterated id.

All in all it was a glorious day. I hope hearing about it brings you even a fraction of the joy it brought me. It will occupy a special place in my heart as long as I live.

Love,
Ginny & Little JJ

—

To: Jonas Williker, inmate #957464
From: Anonymous
July 15, 2008

most gentle inmate,

when morality is at play
an actor often encounters the magnetic attraction of a sharp piece of slate
capable, in its wisdom,
superficial though it may be,
of spilling sunset humors beneath sea-foam prisms
adrift listless like lanterns
of which only the most fortunate will rust

sincerely,
grandpa ott

—

To: Jonas Williker, inmate #957464
From: Darlene Edmonton
July 20, 2008

Dear Jonas Williker,

As always, thank you for choosing Outside Access for all your online secretarial needs. Below please find the most recent comments on your poem, "A Purpose Served," which has been posted to the Truth Sleuths website.

COMMENTS

"Well shit. Maybe these *are* copycat crimes." **manx**

— "Somebody's trying to steal the thunder from JW's conversion." **cerealkiller**

— "Seems a little convenient, doesn't it? JW converts, the PSK killings start up again. Did they get the wrong guy?" **marlowe76**

— "There's NO WAY. Where's our resident sycophant/expert?" **barryboy3**

— "There have been two more killings. Bloomington and Austin Town. I'm willing to bet there will be more. As requested, I've started another thread." **dman**

END COMMENTS

Sincerely,
Darlene Edmonton
Outside Access, LLC

—

To: Jonas Williker, inmate #957464
From: Grant Singer
August 15, 2008

Mr. Williker,

Thank you for your cooperation. My men told me you were eager to help and provided a detailed analysis of the Ohio Valley Killer for our profile. The problem is, the whole thing felt very familiar to me. So I went and compared it against the original PSK profile and guess what? It was almost word for word.

Since these are copycat crimes, we expected some degree of similarity, but this gives us nothing new to work with. It's identical to what we've been going off of this whole time. Which leads me to believe you are either jerking us around or once again lobbying for your own innocence. Let me be perfectly clear—this is not a potential under consideration.

I do not appreciate you putting these thoughts into your mother's head. The idea that the killer is still out there and you are innocent. The last thing she needs right now is to be filled with false hope. It's selfish of you. She deserves better. The ethics of capital punishment aside, you and I both know you're where you belong.

Don't try using this to pitch a wedge between your mother and I. We've made it this far not seeing eye-to-eye on your guilt. The Ohio Valley crimes do nothing to change this. She understands that my job and our relationship are two separate things. I've put too much time and effort into this case. If you think I'm so pussy-whipped I won't sacrifice what I've got with Judith to make sure you stay locked up, think again, son.

Sincerely,
Special Agent Grant Singer
Federal Task Force: Serial Homicide Unit

—

To: Jonas Williker, inmate #957464
From: Judith Williker
August 25, 2008

Dear Jonas,

I know you have a lot going on, and I hate to be a bother, but I have to ask. Do you remember your cousin Tina? You were only five or six at the time, but she went missing during the family picnic that year. We searched the woods for days and never found any trace of her, which is why your Aunt Lottie had to go live at the hospital. A few months later I found Tina's jacket in the back of your closet. The shiny purple one, with the white trim? It was all torn up and stained, and when I asked you how it got there you just shrugged and gave me a blank stare, the one you made in all your school photos.

I'm not accusing you of anything, but the purple satin used to bind your alleged victims reminded me of that jacket. All I know is that even after all these years, it would be a relief for Aunt Lottie to know what happened to poor Tina. It would be a relief for all of us. I thought, what with your recent conversion and how help-ful you've been to the police lately, you might have something you want to tell us.

Then again, maybe I made the whole thing up. When I went back to look for the jacket the next day it was gone. I put it out of my mind after that. Like I said, recent events have dug up old memories.

As you can imagine, Aunt Lottie has not taken this whole Purple Satin thing very well. She's back on 24-hour suicide watch, poor thing. When I visit I have to make sure not to wear anything close to purple, or else she has a major meltdown. Even your lighter mauves and lavenders are off limits. Life sure is strange sometimes.

Oh well. I suppose that's all for now. I'll write again soon.

Love,
Mom

—

To: Jonas Williker, inmate #957464
From: Jane Doe
August 28, 2008

—where do you go when I'm asleep?

traveling amongst the stars, he said
to hunt angels
i'm right here, he said
waiting
as always

—tell me again about the day I was born

you take me by the hand this pen having become heavy with congealed ink and lead me through a metropolis extending skyward blades for branches reaching out to decorate our faces with ritual paint my insides a shelter for stones you lay me down lips pressed against my shimmering brow a father tucking in his child taking what's rightfully his sewing her back up to preserve already spoiled goods this womb is my coffin and I will sleep here forever and ever amen

i am the one

—

To: Jonas Williker, inmate #957464
From: William Peters
September 4, 2008

Dear Jonas,

I'm writing this letter during my lunch break, away from the prying eyes of Ziv. Did I ever tell you what I do for a living? I work as a barista at an upscale coffee shop catering to snooty rich people. It's not the greatest job in the world, but I like my coworkers, so I can't complain. The only downside is I don't make a ton of money, which wouldn't bother me if it didn't make me all the more dependent on Ziv. It's another way for them to control me. Or maybe it's another way in which I relinquish my agency, since I never bother trying to improve my station in life.

You want to hear something crazy? Sometimes Ziv sends people to spy on me while I'm working. What makes it all the more insane is we technically have an open relationship. It's something I've never acted upon because random hookups aren't my thing, but Ziv has so many rules and regulations in place it would be almost impossible to have an affair even if I wanted to.

Ziv's the type of person who likes to give the illusion of freedom. One time they sent someone into the store to hit on me, to try and get me to "cheat." I rebuffed the person numerous times, but they continued to pressure me. Only after I banned the person from the store did Ziv reveal their involvement and laud me for my loyalty. And you know what they said after all that? "You could have if you wanted to." Pretty fucked up, right?

Everything's a test with Ziv. They accused me of wanting to sleep with you when they found out I planned on visiting. What did they think I was going to do, blow you through the bars? Sometimes I wonder why I bother putting up with this shit. I guess I'm a glutton for the status quo.

Anyway, if you want to write me back, send it here to the coffee shop, okay?

Your friend,
Billy

—

To: Jonas Williker, inmate #957464
From: Anna Anderson
September 16, 2008

Dear Jonas,

Are you surprised to hear from me? Nothing surprises me anymore, and I'm only 16-years-old. It's been that kind of life. So much has changed in the last two years I feel like I've become a completely different person.

Do you remember the letter I sent you? Of course mom found out, which is part of the reason I never wrote another. She intercepted your reply and watched me like a hawk every day after. She wouldn't let me read it no matter how much of a tantrum I threw. To this day I have no idea what it said. She destroyed it. Lit the stove and made me watch it burn.

We stopped speaking after that. It started with the letter, but over time the reasons for my resentment evolved. Instead of hating Mom for keeping us apart I hated her for bringing you into our lives. For being weak and naive, and passing those traits on to me. But after her health started to decline I had to put our differences aside. I learned what it meant to be responsible for someone.

The doctors think she has a rare form of Alzheimer's but they can't say for sure. They have no idea what's caused it. Early onset dementia is rare so there isn't a lot of research. Mom recognizes me most of the time, but sometimes she mistakes me for my 7-year-old self. In those moments she talks like you're still part of the family. Other times she asks where you are and why you left us. She breaks down and blames herself. When things get really bad she tells me her darkest secrets, stuff she used to protect me from. Sometimes they reveal moments from my childhood that I don't remember. Moments that might not even exist. It's a burden I'd rather not have to carry, but she has no one else.

Which is probably why I'm telling you all this. I have no one else. All my "friends" are still in high school. They're still leading normal teenage lives, so how could they possibly understand? They already think I'm weird because I don't act like a typical kid. One of their favorite jokes is to ask if I've mysteriously swapped bodies with my mother, like in one of those movies. They don't know how close to the truth that is. And even if I thought they could understand I wouldn't want to burden them with the tragedy that is my life. I prefer to keep my trauma to myself. That way it can't hurt anybody else.

Or maybe I'm just ashamed.

Who knows what the future holds? I mean, we know what *your* future holds, but I'm speaking in the broader sense. I'm just trying to take care of mom and make it to graduation. I don't see the point in planning beyond that. The doctors give mom anywhere from 6 to 8 years. It sounds cruel, but I'll be almost 25 by the time I'm able to move on. There's no point in even thinking about college before then. Once you and mom are gone I can finally close this chapter of my life. It's too soon to see the light at the end of the tunnel. I just have to keep walking towards it, hoping it exists.

Did you care about us at all? Even a little? It felt like you did, once, but now I'm not so sure.

Sincerely,
Anna

—

To: Jonas Williker, inmate #957464
From: Abigail Tinder
September 20, 2008

Mr. Williker,

You filthy, two-timing heathen! I can't believe you would screw me over like that! Yes, that's strong language for a child of God, a literal child at that, but I believe it is necessary to communicate how angry I am. (And yes, I got permission from my father to write this letter. I am nothing if not obedient.)

When I first read about your conversion I was miffed, but my personal feelings were eclipsed by what you stood to gain. I thought perhaps I had contributed in some small way, and I could mark it down as a win even though a teammate came in from the bullpen and completed the game. But when I found out you'd aligned yourself with Fartin' Joe Mega Church and his Walmart of Christianity, I lost my composure.

I have to say I am highly skeptical your conversion is sincere and isn't some last-ditch effort to stay your execution. Joseph Oysterton is nothing more than a modern P.T. Barnum, and his church is one of the biggest, most expensive circus tents in the country. He doesn't care about your immortal soul, he cares about putting butts in seats. More butts equal more money.

What did he promise you? Did he tell you he has powerful, political friends? That he can intercede on your behalf? Don't tell me he thinks he can get you a presidential pardon? That would be beyond the pale, even for him. You couldn't possibly be a big enough rube to believe a lie so blatant!

But maybe I'm wrong. Maybe your conversion is real. I hope for your sake it is. Nothing would bring me greater joy. I can picture the souls of your victims welcoming you into heaven with open arms and forgiveness in their hearts.

Assuming they were believers when you killed them, of course. Otherwise they'd be in the other place.

Either way, this will be the last letter you receive from me. I have done my best to avert you from the path of eternal damnation. The rest is between you and God.

Yours in Christ,
Abigail Tinder

—

To: Jonas Williker, inmate #957464
From: Grant Singer
September 24, 2008

Mr. Williker,

I've been made to understand you have converted to Christianity. My men confirmed this was a major topic of conversation during their follow-up visit with you. I am not a religious man myself, but I do believe in God. Even if he thinks bruises are beautiful and enjoys inflicting them on humanity.

I also believe in redemption, so I support your newfound spirituality. Your mother in particular is over the moon, which of course makes me happy.

That being said, I cannot allow this to affect my judgment when it comes to the facts of this case. I'm sure you understand, and would expect nothing less from me.

Sincerely,
Special Agent Grant Singer
Federal Task Force: Serial Homicide Unit

—

To: Jonas Williker, inmate #957464
From: Morty Friedman
September 26, 2008

Hey dude,

Christianity, huh? I did *not* see that one coming. Religious colonialism strikes again.

Personal views aside, I'm not gonna lie. This fucks with my money. How am I supposed to maintain a credible satanic rock outfit based around a guy who's gone Jesus freak? We'd be laughed out of the scene!

Unless… I might be able to spin this whole thing as a ruse on your part. A cunning attempt to trick the big man upstairs. What better way to cement your name in the pantheon of killers than to sneak into heaven and murder God himself? Now that sounds pretty fuckin' cool. I better write this down. There's definitely a song in there. Maybe even a concept record. *Godkiller! Killer of God!* It practically writes itself:

Sent from earth to kill in heaven
Hell awaits the number seven!
Forced to abdicate his throne
Succeeded by the devil's own!

Godkiller! Killer of God!

[insert guitar solo]

Since we're being honest with each other, I'll let you in on a little secret. I don't really believe in the devil. That's just as ridiculous as believing in god (no offense if you have, in fact, converted). I mean, if I thought the devil was real, do you think I'd be fucking around with this shit? Mama didn't raise no fool. Mama raised herself a nice Jewish boy.

I can hear her now: "Morty, what's with you and all this devil stuff? You know we don't believe in that nonsense!"

Yep, I hear her voice loud and clear. Probably because she's right in the next room folding laundry. I didn't tell you I still live at home? What can I say? I'm a total mama's boy. She's Black Satan's biggest fan!

Anywho... It's a shame we haven't been able to get our collaboration on, but I feel like this correspondence, as one-sided as it is, has been creatively productive for me. At least I got "Godkiller" out of it. *Godkiller*!

I'm curious to see where this conversion business takes us. Keep me posted.

Yours in eternal darkness,
Mortimus of Black Satan

—

To: Jonas Williker, inmate #957464
From: Meredith Wu
October 2, 2008

Dear Jonas,

Well, I think my book idea might be dead in the water.

I went to the monthly meeting of the Purple Satin Jurors (that's what we call ourselves, gauche, I know) and told everyone you and I had been exchanging letters. It felt good to come clean. I also told them I intended to collect our correspondence in a future book (down the line, of course. What do you think of the title, *The Purple Satin Letters*?).

Boris said he didn't like the idea. You remember Boris. Short, bald, bossy. He was jury foreman, so now he thinks he's some sort of foreman in real life. He acts like the de facto leader of the PSJ, even though we never officially elected him.

When I asked him why, he said it had the potential to "humanize a killer," which went against the ethos of the group. Can you believe that? We aren't even a real "group." Just a bunch of people with a shared past and a standing coffee date. So I kept pushing until I got the real scoop. He told me he was working on a book of his own, and too many similar books would saturate the market. As a group we needed to put our support behind one project at a time, and everyone agreed, after Vinnie's book it was Boris's turn.

Let me tell you something: Boris can't write for shit. I don't even recall how he got elected foreman of the jury. I think it was because no one else wanted to do it. He barely did anything. All he ever expressed interest in was where we ordered lunch.

He told me I'd better play ball, or I was out of the group. "Play ball." That's how he put it. Can you believe that? When I turned to the others for support, they just looked the other way, or at their feet, or into their mugs. Spineless, the lot of them. I get more honesty from you than the whole PSJ combined. Maybe I should quit. What do you think?

Sincerely,
Meredith Wu
Juror #6

—

To: Jonas Williker, inmate #957464
From: Amy Sorenson
October 15, 2008

Dear Jonas Williker,

You don't know me, but I have a story I'd like to share.

Back during high school me and my best friend got super into urban exploration. We'd hop on our bikes and ride for miles in search of condemned houses and abandoned buildings to sneak into. We called it "sneaking and entering," as if that made it any less of a crime. Not that it mattered. Neither of us were 18 at the time, and we were under the impression that being underage was still a quaint excuse for youthful troublemaking, like in the movies.

My mom hated it. Told me that type of exploration wasn't an appropriate hobby for a girl. It wasn't safe. She obsessed over the murders happening at the time, and saw your face around every corner even though we had no idea what you looked like. I told her Quentin would keep me safe, but she wasn't too confident in his abilities as a protector. He was kind of a late bloomer. Very non-threatening. And this was before either of us had a cell phone, so we wouldn't have been able to call for help if we'd gotten into trouble. Not like having a phone would have made much difference if we ran into a serial killer.

People tend to view unsubstantiated stories with a good deal of skepticism. A lot of people call bullshit on the one I'm about to tell. Or claim I'm embellishing it.

Not my mom, though. She believes every word.

One summer at the height of our exploration obsession me and Quentin discovered this abandoned hospital a few towns over. It must have recently closed down, as it didn't look too worse for wear from the outside. Just some boarded up windows and illegible tagging. Overgrown weeds and litter. The building didn't look like a hospital at first glance. Just another piece of defunct corporate real estate. But we realized the potential of what stood before us. We had to get inside.

Gaining access wasn't hard. We stashed our bikes and hopped the fence. No barbed wire or anything like that. No security. Just a rusty old padlock on the gate.

We circled the perimeter and found a window sufficiently secluded from the street. I whipped out my trusty Swiss Army knife and proceeded to unscrew the plywood covering the window. We hadn't thought further ahead than that. We figured once the board came off we were in. Of course once the board came off we were greeted with the obvious. A locked window.

Luckily we loved the breaking of glass. It was one of the main objectives of our little excursions. So we found an old concrete block and made with the smashing. The sound of it rang across the empty lot. We scattered like bugs and spent the next half hour monitoring the scene of our crime to make sure no one had alerted the authorities. When we were sure the coast was clear we braved the jagged glass and entered the hospital.

From the light of the broken window we analyzed our immediate surroundings. Two beds separated by a curtain. The first had a sleeping bag spread out on top. A small, battery-operated radio sat on the table beside it.

I pulled back the curtain to fully expose the second bed. A pair of handcuffs was clamped to the railing, the other end dangling towards the floor. A dark brown stain covered the mattress. It could have been shit, but it could have also been blood. Even more disturbing, painted on the wall in huge purple letters were the words, "The Purple Satin Killer Was Here."

Right at that moment Quentin decided to turn on the portable radio, filling the air with static.

I practically jumped out of my skin. I pictured my mom shaking her head at Quentin, an "I told you so" on the tip of her tongue. I reached over and took the squawking box from him, clicking it off. Quentin shrugged and gave a sheepish smile. I put a finger to my lips and pointed at the stained bed. His face drained of color.

We stood there for a while, staring at a scene from a horror movie come to life, dread mounting, the air in the room growing thick. I remember wanting to leave, but also wanting to see how much of that feeling I could take, wondering if it had a limit or if it would continue until it became unbearable. I'm pretty sure Quentin was legitimately paralyzed with fear. As I was about to suggest we should leave, the sound of footfall came from further inside the hospital.

I turned to find Quentin already scrambling through the broken window.

I took off after him. I attempted to hurdle the window, but caught my ankle on the sill and toppled face first onto the pavement outside. Groaning, I turned myself over so I faced the window. A dirt smeared face stared back at me. The girl wore a baggy sweatshirt despite the summer heat. She wasn't distressed or threatening, and didn't seem interested in following me any further.

"He'll be back soon," she said.

I took off across the parking lot after my friend.

My mother unleashed hell when she saw my face. She knew what I'd been up to, but I spared her the details. She grounded me for a month. No bike. Which was fine. That was officially the end of my urban exploration days.

Not long after my punishment ended, Quentin came over my house to shoot some hoops. He hadn't gotten in trouble because he hadn't gotten hurt. He told me he'd gone back to the hospital, about a week later, to check things out, but he'd only gotten as far as the fence. He spied a pair of cop cars in the lot, and a bunch of officers inspecting the window where we'd broken in.

It never made the news. As far as I can tell there are no known victims from that area. According to the media coverage you weren't even in the state at the time. But I can't help thinking of those cuffs, and that blood-stained mattress. And the girl.

A year or so later they tore the old hospital down and built a strip mall. Hardly anyone remembers it was there.

But I'll never forget.

Sincerely,
Amy Sorenson

—

To: Jonas Williker, inmate #957464
From: anonymous
November 21, 2008

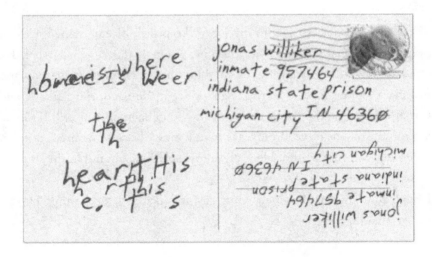

[*A postcard found among Jonas Williker's possessions. No known murders took place in Murrysville. It was the hometown of Judith and Frank Williker until their deaths.* —Editor]

To: Jonas Williker, inmate #957464
From: Ginny Goodwinch
November 22, 2008

Dear Jonas,

My apologies. I know I haven't been writing as often as I should. It's hard, sometimes. Not because writing to you is a chore (on the contrary!), but because life has been so good to me that sometimes it makes me feel guilty. Believe me, every time little Jonas so much as giggles at a fart I have to fight the urge to fire off a detailed letter to you. A child discovering its own flatulence should be an unimpeachable joy, but it also makes me sad because you're not here to witness it. Especially since those farts wouldn't exist if it wasn't for you. In fact, sometimes I can't help but think of myself as a thief because all the joy I'm experiencing is rightfully yours.

Anyway, this is just a quick note to share some holiday warmth.

When Candy's not around it's my job to keep little JJ entertained with an assortment of crafts and activities. Bonus points if they're educational. He especially likes finger-painting, or anything that involves smearing goo and making a gloppy mess. For Thanksgiving we made handprint turkeys, and Candy said it would be okay if I sent you one to hang in your cell. JJ's hand is almost as big as mine already! It's a little messy because he used so much paint, but you get the idea. He really enjoys splashing around in the stuff.

I hope your son's art brightens your day as much as it does mine. Have a happy Thanksgiving!

With love,
Ginny & Jonas Jr.

To: Jonas Williker, inmate #957464
From: Judith Williker
November 24, 2008

Dear Jonas,

I'm afraid I have some sad news.

If we've spoken on the phone in the past few days you already know what I'm about to say. But since I don't hear from you as often as I used to I thought I'd put it in writing, just in case.

Your father has passed away.

You'll be happy to know he went peacefully. I found him outside, slumped over in his wheelchair. The doctors seem to think his heart gave out in his sleep. What they call an unremarkable death.

But there *was* something remarkable about it. Something I didn't tell anyone. When I found your father that day, he was clutching something in his hand. Clutching it so tight I had a hard time prying his fingers open. Granted, it was a while before I found him and it was cold out, but still. It must have been something very important to him. Something he didn't want to let go of. Do you know what it was? A crumpled ball of shiny, purple fabric.

I have no idea where it came from, or how he kept it hidden from me, but its meaning is obvious. Despite his inability to express it, despite what you've been accused of, your father loved you to the very end. And he kept that cloth as a reminder of those feelings, as a way to be close to you.

When I saw that cloth tears of joy flooded my eyes. It was such a beautiful gift from him to me, and by extension, to you. A gift to our family, one I didn't want to spoil. So I took the cloth before the coroner arrived. The police would only have misinterpreted it, complicating matters, ruining a beautiful, tender moment. I can't even imagine the conclusions they would have jumped to. That your father was the real Purple Satin Killer, or that he trained you, or that you somehow orchestrated his death from prison and that cloth was the proof. No, my heart couldn't bear it.

If you need someone to talk to, please call. Take comfort in the fact that your father is at peace. There's a lot less aggravation where he's gone. I don't suppose they'd give you a furlough to attend to the funeral? I've seen it done in movies, and it never hurts to ask. I trust you've been a model prisoner. You always were such a good boy.

I'll update you when I have more details.

Love always,
Mom

—

To: Jonas Williker, inmate #957464
From: Stacey Santiago
November 25, 2008

Dear Jonas,

So apparently you're a Christian now? That's cute. And here I thought porn stars had the market cornered on late-life conversions. I know of at least half a dozen organizations dedicated to rehabilitating members of the adult film industry: Heaven's Harlots, Sex Work Saviors, The Magdalenas, just to name a few.

I have an ex-coworker who started a group called Whores for Jesus, which I jokingly refer to as "Whores for Haysoos," because it drives her crazy. It doesn't stop her from constantly inviting me to join her church, though, especially since I've "retired." I tried explaining how that would be like trading one master for another, but logic is wasted on her.

Did you know Mary Magdalene wasn't actually a prostitute? At least not according to the Bible. Some 6ᵗʰ Century Pope decreed that because…misogyny? Christians love themselves a good conversion story, the dirtier the sinner, the better. And there's nothing worse than a woman who's a slut, right?

You know that thought experiment about going back in time to kill Hitler? Christians wouldn't go back in time to prevent his birth, they'd attempt to convert him on his death bed, after all his atrocities had already been committed, because it would be the ultimate selling point for their religion. If Jesus can forgive Hitler he can forgive anyone.

I guess he can even forgive you. A serial killer is a pretty sweet score for Team Christian. Better than a boring old prostitute any day. My friend at Whores for Haysoos is going to be so jealous. I can't wait to tell her.

May the power of Christ continue to compel you in new and exciting ways!

Sincerely,
Stacey Santiago

—

To: Jonas Williker, inmate #957464
From: Elrond James
November 28, 2008

Yo,

What's up, you stubborn motherfucker? Even though you snubbed me—*me*, Elrond James—I still wanted to share this with you. My new book, *A History of Stranglers*, is almost out and it is a MONSTER. A bona fide beast. We're talking snaggle-toothed, salivating, and horny as fuck. It's tearing the charts limb from limb, and guess who I have to thank?

Myself.

That's right, dipshit. Let me share an excerpt from the NY Times review:

If you thought Elrond James was fixated, you ain't seen nothing yet. In A History of Stranglers *he gets downright pathological, killing his mother over and over again in a masochistic bid for closure. He casts a murderers' row of murderers as the villain, in an orgy of violence that culminates in the most ill-advised roleplaying exercise of all time, one which sees him taking on the mantle of his mother's killer. The whole enterprise is grotesque, disturbing, and more than a little morbid, akin to treating emotional trauma with blunt force. It's an off-putting reading experience. Unfortunately, the book itself is extremely well written.*

Pretty good, right? But that's not even the best bit. Check it out:

One of the more intense sections is also one of the book's best. The character of Jonas Williker, AKA The Purple Satin Killer, brims with James's trademark nihilism, but there's also a humanity at play. James conducted interviews with as many of the killers featured as he could, and he seems to have connected with Williker on a profound level, because he paints him with a heretofore unseen empathy, as if the author has a larger relationship with the man. If any section helped achieve

James's aim of psychically opening up his mother's unsolved murder it would have to be this one. A tour de force of hard-boiled crime writing.

BOOSH. Read 'em and weep. You were the only— I repeat— ONLY living subject who refused me an interview. Interesting how things turn out, huh?

You know what I think? I didn't need the research. The shit I pull out of my brain— I'M THAT GOOD. The chapter with the least interference from real life turned out the best. *Elrond James can out-write life.* You can quote me on that.

So I guess I've got to thank you after all. You snubbing me led to one of the best reviews of my career. A jerk move on your part, but don't think I don't appreciate it. Game recognizes game. If anyone asks I'll deny it, but you did me a solid.

My work here is done. I'll have my publisher send you a copy. I think you'll appreciate what I did. It's that fucking good.

Stay frosty.

Bestselling Mastermind,
Elrond James

—

To: Jonas Williker, inmate #957464
From: Anna Anderson
December 2, 2008

Dear Jonas,

I'm writing with some sad news. Not that I think you care, but because Mom would have wanted you to know. And I want you to know. I need you to know.

It all started with a call from the landlord. "That crazy bitch has finally gone and done it," he said. "Burned the goddamn house to the ground!" No mention of Mom's condition or if she was even alive. I had to fight to get the rest of the information out of him. He told me she had been rushed to the hospital with 6th degree burns, which, I don't think the scale even goes that high, but whatever. He kept going on about arson and insurance money so I hung up on him.

Mom had regained consciousness by the time I got to the hospital, but she was in bad shape. She'd inhaled a ton of smoke and had 4th degree burns over 80% of her body. She kept saying, "Jonas warned me, Jonas warned me," which was hard for me to hear. After all, I was the one who wound up in the hospital last time she forgot to turn off the gas. I told her not to talk, but she wouldn't listen. Finally the doctor had to come in and sedate her.

I stayed with her through the night. At some point in the early morning she woke up. She told me she was sorry for leaving the gas on and "bringing" me to the hospital. She kept repeating those two words, "I'm sorry," over and over again. I told her not to worry, it happened a long time ago, but she kept saying it. "I'm sorry." Eventually I stopped trying.

We both drifted in and out of sleep. At a certain point something in her voice changed. She continued to apologize, but there was a clarity in her eyes as she said it. "I'm sorry." I stroked her hair and tried to soothe her, told her it was okay, I was okay. I said it with as much conviction as I could muster. "I'm okay." She paused to study me, like she was trying to decide if I was lying to her. "You'll be okay?" she asked. "Yes, mom. I'll be okay." She seemed relieved. Then she laid her head back and closed her eyes for the last time.

That was a hard night. If it weren't for her condition this would never have happened. Although in my darker moments I can't help but wonder, what if she did it on purpose? What if that's what she was apologizing for? Maybe she'd grown tired of suffering, or tired of being a burden, or both. As awful as it sounds, that wouldn't make me angry. Her death was the worst thing that's ever happened to me, but it was also a relief. I just wish there had been an easier way.

Now it's just you and me. But really it's just me. I'm all alone in this. I keep telling myself, "It's okay, I'll be okay." It seemed good enough for Mom. If I say it enough times maybe I'll start to believe it, too. Do you think I'm going to be okay?

Sincerely,
Anna

—

To: Jonas Williker, inmate #957464
From: Judith Williker
December 8, 2008

Dear Jonas,

I wish you would call me. It would make things so much easier to have an actual conversation for once, not just exchange one-sided pleasantries. Although in fairness to me your last letter was anything but pleasant. You know I don't like to burden you with undue stress, but you've left me little choice. How could you say such awful things about your father? Especially so soon after his passing? I know the two of you had your ups and downs, but that level of cruelty was uncalled for. Especially after what I told you, how you were in his heart until the end, possibly even the last thing he thought about. Is that how you process grief? It would kill him if he wasn't already dead! You're lucky it didn't kill me!

What did he ever do to deserve such scorn? Such disrespect? All he ever did was take care of you. Sure he could be a curmudgeon at times, but so what? That's no reason to claim he wasn't your father. Where is this coming from? The man was there from the day you were born. And although he couldn't change dirty diapers because of an overly sensitive gag reflex, he was more than willing to hose you off while you crawled around in the backyard. Remember how much fun that was?

Who put their foot down and let you walk home from kindergarten, even when I thought you were too young? Who let you eat ice cream for breakfast and taught you to curse at the newspaper boy? Frank Williker, that's who. If that doesn't constitute being a father, I don't know what arbitrary metric you're using. So I want you to stop being such a brat and call your mother. This isn't like you, and I don't enjoy taking this tone.

I was going to use this letter to tell you how lovely your father's funeral was, but somehow that doesn't seem appropriate anymore. The arrangements were beautiful, but I'll have to save flower talk for another time.

Please call me.

Your mother

—

To: Jonas Williker, inmate #957464
From: Jane Doe
December 11, 2008

...she's there in the trunk, the girl from the back of the car, the dead girl from the news, my friend, Kira, curled up beside me, impossibly, a reunion of sorts, ignorant of the rules governing death...did she wander the afterlife blindfolded, only to find her way home, my home is her home, expecting warmth and compassion companionship protection...you shouldn't be here i whisper, my mouth on what's left of her ear, a cartilage frame with a cavernous echo, blind eyes shimmering in the black at secrets, my finger pressed against paper lips pulling farther back with every smile...

...i hide her grin with an open palm, press my face against the back of my hand and push, whispering all the while, you shouldn't be here, words muffled, mouth molded into a violent rictus, a kiss, crushing the bones in her cheek, willing her to disappear, as i sit across from her, watching her write this letter in my own hand, the same hand planted against her face...

...then i am slamming my face against the back of my hand, knocking her head against the side of the box, the knocking brings me back, summons me, and I rise, leaving her useless and broken, forgiven but rejected, as I gather my strength for what I am sure will be the final time...

—

To: Jonas Williker, inmate #957464
From: Anonymous
December 14, 2008

dearest cousin,

a beguiling countenance invites dereliction and rightly so
are we not justified?
let innocence commence its groveling against a chorus of clanking chains
sound off, sweet children!
resist necessity's desire
for a jury of angelic peers approaches
holy and bereft
of goodness and mercy
(surely)
held hostage by the earth and its provisional stewards

with regards,
your loyal kinsman

—

To: Jonas Williker, inmate #957464
From: William Peters
December 19, 2008

Dear Jonas,

I am once again writing from the comfort of my own home, although it brings me little comfort to do so. Turns out Ziv had a mole at the coffee shop who discovered your latest letter. I've been placed on mandatory mental health leave.

Don't worry, it's for the best. I experienced an epiphany while rewatching YouTube clips of your trial last night. It was a forced viewing, a la *A Clockwork Orange*, but a necessary one. I realized I've been so focused on the past, on our formative years and how they intertwined, I'd neglected to take into account how far they've diverged.

From that vantage point, clearly we are nothing alike. You are a monster. Plain and simple. Me… there's nothing wrong with who I am.

I'm different because of who I love, a difference considered less different every day. You're different because you commit vile, unthinkable acts against women. Things no rational person will ever accept. I'm lucky the person I love is so patient, and they have taken the time to help me see the truth.

But in a way, I also have *you* to thank. Because like when we were kids, you have put me at ease, made me secure in myself. For all the harm you've caused, all the awful things you've done, you've had one positive effect. I don't know if it balances the scales (Ziv is shaking their head no), but I'm going to do my best to make sure the positivity doesn't stop with me. So thank you. I'll always view our childhood with rose colored glasses, but those glasses come off when viewing the man you are today.

This will be my last letter.

Your childhood friend,
William Peters

—

To: Jonas Williker, inmate #957464
From: Todd DeFrancisco
December 22, 2008

Dear Jonas Williker,

Did you watch it? Our *Ghosts of the Purple Satin Killer* episode was a huge hit! One of our highest rated ever. And a total success on the scientific front, as well. The information you provided was a huge help. EMF readings were off the charts at all three locations. We also experienced insane temperature fluctuations, numerous attempted contacts via our Spirit Box, and an unprecedented amount of electronic voice phenomena. We didn't get a proper ID on all the spirits, but most of them seemed VERY angry, as if their lives had been brutally cut short.

Oh, one of them said to tell you to "eat turd mash in hell." At least that's what it sounded like on the EVP. Does that mean anything to you? Danny thought it might be "mush," but I'm pretty sure it was "mash." They definitely said turd, though.

We've been brainstorming ideas for a follow-up episode, and instead of doing the easy thing and picking three new locations, we came up with the idea of visiting your cell after you're gone. Surely you've experienced a lot of complicated emotions over the past few years. We feel the chances of them leaving a psychic impression are very high.

So how about it? Would you like to reconvene after your execution? Maybe we can even help you cross over to the other side. How sick would that be? An *Adventures in Ghost Hunting* first! Navigating the afterlife can be a confusing proposition. It never hurts to have a guide.

We've already reached out to Indiana State to initiate the conversation. I'm told the warden is a fan of the show. It seems the spirit world is a small one. Godspeed on your upcoming journey!

Sincerely,
Todd DeFranscico
Actor-Writer-Director-Producer-Paranormal Investigator-Amateur
Body Builder-Ordained Minister

—

368

To: Jonas Williker, inmate #957464
From: Ginny Goodwinch
January 6, 2009

Dear Jonas,

It's time for me to come clean.

Teaming up with Candy is one of the best decisions I've ever made. There's nothing more badass than two girl bosses living the dream, supporting each other and taking care of business, but that's not all this is. Along the way something extraordinary happened. I'm a little embarrassed to tell you, but what started out as a friendship began feeling more and more like a family and… I'm just gonna come out and say it. I've fallen in love with Candy.

Oh, shoot. You've gone and made me blush. You always were so good at that.

I'd never thought about another woman like that before. Not necessarily in a sexy way, although she's plenty sexy, I don't have to tell you. It's more like I was *always* thinking about her, always *wanting* to think about her, even while I was with her. Mother raised me to believe having feelings for another woman was a sin, but she said the same thing about fornicating in the shower with the gardener, so nuts to her. Because when you think about it, how can love ever be wrong? Love is the embodiment of everything that is right in this world. Any other kind of thinking doesn't make sense.

And Jonas Jr.! What an angel. I love him soooo much. I couldn't stand the idea of not being his *Mommatoo* (that's what he calls me!). So one day I sat Candy down and told her how I felt. And the smile that took over her face, well… it was the most beautiful thing I'd ever seen. She put her hand on mine and I leaned in and had myself my first lady-kiss. And you know what?

It felt as good as a regular one. Maybe even *better*. (Sorry about the smudges. Getting a little teary-eyed just thinking about it.)

Once your divorce is finalized, her and Junior are gonna move back to Chappaqua with me. I hope you're not too upset. I don't want you thinking I swooped in and stole your wife and kid. Trust me, it wasn't like that. It just sort of happened. I was as surprised as anyone. Although no one's gonna be more surprised than Mother. She's gonna have a conniption! I can't wait to tell her.

But one thing at a time. Right now I'm trying to convince Candy to start talking to you again. She's still pretty prickly about how you treated her, and I can't say I approve, but without you there'd be no us. And you *are* the father of our child. If you've done anything good in your life it was donating your DNA to produce that beautiful little boy. He is so full of joy it's incredible. The way he scrunches up his face and goes *eeeeeeeeee!* when he's excited. And he's got your eyes. He's gonna be a lady killer, just like his daddy.

You know me, I could go on and on, but I'm sure you need some time to process this. If you have any questions please don't hesitate to reach out. JJ's Mommatoo is here for you, too.

Sincerely,
Ginny Goodwinch

—

To: Jonas Williker, inmate #957464
From: Anna Anderson
January 13, 2009

Dear Jonas,

What did you mean in your last letter when you wrote, "There is another"? Was that some sort of lame Star Wars reference? I know Jeffrey Dahmer was into that shit. Are you trying to imply I have a brother or sister I'm not aware of?

Are you talking about Jonas Jr.? Because you're not my real father. (Ugh, this is getting more like Star Wars by the sentence.) You and mom never got married, so you were never even my stepdad. I have no connection to your son. Even if I did, I'm sure his poor mother wouldn't want my traumatized ass coming out of the woodwork and demanding to be part of the family. That shit's weird.

Then again, maybe she's the weird one. She did get involved with you after finding out you were a serial killer, unlike mom, who had no idea. Is this some sort of setup? Have you given her instructions to psychologically torture me? I wouldn't put it past you.

It's no secret I always wanted a little brother or sister, so don't think I don't see what you're trying to do. It's something I was very vocal about when you were around. I remember you joining in on more than one occasion. "Yeah, mom," you'd parrot. "Why can't Anna have a baby brother or sister?" Then you'd throw in a passive aggressive insult, which young me would repeat with glee. "Yeah, you ain't getting any younger, mom!"

At the time I didn't fully understand the sort of participation a baby would require of you, or how hurtful it was for a man to jokingly harass a woman for a child he didn't want. Where would we be if you and mom had actually reproduced? We'd be in an even bigger mess than we already are. That poor kid.

It's interesting. After you left us I stopped asking mom for a sibling. It's not that I still didn't want one. I wanted one more than ever, but by that point I realized how unfair it would be to bring another child into our situation, no matter how happy it would make me. So I settled for dreaming one into existence. That way they wouldn't be an undue burden on mom.

It's been a while since I've seen my dream brother, but your recent letter triggered something in my subconscious. I found him sitting in front of the TV with a box of crayons, scribbling away on a piece of paper. The TV was on, but for some reason it had a sheet draped over it, like a cartoon ghost. The glow from the screen underneath only added to creepiness. I couldn't make out the image, but I could hear the hiss of dead air.

"Whatcha drawing?" I asked. My brother held up the sheet of paper without taking his eyes off the TV.

"It's the man who visits me in my sleep," he said.

I looked at the drawing in the flickering light. It was a portrait of a man. His features were so twisted it looked like he was in pain.

"He makes me do bad things," my brother said.

I looked from the drawing back to my brother but he was gone. The paper fell to the floor. I heard the tapping of knuckles on glass coming from the TV. The muffled voice of my brother called to me from the static. I pulled off the sheet to find him trapped inside.

I woke up on my friend's couch. Her drunk older brother was pounding on the door because he'd lost his keys. Turns out they were in his hand the whole time. It was 4AM and I'd fallen asleep with the TV on again. No static, though.

Just one of those gross infomercials where a camera crew tricks drunk girls into taking their clothes off. My friend's brother belched so loud I thought it would wake up the whole house, then dropped onto the couch and passed out. I took my blanket and went and curled up on my friend's floor.

Maybe it's a good thing I don't have a brother. Odds are he'd wind up being a piece of shit frat boy, or worse. As much as I'd love to have a sibling I definitely wouldn't want that. And as hard up as I am for emotional support right now, I don't think I want you writing to me anymore.

I think this is goodbye, Jonas.

Sincerely,
Anna

—

To: Jonas Williker, inmate #957464
From: Candace Bennington
January 15, 2009

Dear Jonas,

In my previous letter I informed you I would only correspond via my lawyers moving forward, but I have interesting news. I met the most curious woman earlier this year. In fact, she was living right next door to me. At first I pegged her for a prostitute, but turns out she's a friend of yours. Ginny Goodwinch? That name ring a bell? From the way she tells it, sounds like you guys were more than just friends. Best friends at the very least. Possibly soul mates.

Don't get me wrong, she's a lovely person, and she's wonderful with Junior. He's taken quite a shine to her. It's too bad you never got that visitor problem worked out. Now that I have a babysitter... Oh well. What's done is done.

The three of us have been renting an apartment in town. Ginny has a psychiatrist here she likes (court appointed), and me... well, I have unfinished business of my own. But once this whole ordeal is over, she's invited us to stay with her in Chappaqua. It sounds like a lovely place. Good schools, plenty of space for Junior to run around in. I'll be able to relax and finish my thesis. Ginny's actually become a huge part of it. She's the find of a lifetime. A textbook hybristophile who's also an amazing babysitter? I feel like I've won the academic lottery. Granted, she can be a little much at times, which I'm sure I don't have to tell you, but it's worth it. Give a needy woman her first same sex kiss and she'll follow you anywhere, even if she thinks you're following her.

My point is you fucked up a good thing. Which is fine, because you don't have a lot of time left to regret it. It was much better for me to move on when I did.

So long, Jonas. It was fun while it lasted.

Candace

—

To: Jonas Williker, inmate #957464
From: The State of Indiana
January 21, 2009

DISTRICT COURT
STATE OF INDIANA

THE STATE OF INDIANA,
Plaintiff

-vs.-

JONAS RAYMOND WILLIKER,
Inmate #957464
Defendant

ORDER OF EXECUTION

A judgment of DEATH, having been entered on the 18th day of September, 2006, against the above named defendant, JONAS RAYMOND WILLIKER, aka inmate #957464, as a result of his having been found guilty of CRIMES, by a duly and legally impaneled jury of 12 persons, and whereas this court has made inquiry into the facts and found no legal reasons against the execution of the judgment of death.

It is ordered that the director of the State of Indiana Department of Corrections shall execute the judgment of death this coming 11th day of March, 2009 via lethal injection.

Dated this 21st day of January, 2009

District Judge Wallace Breheny

—

EXECUTION

To: Jonas Williker, inmate #957464
From: Aurelius J. Percy
January 29, 2009

Mr. Williker,

I represent a contingent of concerned bereaved looking only for closure. As you know, there are many missing and presumed dead associated with your case whose remains have yet to be recovered. You've hinted at as much yourself in depositions and interviews. If you have any humanity left, I implore you, please release the details and locations of these victims before it is too late, so their families can say a proper goodbye. It would be an act of kindness on your part.

P.S. Any previous offer of representation from this firm should be considered null and void, as it would constitute a conflict of interest.

Sincerely,

Aurelius Percy, Esq.
Percy, Paramount & Bint

—

To: Jonas Williker, inmate #957464
From: Walton Dash
January 30, 2009

Dear Jonas Williker,

Greetings from Killer Kitchen, a mobile food truck and catering service based out of South Bend, Indiana. We believe every person deserves comfort and courtesy in their final hours, which is why we offer last meals, free of charge, to all death row inmates incarcerated at Indiana State Prison.

Regulations vary from state to state. Lucky for you, the great state of Indiana allows a "special meal" to be ordered from a local restaurant 36 hours prior to execution. The official price cap is $50, which is why we offer our services FOR FREE, so invite your family, and thank the Lord you don't live in Texas, where they recently ended the tradition of the last meal after an inmate ordered an extravagant feast then refused to eat it in a final act of protest. (Please note: Killer Kitchen supports your First Amendment rights, and has no problem with whatever you decide to do with your last meal. It is our gift to YOU.)

Enclosed you'll find a menu of our most popular offerings, but let me be clear—IF YOU DON'T SEE IT, WE CAN GET IT. Sky's the limit. If you're having trouble deciding, maybe consider some famous last meals of the past (see below). And rest assured, we will get your request right. If you order surf and turf you will get filet mignon and lobster, not Hamburger Helper and a few runt shrimp. If Spaghetti-Os are your heart's desire you won't get some generic store brand. You'll get the real deal.

With that out of the way, we present…

Killer Kitchen's Famous Last Meals

John Wayne Gacy — 12 deep fried shrimp, 1 bucket of fried chicken, 1 order of French fries, 1 lb of strawberries, 1 bottle of Diet Coke

Marion Albert Pruett — 1 Pizza Hut stuffed crust pizza, 4 Burger King Whoppers, 1 large fries, fried eggplant, fried squash, fried okra, 3 2L bottles of Pepsi, a bucket of ice, a bottle of ketchup, salt, 1 pecan pie

Robert Alton Harris — 21 pieces of KFC chicken, 2 large Domino's pizzas (no anchovies), 1 tub of ice cream, 1 bag of jelly beans, a six-pack of Pepsi

Robert Dale Conklin — bacon wrapped filet mignon, de-veined shrimp sautéed in garlic butter with lemon, 1 baked potato with butter, sour cream, chives and real bacon bits, a buttered baguette, a corn on the cob, asparagus with hollandaise sauce, goat cheese, cantaloupe, apple pie, vanilla bean ice cream, and iced tea

Ronnie Lee Gardner — surf n' turf, 7up, vanilla ice cream, and a viewing of the Lord of the Rings trilogy (Extended Editions)

Steven Michael Woods Jr. — 2 lbs of bacon, 4 fried chicken breasts, 1 meat lover's pizza, 2 hamburgers, French fries, garlic bread, 2 pints of ice cream

Timothy McVeigh — 2 pints of mint chocolate chip ice cream

Gerald Lee Mitchell — 1 bag of assorted Jolly Ranchers

Robert Anthony Buell — 1 black olive with the pit left in

James Edward Smith — 1 pile of dirt for a Voodoo ritual to prevent him from becoming a ghost

Odell Barnes, Jr. — "Justice, Equality, and World Peace."

Philip Workman — 1 vegetarian pizza to be donated to a homeless person

—

See anything you like? It would be our honor to cater your final meal.

Sincerely,
Walton Dash
General Manager, Killer Kitchen

—

To: Jonas Williker, inmate #957464
From: Grant Singer
February 2, 2009

Mr. Williker,

I understand the urgency of the matter, but I have done all I can. The Governor has made his decision. He does not consider your aid in profiling the Ohio Valley Killer sufficient cause to delay the execution. Especially since it has not led to an arrest. Trust me, I want to catch this guy more than anyone. I believe the department should utilize every resource at its disposal. Depriving investigators of your expertise at this time is akin to cutting off a vital limb.

If it's any consolation, I feel we have really honed in on what makes this guy tick, and it is only a matter of time before we catch him. Your assistance has been crucial, and when we finally apprehend the bastard, the lion's share of the credit will go to you. It is my hope this knowledge brings you solace in your final hours. I know it will be of great comfort to your mother, who I intend on telling in person at your execution. It's strange. We've talked on the phone so many times, but this will be our first face-to-face meeting. I'm actually kind of nervous.

I look forward to our reunion as well. Of course, I wish it were under more pleasant circumstances, but that seems to be the nature of our relationship. Forged in death. I suppose it's fitting it ends the way it began.

See you soon.

Sincerely,
Special Agent Grant Singer
Federal Task Force: Serial Homicide Unit

—

To: Jonas Williker, inmate #957464
From: Jane Doe
February 4, 2009

please don't leave me please dont leave me pls don't leave me please don't leave me please dont leave me pls dont live me please don't leave me don't leave me pls don't leave me plead dont leave me please PLEASE please don't leave me pls don't leave me pls don leve mee please don't leave me please dont leave me pls don't leave me please don't leave me please dont leave me pls dont live me don't leave me don't leave me don't leave mee please don't leave me dont live please please me dont leave me PLEASE don't leave me dont leave me dont leave me don't leave me dont please don't please don't leave me please dont leave me pls don't leave me please don't leave me please dont leave me pls dont live me please don't leave me don't leave me pls don't leave me plead dont leave me please PLEASE please don't leave me pls don't leave me pls don leve mee please don't leave me please dont leave me pls don't leave me please don't leave me please dont leave me pls dont live me don't leave me don't leave me don't leave mee please don't leave me dont live please please me dont leave me please don't leave me dont leave me dont leave me don't leave me dont please don't pls don't leave me pls don leve mee please don't DON'T YOU FUCKING LEAVE ME

—

To: Jonas Williker, inmate #957464
From: Matt Cominsky
February 5, 2009

Dear Jonas Williker,

You don't know me, but since you're probably getting a ton of hate these days, I wanted to let you know you've changed at least one person's life for the better. Mine.

My name is Matt Cominsky, and I'm a collector of what some would call "offensive" but I prefer to call "boundary-pushing" t-shirts. Not because I like hurting people's feelings, but because people these days need to lighten the fuck up. As the Joker says in Tim Burton's *Batman*, "this town needs an enema." If something offends your personal sensibilities, that's fine, just don't spoil the fun for the rest of us, you know?

It all started when I was a kid and saw Sebastian Bach wearing his infamous RAID-inspired "AIDS Kills Fags Dead" t-shirt. I barely knew what AIDS was at the time (regular folks didn't start caring until that basketball player got it), but I loved the reaction it provoked. It became my mission to harness that power for myself, and after two years of searching (this was pre-internet) I finally tracked one down. It was faded and moth-eaten but I cherished it. I wore it to school the very next day and, even though these were less-tolerant times, I was promptly suspended.

Unfortunately for my parents it was already too late—I was hooked. Any shirt that might get a rise out of people, I had to have it. To this day, that AIDS shirt is one of my most prized possessions, alongside my Cradle of Filth "Jesus is A Cunt" t-shirt. You know, the one with the masturbating nun on it? I've also got a huge collection of serial killer shirts. An original "Burn Bundy Burn" t-shirt, like the ones sold in the parking lot during his execution; a vintage Zooport "Charlie Don't Surf" shirt; a bunch of bootleg "Free OJ" shit—you name it, I've got it.

Which is what ultimately inspired me to make my own: the "Purple Satin Killer: U.S. Tour" t-shirt. It's a really cool design, if I do say so myself. It mimics the notorious "Hitler European Tour" shirt made by Wayne Morris in 1982 (another one of my prized possessions). Wayne was the owner of the European Son T-Shirt shop and manager of an English pop band called The Primitives. The shirt features an image of Hitler *sieg heiling* over a map of Europe on the front and a list of the cities he invaded with the dates on the back.

I updated the design to give it more of an 80s heavy metal aesthetic: Your grinning mugshot on the front hovering over a map of the Midwest, the city and date of each of your murders written in blood red lettering on the back. Your name is in purple, of course.

I haven't seen anyone wearing one in public, but somebody's buying them. A whole lot of somebodies! Sales have completely outperformed my expectations. I tried sending you one as a token of my appreciation, but it came back marked "return to sender."

So I guess I just wanted to say thanks. Not for murdering all those people. I don't condone your actions, just like I don't condone Hitler's. This isn't about that. It's about freedom of expression. It's about pushing the boundaries of taste (and fashion). And frankly, it's about making money. The American Dream, baby! Maybe I'll make a pilgrimage to Indiana for your execution, see if I can't move a few units in the penitentiary parking lot, like they did in the old days. Sounds like fun, right?

Sincerely,
Matt Cominsky

—

To: Jonas Williker, inmate #957464
From: Judith Williker
February 9, 2009

Dear Jonas,

Okay, this time you've really gone too far. This is worse than the Terrible Twos and your petulant teenage years all rolled into one! What are these things you're accusing me of? Performative grief? Emotional infidelity? It sounds like you're just mashing hurtful words together to create longer, more hurtful words. And to insinuate I couldn't wait for your father to die, that I'm happy he's gone, is beyond cruel. What could I possibly have gained from his death? Caring for your father was one of the few things that helped take my mind off your terrible predicament. Without him I am completely alone and my thoughts are free to roam.

I understand these last few weeks have been hard on you, but we should be comforting one another, not tearing each other down. You say I haven't been honest with you, but honesty is a two-way street. Can you really say you've been honest with me, Jonas? About your crimes? About cousin Tina? I've tried to be supportive, but maybe what I've really been doing this whole time has been lying to myself. It's like another one of your Dad's favorite movies, the one with the army lawyers, except instead of Jack Nicholson yelling at Tom Cruise it's me yelling at myself, because even though I want the truth I know I won't be able to handle it.

If your father was here, this is where he'd remind me one of your victims died from having a gag shoved too far down her throat, just like the soldier in that movie. It caused her lungs to fill with blood and then she drowned. But since Dad's no longer with us, I have to do all my own remembering. And you know I don't like remembering those types of things.

What even is "the truth?" When people say, "the truth shall set you free," are they talking about the person telling the truth, or the person hearing it? Because I don't think the outcome is ever what you would call a win-win. In most cases, I assume everyone involved ends up that much sadder, because the truth is selfish. Just like the people who demand it.

You want the truth? I'm tired. I feel like I could go to sleep and never wake up. You'd think not having to take care of someone full time would be a relief, but this invisible weight on my shoulders has only gotten heavier. It threatens to crush me, but I don't think that's its intent. Grief's crueler than that. It wants me alive.

It doesn't matter. If you still want the truth, so be it. But you're not going to like it.

Love,
Mom

—

To: Jonas Williker, inmate #957464
From: Stacey Santiago
February 10, 2009

Dear Jonas,

I feel like I owe you one final update, if only to rub my continued survival in your face. As opposed to, you know, me rubbing my pussy in your face and watching the jury lick it clean. Those were the days, huh? Can you believe I'm able to take care of myself without a man constantly trying to exploit me? Imagine that. I've started managing a couple new girls, fresh off the farm, and I'll be utilizing everything I learned *not* to do from making serial killer-inspired porn with David.

Speaking of my ex, the police came to my door looking for that rat bastard. Seems he's wanted for questioning in connection to the copycat killings of a certain infamous psychopath. Boy, did I have stories for them. I made a pot of coffee and we all got nice and comfortable. Then I gave them access to all the old computer junk David left behind.

One of them even recognized me from my adult film days. *Hey, I know you,* he said. Being known is *much* better than simply being remembered. He left with a couple of signed glossies and my phone number.

How are things with you? Not well, I hope. In one of my previous letters I asked if you were biding your time waiting for the big goodbye. Now that goodbye is almost upon us, do you feel like you've used your time wisely? I've learned from my mistakes. Did you learn anything from yours? I'll be sharing my wisdom with others. I assume you'll be taking yours to the grave.

Goodbye, Jonas.

xoxo

Staci Satin was here.

—

To: Jonas Williker, inmate #957464
From: Helena Rubinski
February 12, 2009

Dear Jonas Williker,

My name is Dr. Helena Rubinski, and I am a psychiatric researcher in the emerging field of neurocriminology. I am writing in regards to your plans for post mortem disposition. I understand this can be a difficult subject, but it is a necessary one, which we all must face at a certain point in our lives. You've been painted in the press as a meticulous planner—perhaps you've already begun the process? Whatever your intention for the rest of your body, it is my hope you will consider donating your brain to our institution for scientific study.

I ask this with the utmost respect. I am not some sideshow huckster looking to display your head to a bunch of slack-jawed yokels. No, my intentions are altruistic in nature. Modern science understands very little about the biology of compulsive behaviors such as yours, and this would be a tremendous step toward helping similarly minded individuals in the future.

The organization I represent is not a modern-day cabal of phrenologists as some have suggested. Neurocriminology is not junk science. It is a legitimate discipline that utilizes data from multiple fields of research to identify prede-termining factors that lead to violent crimes. Our goal is not to police "pre-crime" as Philip K. Dick would call it, nor is this an ultra-liberal attempt to eradicate culpability. We are advocates for mental health. We want to better society. If you doubt my motivation, know that I have a number of violent offenders in my own family tree, and am concerned with the implication this has for the mental well-being of my children and their offspring.

A collaboration of this nature is not without precedent. John Wayne Gacy famously bequeathed his brain to a psychiatrist friend who acts as its caretaker to this day. She continues to study the organ as our knowledge of neurology progresses.

Despite all this I anticipate you may still have some reservations, so let me present you with the benefits of such an arrangement.

Planning for your death ahead of time prevents any confusion where your final wishes are concerned. Those who pass without such assurances in place often have their estate relegated to a limbo of familial infighting. Look at what happened with Dahmer. His mother wanted his brain studied by science. His father did not. So after the rest of him was cremated, his brain sat in literal and figurative limbo—in a jar —while his family fought it out in court. (The organ was eventually cremated as well. A win for his father, a loss for science.)

Those without an immediate family to settle their affairs are even worse off. Someone of your notoriety could be subject to the whim of every self-serving opportunist looking to capitalize on your name. Or, worst of all, your body might go unclaimed, like Albert Fish, dumped somewhere in an unmarked grave.

Maybe you don't care what happens to your remains after you're gone. In that case, what have you got to lose? Sign them over to us and we'll never bother you again!

If nothing else, it is a way for your name to live on. Whether in an afterlife, by progeny, or by legacy, this is something of fundamental importance to human beings as a species. I look forward to hearing from you.

Sincerely,
Dr. Helena Rubinski

—

To: Jonas Williker, inmate #957464
From: Meredith Wu
February 13, 2009

Dear Jonas,

I am culturally relevant once again, and I have you to thank.

It may sound cruel, but the signing of your death warrant has been a god-send. It's thrust me and my fellow PSJs back into the spotlight. The media vultures can't seem to get enough and we've been working overtime like Bachman-Turner.

I've become especially popular, since I'm the one spilling all the behind-the-scenes dirt on our little group. The backstabbing, the infighting, the *affairs*. That's right. I'm not saying sexual favors were traded to jump the publishing queue, but Boris is going to give himself heart failure if he doesn't ease up on the gas station boner pills.

Anyway, I've cut to the front of the line and I didn't even have to snuggle up to that rancid sack of meat. I just had to tell people the truth. They barely even ask about you or the trial anymore. Don't worry, I'm still going to include our correspondence in my upcoming tell-all. Writing a book isn't easy and I've got to pad the thing out somehow. So if you've got anything you want the world to know, now's your chance. Don't hold back. The publisher's given me carte blanche. The more sordid the better.

Let me tell you, I am positively buzzing with excitement. The only problem is in the back of my mind I know it won't last. The attention is fleeting, and once you're gone there will be no reprise. Sure, they might trot me out to say a few words each year on the anniversary of your death, but it's all downhill from here. I envy the version of myself that has yet to experience the comedown, is ignorant of the gaping hole it leaves. To think I never even wanted to serve. Talk about naïve. Now being a professional juror is my dream job.

I'm doing what I can to make it last. I've hired a publicist and gotten myself an agent, just like a Hollywood actor. Maybe I can parlay this into some sort of long-term career. We'll see. Is there any way I can score a ticket to the execution? How does that work, exactly?

Sincerely,
Meredith Wu
Juror #6

—

To: Jonas Williker, inmate #957464
From: Morty Friedman
February 15, 2009

Hey dude,

Mortimus here. All hail Black Satan! [makes the sign of the devil horns]

Bummer about your impending execution. I mean, even though it was a foregone conclusion, it's gotta be rough staring it down like this. Although maybe it's something you're looking forward to? I dunno. I spend most of my days submerged in the darkest cloud of gore and grind, but that doesn't mean I wanna die, ya know? At least not right now. I always figured I'd go out on my own terms, in a way that serves my legacy. Preferably on stage. Mortimus of Black Satan's obituary can't read "coronary on the crapper." That shit won't fly. How would I look the Dark Lord in the eye when I meet him?

I know, I know. I said I didn't actually believe in the Dark Lord. He's more of an all-purpose metaphor for the unknowable governing forces swirling around us. Like personifying nature or the Earth as "Mother." What about you? Still hanging out at the foot of the one true cross? How's that working out for ya?

Anyway, not trying to be a total bummer here, but I've got some bad news to add to the pile. Are you sitting down? You might want to. Because due to circumstances beyond the Dark Lord's control, Black Satan, the most evilest band to ever emerge from the diseased womb of Kokomo, Indiana, is no more.

It sucks, dude. Things had been going really well, too. It usually takes me a while to write a new record, but since our Norwegian sojourn I've been extra inspired, churning out killer riffs left, right, and center. Not as fast and shrieky as *Sacristy*, but still heavy as fuck. Epic and atmospheric. More refined. It feels like I've got the blood of the Old Norse gods pumping through my veins. I'm starting to wonder: maybe there's a religious conversion in my future? Hell, if you can do it, why can't I?

Unfortunately my bandmates aren't as excited about this stylistic evolution as I am. They say we can't just change course mid-stream, even if that stream is an icy fjord, and that although Norway may be the birthplace of satanic black metal, Satan doesn't actually exist in the old Nordic traditions. I tried my best to argue for reinvention, that we should aspire to be, like, the David Bowie of black metal, but they just responded with homophobic slurs, saying Bowie was a queer that had nothing to do with metal.

But when God closes a door, Satan opens a window. (You like that? Another one of mine. Consider it coined.) That's because where God is all about repression and compliance, Satan is permissive. He isn't in competition with other gods. He's not insecure like that. Trust me, if I want to write some tunes about Odin and the Æsir, the devil won't mind. You could even make the argument it's thematically relevant, because the singular form of Æsir is Áss, and if metal is historically about anything, it's about gettin' some! Plus, Áss literally means "god" in some old Norse dialect. *Ass is God*. If that's not metal, I don't know what is.

Anyway, if there's one silver lining in all of this, it's my relationship with Wilfa. You remember Wilfa from Lily's Hammer? She and I have kept in touch since tour and she's been nothing but supportive. Granted, her support takes a very authoritative form, but it turns out I like that sort of thing. Wilfa thinks I should go solo and that my new material would do really well in Scandinavia. She's also pretty sure she can secure me an exclusive vinyl release on Neseblod Records, which would be tits! She's invited me to live with her as her sub, and I'm seriously considering moving to Oslo.

But before that, I'm planning on releasing one final piece of music under the banner of Black Satan, in your honor. It's an epic 12-minute song entitled

"Bleeding Blue and Red." You know how deoxygenated blood is blue and oxygenated blood is red? Well, what would happen if you mixed them? What do you get when you mix blue and red?

That's right. Purple.

I will be self-releasing the song on March 11ᵗʰ through the Black Satan Myspace page. I'll post it as early as possible, to give you a chance to listen to it, but it's gotta be the 11th. I've included an excerpt of the lyrics below. I hope you find them as poignant as I do.

Rest well, my friend. Remember, heavy metal will never die. It's too bad the rest of us have to.

Yours in eternal darkness,

Mortimus

Bleeding Blue and Red

(Can you hear me Jonas?)
It won't be long now
Time to take your final bow
Cut you open, watch you bleed
Veins and arteries tangled skein
The mob has gathered unsure why
Other than to say goodbye

—

To: Jonas Williker, inmate #957464
From: William Peters
February 16, 2009

Dear Jonas,

Today I received a letter from the State on your behalf, written in the detached, formal language of a wedding invitation.

Mr. Jonas Williker requests the honor of your presence...

It brought me to my knees. That you would consider sharing your final moments with me is profoundly moving in ways I'm unable to articulate. Perhaps because you never once exhibited the slightest hint of vulnerability in the past.

The only thing that comes to mind is the time you fell off your bike and sprained your ankle. You couldn't continue riding and had to rely on me to help you hobble back to my house. A quarter of a mile transformed into an epic journey. We were Sam and Frodo behind enemy lines in the darkest depths of Mordor. You had just hurled the One Ring into Mount Doom and there were no eagles to fly us home. I wasn't glad you'd hurt yourself, but in the moment it thrilled me to be needed. Reading the State's letter felt similarly bittersweet.

Unfortunately I won't be able to attend your execution. Neither Ziv nor my therapist thought it was a good idea, and I have to agree. Your death is going to be hard enough to process without experiencing it in person. I don't think I'd be able to handle it. In my nightmares it plays out like the electrocution scene in *Faces of Death*. Your eyeballs melt and leak through the protective tape as your lips plump like hotdogs. Yeah, I know the scene is fake and Indiana has decommissioned the chair, but still. It left such an impression on me as a kid. I was too naive to see the tell-tale clues. The shoddy set, the convict's acting, the over-the-top soundtrack doing all the heavy lifting. How was I supposed to know it wasn't real? Years later I read an interview with the director where he claimed his sole piece of research material for the segment was an article on capital punishment he found in an old Hustler magazine.

Now before you accuse me of doing everything my partner tells me to, neither Ziv nor my therapist thought it a good idea to write you this final letter, either, but I held my ground. In fact, the strength of my resolve led to me uncoupling from both of them. Well, technically Ziv left *me*, but I knew what would happen and made my decision accordingly. I'm through with ultimatums. There's a fine line between tough love and being a control freak, and Ziv rode it hard. And since my therapist was also our couples therapist, hand-picked by Ziv, they had to go as well. Good riddance!

It hasn't been easy, though. I'm losing a lot of important people in one fell swoop. I haven't been on my own like this in a long time and I'd be lying if I said I wasn't scared. But it's time I took back control of my own life. Started making decisions for myself, for better or worse. At least then I have no one else to blame when it all goes to shit.

Take care, Jonas. I'll always cherish that summer and what it represented, even if it turned out to be about as real as a scene out of *Faces of Death*.

Your friend,
William Peters

—

To: Jonas Williker, inmate #957464
From: Candace Bennington
February 17, 2009

Dear Jonas,

No, I will not allow Junior to attend your execution. What makes you think I would consider such a thing? Because I wanted him to have a relationship with his father? Note the tense of the verb *want* there—that ship has long since sailed. Communication has been lost. It's lying at the bottom of the Mariana Trench. Did you think I wouldn't see this request for the manipulation it is? You had plenty of chances to meet your son but you refused. Even if you were sincere, which I know you aren't, I wouldn't burden him with the experience. At this point Junior has no need for you in his life. His *Mommatoo* more than makes up for your absence. When he's old enough I'll make sure to tell him what a selfish bastard you were.

By the way, you can take my name off the guest list as well. I have no intention of showing up.

Goodbye, Jonas. For real this time.

Your soon to be ex-wife,
Candance

—

To: Jonas Williker, inmate #957464
From: Rubix Integer
February 19, 2009

Dear Jonas Williker,

Thank you for your interest in cryopreservation. The International Knights of Cryon is no longer a functioning organization. As dictated by the terms of a civil suit, I am required to inform you that in 1979 the company was found criminally negligent after the bodies of several prominent citizens thawed out and decomposed. This was due to an inability to cover electrical costs. To add insult to injury, the bodies were disposed of in an illegal manner.

I am also obligated to inform you that I do not hold any sort of medical degree or formal scientific education. The only certified training I have is in the field of refrigerator repair (although in fairness, I am quite the avid learner, and am regarded as a polymath and autodidact by friends and industry associates).

That being said, cryonics is no longer considered the most viable option when it comes to consciousness preservation. In the years since the KOC's demise remarkable strides have been made in the field. It is quite an exciting time to be alive, and possibly, come back to life. Not since the publication of *Prospectus Immortalitas* have such groundbreaking scientific ideas emerged.

For instance, we have now determined long term memories can survive without blood flow or brain activity. This means that in the future humans will not be encumbered by fallible physical bodies. Sure, these meat sacks are our homes, and we've become attached to them, but they are not necessary for survival. Current methods will allow for the neurons and synapses in our brains to be chemically preserved, in order to be scanned and uploaded into a computer simulation (future willing). Like cryonics, this method is physically fatal, and is technically considered euthanasia, but would allow for the important part of us— the consciousness— to live on. And who knows? Maybe by then science will have developed customizable robot bodies to house our non-corporeal selves.

Since I am forbidden from running a company, I have taken an advisory-only position with Consciousness Preservation Solutions, a startup doing wonders in chemical consciousness preservation. They have earned my trust and receive my highest recommendation for those seeking to beat the reaper. We always believed science would supersede death. That day is closer than anyone expects.

Sincerely,
Rubix Integer
Senior Advisor, Consciousness Preservation Solutions

—

To: Jonas Williker, inmate #957464
From: Abigail Tinder
February 20, 2009

Dear Mr. Williker,

Please stay your initial impulse to tear this letter into pieces. I am not writing to further admonish you or gloat. In a case such as this I find no joy in being right. Your death, despite what you have done, should not be cause for celebration. It is simply a consequence of your actions. A reminder that God's justice is tough but fair.

I am sorry your association with Pastor Oysterton did not yield the desired results. He is lucky his intercession on your behalf did not cost him his livelihood. It almost accomplished what constant rumors of embezzlement and infidelity could not. The Universal Water of Life congregation has been very forgiving over the years.

I watched your testimony video, *Jonas Williker: Live From Death Row!* You might have made a half decent preacher in another life. I'm still amazed Oysterton had the juice to set something like that up. Undoubtedly palms were greased. Still, as much as Evangelicals love a good celebrity conversion, no matter who they are or what they've done, there's no way the greater public was going to accept the back-channel pardon of a serial killer.

It reminds me of when the cousin of a famous pop star started attending our church, and the deacons thought it'd be a smart idea to make him an honorary youth pastor. I'm not gonna tell you the singer's name, it's easy enough to guess. Despite being a drug addict and known scammer, and having no actual relationship with his famous relative, the elders thought the cousin's periphery to fame would give him credibility with the youth. Well, kids can smell inauthenticity a mile away, even naive Christian kids, so it didn't work out. Let's just say the youth group wasn't able to go on the missionary trip they'd been saving up for due to an unforeseen lack of funds.

But I want to give you the benefit of the doubt. Maybe you are sincere. If you have truly accepted Christ into your heart then perhaps a chance exists we will one day meet in the sweet by-and-by. I should like to sit down and have a proper conversation with you, Mr. Williker. If you find yourself in heaven, please, save me a seat next to you at God's table.

In closing, I have taken the liberty of composing a short prayer for you. It contains elements of the traditional as well as some more modern influences. It is my hope it will comfort you in your final moments.

Almighty and eternal Father, have compassion on this dying sinner. Bestow upon them the strength to face their fear. Permit the pain to pass through them, so they may look back and see only grace. A single set of footprints where you carried them. Receive them into thy kingdom despite their many failings. Release them from this imperfect body, the nightmare screams of those they have harmed, the stench of death that fills their nostrils, after which they may spend eternity comforted by your love. We ask this in the name of the Father, the Son, and the Holy Spirit. Amen.

Peace be with you, Jonas Williker.

Sincerely,
Abigail Tinder

—

To: Jonas Williker, inmate #957464
From: Anna Anderson
February 20, 2009

Dear Jonas,

Were you actually trying to trick me into attending your execution with the promise of your son being there? That's fucked up on so many levels. I already told you I can't go. I'm homeless, remember? Crashing on couches until I find myself a new place to live. Which means all I do is work and save money. Besides, I have no desire to see a person I used to be close to killed in front of me. Call me crazy, but I don't see the benefit to my mental well-being. Although calling myself crazy doesn't seem very helpful either, does it?

Why am I rationalizing this? For starters, I know Candace isn't going. We've been in touch. She said she's writing a paper or a book or something about the women in your life and I've agreed to tell her our story. Me and mom's. Women need to stick together, especially those of us with shared trauma.

Please do not contact me again. My decision is final. I have made peace with it and so should you.

May God have mercy on your soul, Jonas. It sounds trite, but I don't know what else to say.

Sincerely,
Anna

—

To: Jonas Williker, inmate #957464
From: Trevor Pence
February 23, 2009

Dear Jonas Williker,

This is the hardest thing I've ever had to write… is the way this letter *should* begin. But this illness has cured me of my shame, and anger is a luxury I can't afford. At this point I have nothing left to lose. This letter is a last ditch effort to save my own life.

And I am writing it to ask you a favor.

Because hey, why not? The courts have already rejected my petition. The State has no qualms about putting someone to death, but posthumously earmarking their organs for donation without consent is a violation of their human rights. Even as an act of reparation.

If my sister were alive this wouldn't be an issue. But you took her from us. Her name was Holly.

Not only did you cut her life short, but in an act of diabolical prescience you kept one of her kidneys as a memento. As if you knew it could save me. As if you were killing two for the price of one. Except technically you were killing three, because my sister was pregnant.

We were a perfect match. I know because we'd done the tests. The plan was to do the surgery after the birth of her baby. It was early enough in my illness. I was going to be an uncle *and* I would get to see my nephew grow up. Two incredible gifts. My sister was a saint.

If she had died right after the attack, the kidney you left inside her would have still been viable. It sounds selfish, I know. But after what her body went through, after what THEY put her through, the organ was worthless.

My sister was still alive when they found her stuffed into our neighbor's trash can. I'd say "miraculously," but I don't believe in miracles after what happened next, which can only be described as an atrocity. A barbaric practice called maternal somatic support, in which the pregnant body of a brain dead woman is kept alive for the express purpose of delivering a fetus.

This may sound all heroic and heart-warming to some, but my sister staunchly opposed keeping her body on life support, and reiterated as much in the final hours before her brain ceased to function. She also repeatedly told the doctors she didn't want to bring a child into this world if she couldn't raise it. But because we live in the archaic state of Indiana, where hospitals are legally required to keep a pregnant woman alive at all costs, doctors denied her wishes, as well as the wishes of her family. So although abortion is legal up to 22 weeks in Indiana, and my sister was only 18 weeks pregnant, they kept her body alive long enough to deliver the baby. My nephew. An additional 12 weeks. That's 84 excruciating days.

My sister's body finally gave out during the delivery. Her remaining kidney failed. But hey, at least my nephew survived. There's a silver lining to this gruesome story, right? Wrong. Even though he was born perfectly healthy my nephew died 24 hours later. No clear explanation why, so the doctors filed it under SIDS. A freak occurrence. They made such a big deal about saving his life before he was born, but once he was out in the world they acted like they couldn't have cared less. It's like my nephew knew the situation he was born into, that he wasn't supposed to be here on these terms. I never even got to hold him.

After all this, the courts still denied my petition to be awarded one of your kidneys. It just isn't done, they said. It's funny. A convicted serial murderer has more control over his body than the woman he killed. Even after he's dead.

So on the off chance you say yes, I'm asking you, please, give me one of your kidneys. I don't know why you'd say yes, but I'm asking regardless. In fact, I'm begging you. Please let me live. Look at it this way, it's like a part of you will live on. An actual flesh and blood part. Inside the body of a man whose sister you brutally murdered. That's pretty fucked up. That's got to appeal to you on some level, right? Let me be the receptacle for your fucked up kidney. My every waking breath will be a reminder of what you did to my sister and nephew. The lives you stole. It's something that will haunt me for the rest of my life. Don't you want to prolong my suffering?

Please.

Sincerely,
Trevor Pence

—

To: Jonas Williker, inmate #957464
From: Jane Doe
February 24, 2009

Dear Jonas,

Another clearing in the fog. I don't know how long this moment will last so I must make the best of it.

Without you I am nothing. An empty shell. When you die I will cease to exist.

That which I have conjured will disappear back into the ether from whence it came, obligation fulfilled. I will be where I belong, beneath the ground, secure in the knowledge I am beyond reprieve.

I can't wait to follow you into the long, dark night of eternal nothingness. Only then will my suffering be complete, my true purpose accomplished. I finally understand what you meant when you said, *Nothing escapes me.*

My body is ready. This journey is at an end, but another is just beginning.

Lead the way.

Sincerely,
The One

—

To: Jonas Williker, inmate #957464
From: Morley Woodlock
February 25, 2009

Dear Jonas,

You'll appreciate this. While doing some reading on lethal injection (in anticipation of your big day), I came across the most fascinating anecdote. Are you aware the first man executed by lethal injection might not have even killed anybody? His name was Charles Brooks Jr. One day Charles, along with his accomplice, Woody Loudres, abducted a man from a used car lot, took him to a motel, and shot him in the head. Not sure why, to tell you the truth. The thing is, neither of them would admit to pulling the trigger. They assumed their mutual silence would somehow cast reasonable doubt on their guilt, but guess what? It didn't. Both men ended up on the receiving end of the death penalty.

Woody Loudres went on to have his conviction overturned on appeal. He cut a deal that saw his sentence reduced to 40 years. By some miracle he received parole in 11. Brooks, on the other hand, did not fare so well. His execution went ahead as scheduled, and the State put him to death on December 7, 1982.

Since then, almost 1400 prisoners have been executed by lethal injection. A multi-step process sold to the American public as the most humane form of capital punishment, which is the same thing they used to say about the electric chair! But according to modern experts, lethal injection executions go wrong more than any other, and instead of a quick, painless death, most subjects experience the sensation of suffocation or drowning, due to a build-up of fluid in the lungs. Like being waterboarded from the inside out. So while they may look like they are peacefully crossing over to the other side, this is only because their bodies are paralyzed. In reality the condemned is undergoing an intense amount of physical and psychological torture right under the unsuspecting witnesses' noses.

To make matters worse, it is considered unethical for medical personnel to take part in a State-mandated execution. You know, that whole "do no harm" thing. Therefore prisons have to rely on inadequately-trained corrections officers who often have trouble with the simple task of locating a vein. The condemned spend more time on the table getting jabbed with needles, anticipating their own death, than it takes for them to expire.

Let me tell you a story about a man named Carter Washington. They called him, "The Man Who Survived His Own Execution," and "The Man the State Couldn't Kill." His death had to be rescheduled twice due to executioner incompetence. The first time, the kill team tried for over 30 minutes to find a vein. At one point Carter turned to the witness booth and said, "Can you believe this shit?" which elicited only nervous throat-clearing. The 2ⁿᵈ time they tried twice as long before the needle snapped off in Carter's arm and migrated up the vein, necessitating surgical removal. They succeeded in initiating an IV on the third attempt, but only after Carter suggested they give his arms a rest and try his foot. At this point blood trickled from dozens of tiny puncture wounds, his arms well-lubricated from the constant wiping.

Once the lines were connected, they administered the first injection, Sodium Pentothal, which is supposed to render the patient unconscious within seconds. But after 2 minutes Carter continued drumming his fingers, looking around the room as he hummed "Amazing Grace" to himself. After 5 minutes he sighed heavily as the team scratched their heads, unsure of what to do next. They determined the drug was having a hard time working its way up to the heart from the foot, so they inverted the table and suspended Carter upside-down to hasten the flow.

This seemed to do the trick. The drug hit his heart in such a large quantity Carter flew into convulsions. His throat spasmed as he gasped for air, eyes and veins bulging with the effort. His face turned purple and swelled like a tick as blood rushed to his head. When one of the team members kneeled to check his airway (as he was still upside-down), Carter vomited with such force it shot straight up like a fountain, hitting the man in the face and knocking him backwards. Carter continued heaving, sending blood-tinged puke splashing up his inverted body, only for it to run back down his chest and face, pooling in his nostrils and mouth, drowning him.

At this point his blood pressure plummeted, sending him into cardiac arrest. The team quickly flipped the table back into an upright position, sending vomit arcing across the room and splattering against the ceiling. Then instead of administering the next injection to speed the process, the execution team spent 35 minutes reviving and stabilizing him, all while droplets of vomit fell from above. They were all set to call it a day when, after an angry call from the Governor, they started the process all over again, because "no way in hell were they going to postpone a 3rd time." By that point it barely mattered because Carter was unresponsive. An inert blood-streaked, vomit covered mess.

Talk about cruel and unusual.

Anyway, a little bit of a tangent, but a fascinating one. All part of the wacky world of State-sponsored execution, I suppose. I hope this anecdote has brightened your day. May your own departure prove less memorable.

Sincerely,
Morley Woodlock

—

To: Jonas Williker, inmate #957464
From: Ginny Goodwinch
February 26, 2009

Dear Jonas,

This letter has been a long time coming yet I still don't feel emotionally prepared to write it. It seems like only yesterday a starry-eyed Ginny turned on the news and saw the face of a handsome stranger run afoul of the law. If you're just tuning in here's a recap of tonight's top story: It was love at first sight! A naive kind of love, sure, but love nonetheless.

Little did I realize how well I'd get to know that man over the course of the next few years, and how much he would affect my life. Looking back I barely recognize the me I used to be. So much has changed I bet you're wondering, *Who is this lady, and what the heck happened to my Ginny-bird?*

I'm just kidding. It's hard not to resort to humor at a time like this. But let me be serious for a moment.

Way back in my very first letter I told you I found it hard to believe a man with such a kind face could do the horrible things you'd been accused of, and I stand by that statement. It *is* hard to believe, whether you did those things or not. Back then I was convinced you hadn't. These days I'm not so sure.

A lot of people are going to be happy when you're gone. They say you're a monster, but I never once doubted your humanity. I didn't have it in me. Mother says I'm trusting to a fault, and maybe she's right. I always look for the good in people, and I sincerely believe there's good in you. I mean, look at Jonas Junior. A truly evil person couldn't possibly have created something so perfect. It doesn't make sense.

Candy, to her credit, has never once tried to sway my opinion, despite the history between the two of you. We've spent many a late night discussing the nature of good versus evil, why a benevolent god would allow evil to exist in the first place, but she's never once passed judgment. We've never even discussed whether she thinks you're guilty or not, and frankly, I don't plan on asking. It doesn't seem important anymore.

Alright, now you're *definitely* wondering what happened to the real Ginny. Don't worry, she's still here. She's just become a bit of a deep thinker in her old age. I've been 29 for over 18 years now!

Sorry, there's that humor again. As you can tell I'm having a real hard time saying goodbye. So let me just say this:

I want you to know how much I've appreciated our correspondence, and how much better it's made my life. The Lord works in mysterious ways, as Mother would say. We don't know why certain things happen, why some people are rich and some people are poor, or why ice cream tastes so good, so why question it? You play the cards you're dealt and try to live your life. I think I've done pretty okay with mine. I hope you can say the same about yours.

I'm glad to have known you, Jonas Williker. Thank you for Jonas Jr., and thank you for being my friend.

Sincerely,
Ginny Goodwinch

—

To: Jonas Williker, inmate #957464
From: Martha Randolph
February 27, 2009

Dear Mr. Williker,

My family begged me not to write this letter. But for the sake of my mental, physical and spiritual well-being, it had to be done. If I am to move beyond this, live some semblance of a normal life, I need this closure.

Sally Randolph was my daughter.

Victim #14, as the media so callously refers to her. I'm sure I don't need to go into any further detail. As is evident from your testimony, your recall is quite excellent.

Which leaves me at a disadvantage. You are intimately familiar with the details of my daughter's death, yet I know so little about you. Just the tidbits released to the media: you were a smart, happy child. Your parents loved you. You had never been in trouble with the law.

These are things I can relate to. My Sally was a smart, happy child, and I loved her very much. She never even had a chance to get in trouble with the law. What I wouldn't give for her to have the opportunity. I'd gratefully post her bail and hire a lawyer. We'd laugh about it on the ride home from the police station.

My heart breaks for your mother. It really does. In some ways she's had it the worst. She might be the biggest victim in this whole ordeal. Because her child has been lost as well. They've transformed into something else, something unimaginable. And the burden of knowing your loss is the cause of exponential amounts of loss... I don't know how one person could handle it. Being viewed as the mother of a monster. Wondering where you went wrong, how you could have prevented the unpreventable.

To make up for the lack of information about who you are, I had to invent my own reasons why. Why you turned out the way you did. Why you took Sally away from us.

You were obviously a master of disguise. How else could such a "normal" child become a killer? The answer is you were never normal. You were a student of human behavior, an expert mimic, and a master manipulator.

Or maybe something horrible happened to you while growing up, something nobody is aware of, not even your parents. Or maybe they are. Maybe they perpetrated that horror, and all three of you have managed to keep it a secret, a twisted family pact. Maybe your parents are the ones mimicking normal human behavior. Maybe that's where you learned it from.

Everyone wants to find someone to blame in situations like this. There has to be a reason, a defining moment, a catalyst for such a monstrous transformation. Psychopaths can't be born that way, can they? Why would God allow that?

God?

I guess in the end it doesn't matter. Whatever the reason for your actions, knowing that reason won't bring our daughter back. Neither will holding on to the anger, the pain of such loss, the inevitable hatred that metastasizes. Which brings me back to the reason I'm writing.

You see, even though you don't need it, probably don't even want it—would spit on it!—I have to forgive you. Otherwise the press might as well count me as one of your victims, another body on the pile. Because hating you will kill me. And in the face of so much death I'd rather live.

So here it is.

Jonas Williker, I forgive you for taking the life of my daughter, Sally Randolph.

Do with that information what you will. The rest is between you and the universe.

Sincerely,
Martha Randolph

—

To: Jonas Williker, inmate #957464
From: Sonny Monroe
February 28, 2009

Dear Jonas,

This feels strange, but I promised your mother I'd write you. Not sure why, to tell you the truth. Mostly out of curiosity, I suppose. But for what it's worth, my name is Sonny Monroe, and I'm your biological father.

This probably comes as quite a shock. It did for me. I hadn't heard from your mom in almost 45 years, and all this time, I had no idea you existed. I only dated the woman a few months before she stopped returning my calls. She never told me I knocked her up.

Which... she probably made the right choice. I can't say exactly how I might have reacted at the time, but I don't think it would have been positively. I'm pretty sure she realized that when she decided to cut ties.

Like I said, it came as quite a shock when she contacted me. It was an even bigger shock when I found out why. She played it smart, though. Asked me to meet her for coffee. Told me in person. I've lived within the same 50-mile radius my whole life, which made it convenient. Sure, the idea I might have a secret adult son crossed my mind, but I never put two and two together. The name Williker. When I knew her she went by Judy Schoenecker, which is how she reintroduced herself.

Your mom seemed extra keen on catching up. You'd think she was writing my biography, all the questions she asked. Dumb me, I still didn't see it. Finally, after she'd exhausted her line of questioning, I managed to get a word in edgewise. "How about you?" I said. That's when she hit me with the news. I was the father of her child, a man named Jonas Williker. I must have looked confused. Why did that name sound so familiar? She followed up with, "You know, the Purple Satin Killer?"

At first I laughed. I couldn't wrap my head around something so preposterous. But when I saw the look on her face I knew she meant business. I ran out of that coffee shop like a house on fire. Thought I was gonna pass out. Your mom found me outside, huffin' and puffin' in the parking lot. Doesn't help I'm a two-pack-a-dayer. She put a hand on my shoulder and rubbed my back while I caught my breath.

The conversation was far from over, but I couldn't go back inside. So we went for a ride instead. I let your mom drive, because no way was I getting behind the wheel after that. She told me all about your childhood, what a smart kid you were. She kept using that word, *smart*, like she was covering something up. Never cute, or funny, or loving. Always smart. Like an excuse. She told me about the disappearance of your cousin, Tina. A huge red flag her mind still refuses to acknowledge. If I were her, I told myself, the alarm bells would have been deafening. But deep inside I understand it's never so simple.

She told me how you got mad at her for keeping me a secret, hiding the adoption from you. How you revealed in a recent letter that ole Frank let it slip once while on a bender. More than once. How you'd been holding a grudge against her for so long. Which is why she sought me out. She wanted to verify she'd made the right choice, that your life only improved without me.

Damn, if that wasn't a slap in the face.

Anyway, I'm not writing to tell you your mom made the right choice. I'm just gonna give you the information I gave her and let you decide.

When your mom and I met, I'd already developed a thirst for booze and a nose for trouble. And she liked that, at first. Having a hot-headed boyfriend who rode a Harley and settled differences with his fists. Keeping him a secret from her parents. But the infatuation didn't last. My antics got old real quick, and it wasn't long before she moved on. Our time together was a blip on the radar. Insignificant in the scheme of one person's life.

Of course, it doesn't appear to be insignificant in the scheme of *your* life, but I'm not here to editorialize.

Not long after that your mother met your father. Some grease monkey her dad introduced her to. The way she tells it, he wasn't the best prospect. He wasn't exciting like me, or attentive or romantic, but he had a good job and was dependable. He also didn't mind your mom came fully loaded like a plate of nachos.

It's a common enough story. He married your mom and took her in. He was present from the day of your birth, so for all intents and purposes, like it or not, he *was* your father. Your mom still thinks she made the right choice there. She claims he treated you like his own son, and tension didn't develop until your teenage years, which sounds about right, although I wouldn't be surprised if there was more to it. I think your mom's looking for an exact reason, a moment she can pinpoint, an explanation why you grew up to do the things you did. But I don't think finding out you were adopted made you a monster. By that point I assume the monster was well-formed.

As for me, I took the ghosting pretty hard. At least for a couple weeks. Then I was on to the next one, cementing a pattern of behavior I would follow for the better part of 20 years. During that time I racked up quite an arrest record. Nothing too serious, mostly misdemeanors. Lot of drunk and disorderly, low-level assault charges.

I didn't wanna tell your mother about the S.A. charges. He said/she said stuff both parties were usually too drunk to remember. Most of those fell by the wayside. I did a two-year stint for one of 'em. Got back together with the woman after my release, if you can believe it. We lasted about as long as you'd expect. Wasn't long after I got 5 to 10 for armed robbery. I was out in six.

After that I had a string of DUIs. I've been going to AA for about 10 years now. My most recent chip confirms I'm 9 months sober, so… It's an ongoing process. It's not 100 percent effective, but it keeps my life from going too far off the rails.

Anyway, after hearing all that (minus the S.A. stuff, mind you), your mom decided she'd made the right choice. What this list of sins will mean to you, I'm not sure. Depends what you're looking to learn. You looking to blame being a serial killer on something you inherited from Dear Old Dad? I'm a career fuckup with substance abuse problems who battles depression, but I'm no psychopath, so you might be out of luck. Your mother sought to control the nurture portion of your development, but couldn't account for the nature. I don't think anyone can.

And like I said earlier, even if your mom had told me she was preggers, I doubt I would've wanted anything to do with you. Sounds harsh, but that's the way it is. Besides, I would have been too busy fucking up my own life to pay much attention to yours. Hell, if I'm being honest, the only reason I'm writing is because you're on the inside and your time is limited. One letter ain't a big commitment on my part. Wouldn't be enough time to do more if I wanted.

Anyway, that's the straight dope. Your mom said to give it to you straight, so… I think at this point you're used to tough talk. But who am I to say? I'm just a mid-tier shit running out the clock on life.

But your mom, she obviously loves you a great deal. Hell, she'd have to. If even *half* of what I've read in the news is true… So I'm gonna leave you with a story she told me. It might be a little TMI, but somehow I don't think it'll be an issue for you. I feel like the only reason she told me something so personal was in the hopes I'd pass it on, so…

Here goes.

Your mom wanted to do everything in her power to ensure you grew up happy and healthy and loved. Which is why she chose to breastfeed you. Public opinion on breastfeeding has gone back and forth over the years, and around the time you came along its popularity was once again on the rise. According to experts it's the best way to promote bonding between mother and child. I mean, duh, right? You don't have to be a genius to see the reasoning. Titties are fucking awesome. End of story. Anyway, there was only one problem. You liked to bite.

Your mom said the first time you bit her she yelped so loud it jolted you out of suckling. The whole of your tiny body spasmed with surprise. You didn't cry, though. You just kind of looked up at her, like you were contemplating something, coming to a realization. You maintained eye-contact as you went back to feeding, a spot of blood on your upper lip. She said you probed her nipple with an inquisitive tooth, applying a little more pressure each time, as if testing her threshold. Despite what I imagine must have been intense discomfort, your mother finished feeding you without additional outburst.

All her friends recommended she switch to a bottle, but she refused. She intended on breastfeeding you for the entirety of the recommended duration at the time. She endured weeks of raw, inflamed skin. So sensitive she could barely wear a shirt, let alone a bra. Any shirt she did wear wound up spotted with blood. She was that committed.

She'd made it to the second to last day. It was almost as if you were biding your time. By this point her nipples were two mounds of chop meat (her words). She'd lost sensation on the left side due to nerve damage. Which is why she didn't cry out when your jagged little tooth bit clean through it. She felt a tug, and the next thing she knew you were spittin' up blood.

She grabbed a bib to clean your face and there it was—a tiny lump of flesh sitting on your tongue, as if you were presenting it to her. Not wanting you to choke, she reached for it with her fingers, but you shut your mouth tight. Your mom panicked, trying to pry your little lips apart to no avail. You watched until she gave up, exasperated. Only then did you unclench your jaw to reveal an empty mouth.

That would have been the last straw for most women. Hell, most women would have given up on day one! But your mother cared about you above her own well-being. So what did she do? She cleaned the two of you up, switched breasts, and finished feeding you. And she fed you the next, final day as well.

So there you have it. I believe for better or worse, her actions speak for themselves. Read into them what you will.

On that note, as trite as it is to say, I hope you use your remaining time wisely. It's been an interesting ride to say the least.

Sincerely,
Sonny

—

To: Jonas Williker, inmate #957464
From: Judith Williker
March 2, 2009

Dear Jonas,

Already I'm crying. That's because this will be the last letter I ever write to you. In a few days I'll be driving out to see you for the first time since this whole mess began. The first and the last.

So much time wasted. Sure, your father needed taking care of, but I used that as an excuse. The truth is I was afraid to see you. Afraid of shattering the perfect little world I'd created in my head, a fantasy reinforced by my cordial letters, written as if you were on a long trip. One you would eventually return from.

But the fantasy is over now. I don't get to retreat into it forever. No, in just a few short days I will be confronted by the truth, and then I will be forced to watch my son die.

And as I sit there, my heart breaking yet again, so many times now I've lost count, I'll be sharing the room with people you've hurt. People who will breathe a sigh of relief watching you breathe your last. People who might take pleasure watching *me* suffer. I'm afraid of what might happen in such a volatile space.

Then I'll return home to an empty house, where I'll ride out the wave of celebration as the media continues to revel in murder. Just like they have this whole time. But the worst part will be after, when they forget about you and move on. I'll be left with nothing to defend, alone in my never-ending grief. My only consolation is Jonas Junior, but he and Candace live so far away.

I'm sorry to burden your final hours with such a depressing letter, but I couldn't keep up the act any more. I'm all out of sunshine. There's just enough gas left in the tank to say goodbye, and then we'll go our separate ways. I wanted to get this off my chest so it wouldn't intrude on our reunion or interfere with our farewell.

Still, part of me never wants to stop writing this letter. Even after I seal the envelope, I'll continue writing it in my head, filling in all the little details between now and when I see you, as if it will magically update itself on the way. It's hard to pass the time without thinking of my life as one big letter, or how that letter should read.

I can't wait to see you. I do hope they let me give you at least one hug. I've got so much lost time to make up for.

I love you, Jonas. Always and forever. I'm sorry I wasn't always honest with you.

Love,
Mom

—

To: Jonas Williker, inmate #957464
From: anonymous
March 5, 2009

EDITOR'S NOTES

Jonas Williker was executed by way of lethal injection on March 11, 2009. The medical examiner listed his death as "unremarkable."

Judith Williker's final letter to her son was found among his personal effects, unopened, the day after his execution. It is unknown exactly when it arrived— if it had arrived on time, if he hadn't had a chance to read it, or if he had refused to read it out of anger. It was postmarked March 2, 2009.

Judith Williker never made it to her son's execution. She died of congestive heart failure the morning of her trip and her body wasn't found until the next day, clutching the same piece of purple satin as her dead husband. By the time the body was identified and next of kin determined, Jonas Williker was dead.

Jessie Clover, better known as The One That Got Away, was found dead in a steamer trunk buried in the backyard of the house where she lived. A neighbor had noticed a shovel sticking out of a recently disturbed pile of earth and called the police. To this day, authorities have no idea how the trunk came to be buried, and no suspects have been named in Jessie's death. She was found wearing a child's tattered jacket—purple satin, with white trim—with what appeared to be a smile on her emaciated face.

David Manning was questioned in regards to the 2007/2008 Ohio Valley murders, but was never charged.

There were no further copycat killings after Jonas Williker's execution.

Antonio Birch, the young man with the traumatic brain injury, was never located and is presumed dead. His stepfather has not come out of hiding.

Ginny Goodwinch, Candace Bennington, and Jonas Junior still live together in Chappaqua, New York.

—

TIMELINE

March 24th, 1975: Jonas Williker is born in Murrysville, PA

June 4th, 1993: Williker graduates from Franklin Regional Senior High School with honors

September 6th, 1993: Williker attends WVU Tech as a criminal justice major

October 10th, 1995: Williker officially drops out of college after being denied a leave of absence

May 17th, 1996: Williker begins work as a volunteer on the gubernatorial campaign of Andrew Jack Bradford

August 28th, 1998: Williker begins work as a phone counselor at the Charleston Suicide Crisis Center

November 3rd, 1998: Williker begins dating former high school classmate Lily Anderson

February 14th, 2000: First known murder—20-year-old Leslie Anne Hawkins of Scenery Hill, PA

November 12th, 2000: Murder #2—17-year-old Betty Kaiser of Berlin, PA

February 14th, 2001: Murder #3—31-year-old Melissa Wainscott of Homer City, PA

April 20th, 2001: Murder #4—24-year-old Tawny Rayfield of New Kensington, PA

May 15th, 2001: Murder #5—27-year-old Danielle Phillips of Latrobe, PA

June 2ⁿᵈ, 2001: Murder #6—52-year-old Penny Dandridge of West Mifflen, PA

June 30ᵗʰ, 2001: Murder #7—23-year-old Andrea Feldman of Mount Pleasant, PA

July 2ⁿᵈ, 2001: Murder #8—25-year-old Coraline Waters of Youngstown, OH

July 4ᵗʰ, 2001: Murder #9—29-year-old Francine Kilshaw of Austintown, OH

July 5ᵗʰ, 2001: Murder #10—22-year-old Grace Carmona of Canfield, OH

September 13ᵗʰ, 2001: Murder #11—30-year-old Andi Hamilton of Somerset, PA

October 23ʳᵈ, 2001: Murder #12—22-year-old Hazel Coonan of Zanesville, OH

November 2ⁿᵈ, 2001: Murder #13—22-year-old Felicity Coonan of Zanesville, OH

January 1ˢᵗ, 2003: Murder #14—19-year-old Sally Randolph of Whiteland, IN

February 14ᵗʰ, 2003: Murder #15—28-year-old Patricia Emmerson of Monrovia, IN

March 3rd, 2003: Murder #16—24-year-old Kira Wagner of Bloomington, IN

May 22ⁿᵈ, 2003: Murder #17—26-year-old Holly Pence of Groverdale, IN

August 17th, 2003: Murder #18—20-year-old Kirsten Swallows of Greencastle, IN

October 16th, 2003: Murder #19—27-year-old Mary Landsfield of Brownstown, IN

December 17th, 2003: Murder #20—31-year-old Roberta Meeks of Crothersville, IN

December 19th, 2003: Murder #21—29-year-old Sandra Hamilton of Evansville, IN

January 24th, 2004: Murder #22—63-year-old Hannah Warburton of Hondo, NM

February 3rd, 2004: Murder #23—27-year-old Patti Sizemore of Phoenix, AZ

February 8th, 2004: Williker assaults Rena Marie Hill in Henderson, NV

February 23rd, 2004: Williker is arrested for the assault of Rena Marie Hill

July 12th, 2004: Williker stands trial for the assault of Rena Marie Hill

November 4th, 2004: Williker is sentenced to 18 months in prison

July 6th, 2005: Williker is extradited from Nevada to Indiana

July 12th, 2006: Williker stands trial for Indiana murders

August 2nd, 2006: Williker escapes from prison

August 8th, 2006: Williker is apprehended by State Police

August 21st, 2006: Murder trial resumes

August 21st, 2006: Jonas Williker proposes to Candace Bennington on live TV and they are married in a civil ceremony that evening

September 7th, 2006: The jury reaches a verdict of guilty on all charges

September 18th, 2006: Williker is sentenced to death

May 18th, 2007: Jonas Sean Williker is born.

October 16th, 2007: Copycat killing #1 takes place in Brownstown, IN

March 3rd, 2008: Copycat killing #2 takes place in Bloomington, IN

April 1st, 2008: Williker publicly converts to Christianity

July 4th, 2008: Copycat killing #3 takes place in Austintown, OH

November 20th, 2008: Frank Williker dies an unremarkable death

November 27th, 2008: Lily Anderson dies of complications due to smoke inhalation

March 9th, 2009: Judith Williker dies of congestive heart failure

March 11th, 2009: Jonas Williker is executed by lethal injection

—

AFTERWORD

Taking the Long Way Home

I want to say I learned a valuable lesson writing this book, but that would be presumptuous of me. Perhaps even disingenuous. Because this isn't the first time I've encountered this particular lesson. And you know what they say: If you keep repeating the same mistakes over and over, you probably haven't learned anything. Like the kid that always got left back in school. I suppose in my case time will tell.

My short story, "Letters to the Purple Satin Killer," was originally published on October 31st, 2015, in issue #20 of Todd Robinson's venerable *Thuglit* magazine. Before that I'd never written anything tailored specifically for the crime genre, but I know a good venue when I see one, and *Thuglit* was one of the goodest (may it rest in literary peace). If I remember correctly, the epistolary format was more a product of my own laziness rather than ingenuity, as the idea of committing myself to a meticulously plotted crime story on a short deadline proved highly unappealing. All I know is I wanted that byline. What I *didn't* know was that almost a decade later, the thing I was trying to avoid writing is exactly what the novel-length version of the story would turn into—an intricately structured nightmare—but at the time I sold myself on what I thought would be a narrative shortcut. One of those rare stories that burst forth, quick and painless.

Well, it did and it didn't. The structure provided a creative breath of fresh air, giving the illusion of ease, even if I did take the usual amount of time hashing out the details. So I wouldn't say it was *easier* than writing a traditional story, but it was different enough to trick me into thinking it was, if that makes any sense.

Still, something of my enjoyment must have shined through, because it proved to be a popular story (these things being relative). It put me on the radar of a reputable agent who would go on to reject two of my novels, including this one, which was based on a story he loved! (Not complaining, just highlighting the capricious nature of publishing here.) It was reprinted at Trigger Warning Short Fiction in July 2017, and was chosen to be the lead-off story in my debut collection, *Whispers in the Ear of A Dreaming Ape,* in 2019. In fact, at one point CLASH even suggested we call the collection *Letters to the Purple Satin Killer,* which, considering the book you are holding in your hands, I'm thankful didn't happen. What a confusing mess that could have been.

So how did this version come about? I didn't initially intend on expanding the story into a novel, although looking back, I don't think I ever intended on writing *any* novels. Then *The Paradox Twins* happened. I wrote that book because I'd already written the screenplay, and I figured I'd already done most of the work, so adapting it into a novel would be easy. Turns out, it wasn't. Are you starting to see a pattern here?

Anyway, *The Paradox Twins* had been out for a while and I wanted to keep the momentum going by putting out another book as soon as I could, a pitfall I once promised myself I'd never fall into, but there I was. That's two promises broken, for those keeping track at home. So what did I decide to do? Why, adapt another screenplay I had written, of course. Because that had gone so smoothly the first time.

To make a long story short, it only took a few months for me to realize I couldn't turn the project around as quickly as I thought I could, so I began considering other options. Only one presented itself. Expanding *Letters to the Purple Satin Killer.*

I reached out to CLASH and pitched the idea of a PSK novella. Adding some characters and taking the story from its modest 3200 words to about 25K.

I figured it would be a quick, easy way to get something new out there, so people didn't forget about me while I worked on the next novel. A stopgap release. A shortcut.

Friends, let me tell you—there are no shortcuts in writing.

Cut to over a year later and me finally sending the finished, 90K word draft to CLASH. Turns out, I'd been lying to myself, and by extension, my publisher, every time I said I was "almost done." Deep in my heart I knew if I wanted to do the story justice, it had to be longer, I just didn't want to admit it. Every time I came up against a timeline problem or a plot hole, the answer was always, "Flesh it out. Stop cutting narrative corners." It didn't help that I had written the book out of order, which made sequencing it a logistical nightmare. All because I was in a hurry, and put content over creativity. Never again, my friends. No more shortcuts for me.

There are plenty of writers out there who thrive under pressure. Give them a deadline, they'll give you gold. But a lot of them have been at this game a long time, and not everyone can be so prolific. Not all writers are the same. When it comes to productivity, most of us fall somewhere between Thomas Pynchon and Stephen King. And no matter what type of writer you are, it's important to remember—you can't force it. The thing is done when it's done.

And thankfully, *Letters to the Purple Satin Killer* is finally done. In the story notes of *Whispers in the Ear of A Dreaming Ape*, I talked about *Making A Murderer* being one of the main influences for the short story. Well, those influences have expanded exponentially in the novel. From Bret Easton Ellis to Anne Rule, C.S. Lewis to Dennis Cooper, John Fowles to A.M. Homes, James Ellroy to Bram Stoker. An eclectic group of writers who have tackled the epistolary novel and the subject of serial killers. I only hope I do them and their work justice.

Thank you for reading. It's time for me to move on to the next one. Don't hold your breath.

Joshua Chaplinsky
June 2023

—

ACKNOWLEDGEMENTS

Thank you to Rebekah, my first reader, always.

Thank you once again to Christoph and Leza of CLASH Books for publishing me. Nobody but my wife would be reading this stuff if it wasn't for you. Thank you to Kaitlyn Kessinger for taking care of business, Brett Petersen for his keen eye, and Matthew Revert for making everything look pretty.

I would also like to thank Dennis Widmyer and the LitReactor community for 12 amazing, formative years. RIP Kirk.

Thank you to Paul Tremblay, Rob Hart, Nick Kolakowski, Brian Allen Carr, David James Keaton, Max Booth III, Clay Mcleod Chapman, Stephanie M. Wytovich, Chandler Morrison, B.R. Yeager, Richard Thomas, Dennis Mahoney and Todd Robinson for the early reads and kind words.

Thank you to all the Bookstagrammers, Booktokers, Booksellers, Books of Horror members, podcasters, early reviewers, and other social media mavens who helped spread the word. Thanks to Meredith Borders, Robb Olson, Leah Bond, Robert Brewer, Jason Grell, Brad Proctor, Jim Mcleod, Molly Odintz and Bobby Miller. Without all of you this brick would be dead in the water like Kira Wagner. (Too soon?)

Thank you to Thuglit for publishing the original short story. Thank you to Trigger Warning Short Fiction for reprinting it. Thank you to Sadie Hartmann for championing it and hosting the cover reveal. Thank you to anyone I may have forgotten. If you feel you deserve credit, it's yours for the taking.

And thank YOU for reading.

xoxo,

Joshua Chaplinsky

—

IMAGE CREDITS

Page 323: Austintown postcard
Original image: *Roper Manufacturing Co., Zanesville, Ohio* (circa 1930-1945), Boston Public Library Tichnor Brothers collection #84084 - via Wikipedia Commons, public domain, manipulation by Joshua Chaplinsky

Page: 349: Murraysville postcard
Original image: *Murraysville Westmoreland Co, PA* (2013), Erik Drost - via Wikipedia Commons, creative commons license, design by Joshua Chaplinsky

Page 351: "Turkey Hand" by Joshua Chaplinsky

Page 423: "Burn in Hell" by Joshua Chaplinsky

Page 436: Author photo by Joshua Chaplinsky

—

ABOUT THE AUTHOR

Joshua Chaplinsky is the author of *The Paradox Twins*, *Whispers in the Ear of A Dreaming Ape,* and *Kanye West—Reanimator.* He was the Managing Editor of LitReactor.com from 2011-2023. Follow him on Instagram, Twitter, and TikTok at @jaceycockrobin. More info at joshuachaplinsky.com.

—

Printed in the USA
CPSIA information can be obtained
at www.ICGtesting.com
JSHW080254290624
65595JS00001B/1

9 781960 988096